PREFACE.

The following narrative first appeared in the columns of the *Halifax Courier* about ten years ago, in a series of papers entitled " Evenings with Sam Wild."

" Sam," the principal hero in these pages, and whose reminiscences they are, was then living in Halifax but in needy circumstances, and the interest which his simple story created was manifested from time to time during its progress, and subsequently, in pecuniary aid and in letters of sympathy from his readers. These cheery and timely remembrances reached him (in some cases direct, and in others through the proprietors of the above journal) not only from many parts of England, but also from beyond the Atlantic, the correspondents in the latter cases being former patrons of " Old Wild's " who had gone out and settled there.

To see, like his old friend Wallett, his adventures in print, had been with the stroller a long-cherished ambition, and his joy as the published results of our successive interviews appeared was unbounded. His existence brightened, for he had now emerged out of his enforced obscurity and had become a hero again.

Since the first appearance of these papers in the *Courier* selections and data from them have, with the writer's permission, appeared in the productions of two local authors,* but he has been so repeatedly asked to republish

---

* *Yorkshire Stories Retold (A Yorkshire Stroller—" Old Wild's ")* by James Burnley. *Stray Leaves on the Old Bradford Theatres,* including a Sketch of Sam Wild (in the *Yorkshireman*), by W. Scruton.

the narrative in its entirety—the several issues of the *Courier* in which it appeared being long since out of print —that he has at last decided to do so.

That there is at the present time an insatiable thirst for the reminiscences of stage heroes is abundantly evidenced by the numerous autobiographies which have appeared of late from the pens of Thespian celebrities. Nearly every succeeding month for some time past, and latterly about every succeeding fortnight, has recorded a new contribution to this popular class of literature. And the cry is " Still they come ! "

Herein, then, may be found, perchance, further reason and inducement for the publication of this little volume.

While of admittedly lesser magnitude and import than those to which allusion has just been made, and imperfectly though the writer fears the stroller's story has been told for him, this history of " Old Wild's " it is believed will, nevertheless, appeal largely to the community. For who that does not himself remember that once famous temple of the drama has not heard his elders speak of it ?—and, it may be, too, declare, in reference to some modern performance which they have been prevailed upon to sit out, that they have " seen better acting at ' Old Wild's ' years ago ! "

But even to those who do not remember that establishment in its palmy days, these reminiscences of its chief and last proprietor will be found not altogether devoid of entertainment. The stroller's adventures are " adventure-y " enough as regards the ups and downs of life and the vicissitudes of theatrical *entrepreneurs,* and it seems but justice to say that they claim a place in the history of the Provincial drama ; for, as will be seen, " Old Wild's " was unquestionably a pioneer in that great march of improvement which led to the permanent establishment of theatres in the provinces.

Then again, from a strictly historical point of view this narrative may, it is hoped, not be unacceptable ; for the

THE ORIGINAL, COMPLETE, AND ONLY
AUTHENTIC STORY OF

"OLD WILD'S"

*(The Yorkshire "Richardson's," and the Pioneer of
the Provincial Theatre) :*

A NURSERY OF STROLLING PLAYERS

AND THE

CELEBRITIES WHO APPEARED THERE.

BEING THE REMINISCENCES OF ITS CHIEF AND
LAST PROPRIETOR, "SAM" WILD.

EDITED BY "TRIM."

REPRINTED FROM THE "HALIFAX COURIER."

LONDON: G. VICKERS, ANGEL COURT, STRAND.
BRADFORD: J. MORGAN, DALE STREET,
AND ALL BOOKSELLERS.

This book was edited by William Broadley Megson
and originally published in 1888.
This edition is published in 1989 by
The Society for Theatre Research
c/o The Theatre Museum
1e Tavistock Street
London WC2E 7PA.

This reprint is issued in conjunction with
Victorian Portable Theatres
by Josephine Harrop
from the same publisher.

ISBN 0 85430 048 1

Printed and bound in Great Britain by
Biddles Ltd, Guildford and King's Lynn

writer begs to assure his readers that THIS IS THE
ORIGINAL, COMPLETE, AND ONLY AUTHENTIC HISTORY OF
THE PEREGRINATIONS OF THE WILD FAMILY, and that it
was narrated to him personally by the late "Sam" Wild,
who placed the whole of his voluminous papers at his (the
writer's) disposal.

And further, inasmuch as the aged stroller and his still
elder brother, Tom, have both "shuffled off this mortal
coil," this remains the *only account now possibly
procurable*.

It was only to be expected that our old broadsword
friend, taking in so great a period as that covered by his
narration, should occasionally have to go back in his
dates. With a view, therefore, to the rearrangement of
the events in, as nearly as possible, chronological order,
some entire chapters, and portions of others, have had to
be transposed; but the original text (subject only to
minor corrections) has been carefully adhered to
throughout.

While fully conscious that viewed in the light of
to-day, with our almost palatial theatres and general
efficiency in things theatrical, these are but the simple
records of a somewhat primitive form of entertainment,
and one at which the rising generation can afford to smile,
the writer feels bound to confess that this labour has not
been without considerable interest to him. Carried back
in memory to that sanguine, impressionable period of life
when happiness is readily extracted from what in later
years would fail to impart it, old sympathies have been
quickened, and pleasurable recollections aroused which
long had slumbered.

"TRIM."

20th October, 1888.

"OLD WILD'S."

CHAPTER I.

INTRODUCTORY.—VISIT TO AN OLD STAGE HERO IN
DISTRESS—BOYHOOD IMPRESSIONS OF " WILD'S "—
HOW WE FOUND THE STROLLER KING.

"I am surprised," said the barber to the player. "to see you in
such indifferent circumstances; for a stage hero, methinks you have a
very needy appearance."—*Gil Blas.*

The periodical visits of the old showmen are probably
amongst the most delightful recollections of childhood;
nor can it be doubted that the histrionic tastes of many
lovers of the drama of the present day were first awakened
under the canvas of wandering Thespians.   To this let us
add, the older we grow the more tenaciously we seem to
cling to the memories of the past; the slightest allusion
to early days serving only to prove the tender regard we
have for old associations.

It was unquestionably the remembrance of old times—
the short jacket and frill days of their writers, when they
used to number amongst the juvenile patrons of " Old
Wild's "—that recently* prompted certain knights of the
pen to call attention, through their journals, to the necessities of an old favourite at the once famous theatrical
establishment just alluded to, and a desire to obtain
assistance for that same old favourite, arising out of pleasant recollections of him years ago.

Through one of these media it was that we first became
aware ourself of the infirmity and extreme poverty of one
whose varied performances had charmed and delighted us
in the days of our youth; and also of the fact, concerning

This paper was written in March, 1878.

which, strange to say, we were previously in ignorance, that such person was actually resident in the same town with us.

It was one Saturday evening, while chatting with Mr. Lumb, at his bookstall in the Market House, Halifax, that the subject of the old player's destitution was broached, and having expressed a desire to see the quondam hero of the broadsword, the bookseller, being a very old acquaintance of his, promptly and kindly offered to take us at any time to the old man's place of abode. So the end of it all was that one beautiful starlight night, not long ago, our bibliomaniac friend, who, when all is said and done, was the prime mover on behalf of the old stroller, having closed his shop betimes (further testimony, if you will, to the respect we entertain for the memories of early days), we found ourselves wending our cheerful way to Caddy Field.

As we jogged along together, we talked of the time when the Wilds were in their prosperity; of the high esteem in which their establishment was held by the rising generation years ago; and of the vicissitudes through which the family had since passed. Of the influence which their histrionic performances exercised over the minds of youth in days gone by it was needless then to speak, for who amongst us, arrived at man's estate, cannot testify to their once fascinating power? And we believe the little pilgrimage that night was in some sort testimony so far as two persons were concerned. For do we not remember, aye, as though it were but yesterday, how—long before we could summon up courage to cross the outer stage of their portable theatre, which, regularly as the fair season came round, used to spring into existence as if by magic—how we used to stand watching with intense admiration a magnificent personage in buskins and tight ineffables (and whom we afterwards learned was the tragedian) pace majestically before the outer proscenium, to and fro? In fancy we see him now, frowning ominously as he holds some mysterious conversation with himself; now pausing, as one absorbed in deep thought, and now awakening from his reverie to address the wondering spectators below in the brief but never-to-be-forgotten words, "Be in time! be in time!" We have still in our mind's eye, too, that ruddy-complexioned but delightfully facetious man, who

was continually appropriating other people's property, and
stowing the same, no matter how bulky, in his capacious
pockets ; besides getting into no end of mischief when his
kleptomaniac tendencies were in repose—which was but
seldom—which acts of commission, however, nobody liked
to take exception to with any degree of severity, because
he was such a funny, good-natured rogue after all. And
we recollect how, in common with other admiring spectators of a tender age, we listened with breathless attention
to his excellent jokes, storing our young mind therewith
for retail purposes by and bye. Then, can we ever forget
the honest face and stalwart form of that noble tar, the
victor, as we learned anon, in a thousand broadsword
combats ? We see him still, his trusty cutlass swinging by
his side, walking leisurely about the stage, or pausing to
hold cheerful converse with that winsome creature, the
femme de chambre. But when memory recalls the forms of
certain fairy-like beings in muslin and pink stockings, and
who frisked about in youthful gaiety to the dulcet sounds
of trombone and drum, description fails, and words
become powerless to interpret the tender passion which
used to fill our youthful breast.

Then, having advanced in years just a little, having
improved in worldly circumstances to that extent that we
were able to pay for admission into the show, and having
conquered bashfulness so far as to ascend the miniature
staircase outside, what shall we say of the wondrous doings
of the interior ? Vain indeed would be any attempt to
describe the impassioned eloquence of the lover; the
sublime pathos of the tragedian ; the glorious broadsword
achievements of the nautical hero ; the stern parent's
wrathful indignation, and the touching appeals of that
virgin fair, his daughter. Then the dancing, and the singing, and the downright rollicking fun ! Alas ! that we
should ever grow old.

We had now reached the humble dwelling of the
veteran player. By the side of a small but cheerful fire,
in a narrow and poorly-furnished room, sat the veritable
" Sam." On the opposite side of the hearth was one of
his sons, who had called in to see him ; and, busied about
domestic duties, his eldest daughter, Louisa. He had a
large red muffler about his neck, and had thrust himself
into a coat, which, like its owner, had seen better days. A

roll of coloured silk and satin play-bills lay upon the table : he had been looking over them, and musing upon his old stage triumphs, thinking of what might have been.   His trusty fiddle was there, too — the same old fiddle, as he afterwards told us, that his father used to play upon when they were all children, learning the first rudiments of professional art.   A priceless relic this of an eventful past, and about the only solace of its master, whose way of life had

> Fall'n into the sere and yellow leaf.

Yes ! there was the old champion of the broadsword, who, as the William of *Black-eyed Susan*, as Harry Helm in *The Ocean Child*, as Jack Junk in *The Floating Beacon*, and as Mat Meriton in *Every Inch a Sailor*, had, years ago, fired our youthful bosom with emulative zeal for the stage. He rose to greet us as we entered, and his daughter having placed seats for us, he bade us be seated, with a touch of the old theatrical gracefulness.

Seeing that we evinced some desire to know his history, he took us thus far into his confidence.

CHAPTER II.

CONCERNING THE ORIGINAL "JEMMY" WILD –HIS FIRST
AND SECOND MARRIAGES — ISSUE — HIS CHILDREN
TRAINED AS ACROBATS—THE FORTUNE-TELLING PONY,
"BILLY"—A DISTRAINT FOR TAXES—WILD LEFT
PENNILESS — OPEN-AIR ENTERTAINMENTS — UNDER
CANVAS AGAIN—LOTTERY PRIZES, AND AN INFRACTION
OF THE LAW—A TEMPORARY RETREAT—VERY KIND
RELATIONS — HELP IN DISTRESS — LAUNCH INTO
THEATRICAL LIFE—"JEMMY'S" FIRST APPEARANCE
AS AN ACTOR—A LAPSUS LINGUÆ AND A SUCCESSFUL
GAG.

> Yet hath my night of life some memory,
> My wasting lamps some fading glimmer left.
> — *Comedy of Errors.*

"My father, James Wild, born in the year 1771, was
the eldest of three sons; two of whom, Frank and Samuel,
were placed in their youth to work at a colliery at
Wrenthorpe (or Potovens), near Wakefield. An occupation of that description was not congenial to the mind of
James; so, leaving his brothers, who, poor fellows,
subsequently perished, while sinking a shaft somewhere
near Wakefield, he was sent to Lee Fair, near Cleckheaton, to a ropemaker called Wilkinson, and to whom he
was finally apprenticed. But though in after years he took
great delight in rope dancing, he had never a very great
liking for ropemaking. So he left the business at the
earliest opportunity. Being passionately fond of music,
and an excellent player on the clarionet, he became a
member, and eventually the leader, of the Cleckheaton Old
Band. Some time afterwards Kite & Morris's Circus
paid a visit to Cleckheaton, and musicians at that day
being a rarity, he was persuaded to join the band of the
circus. Here, too, he soon rose to the position of
conductor, and at length married Mrs. Kite, the senior
partner, who was a widow. Upon this, Morris withdrew
from the concern. My father, from boyhood, had always

a taste for juggling and the like, and he now set himself to work and practised it, as also vaulting and slack-rope dancing, and performed in the circus. His wife died before they had been long married, and he was left sole owner of the establishment. There was no issue of that marriage. His second venture in matrimony was with one Elizabeth Atkins, whose father was a master boot and shoe maker at Coventry. She presented him at various times with, in all, six children. Elizabeth and James, both born at Nottingham; Thomas, born at Newark, about the year 1812; your humble servant, Sam, who first saw the light of day at Huddersfield, on the 4th of July, 1815; Sarah Ann, born in Petticoat Lane, now Russell Street, in this good old town of Halifax; and Selina, born at the second of those three places from which the rogues of olden time used to pray to be delivered, namely, Hull. As the circus was still my father's means of livelihood — and his wanderings with his equestrian troupe will account for our having been born at different places — we were all educated at a very early age in the various arts of tumbling, and tight and slack rope dancing, and each of us performed in public when he, or she, was five years old, if not before. Amongst our other attractions we had a performing pony. The authorities (tax collectors I suppose they would be) having discovered that my father kept more horses and carriages than had been registered in their books, he was surcharged to such an extent that his effects had to be disposed of. Though he was now left penniless, he did not despair, but, turning his own and the ability of his young family to account, we became mountebanks and gave entertainments in the open air, and sometimes in a sort of tent, constructed with stakes and ropes. Nothing was charged for admission to the entertainment, but we sold tickets for prizes, which were drawn for. The prizes consisted of sacks of flour, tea trays, pocket handkerchiefs, gown pieces, snuff boxes, pigs, and even horses, though with regard to the animals last-named it was a case of *presto man jacko*; that is, the horses were generally won by somebody with whom we were on speaking terms, to say the least of it. After this mountebank fashion we have performed here in Winding Road. We did pretty well out of the business, and I have heard my father say that on Dog Green, Hull, we have taken at one time well on to £100, but, of course, the prizes (saving the animals already mentioned) had to be provided for out of the receipts. Things went on smoothly until one day, when we were performing some two or three miles from Wakefield, I think it was Loftus Gate, the Chief-constable, John Brearley, paid us a visit, and, discovering in our system of giving prizes what he considered was a violation of the law, he caused a summons to be issued against my father, and he was sent for three months to Wakefield House of Correction—the only retirement he had been allowed for many a long year. This misfortune plunged our poor mother alike into sorrow and difficulties. Brother Tom and I (we were still very young) were sent to an aunt in the country, who, in consideration of so much per head per week, undertook, kind creature, to do her duty by us. But mother, poor soul! being unable one week to raise the wind, as we say—it was her first default mind—our affectionate relative consigned us to the tender mercies of the Workhouse custodians at Alverthorpe.

There's your relations, nice relations, very kind relations !

But this Workhouse was not such a cheerless place to look at outside as the one here in Halifax, for example, is (and God grant I may never be compelled to compare its internal arrangements), but it was a sort of old fashioned farmhouse. We ate our dinners from wooden trenchers, I remember ; it was so homely as all that. While here we were sent to the village school at Alverthorpe. I am afraid Tom and I did not take kindly to book learning, for I recollect we once or twice wandered forth into the fields instead of going to school; and the subsequent ' wolloping ' with cowtie I received has, I doubt not, served to impress the fact of our truant-playing strongly on my memory. My mother, who, on her husband's incarceration, was left with a pretty fair share of responsibility of one kind or another, struggled hard and got together a little booth (but it was not much bigger than a pea saloon), and her children, Elizabeth and James, probably assisted by Big Ball, a tumbler, who had joined us previously, helped to keep her from starvation. She no sooner heard, however, of our removal to new quarters than she at once set about having us away. What a prospect for a mother of five little cherubs! Two of them in the Workhouse and husband in jail. But she fetched us out before we had been there very long. How she raised the money God knows. Henry Adams, grandfather of the present Charlie Adams, was then travelling with his circus company, and being somewhere in the vicinity, his artistes, who would be sure to hear of her distress, helped her no doubt. That is the only way I can account for it. For I must tell you that our parents were very highly respected by the members of the profession. In fact, my mother used afterwards to be called the ' Queen of the Travellers,' because of her courtesy and kindness to everybody about her.

" Father's term having expired he lost no time in rejoining his family. Life in the little booth seemed brighter now, and our prospects reassuring. He was a clever man was my father, though perhaps I oughtn't to say so, but pride of this sort is pardonable, I hope. As a conjurer he was undoubtedly clever ; as a slackrope and wire performer he stood very high (in a double sense, if you like), and as a ventriloquist and imitator of birds, &c., he was universally acknowledged to be unrivalled. So with him as principal performer—and indeed he was a host in himself—with his children as acrobats, rope-dancers, and so forth, and with ' Billy ' as fortune-teller (the pony, which we managed to get back again after it had been sold, and which we regarded always as one of the family), we contrived to get up a good entertainment. And so, like rolling stones, we wandered about, gathering but little moss truly, but acquiring considerable experience.

" Our brother James had now developed into a smart young fellow, and his aspirations had kept pace with his development. He had visited Adam's Circus while we were at Huddersfield, and fascinated by the cream-coloured horses, the elegant dresses of the performers, etcœtera, etcœtera, went and joined himself as a clown and vaulter to that establishment. Then besides the grand horses there was a good band there too, which played music altogether different to what was discoursed at our little place. We had simply a clarionet for the outside of the show and a fiddle for the inside, both played by one performer, my father.

"And so James the younger left us. A serious blow to his mother, who lamented it much, and a loss to the concern generally. He achieved considerable popularity in his time as a clown. He travelled with Batty, Cooke, and Pablo Fanque. His last engagement was with Hengler, with whom he remained until his death, which happened about five years ago.

"We still kept travelling from place to place with our little booth, and by way of variety introduced ballet dancing and circus farces, without scenery of course. When we came to Halifax we pitched at the bottom of the market. It was then called Market Croft. But the fair was not always held there. It was sometimes held in Horton Street, in Cadney's Croft (where the West Riding Court now is), in Red Tom's Field (the site of the Halifax Industrial Society's present buildings), and once in Grace-field. At this last-named place, when we visited it in 1838, we remained only a week, but Ryan's Circus, which was there too, had a stay of three or four months.

"To return.

"Our first launch into theatrical life was during one of our visits to Halifax. Our show was on the site of Stocks's Eating House, near the Mitre Inn. An old actor, Henry Douglas, a friend of my father's, persuaded him to try the sock and buskin. He agreed, and Douglas joined us. We lodged then in a house where the Saddle Vaults in Russell Street now are, and in that house our first scenery was painted by a native of this town called Wilson. We had three scenes—a street scene, a room or parlour, and a wood or shady grove. With such a fertility of scenic resources we could play a great many pieces. We were indoors, out of doors, and in a wood directly.

"At first we commenced with a farce called *The Village Lawyer*. Henry Douglas played the lawyer and brother Tom, Sheepface; and I recollect they wanted somebody to sit for the judge. My father having received from his company that appointment, he was, after some reluctance, persuaded to respond, and ultimately accepted it. In the absence of robes he sat, as Justice Mittimus, attired in a large white sheet (emblem, no doubt, of his own unim-peachable character), and powdered his hair that he might look venerable. But he was either so tickled at the thought of his own appearance, or else impressed with the serious

nature of the case before him, that he quite forgot
the words previously put into his mouth. He quietly
summed up the whole matter, however, upon his own
responsibility and without reference to precedent. 'After
carefully considering the facts of this case and the testimony of all parties concerned, I can only see one course
before me under the circumstances, and that is to send you
all to Wakefield House of Correction for one calendar
month.' Never was the dictum of a judge received with
more evident signs of satisfaction than was this impromptu
by the old man's audience.

"We, the younger branches of the family, were
impressed into stage service whenever an opportunity
offered. I should be only ten or eleven when I appeared
behind the footlights, but I had performed as a tumbler
and posturer ever since I was five years old. At that early
age I could stand on my head at the top of a ladder
balanced by my father (it is as much as I can do now to
keep well on my feet, through my infirmity), and made a
sort of serpentine descent, by threading my way downwards
through the staves. I forgot to mention before concerning my father, that he was a man of extraordinary
strength. He could bear eight persons on his body at one
time, and as for us little chaps, he threw us about like
ninepins.

"So, with our 'Star Company' of theatricals, we
attended all the feasts, fairs, and races, far and wide;
sometimes staying three or four weeks at one place, at
others as many months. In this way we have travelled
through Yorkshire, Lancashire, Derbyshire, Leicestershire,
and, indeed, through almost all the other shires in England;
but we never as a company went out of it, though I have
done so in my capacity as comedian.

"I believe my first character was one of the farmers in
Cherry Bounce, whose misfortune it was to take a copious
draught of horse medicine, under the delusion that they
were imbibing a delicious potation.

"All our family, including my mother, played in one
piece or another. But Elizabeth, woman grown, married
and left us. So, besides our parents, and any strollers we
might hire, there were only Tom, Sarah Ann (Sally we
usually called her), and myself to sustain the minor parts;
Selina being as yet too young to appear.

"We were considered tall children for our years, and being excellently trained by our parents, were enabled soon to take parts usually sustained by adults.

"Things went on, and our plays went off with the public, for that we were improving wonderfully was testified by the increased support that was accorded us on every return visit we made to towns at which we had played before."

CHAPTER III.

PARTNERSHIP WITH "PEP" DAWSON—ANDERSON (AFTER-
WARDS PROFESSOR AND "WIZARD OF THE NORTH")
RECEIVES LESSONS IN CONJURING FROM "JEMMY"
WILD—ALSO DAVID PRINCE MILLER AND JOE MORTON
— MALABAR, THE EQUILIBRIST — "UP GOES THE
DONKEY" — BATTY (AFTERWARDS OF ASTLEY'S)
RECEIVES HELP FROM WILD—JOE BREARLEY AND THE
HARLEQUIN'S BOX—A DESCRIPTION OF THE BOOTH—
PARTNERSHIP WITH POWELL.

The better part of valour is—discretion.—*I. Henry IV*.

"For a period of perhaps eighteen months (commencing when I should be about fourteen years of age) we
suspended the theatrical business, and in lieu of tragedy,
comedy, and farce, returned to the old feats of leger-
demain, and the like; 'Billy,' the fortune-telling pony,
being still with us. One 'Pep' Dawson, a juggler,
entered into partnership with my father at the time I
speak of, and there were added to the attractions of the
booth, Punch and Judy and a Chinese shadow entertainment. Our staff of performers now consisted of the two
principals, our own family, an acrobat called Lightwood,
and also his wife, who was a capital singer and dancer.

"You have heard of Professor Anderson, the 'Wizard
of the North?' Well, my father at this very time gave
him private lessons in conjuring. Anderson, previous to
this, had travelled with a theatrical company; but it was
said of him that he could only play two characters,
William Tell and Rob Roy. Of his subsequent success as
a magician I need not speak.

"David Prince Miller also received similar instructions
from our worthy parent, and, as a conjurer, travelled with
us, I should say about twelve months. He afterwards
turned his attention to the stage; got together a dramatic
company, and erected a wooden theatre at Glasgow. It
seems, however, that he offended the proprietor of the

Theatre Royal in that city in some particular (probably playing the same pieces as the company at the Royal did, and at the same time), and the magistrates, before whom the matter would doubtless be laid, declined to renew Miller's licence. He continued to play, however, in open defiance of those authorities, and the end of it was they put him in 'durance vile.' It was while in prison that he wrote his celebrated book, 'The Life of a Showman.'

"My father also brought out the famous Joe Morton, otherwise Joe Jowett, *alias* 'Curly Joe.' The old man met with him at Flockton, and brought him away, a young man, with him. He was quick and apt, notwithstanding that the greater part of his life had been spent in a coal pit. He soon surpassed his teacher. He could do more varied and clever tricks with cards than any man whom I ever saw, and was a master at twirlabout or 'devil sticks.' He was always at those sticks ; you never saw him without them in the daytime, and I do verily believe he slept with them under his pillow at night. By and bye he left us and set up an establishment of his own. He had a contrivance—*camera obscura* we called it ; I think it was Sir Isaac Newton's invention originally—by which the crowd outside the show could, by means of mirrors on the roof, be distinctly seen, and all their movements watched. Through this agency more than one of the light-fingered gentry has been detected at work and captured. Joe afterwards got married, and turned to conjuring solely. Like us he travelled ; and though his establishment was a small one, and his juggling paraphernalia meagre, he was undoubtedly a clever man.

"Messrs. Wild & Dawson also engaged an equilibrist called Malabar. He balanced coach wheels, a plank twenty-one feet long, and a live donkey on a ladder. After leaving our place, he became a 'pitcher' in the streets. 'How much have you got?' he would ask of his wife and the youth who went round 'nobbing' amongst the spectators. 'Ah, we must have just another shilling, ladies and gentlemen, and then up goes the donkey.'

"Batty (at this time much reduced in circumstances) had a small portable circus. During the winter season of the period I am referring to he came here to Halifax, and pitched his 'roving tent' beside our booth on Market

Croft. Father and he were great friends, and it was because of this friendship, and to give poor Batty a lift, that Tom and I and Barry (afterwards the clever Hibernian clown who performed at Astley's Amphitheatre), after we had finished our duties at our own place, used to pop into Batty's circus and do a little extra there.   Batty had an apprentice to the equestrian business, who was about my own age, one Edwin Hughes.   My sister Sarah Ann and he, both children tben, saw much of each other, and the acquaintance then formed ripened into love as they grew older, and ended in matrimony.

" George Parrish, I remember, was also an apprentice of Batty's. He performed outside on the slack rope, and had a wonderful knack of throwing himself off it and catching by a sort of sling which passed round his neck.   But he went in for an unrehearsed effect one day, for the sling unexpectedly drew up tight as he put his head through it, and it is difficult to say what sort of a verdict would have been given in had not speedy assistance arrived.*

" During his stay at Halifax, Batty was very unsuccessful.   The weather was against him, and his tent was damaged by storm and tempest.   But he met with better luck, as we say, at Keighley, and came over to redeem two horses which he had left as security for debt (stabling and horse keep), when his funds were exhausted.   What ups and downs there are in life to be sure !   This man afterwards acquired considerable wealth, and rebuilt Astley's Royal Amphitheatre at his own cost.

" As I grew up to be a young man I took an affection to nautical characters, such as Harry Helm, Jack Junk, &c. I practised fencing and was counted one of the best swordsmen in the profession.   I used to fight against six

---

* A Bradfordian, and a patron of " Old Wild's " in these early show days, told me recently an amusing anecdote. One evening while the outside fun was in full swing it suddenly began to rain heavily, The performers, of course, summarily retired. In spite of the continued downpour, however, the juniors still hung about the front hoping for fair weather and a resumption of the free entertainments. " There is no saying (my worthy friend remarked) how long we should have lingered there had not a member of the company reappeared, and, with that consideration for his patrons which ever distinguished the management at ' Old Wild's,' dispersed the expectant crowd thus :—' Ladies and gentlemen, I am desired to state that there will be no more amusements outside this evening, in consequence of the wetness of the rain.' "—" Trim."

men at one time ; using two swords, one in each hand.
At the age of eighteen or nineteen I was a leading man
and could do almost anything. Yet I never aspired much
to tragedy. Shaksperian characters such as Richard III.,
Macbeth, Othello, I rarely attempted, though I have
several times played Macduff, the ghost in Hamlet, and
similar characters.

"In 1832 or 1833 we were stationed at Rotherham, at
the Theatre Royal there. The building had been a chapel
formerly but had fallen into disuse, under what circumstances I cannot say. I remember our sojourn at Rotherham because our band, of which I was then a member,
used regularly once a week during our stay, to pay a visit
to Wentworth House, the seat of Earl Fitzwilliam, and
about two miles from the town. This allusion to my Lord
is full of sound, but ' signifying nothing,' inasmuch as we
never had the honour of his patronage. We were the
guests of the men servants and maid servants. They sent
for us while my Lord was in town, to ' cheer them up
with our music.' They treated us always with the
greatest kindness. The butler was a good old soul and
returned cheer for cheer.

"While at Rotherham we held a grand masquerade in
the theatre. It was a public affair, of course. The pit
was boarded over to a level with the stage, the back of
which conducted to the White Hart Hotel, where the
revellers adjourned from time to time for refreshment.
There were no restrictions then upon public-houses, and
the White Hart kept open until the masquerade was
brought to a close, which was about two a.m. next day. A
great many persons who wished to be present, but who
had not suitable costumes to appear in, applied to us to
lend them some. Our theatrical wardrobes were as a
consequence thoroughly ransacked, and we did a capital
business in this line, for, of course, we charged the appli-
cants for them. We had distinguished guests that night,
I assure you. Most of Willie Shakspeare's heroes and
heroines were there, as were also Rob Roy, William Tell,
The Stranger, Mrs. Haller, William, and his Black-eyed
Susan. The last two characters, I may here remark,
were represented by Mr. and Mrs. Thornes, who were
playing in our company at this time, and to whom, upon
their setting up an establishment of their own, Wallett

went on leaving us.   Then we had clown—we couldn't get on without him at all, so brother Tom answered for him ; I followed up as pantaloon, and Joe Brearley represented harlequin.   But there were numerous characters which I cannot now remember.   It appeared that at a masked ball given some time previously in Sheffield, there had been either some irregularity or impropriety in dress, which, becoming known, put the police upon the alert in other towns whenever exhibitions or entertainments of this sort were held.   The Rotherham authorities, to their credit be it said, lacked no part of their duty upon this occasion, for just when 'the mirth and fun grew fast and furious,' they appeared, though uninvited guests, in their own peculiar livery, at our ball.   There was at once consider- able agitation, especially amongst the ladies.   Joe Brearley, the harlequin, as I have said, the moment he saw a real constable—whom, by the way, you can never take the same liberties with that you can with a stage ' bobby '—became so alarmed that he was *non est inventus* in an instant.   The police, however, having satisfied themselves that all was orderly and regular (and those who have known ' Old Wild's ' will remember very well that nothing improper or disorderly was ever allowed), withdrew, and the ball was resumed.   But where was glittering harlequin ?   A search was made, but Joe could nowhere be found.   ' Joe Brearley ?' inquired for everywhere about the room.   ' Joe Brearley ! ' bawled all over the stage.   ' Joe Brearley !! ' echoed in every corner in the White Hart.   ' Joe Brearley !!! ' shouted from more than one pair of sten- torian lungs outside the theatre.   But no response.   So we gave him up for lost—a rational and safe conclusion when a person cannot be found.   At length, say about an hour and a-quarter after this interruption, and when the recollection of it had almost died away in the excitement of the dance, somebody crossing the stage fancied he heard a slight noise proceeding from the harlequin's magic box, stowed away at one of the side wings.   So he called some of us to him quietly, and we at once overhauled it. Whereupon—would you believe it?—Joe was suddenly dis- covered, considerably crumpled and dusty and trembling like a leaf.   He had been there ever since the advent of the constables.   How long he would have remained there but for this accidental discovery, nobody can tell, for he seemed, in spite of all our assurances, very reluctant to leave his quarters. It might have been another 'Mistletoe Bough' affair for aught I can see.

"Shortly after this we left the old chapel premises and took to our booth again. The size of it at this time was, as near as I can remember, some 80ft. long and 45ft. wide. We had only a promenade outside at fair time or feasts, and always took it down when the festivities were over, notwithstanding that we might remain in the same place for weeks afterwards. Along the outside were painted shutters, with canvas for the roof. The inside was lined with green baize. Our footlights were candles, or 'Russian gas,' as Tom called those modest luminaries. At one end of the booth was the stage, and immediately before it a circle brilliantly illuminated by more Russian gas, in the shape of a chandelier of forty candles, for equestrian and other performances. On one side of the booth was the pit, upon the other side the boxes, the seats of which were carpeted. At the other end of the booth, opposite the stage, was 'Olympus top,' the gallery.

"Somewhere about this period my father entered into partnership with one Anthony Powell, formerly a large circus proprietor, but then much reduced in circumstances, Powell had several horses, and so with a 'grand combination of talent,' as they put it even at this day, we opened as amphitheatre on a small scale. This partnership, however, was but of short duration."

CHAPTER IV.

WALLETT (AFTERWARDS THE QUEEN'S JESTER) JOINS
WILD'S ESTABLISHMENT — HIS REMINISCENCES OF
" OLD WILD'S " — AN OLD PLAY BILL — "SAM"
WILD'S GROWING POPULARITY — WALLETT AS A
SCENIC ARTIST—PLOT OF ONE OF THE STOCK PIECES.

" A fellow of infinite jest."—Hamlet.

At this point reference was made to Wallett's autobiography, which being produced we read extracts therefrom,
referring to this period of the career of the Wilds. During
the reading, the old man's eye glistened with delight as the
recollection of his early friendship with that world-
renowned jester was revived, and as he testified to the
accuracy in the main of Wallett's reminiscences, we cannot
do better than quote from them here :—

I started for Leeds. There I joined a theatrical booth belonging to
Mr. Wild, better known as " Old Jemmy." This concern was a sort of
amphitheatre, being made up of a fortune-telling pony, a tight-rope
dancer, and a slight theatrical entertainment. . . . . I instantly
set to work to remodel the establishment, and get it in order for the
coming fairs. Towards the end of the first week, the band, consisting
of the manager, his sons, and myself (promoted to the rank of drum-
major) promenaded the district, to acquaint His Majesty's lieges of the
great and intellectual treat in store for them at the moderate charge of
threepence. . . . . The manager, a very old man with a loud voice,
persisted in announcing the performance in the intervals of the music.
The piece to be performed was *The Floating Beacon*, which he proclaimed
as follows :—" This evening will be represented a drama called *The
Floating ' Bacon,' "* to which a wag replied, in the Yorkshire dialect,
" And a very good thing too, Jemmy, wi' a bit o' cabbage to it." The
farce for the evening was *Raising the Wind*—rather an ominous title, for
a storm came on after the conclusion of the performance. At four in the
morning I and others were called up to disentangle the wrecked theatre
of its sails and tackle. The canvas roof and the new scenery I had
painted were torn to rags. While sitting upon the ridge-pole of the
demolished roof clearing the *débris*, the factory bells rang out the hour
for work. Then hundreds of the workpeople passed by, and many
stopped to look at the ruin. I believe I gave vent to my feelings in
emphatic language, for a small urchin called out, " Eh, Mr. Wallett,
don't grumble ; ye were raising the wind yourselves last night." Our
booth, however, was somewhat dilapidated before, and the rain coming
through the roof rendered it impossible to keep the violins in tune. On

one occasion the leader of the orchestra, a talented but eccentric character, called Dr. Down, hearing the manager's daughter sing "Buy a Broom," stopped playing and looked up, exclaiming, "Better tell your father to buy a new tilt to the roof."

We soon recovered from our disaster, owing to the happy disposition of Mr. Wild and the industry of his sons, backed by my judgment and energy, and all encouraged by Mrs. Wild; and the establishment became one of the most prosperous in the country.

"Wallett was our scene painter," the old man continued, "and also performed comedy parts. He afterwards became a good posturer. We were inseparable friends and bed fellows. At first he was with us some three or four years, then he left us and joined Thorne, who had a place of entertainment similar to ours, and who, like us, went about to fairs. The Jem Farrar mentioned by Wallett [p. 19] was also with us off and on for many years."

Again quoting from Wallett:

I next joined Mr. W. S. Thorne, the proprietor of a pavilion in huge proportions built in the form of the Towers of Warsaw. He was in opposition to my old friend Wild. Previous to the commencement of the *fête*, four London acrobats arrived, whose names were Heng, Constantine, Morris, and Whitton. This party were engaged by Mr. Wild as a counter attraction to us. Among other entertainments, Constantine represented the Grecian statues, which were then quite new, having been shortly before invented, and introduced by Ducrow, at Astley's. We commenced on Saturday, and the statues were our most formidable rivals; they were exceedingly effective and successful. So much so that I made up my mind to obtain the dress and properties, which were first-class. So on the Saturday night, after the performance, I introduced myself to Constantine. He concluded to accept my liberal offer for his costume and the appointments of the statues. On Monday morning the strife between the rival establishments was resumed. Of course I lost no time in making proper arrangements, and advertising the representation of the statues at our establishment that had been so successful at the opposition shop. The plan succeeded; we carried the day. In the height of the professional battle Mrs. Wild sent for Constantine. "Why, they're doing the statues at the other place, and carrying all before them. Go and get your dress, you must do the statues." "But I cannot," he said. "You must." "Impossible; I've got no dress, no properties." "Why, where are those you had on Saturday night." "I've sold them." "Sold them!" "Sold them! sold them! to whom?" "Why, I sold them to Mr. Wallett, at the other establishment." The old lady's face flushed like a thousand roses. "Dolt! fool! idiot! you've ruined me? Pack up your traps, and leave at once." . . . Soon after this, I transferred my services from Thorne's to the opposition establishment, Old Wild's, where I formed an intimacy with one of the sons, Sam, that has lasted through life. In fact, I may say, as Burns, "I lo'ed him like a very brither." As we had a very happy and prosperous time, Sam and I saved a few pounds. We determined upon a trip to my native town, to see my parents, brothers, and sisters, a goodly array, as I am the eldest of twenty-four children. Being young fellows, and fond of life, our funds were soon exhausted. We did not like to write to his mother for money, as we had run away and were neglecting our business, and my mother had none to give us. But there's always balm in Gilead, It was within three days of Hull fair ; and, to our unspeakable joy, old Jones arrived with his booth. We were immediately engaged as stars in this small firmament, at the princely salary of one guinea each per day. It was on the evening after we made this engagement, when Sam and I were seated in the bar of Glover's Hotel, that an elderly gentleman, with either a very high forehead or a partially bald head, attracted our attention by his steadfast gaze upon me. He made himself known to us as Mr. Gifford, the stage manager of the Old Theatre Royal, Hull. It appeared that they were producing a pantomime for the Hull fair, and had engaged artists from London, Signor Garcia and young Masoura, as clown and pantaloon. The pantomime was to be produced on the following night. The steamboats from London were all in, and there was no railway at that time. The management had given up all hope of the party arriving by mail coach ; the journey being long and expensive. This then was my first essay in management, for I forthwith made a contract to supply the pantomime characters for £8 a night. I played the clown, and Sam Wild the pantaloon. We instantly waited upon old Jones, and told him the nature of our engagements. We said we would work at his establishment from noon till nine at night, when we must leave to appear in the pantomime. He said, "Bless you, my boys, I have children of my own. Don't let me be any bar to your preferment." So, as Wallett and Wild at the show, and as Signor Garcia and young Masoura at the Theatre Royal ; receiving two guineas from the show, and eight pounds from the theatre, and paying one pound a night to harlequin and columbine, and two pounds to my chum and brother Sam for his day and night, I was left with a handsome margin of profit. All went on merrily as marriage bells for some time. But my luck again ! Old mother Wild arrived with a policeman from Hull, to snatch us from prosperity, and drag us back to that theatrical factory where labour was certain and payment rather doubtful. With much ado we persuaded the old lady to allow us to remain till the end of the week, undertaking to return on the following Monday, which we accordingly did,"

Here again we resume " Sam's " narrative.

" In 1835 we were staying with our theatrical booth at Holbeck, near Leeds. Wallett was then with us. He and I were as firm friends as ever, and he still shared my bed. When we arose on the morning of the 26th of September in that same year (it was a Saturday, I remember), I said to Wallett, ' Well, my friend and brother, as I am going to enter into an engagement of a matrimonial nature to-day, I am compelled most reluctantly to give thee notice to quit.' Poor Wallet ! I wonder if he remembers it?

" Now I came upon a very interesting thing in its way, a day or two ago. It is one of our play bills over forty years old. Indeed, it is dated the very same year in which Wallett joined us at Leeds, and his name occurs in it. See, here it is.

Imps !   Imps ! !   Bottle Imps ! ! !
WILD'S
Royal Theatrical Pavilion, Marsh Lane.
This present Wednesday evening,
November 25th, 1835, will be Performed the Grand Romantic
Drama, entitled,
THE BOTTLE IMP !
Or the Fiend and the Sorcerer.

Albert, a young Neapolitan on Travel ....Mr. Butler.
Willibauld, his Valet, and very much alarmed at Imps ......Mr. Wallett.
Nicolo, a Spendthrift, supposed to have sold himself to the
    Imp .... Mr. Parry.
Waldeck, an aged Farmer ....Mr. Asgill.
Conrade, his son, in the Neapolitan Service ....Mr. Zadi.
Mordecai Cracow, an Itinerant Jew, rather uneasy at having
    purchased the —— Imp......................................Mr. Hall.
Jomelli, a Drunken Corporal of the Guard ....Mr. T. Wild.
Officer of the Inquisition...Mr. Hume.
And the Bottle Imp................... ....Mr. S. WILD.
Marcelia, Conrade's Sister, attached to Albert.....................Miss Wild.
Phillippa, a Lady very fond of Rougiet Noir, &c. ....Mrs. Ansell.
Lucretia, ditto of the same stamp......................................Miss Ball.
Ladies, Guards, Inquisitors, Gondoliers, &c., &c.

☞ The following are among the many Scenes Painted expressly for the
" Bottle Imp " by Mr. Wallett :—
A Beautiful View of Venice by Sunset.
" Hail, smiling Venice, thou widely celebrated scene of luxury and
revelry ! thou lovely queen of the Adriatic."
An Illuminated Saloon.
" Come, Gallant Cavaliers, you were not wont to be so indolent—Ladies,
try your skill, and urge again the merry dance."
The Chamber of Albert.
" Demon ! Demon, I call upon thee—aid me." " Behold and the
Bottle Imp appears encircled by a superb cloud of
Blue and Red Fire ! "
A Street in Venice
" Vat the —— is in my box.—I tink someting is dere,—I feel so
comical since I purchased 'tis —— bottle,—I vish mit all my heart I
could sell it,—I vould give all my goots and box to any pody that vould
buy it."
Dungeons of the Inquisition on Fire.
" Nicolo, thy time is come and thou art mine. The coin with which
thou hast purchased me is of the least value in the world. Parricide !
thy hour is come and thou art mine, Ha! Ha! Ha!" Agony of Nicolo,
—appearance of the Imp, who seizes his victim and dashes him to the
earth, encircled in volumes of
Red, Blue, and Green Fire !
To be followed by the performance of
Mr. Hunter on the Tight Rope.
Duet ...... " Polly Hopkins and Tommy Tomkins," ...... Mrs. Ansell and
Mr. Hall.
Comic Song, Mr. Wallett.
To conclude with the very lively farce of
SCANDAL HATH A BUSY TONGUE.

Henry ....Mr. Butler.
Oliver ....Mr. Hall.
Junot ....Mr. Zadi.

Mr. Nicholas Dovetail ....Mr. T. Wild.
Madame Manette, a lady after the manner of Mrs. Paulina Pry,
    with not the tongue that "never told a lie" ....Miss Wild.
Jacquette ....Miss Ball.
Louise..Mrs. Hume.
Jane ....Mrs. Zadi.
Therese, Oliver's adopted daughter ....Mrs. Ansell.
    Doors open at half-past six, and performance to commence
        at eight o'clock precisely.
        Boxes 6d., Gallery 3d.
    Good Fires constantly kept, and the whole Brilliantly Illuminated
        with Gas.

"You will observe that we opened the doors a full hour and a-half before the performance began. The band played at intervals during the time. By this method crushing at the doors was entirely avoided, our patrons took their seats at leisure. Considering that we opened at half-past six and did not usually close until half-past ten, sometimes not until later, I think we treated our audiences well, and gave them money's worth.

"Wallett, you will see, sustained the *rôle* of Willibauld in the first piece, and is down for a comic song before the farce. But I really cannot now say what that song would be. He had a fair voice, and his style—the main thing in a comic song—was irresistible always.

"The Mrs. Ansell, who is mentioned in *The Bottle Imp* cast, was afterwards my brother Tom's first wife. His second, I may here remark, was a Mrs. Beech (Tom seems to have compassion on the widows), the proprietress of a small theatrical concern. Mr. Hall, the Moses of the piece, was Paddy Hall, that powerful Hibernian who attacked Wallett on one occasion, as narrated by him in his autobiography (pp. 46 and 47). Messrs. Butler and Parry (Albert and Nicolo respectively) after leaving our place went to London, and at one time or another have played in most of the large theatres there. The former subsequently became a theatrical agent. Miss Ball (Lucretia), who had been with us some time, would have been Mrs. Sam had my sentiments on that score corresponded with hers."

"How do you know what her sentiments were, father?" interrupted the old man's daughter, Louisa, at this point.

"Because she couldn't conceal them, my dear," rejoined he, and resumed his narrative as though he had never been interrupted. "But it was hard for me, as the song says,

> To give the hand where the heart could never be.

At the date of the placard, however, I had been taken in and done for about two months. Miss Ball ultimately married a Mr. Caney, of our company. The Miss Wild who is mentioned in the cast of characters in both pieces was my sister Sarah Ann (afterwards Mrs. Hughes). I was the Bottle Imp as you will see. That was a prominent character, and so I was put into prominent type. In fact, if one may speak of himself, I was always counted a 'great gun' as they say, at our establishment, and I believe I was never without the vanity to agree in the reckoning. Up to the very last day of our professional career I always played principal parts, and I have had little colloquies like the following often repeated to me by persons who have overheard them : ' Going to Wild's to-neet, Ned?' 'Doan't knoa. Is Sam actin'?' 'Nay, I doant see his name on t'bill.' 'Wha then I sa'ant goa.' Unvarnished testimony this certainly, but gratifying to a class of people whose livelihood is dependent upon public opinion.

"My costume as the Bottle Imp consisted of a tight-fitting suit of blue, with folding wings also of blue from tip to toe, grotesquely spangled and silvered. My face wore a demoniacal aspect, and concerning my *coiffure*, each particular hair did stand on end with a vengeance. The tight-rope dancer, James Hunter, who was also a clever equestrian, was an American, I believe. The scenery, as you will observe, was painted by Wallett, and it is but justice to say of it that it was beautiful and effective. It was painted in water colours. He kept always by him a portfolio of plates and sketches, and was ready almost at a moment to give us an idea for any new scene we might require. Of course he was paid specially for his painting, so much per scene.

"This *Bottle Imp* is founded, I believe, upon some fairy tale. The piece is written as a melodrama, but as our vocal corps was only limited, we used to 'cut' most of the songs and choruses and call it a Grand Romantic Drama. But in order to afford you some idea of the special efforts required from Wallett, Paddy Hall, Sally,

myself, and indeed from all of us, and as you may not
possibly have seen the play as we only performed it about
once or twice during a season, though it formed one of our
stock pieces to the last, I will attempt to describe the plot.

"Albert, a German, in love with Marcelia, sets out
upon his travels some four years after he has attained his
majority.   He is accompanied by Willibauld, a 'steady
and discreet young man,' who acts in the twofold capacity
of *valet de chambre* and 'general admonisher' to the
youthful traveller.   Arrived at Venice, Albert, fickle and
impressionable, espies on the balcony of a magnificent
palace the forms of Lucretia and Phillipa, and, quite forgetting the girl he has left behind him, suddenly becomes
enamoured of them both.   While he is casting about in
his mind for a means of introduction to these ladies, Nicolo,
the owner of the palace, enters, and falling into conversation with Albert, ultimately invites him 'to add to the
merry group within.'   But Scene 2, which discloses the
study of Nicolo, shows how exquisitely miserable he is
notwithstanding his wealth, into the possession whereof
he came through the agency of the Bottle Imp, for which
he entered into a compact with a certain Invisible Gentleman.   The story is that the possessor of the bottle may
command from it as much gold as he desires on the conditions that, in return for such services, should the owner
desire to part with it he must sell it for less than he gave
for it, and moreover, that should he die with it in his
possession he becomes forthwith the absolute property of
that same Invisible Party.   It is natural, therefore, that
Nicolo should be unhapppy knowing all this ; but in addition, the Imp is continually appearing (to blue and green
fire) and reminding him what a wretched slave he is,
and pointing also to antecedents far from pleasant to
reflect upon.   Nicolo is therefore determined to rid
himself of this terrible fiend, and perceiving in Albert a
ready instrument, assures him that a certain way to
become rich and happy is to possess this 'friendly demon.'
So Albert, who wishes to be both, makes the desired
purchase.   Like the sorcerer Nicolo, or rather as he was—
for since he has parted with the source of his wealth he
has become homeless—Albert becomes at once affluent and
wretched, and is soon desirous, as its former owner was, to
part with the 'dreaded purchase.'   So he employs

Willibauld, still his servant, to dispose of it in the street; but as nobody will buy it, Willibauld, in his despair, gives his master three ducats, the reputed price at which he has sold it, and keeps it himself. Willibauld who, without becoming instantly rich, has nevertheless considerable misgivings as to his purchase, determines also to get rid of his doubtful treasure without delay. He accordingly palms it upon a Jew, who, in turn, meeting with Albert, anxious to escape the Inquisition and get safe back to Germany, sells him his attire, as a disguise, and with it his pedlar's box containing the unfortunate Bottle. Albert discovering the Imp again in his possession, in a moment of anguish enters the army, hoping that some friendly ball may rid him of his weary existence. In a carouse with his brother soldiers he gambles away his canteen—as the soldiers believe it is, not the Bottle Imp, as it afterwards turns out to be—and is sentenced to be shot. Marcelia meanwhile having disclosed to her father the faithlessness of Albert, vengeance is vowed in the usual stage terms, and the old man and the maid set off; the laudable object of the former being to hunt down the reprobate without loss of time. Just as Albert is being led forth to execution Marcelia appears. Strange to say she has become possessed of the unfortunate Bottle, from which Albert, for the sake of 'Auld lang syne,' releases her. His sentence being reversed, Albert is subsequently sent to guard the prisoners in the dungeon of the Inquisition, at which a fire has broken out, and he finds Nicolo there arrested upon a charge of sorcery. Smoke is issuing from the floor of his cell, and he implores Albert to give him drink out of his canteen to allay his thirst. But finding him fixed in his determination to sell it only (for you will readily perceive it is the old bugbear which he has mistaken for a canteen of liquor), Nicolo offers him for it a picola, the coin of smallest value in the world, which Albert accepting, the Demon appears to an extra dose of coloured fire, seizes Nicolo, and the rest (the descent to Pandemonium) is left to imagination. When it was required that the Bottle Imp should speak, I appeared, in a blaze of light of course; on all the other occasions a phial alone sufficed.

"The only thing that can be said for this play is that there is plenty of dramatic effect in it, and that was chiefly what our audiences required."

CHAPTER V.

For tails by nature sure were meant,
As well as beards, for ornament.—*Hudibras.*

" I remember about the time to which I have just been
alluding, that amongst our other entertainments in the
circle we had a four-horse *entree.* Engaged in this were
Charles Adams (great uncle of the present Charlie), my
brother Tom, Wallett, and myself. Wallett rode a blood
mare belonging to Powell, who, as I have before said, was
in partnership with my father, though his name appeared
neither on the show nor in the bills. At one side of the
ring we had a large coat of arms mounted on rollers—I
don't know whose coat of arms it was, it would be impossible for any showman to tell at all times the object and
meaning of every device and ornament he displays—but it
would be put there for show, no doubt. Well, it so happened that Tom's horse, going at a quick pace, somehow
caught the roller with its head, whereupon it shied and
threw its rider in a moment. This occasioned Wallett to
pull up suddenly, when—owing mainly to the fact that
his saddle was loose—down came the great jester that was
to be. My horse, ' Spot,'—who at the best of times
never objected to going down upon his knees,—after such
a sad example shown him by his two equine brethren,
needed no persuasion to make himself shorter by the legs,
and so projected me over his head. And there we three
great stars lay, displaying our elegance in the sawdust to
the intense delight of the audience.

" In those days we used to promenade the streets with
our horses, and sometimes we took our instruments with
us and played. Tom played the key or Kent bugle and I
the trumpet, and two other members of the company
played respectively the trombone and bugle *secundo.*

'Spot' was the horse I always rode on these occasions (for nobody else would have aught to do with him), and a listless rat-tailed animal he was! As I rode him along the street, his barren extremity looking terribly conspicuous, little boys would point to the place where the tail ought to be, and made merry at his expense. It annoyed me very much to hear these reflections cast upon his shortcomings, and so I said to my father one day, ' Father, couldn't something be done to that horse ? '

" ' In what respect, Sam ? '

" ' Why, in regard to his tail ? Couldn't we get him some false hair ? '

" ' Well,' replied my father, slowly pondering the matter, ' I *have* heard before of such a thing as a horse having a false tail. I'll think about it, and then see what can be done.'

" So, by and bye, he made his way to a tannery, and giving one of the men there a trifle in money, induced him to detach from the hind quarters of a deceased mare a beautiful long tail. The curer's aid being next sought, my father had straps affixed to the false tail, which straps were artfully secured to the crupper of the saddle of the rat-tailed gentleman before mentioned. Odd's bodikins! but the animal looked twenty pounds better; in fact, he was hardly himself at all; and when he and I appeared in the ring that evening—'Spot' moving his false hair about with as much vanity as if it had been his own natural produc-tion—the exclamations on every side were, ' A new horse ! Si'thee, Bob, si'thee, Jem, a new horse !' Popular enthusiasm knew no bounds, and I bestrode the animal with a dignity befitting the occasion. But truth will out, and the deception was at length laid bare.

" We were promenading one day at Leeds, and halted for refreshment at a public-house near the New Road End, called the ' Bean Ing.' We dismounted, and leaving our horses in the custody of some admiring boys—for what lad doesn't feel proud to hold a horse? and ours were the ' grand ' circus horses, remember—we went forward into the parlour. While there quietly regaling ourselves, the juveniles, who it seems aspired to be judges of horseflesh, began to examine and direct each other's attention to the good points of the animals in their custody. The short-comings of mine must have been detected, and the necessity of buckles and straps about the tail of a horse discussed. Having each of us refreshed the inner man we remounted, rewarded with coppers the lads (whose joy at their discovery they kept so remarkably well under control that it was never alluded to before us), and, as it began to rain, we went off at a good round pace. I endeavoured to keep up with my fellows as well as I could, but it was all to no purpose. 'Spot,' whom, as I have said, nobody would ride but I, still lagged behind. After we had been jogging along for some time, 'Spot' and I, the sound of voices behind me, 'Hi! Hi!' caused me to look back, when my attention was drawn to 'Spot's' hind quarters. And would you believe it, the ragamuffins had undone those buckles, and there was my horse's grand tail hanging by a single strap, and draggling along in the dirt. Presence of mind is everything in a case like that, so jumping down I cut the strap, put 'Spot's' and the old tan-yard mare's glory in my pocket, and resumed my journey as though nothing had occurred. This affair soon got wind, as you may suppose, and though we still persevered in the use of the tail, and never left our horses in custody of boys any more, it was anything but gratifying to me, as I rode the animal round the ring at subsequent performances, to hear the audience admonishing 'Spot' to keep his tail up.

"It is very natural that you should ask me if we had a special band for the evening, as we couldn't both play on the stage and in the orchestra at the same time. We engaged amateur musicians who lived in the town; they came after their daily labours were over. There were four of them—John Richardson, who played an E flat clarionet; his son Joseph, who performed on a similar instrument, but his was a B flat; Tom Clarke, who uttered his sentiments through a key bugle; and William Gott, who gave vent to his emotions on a trombone. Joseph Richardson was a clever fellow, I assure you. He was afterwards sent to Nicholson, of London, a great flute player, and ultimately became the greatest professor of that instrument in England. He was flautist to the Duke of Devonshire, and for some time soloist in Jullien's famous band.

"When we should have removed from Leeds we could not on account of the severe weather, the uprights of the booth being frozen into the ground. So we left the place a few days, and, dividing ourselves into two companies, took rooms at Armley and Bramley, and gave short theatrical entertainments—little sketches, comic songs, and usually a farce. I went to Armley and Tom to Bramley. When weather permitted we pulled down our booth and came to Halifax.

"Our companies always kept well together, for my mother and father (I put her first, for in business matters the grey mare was always the better horse) would pay them, if only money was forthcoming. Many won't do that. One of our actors was a splendid penman, and he sometimes added a little to his salary by writing out our parts for us; but these we had to pay for ourselves, of course.

"Our repertoire of pieces about this time consisted of *The Sea, or the Ocean Child, Mutiny at the Nore, The Idiot Witness, Rob Roy, Othello, Jane Shore, The Stranger, William Tell, My Poll and My Partner Joe, The Bottle Imp, The Floating Beacon,* and similar plays."

CHAPTER VI.

"Sam's" Marriage—Mrs. "Sam" Comes Out as an Actress—Their Olive Branches.

> Longueville—What! are you married, Beaufort?
> Beaufort—Ay, as fast
>   As words, and hands, and hearts, and priest
>   Could make us.
>   —Beaumont and Fletcher—*Noble Gentleman.*

"As I have before stated, I was married in 1835. My bride was Louisa, daughter of John Worrall, captain of the *Duke* sloop of war. She was a fine woman, I assure you, both physically and intellectually.

"I still kept on at my father's establishment, though I found it rather difficult to keep up with my domestic wants. Eight or nine months after our marriage, my wife, seeing there was plenty to do to make ends meet, decided, though I desired her not, to go on to the stage. In course of time she became our leading lady actress, and was worth any two women we had. She was at home alike in tragedy and comedy, in Irish and in Scotch characters. As Lady Macbeth she was considered excellent; and she gave very fine renderings of Desdemona, of the Queen in *Hamlet,* and characters of that description. We were continually having fresh pieces, but she readily adapted herself to every occasion. The *Green Bushes, Flowers of the Forest,* the *Green Hills of the Far West*—she also played in these. We had, as you must please remember, quite given up the juggling and acrobat business at this time, but we always kept a posturer or clown for the outside to attract the spectators during the fair season. Old Finch was with us in that capacity at the time of my marriage. Our first child was born a year after that event. We christened it Sarah Ann, after my sister. As soon as this little lady was of age to learn anything at all, we sent her to my brother-in-law, Edwin Hughes (he married my sister Sarah Ann, just mentioned), to learn tight-rope dancing. He was the

proprietor of a large circus, and was then staying at
Warwick. But little Sally was only with him some eight
or ten months; the olive branches of the Hughes family
didn't treat her very well. ' You're only pa's apprentice,
remember,' was their continual cry; and the poor child
didn't like it. So she returned to us while we were on a
visit to Leeds. Almost immediately upon her return she
caught the scarlet fever, and in a week afterwards our
firstborn was taken from us. She was nine and a-half
years of age when she died. But she had the makings of
a clever woman in her, had Providence thought fit to spare
her to us. Altogether, we had twelve children, but four of
them died in infancy. Thomas was born 24th May, 1842.
He, like all our children, when they were old enough (except, of course, the four just alluded to) was brought up
to the stage, and he performed along with us for a time.
He is still living, and is married, but has no family. He
is an excellent musician; plays the cornet and the double
bass, in fact almost any instrument. As a comedian he
has travelled with Henri Corri's company, and with others
of note, and at the present time is engaged at the Theatre
Royal, Dudley, in Worcestershire. Louisa, named after
her mother, was born in 1846. She, too, was taught the
performer's art. Her chief aspiration seemed to be
chambermaid parts, though she sustained others; but her
strong point was dancing—she was always our columbine
in the pantomimes. She was married 15th May, 1864,
to a juvenile actor, named Russell, who travelled with us.
They remained with our company seven months after their
marriage, and then, no doubt for the sake of change, they
joined successively the establishments of Pickles, Duval,
Thomas Wild (my brother, he was once on his own
account a short time), McDonald, and others in the same
line. Her husband is now joint proprietor with Mr. John
Scott, of the Victoria Theatre, Bury, Lancashire. The
Louisa in question is none other than my lady there. She
is over on a visit for a little time. Then we had a son
whom we called Samuel after myself. He appeared in pantomime at a very early age, but died in his ninth year.
This was in 1855 or 1856. Our next son, James, was born
at Leeds. There is not much to record of his professional
career, as he, too, died at the same age as Samuel. Then it
was while we were at Halifax, in 1852, that our next son

(Charles Henry) first announced his entrance into the world. He was born in the Old House at Home, at the bottom of Albion Street. Like the rest, when of age, he went behind the footlights, and performed with us until 1868, the time when, owing to failing health and ill-advised speculation in circus property, I broke down. He is married, and now works as a cloth dresser here at Savile Mills. Then we have Elizabeth, born at Leeds two years after Charles Henry. She played little parts in due time, but took her farewell of the stage when we all did, in 1868. You will find her any time, during working hours, at Ogden's Mill, amongst the twisters there. Our last son, William Edwin (now a carpet printer at the Atlas Carpet Works, Halifax), was born 14th May, 1856."

CHAPTER VII.

"OLD FINCH"—ATTEMPT TO LEVY AN EXECUTION—
FINCH TACKLES THE "BUMS"—SEQUEL TO THE
ADVENTURE.

> I cannot find those runagates : that villain
> Hath mocked me.—*Cymbeline.*

"One of the greatest favourites at our establishment, a favourite both with us and with the public, was 'Old Finch,' who from a posturer gradually rose to be a clever actor, and was with us many years, along with his wife, who also performed upon the stage. But at fair times, as I have said before, he always entertained the outside audiences with a little of his favourite art, for at those times competition invariably ran high, and it was the pride of an establishment to show its varied resources.

"Talking of 'Old Finch.' Now I don't know why we should call him 'Old,' for when he came to us at first—and we begun to use that term as soon almost as he did come—he was comparatively young. Yet, somehow, he never objected to the title ; indeed, I fancy he used to consider it a mark of respect, and I am quite sure we never used it in derision. Well, talking of Old Finch reminds me of an incident in which he figured very prominently. It was probably about the year 1837. We were at Preston, in Lancashire, at that time ; and we had been performing in a place built some time previously by Ryan as a circus for himself, and which we had fitted up as a theatre, using our own scenery and whatever other properties we required. A capital business we did there during our eight-weeks' stay. But before we closed, as it was always the old folks' plan to let the company share in their successes, the principal members were allowed benefit nights. Mine, I remember, was the very last night of the season : Donnolly and Snape had theirs shortly before. Now each of those gentlemen on the occasion of his benefit went in very largely for handbills and posters, for which,

as it afterwards came to our knowledge, they quite forgot
to settle with the printer. The season at Preston had just
closed, and we had packed up our effects as usual, and sent
them forward to Blackburn, at which town we had next to
appear. The living van was left until the last. Finch was
securing 'Billy,' the pony, to the back of it, and I was har-
nessing the horses, and putting them to the shafts, while
Donnolly was busying himself by setting things to rights
in the van. The old folks were waiting for us at the Bluebell Inn, at which place we were to call on our way, and
take them up. Just as we were about to start a bailiff
appeared upon the scene, with an execution against my
father's goods and chattels at the suit of the printer. Now
I knew very well that my father had squared accounts with
the printer—he made a point of doing that regularly every
week—and so I suggested to the bailiff the probability of
his being mistaken. Oh, no! he knew his business, he did;
and thereupon produced a paper which he said empowered
him to seize the van. Donnolly asked to see his authority,
and, having cast his eye hurriedly over it, he gave it back
to the bailiff, and said to me, 'Drive on, Sam, you're all
right.' So I cracked my whip and the horses started.
But the bailiff insisted upon the caravan being stopped,
and conducted himself in a manner which, however peculiar
it may be to bailiffs, I considered very disagreeable. I
reasoned with him in vain for some time, until at last he
attempted to stop the horses, when I found myself bound
by the laws of good breeding to knock him down. The
crowd which had gathered round us during our altercation
expressed their entire satisfaction with the course I had
pursued, for, somehow, few people seem to be of opinion
that bailiffs are deserving of sympathy. But as the
knocking down of a bumbailiff was considered to be in
the eye of the law a most serious offence, while the power
of the law to punish was unlimited, I was strongly advised
on all hands to retire as quickly as possible. For the
bailiff, after regaining his perpendicular, had made off in
great haste, looking very desperate, and threatening to
visit me with all the terrors of the law, while it was
commonly believed for the moment that nothing short of
penal servitude could make satisfaction for so great an
offence. As he went along he met two policemen, whom
he instructed to come and seize the van, which they did.

Whereupon, throwing the whip to Old Finch, I acted upon the advice of my counsellors. By and bye, the bailiff returned with another of the same fraternity, and they, and the police together, proceeded to take the horses out of the van. But the bailiffs, in removing 'Billy' from the back of it, used him rather roughly—they had a grudge against me, you know, and 'Billy' was a quiet, little, harmless fellow, who didn't know what it was to retaliate—at which Finch, in a moment of indignation, struck one or both of the cowardly fellows, who, turning round, set upon him in good earnest. Finch was advised, for similar reasons, to make off as I had done, and so took his flight in the direction of the Bluebell Inn. Arrived there, he ran upstairs and into a long room, a sort of meeting or club-room, his antagonists following in pursuit. This room was in course of being cleaned, and all the chairs were placed together at one end of it. Closing the door after him, and instantly seizing a chair, Finch stood prepared to receive the enemy. The moment the door was opened, whiz went the chair, and for a few seconds the enemy beat a retreat. Again it attempted to enter, when whiz came another chair, and it was a second time repulsed. In this way the defence was kept up until poor Finch's stock of ammunition was exhausted. Then, driven now to desperation, he threw up the room window. In the street below, the crowd, part of which had followed him in his flight to see what became of him, cheered him as he opened the window, and told him to jump down. Three or four lusty fellows joined hands, as we used to do in the harlequinade, to receive the clown when he jumped through the pork butcher's shop window, and renewed their invitation. Finch accepted it, and they caught him safe and sound. The enemy's attacks being no longer resisted, a grand triumphal entry into the fortress was arranged, and preparation carefully made for the capture of the vanquished Finch. The open window, however, revealed the direction of his flight, but the enemy did not deem it necessary or prudent to follow that way in pursuit, but retraced its steps, confidently expecting to find the mortal remains of Old Finch lying on the pavement outside. By this time, however, Finch was making off in the direction I had taken, and the crowd, with a view to let him have a fair start, so pestered, and hustled, and bustled the bumbailiffs about, that a hope of ever overtaking him seemed doubtful.

"Meanwhile, I was on the road to Blackburn, and paused to recruit my spent energies at the Old Hall, a sort of half-way house between Preston and Blackburn. Here I had to take my refreshment covertly, and dodge about the out premises as my pursuers (imaginary ones only they proved to be) would be sure to call there and inquire for me. I had a good view of the road, and could see passengers and conveyances pass. When the stage coach came up I felt rather sure then that it would set down somebody in quest of me, and for some time after it had gone I kept close quarters. My fears were groundless it seemed, and so I breathed again, but still kept watch. A carrier's van now drove up, and great was my delight to see my wife and a servant at the front of it. I immediately joined them, and we went forward to Blackburn and put up at our old posting-place, the Golden Ball. But, before we had been there long, I heard a hurried footstep in the passage, and for a moment, in imagination, saw nothing but handcuffs before me. I was agreeably surprised, however, to find nobody more formidable (to me) than Old Finch. And I was surprised in another sense, for where was the van I had left in his custody? Then followed the details of his adventure with the bailiffs, at which we laughed very heartily, notwithstanding that both of us expected at any moment to be arrested.

"By and bye the old folks turned up in the van itself, and this caused us to feel a little easier in our minds. They told us that on hearing the disturbance at the Bluebell they inquired into the matter, and then learned for the first time all about the execution against my father's goods, and what the attempt to carry it out had led to. It appeared, on inquiry, that the printer's claim was for the bills and posters ordered by Donnolly and Snape, and for which, as I said before, they had neglected to pay. The printer, foreseeing the difficulty of getting anything out of two strolling players, who had little more to call their own than the clothes on their backs, thought he might stand a better chance by suing my father, to whose prompt settlement of accounts the printer himself could testify ; so he took that course. As might be expected, my father and mother were justly indignant at having £9 odd to pay for two not particularly indispensable members of their company. But what could they do? To test the legality of the thing would entail expense, and to leave the caravan in the hands of the bailiffs would be more out of my father's way, in a pecuniary sense, than to pay the amount of the execution. So, after weighing well these considerations, he decided to pay the £9 something—a pretty score for a debt of only £2 odd—and the caravan was restored to him.

"At the Golden Ball we all had tea together that night, and though the old folks were worse off by £10 than they had been in the morning, it was impossible for them not to laugh at that day's adventures.

"Neither Donnolly nor Snape ever repaid my father the amount he had laid down for them, yet he never attempted to deduct it from their salaries. But he lost confidence in them, and got rid of them at the earliest opportunity. Donnolly, however, some years later (after my father had died) came to us again for a little while. He presented himself at the theatre at a time when we were one short of our full number of men, and that was how he came into our service again."

CHAPTER VIII.

LAST DAYS OF "JEMMY" WILD—THE OLD MAN AND HIS
PETS—VISIT TO BRADFORD—HIS DEATH AND LAST
JOURNEY IN THE VAN—HIS FUNERAL—"HUMBUG
CHARLIE"—LAST OF "BILLY," THE TRICK PONY.

Tired, he sleeps, and life's poor play is o'er.
—POPE—*Essay on Man.*

"For several years before he died, my father was
unable to take any active part in the business of our
establishment.   He had grown exceedingly corpulent, had
lost his former energy and skill, and the fire had nearly
died out in his eye.   So he did pretty much as he liked,
and wandered about at his own sweet will.   And in his
wanderings 'Billy,' now grown old like himself, but
sheltered and cared for for what he had been, sometimes
accompanied him.   As for his favourite bloodhound,
'Jerry,' which he had owned ever since it was very little
bigger than the palm of his hand, he couldn't move but it
would be by his side.   In fact, 'Jerry' was always lying in
wait for his master.   He would hang about the caravan
(or living van) when father was at home, listening to his
every movement, and would prick up his ears whenever he
heard the old man's voice.   But when he saw him put on
his hat and come to the door there was such a barking and
such a fuss as you never did see.   Then sometimes his
master would say to him cheerily, 'Come, "Jerry," my boy,
let's go for a walk.'   And 'Jerry' needed no second invitation, I assure you.   Nay, he always conceived it his duty to
go with his master without being asked at all, though a
word of encouragement always enhanced the importance
of his trust, and made him the happiest of dogs alive.
Then he would scamper off as though he was never going
to return any more, and then, suddenly wheeling about,
before he had gone forty paces, come bounding back again
to his master's side.   So that, knowing all about this
attachment, it became a very common observation amongst

ourselves, when any one observed that father had gone out, 'Oh, then that accounts for "Jerry's" absence,' and very often it would be asked at the same time, 'Hasn't he taken "Billy" with him too?' for sometimes father would go to the stable and fetch 'Billy' out for an airing; and with the pony by his side, and 'Jerry' running first to his master and then to 'Billy'—with whom he was on the very highest terms of friendship—they would in this way take their constitutional. Three old cronies these, always happy in each other's society, and almost melancholy if parted. Sometimes when they were all out together father would pop in to some wayside inn; but they always followed close at his heels, and when he sat down, 'Jerry' would go and lie under his seat until he was called for—for the old dog knew his business and his place—and 'Billy,' who generally followed the old man into the inn also, would make up to his master and wait patiently until he was ready for going; then, while the old man refreshed himself with his customary two-pennyworth of gin, he would order the animals a biscuit or a sop to keep him company. (Not that my father was by any means a drunkard. He had a bronchial affection, as most old men who have played upon wind instruments all their lives usually have, and he preferred gin because it invariably relieved him in his breathing; but it was about the only liquor he cared for.) Then, if there chanced to be good company in the parlour, they would be sure to want to see the renowned 'Billy's' performances, whereupon his master would just whisper the old nominies to him and give him the old signals, upon which 'Billy' would endeavour to remember some of the fortune-telling tricks wherewith he used to delight audiences twenty good years before; and then if any of the company chose to give him a biscuit or a copper—though happily 'Billy' was far above want—he would go down on his knees and return thanks like a Christian. But he was not so agile as of yore, still his performances always pleased his audience and delighted the old man. As for 'Billy,' he was only too happy to do anything for his master, notwithstanding that he always pointed him out as the 'biggest rogue in the company.' 'Jerry,' however, was not a performer, so he could only look on admiringly from under the chair, and up at his master, and whenever he chanced to catch his eye there was sure

to be a little bit of demonstration with that tail of his.
Then my father would get up, and 'Billy' turn himself
round and make for the door, whither 'Jerry' had preceded
them, watching for them both and wagging his tail. When
they had reached the outside they would all jog along
homewards in the same order as before.   Father would
then conduct 'Billy' to the stable, see that he was well
provided for there, and bestow him a pat on his aged sides,
and a parting word or two. Arrived at the caravan, 'Jerry'
would wait to see his master safe in, then hang about with
a very disconsolate look until the old man appeared again.
But supposing it was night when they returned, 'Jerry,'
without any bidding, would go and take up his quarters
until morning, under the stage inside the theatre.   And
we had never a moment's anxiety about the safety of the
place, so far as thieves were concerned, when he was there.
These were happy times for the old man, and, indeed, for
his pets, too.   In the daytime they were nearly always
together, and at night, when absent from them, father was
always worriting about them — terrified lest anything
should happen to them.

   " In this way the days, weeks, and months came and
went, and the friendship of this trio became stronger as
they grew older.

   " The management of the concern on father's failing
health had devolved on Tom and I, while the treasury had
an able custodian in our mother, who always took care to
appoint herself to that office.

   " In the winter of 1838 we were located at Bradford.
Our wood and canvas establishment was then erected on
what afterwards became the site of Moseley's Theatre.
It was a foggy night in December. The fair season was
just over, and we intended pulling down that night after
the performance, to be in readiness for starting for
Huddersfield next morning.   While my mother was
' counting out the money '—the receipts of the evening—
in the caravan, and while we, behind the footlights, were
in the midst of some important business or other, father
went on to the Manor House, in Darley Street, to have
a quiet chat with some of his old friends who met there,
and perchance to take a little of something to keep out
the cold and the fog that raw night, 'Jerry' being with
him as usual. Not feeling very well, about nine o'clock

he bent his steps homewards. It was only a short journey
he had to perform, but the dense fog made it a trying
one. As he reached the caravan, in an almost exhausted
condition, and dragged himself up the steps as well as
he could—'Jerry' watching and sympathising with him
no doubt—he said to my mother as she opened the
door for him, 'Betty, my lass, I think it's about
over with me.' Seeing that he was much worse than
usual, mother got him to bed and a doctor was sent for.
Upon his arrival he said father was very ill, and had
better be removed at once to some hotel, where he could
be well looked to. The old man knew, however, that he
would receive far more attention in his own caravan than
he could possibly have anywhere out of it, and so declined
to be removed. But there was another reason why he
wished to remain. He wanted to go to Huddersfield with
us because he had an old crony there, whom he loved as
himself, one Charles Healey, generally called, after the
sweets he vended, 'Humbug Charlie.' Charlie had
served twenty-one years in the army, and was then in
receipt of about thirteenpence per day from Government.
His wife kept a small shop, a sort of confectioner's, and
he went about with a little tin suspended before him
selling sweets. Father and he had first met at Huddersfield
many a long year ago, and they had kept up their
acquaintance ever since, and Charlie was now grown old
like my father. So 'Old Jemmy's' delight had been, and
still was, the prospect of another meeting with his friend
Charlie, and on this account, and because he foresaw that
his removal from the caravan would lessen that prospect,
if it did not destroy it altogether, he would on no
consideration be persuaded to leave his quarters in the
van, though he might have had his choice of the best hotels
in the town, for our circumstances at that time were
flourishing.

"Well, after the performances were over that night,
we began to pull down the booth, and put it, along with
our dresses, scenery, and other paraphernalia, on to the
vans. About nine o'clock next morning we started for
Huddersfield, leaving the living van behind us, for the
doctor said if father would not consent to be removed out
of it, he must by no means attempt to make a journey in
it. Selina remained behind with my mother to render any

assistance she could, and also Tom, who was to follow in
the afternoon if matters were no worse. The old man,
however, got no better. The sound of the horses' feet
starting upon their journey only served to make him more
downcast at being left behind, for he had been looking
forward with almost childish delight to our journey to
Huddersfield for some time, and could talk of nothing else
but of that and of Charlie. He began, very soon after we
had gone, to change for the worse, though at intervals he
still talked in the old strain ; then his voice grew weaker,
and his breathing more difficult, and within a couple of
hours of our leaving Bradford there was an end of poor
' Old Jemmy ' Wild.

"But I ought to have said that during his attack it
had become known how dangerously ill he was, and as he
was held in very high esteem by the townspeople, inquiries
as to his health were continually being made at the door
of the caravan. Just at the time when his hope of seeing
the old soldier was for ever set at rest, a friend of the
family—a tradesman in Bradford—called to see how he
was. The moment he perceived how matters stood he very
kindly offered to go and mount his horse and fetch me
back to Bradford. My mother gladly availed herself of
this generous proposition, but advised him when he saw me
to only say that father was worse, and that I had better
go back without delay. Our vans were only just entering
Brighouse when he overtook us. The moment I heard this
sad news (though still ignorant of the worst) I left money
with my wife to pay all dues and demands when they
reached Huddersfield, and, mounting the messenger's
horse at his request, returned with all haste to Bradford.
As soon as I reached the ground where the caravan stood,
a crowd of people gathered about it and talking seriously
to each other plainly suggested the truth to me that the
old showman was no more.

"When I went into the van, there was the old man
stretched out upon his bed, cold and still, and my mother
and sister in tears. It was an affecting sight, and one I
shall never forget ; for you must please remember that
though an actor may, upon the stage, affect distress very
cleverly, he is no more proof against the appeals of real
misfortune than the individual of everyday life.

"Well, I wrote off to my brother and sister, James and

Sarah Ann (both of them at Batty's Circus, Manchester), and to other relatives and friends. This being done, I started for Huddersfield again to bring back Tom's wife and my own. James and Sarah Ann came over the next day, but could only remain with us a few hours, as they were engaged to appear that evening in the arena at Batty's. They were two of Batty's most valued servants, and even in an emergency of this kind couldn't be spared out of the circle. When James learned how anxious his father had been to go to Huddersfield, he said, ' Well, take him to Huddersfield, then. I have a wife and child buried there, in the graveyard attached to Trinity Church, and the vault is my own property ; take him and bury him there ' ; a kind and thoughtful proposition which it was decided at once to act upon.

" So a little before twelve o'clock on the second evening after the old man's death, when all was still, we started upon our journey, the saddest, I think, we ever made. Inside the caravan, and down the centre of it, lay the coffined remains of the old conjurer, and seated around him were his poor widow, Tom, myself, our wives, and Selina, all of us deeply affected. Outside the caravan, and tied to the back of it, was old 'Billy,' all unconscious that he was following his aged master to the grave ; and walking along by the side of the van thoughtfully (for I always fancied he had some idea that the old man had gone), was the faithful watch-dog 'Jerry.' All was still without, except the slow tramp of the horses' feet and the rumbling of the van, and the only sounds within were a whisper now and then from one to another, and an occasional sob from the women.

" We arrived at Huddersfield about three o'clock the next morning. Even at that early hour, cold December though it was, there were hundreds of persons out to meet the caravan, for it had become known there that ' Old Wild ' wes dead, and that his remains were being brought to Huddersfield for interment. And my father did enjoy a popularity in his time, I can tell you. I speak deliberately when I say that his death was as much talked of then, all over the country, as was Sir Francis Crossley's demise six years ago.

" Upon reaching Huddersfield we proceeded to the Druids' Hotel. We had some difficulty in removing the

coffin from the caravan — for my father was broad
shouldered, and weighed over seventeen stones — but when
we had succeeded at last, we conveyed it into the parlour,
and placing it upon a table, locked up the room.   Mother
and Selina remained in the van, with ' Jerry' as watch,
Tom and I lodged at the hotel, and ' Billy' was put into
the stable.

"About nine o'clock Tom and I arose and went into
the parlour.   'Jerry' coming into the hotel at that moment
followed us into the room and threw himself down under
the table whereon his late master lay, and there remained.
I had been thinking about the old man, and felt that I
should like to have a peep at his face once more.   I
expressed my desire to my mother, who at first objected
to the lid of the coffin being removed, but, finding me
still importunate, at length consented.   So I satisfied my
longing eyes.   There was the grand old face, calm and
placid, as though its owner had just composed himself for
his afternoon's nap, the face that we had all looked upon
with awe in our younger days, and with respect and
veneration when we came to be men and women.

"As soon as it became known that the old showman
was to be seen — for, contrary to my mother's expectations,
there was nothing to prevent the lid of the coffin being
left off a short time — hundreds of the townspeople whom
my father had amused in his day came to see him, ' positively for the last time,' and amongst them came Charlie
Healey, father's old crony that had been, and he looked at
his old friend's face until first one tear and then another
started, and the dear old soul couldn't look any longer.

"The moment the coffin was removed 'Jerry' got up and
followed it to the hearse.   As soon as the door was closed
upon it he returned to the parlour, and, resuming his
former position under the table, remained there all the
afternoon, howling mournfully at intervals.

"There was a great concourse of people to see the
funeral.   We had two mourning coaches.   Mother, James,
and Sarah Ann occupied the first, and Tom and I and our
wives the second.   The company, headed by Samuel Kirk-
ham, who was our leading actor at that time, followed in
cabs, and foremost among those who brought up the rear
was Charlie Healey.   He had divested himself of his can
of sweets, along with his weekday clothes, had mounted a

good suit of black, and had staked at least two days' pay from Government in hire of a cab to do honour to his friend's burial.

"The interment took place about two o'clock in the afternoon, in the presence, as I have said, of a large gathering of people. We were all very much affected by the ceremony, and with thinking about the old man; but I do believe that amongst the tears that fell that December afternoon by the side of 'Old Jemmy Wild's' grave there were none more genuine than those of the old soldier.

"For the next two days we did nothing in the way of performing. On the third day, however, we fixed our booth, and, once more throwing the doors open to the public, again took our places behind the footlights. We remained at Huddersfield for three months, and had crowded houses nearly every night, for the good people of that town sympathised very largely with my mother.

"See, here is the old man's funeral card:—

In Memory of

J A M E S   W I L D,

Who died December the 21st, 1838,

Aged 67 Years.

A plain, unassuming affair, like the man. No catalogue of virtues, as you see, though he was not without his good points, as those who knew him best could testify. No grand poetry seeking to assure the reader of what nobody can know, though it is quite right to hope that so and so is the case.

"Following within a couple of years of my father's demise was the death of old 'Billy,' the trick pony. He had travelled with us for about twelve months after he had lost his aged master—for we didn't like parting with him, though he was now of no use to us as a performer. He had got into years, his old black coat began to look dusky, his limbs had lost their expertness and activity, and his love of fun had nearly died out. He no longer delighted audiences in pointing out the little boys who stole their mamma's sugar, the men who were fonder of grog than of going to church on Sundays, and the young lady who was just about to be married ; while, for other reasons, unfortunately well known to us all, he was unable longer to discover the 'biggest rogue of the company.'* Well, as I said, we kept him for old acquaintance' sake until he was unable to get about as heretofore, and then sent him to a farmer at Shelf, Joseph Lister, with instructions for him to see to it that the old fortune-teller was well cared for. But 'Billy' didn't enjoy his retirement more than twelve months—hardly that—and was found dead one morning in a corner of Lister's field. So they buried him there."

---

* This scene, which always created infinite amusement (and which was no doubt partially suggested by the story of Banks and his famous horse, "Marocco," as narrated in *Tarleton's Jests*), was, I am told on the authority of one who has repeatedly witnessed the performance, somewhat after this fashion:—"Now, 'Billy,'" the old man would say, "I want you to go round and pick me out the biggest rogue in the company." Whereupon "Billy" would walk slowly round the ring—this was in the old amphitheatre times—and suddenly stop at his master, to the intense amusement of the audience. "You scoundrel! How dare you, sir?" "Old Jemmy" would ask. "I told you to go round and pick me out the *biggest rogue* in the company, didn't I? Now go round again, sir." To an admonitory crack of the whip, "Billy" would once more set forth on his work of detection, and, of course, again stop at his master. Increased laughter and applause. "Well ladies and gentlemen," "Jemmy" would say, addressing the audience, "I do believe the pony thinks I *am* the biggest rogue in the company"—(roars of laughter)—"and, really, ladies and gentlemen, *I believe you think so, too!*"—"TRIM."

CHAPTER IX.

Enterprises of great pith and moment.—*Hamlet.*

"Of those three, for many years, firm and fast friends, the old man, the pony, and the dog, only 'Jerry' now remained ; though he was no longer the vivacious animal he used to be. Indeed, his health began to fail soon after 'Billy's' death, and disorders peculiar to old age in dogs came upon him, for he was advanced in years. We did for him what we could —for his welfare concerned us all— and finally placed him in the doctor's hands, hoping still that 'Jerry' might improve and have a longer lease of life. But there is—and to this I am testimony myself—no undoing what time has done. The chances were all against the animal, and much as we were attached to him, and he to us, we perceived that the longer we kept him, the more his sufferings must increase, for his aged limbs refused now to support him, and he only became a burden to himself.

"Still we talked about the river long before we could any of us call up courage to send him there. But the necessity to do so came at length, and it was during one of our visits to Leeds that we finally took leave of him.

"'Well, Martin,' we asked of our property man one afternoon, when he and a 'super' joined us at the booth, after having just discharged a painful duty for us, though a kind service so far as the animal was concerned, 'how have you got on with poor old "Jerry"?'

"'Why,' rejoined he, 'as we took him down the river in a boat to Sandy Lobby, he looked up at us from time to time so pitifully that we'd scarce the heart to do anything with him at all, except bring him back again. But we

knew that what we had gone to do was really the best
thing that could be done for the poor old fellow, and tried
not to think about it.   Yet as we took him up, weighted
and bound, in our arms, he seemed so downcast and looked
so inquiringly at us, as much as to say, "You are surely
not going to throw old 'Jerry' overboard?" that we put
him down again and for a moment or two were strongly
tempted to loose him and bring him back with us at all
hazards.   Then we reasoned it over again, Jem and I, and
saw that we should be really performing the animal a good
service; so taking him up once more, without stopping
this time to think about it, we dropped him over the side
of the boat into the river, and pushed away from the place
—a good deal quicker than we went there.'

"Such was the narrative of our property man touching
the last of old 'Jerry,' and I'll answer for it that there
wasn't one amongst his auditors whose eye did not
glisten, to say the least of it, during the recital.

"At this time my mother was the sole proprietress of
our establishment.   The Wild and Powell partnership had
been concluded years ago and in my late father's time, the
season of 1835-6 I believe it would be.   Powell was not an
actor, simply an equestrian.   None of the stage properties
were his: his share in the belongings of the concern was
strictly limited to four horses and their trappings; though
I may add he always received an equal portion of the
money taken at the door.   He had nothing whatever to do
with the stage, his department was the arena.   But considering his somewhat limited stud of horses, he couldn't
introduce much variety into the circle; of the scenes in
which, as we became more proficient in theatrical matters,
our audiences began to tire.   My mother, keen and pene-
trating always, saw this, and decided (this was a year or
so before father's death) that we should do away with the
arena—for a time at least—and see if we couldn't keep up
our houses by dramatic performances alone.   So my father
(through his business agent, my mother) had come to an
amicable settlement with Powell, and the partnership was
dissolved.   Powell, taking with him Charlie Adams,
Hunter (the tight rope performer), and his daughter,
together with his own four horses, went to Leeds; and in
the neighbourhood of that town they 'mountebanked' for
some time; while we, at the booth, having nothing now to

distract our attention from theatrical matters, began to make rapid progress in the player's art.

"The success which always attended our visits to Bradford induced my mother in 1841 to have a wooden theatre erected, and to prolong her stay in that town. John Crabtree, the then landlord of the Market Tavern (which, by the way, was the rendezvous of most of the showmen at Fair time, though the Bermondsey Hotel was also well patronised by the theatricals), was a builder by trade, and had a workshop at that time. Negotiations were opened with him for the erection of the proposed theatre. The land upon which it was to be built was the same that we had occupied for many previous years, and belonged to the Corporation of Bradford, who let it to us. A written agreement was made, under which Crabtree was to put up a wooden erection, according to plans agreed upon, and which we were to occupy for a season of four months or so. He agreed to take back the timber at the close of the season, so that virtually we only paid a little more than the cost of putting up the place. It was a substantial affair, but had nothing grand about it. Our entrances for boxes, pit, and gallery were all at the front. The stage was about thirty feet deep, and in working width about forty-five feet, and down each side of it were the dressing-rooms. Our scenery was fourteen feet high, and about twenty-two feet wide. The building was capable of holding from 1200 to 1300 persons, and a good house, at our ordinary prices of 3d., 6d., and 1s., would yield us something like £27. We called it the Liver Theatre, after a very pretty and well-patronised theatre at Liverpool. We usually commenced the season about November, and packed away on vans the walls of our portable theatre until such season was over, when they were again called into requisition for some other town. Our entire company, including scene-shifters, prompter, &c., consisted of about twenty-five or thirty persons, in addition to which we were constantly engaging for a week or a fortnight—sometimes longer if they took well— actors and actresses of the higher order of travelling players, and whom we denominated 'stars.' For some time we had as our leading lady actress a Mrs. Mansfield, who afterwards, as Miss Rosa Henry, went to Astley's, while it was under Batty's management, and took a leading

position there. Then Mr. and Mrs. John (better known
as 'Jack') Holloway were with us, off and on, for a long,
long time. Mr. and Mrs. Liver, too, were in our company
for three or four years. Mr. and Mrs. Robert Lomas, who
afterwards had a travelling theatre of their own, were also
with us at Bradford and elsewhere for some time, as also
Robert Myers, who afterwards went to New York, and
played at the Broadway Theatre. As I said before, our
company generally kept well together. Some of our
actors and actresses have been with us fourteen and
fifteen years, while old Jacob Henry Williams, a man of
colour, and at the present time attached to Rhodes's
Theatre, I believe, remained with us no less than twenty-
three years. For 'Old Wild's' was considered not only
one of the best training schools, but for paying good
salaries, the first establishment travelling. And a great
many of those who were taught the first principles of the
performer's art with us have become famous in their day,
and their names have passed into history.

"Mr. Liver was our scenic artist at the time I speak
of (1841), and he found plenty of work always, for we had
scenery painted for almost every new piece we brought
forward. He and his wife, as I have said, also performed
with the company. Our orchestra numbered five instrumentalists, *violino primo* and *secundo*, cornopean, flute, and
double bass. The present Charles Hengler, the great
circus proprietor, played the violin in our band at this very
time. He was with us ten months, and was beginning to
learn the trumpet when he left. He never appeared on the
stage, however. As at this day, selections of music were
played before the rising of the curtain, and between the
acts.

"I think it was during our first season at Bradford that
Parrish came to the town, and erected his establishment in
the Hall Ings, and facing to Leeds Road. His place was
much larger, if I remember right, than ours. He had splendid scenery, a capital wardrobe, and an excellent company.
But, notwithstanding all these advantages, we always
drew better houses than he did. About this time the
play of *Jack Sheppard* was having an immense run in some
of the London theatres. Parrish thought that if he could
produce it at his place the thing was bound to be a success,
and would prove a counter-attraction to our nautical

and other new pieces, in the introduction of which to
provincial audiences we frequently stole a march upon
him. So he procured a copy of the play, cast the
characters, and set his artist to work. That nothing
might be wanting in the scenic department, he engaged
a Bradford artist, a Mr. Manners, to produce something
out of the ordinary way. As yet the theatre-going public
was in ignorance of what Mr. Parrish was doing for its
entertainment, but the company at 'Old Wild's' knew all
about it. Certain members of Mr. Parrish's company,
and others of our own, met at the Bermondsey Hotel
every evening, and as there was generally a little rivalry
between the two companies, Mr. Parrish's recent enterprise was, in an unguarded moment, alluded to. 'Oh, oh,
Mr. Parrish, that's your little game, is it?' said the stage
manager at our establishment, Paddy Hall, when he heard
of it. By the luckiest accident in the world, Sharpe, of
our company, the day after the doings of our rival's estab-
lishent were disclosed, happened to see lying upon a book
stall in the market a copy of the very play, *Jack Sheppard*, and instantly purchased it. 'Now,' says Paddy
Hall, 'we'll produce this *Jack Sheppard* without delay.'
So he cast the characters, and divided the book amongst
the company to be written out. Each copied his own part,
and then exchanged for other parts, until the whole of it
was gone through. I know I sat up all night to transcribe
Mrs. 'Sam's' part and my own. Jack Holloway was down
for the notorious robber, and I for Jonathan Wild. The
only new scene we introduced was a view of the exterior
of Newgate, for which view a portion of the outside proscenium did duty, after having been enlivened a little by
the introduction of a few pointed laths by way of spikes.
On the following day—the second after the news of the
enemy's doings had reached us—we had a rehearsal; and
on the third day it was performed before the public.
Up to this very day Parrish had been going on
rehearsing and preparing, quite ignorant of what
was being done behind the scenes at 'Old Wild's'.
But when he saw, to his dismay, our flaming posters
announcing *Jack Sheppard* for the first time in Bradford,
that evening, he rushed back to his own place, called his
manager, Joseph Gould, a sleepy fellow, and accused
everybody right and left of having betrayed him.

" Well, the piece took amazingly. We ran it for four
nights, and had crowded houses every night, and hundreds
went away unable to obtain admission. The part of Jack
Sheppard is a very long one—I should think some thirty
lengths without the cues,—and I remember the first time
we played the piece Jack Holloway hadn't got a line of
the last act off, but he gagged it so skilfully that the
irregularity was never observed.

" The Monday following, Parrish produced his version
of the play, and though, to do him justice, it was most mag-
nificently got up (for some of our company saw it), yet it
went for nothing; we had got the start of him. His Jack
Sheppard was Arthur Nelson (afterwards a clown at Cooke's
circus), and George Currier sustained the character of Jonathan Wild. Currier had, at one time and another, played in
many provincial theatres, and had a fair position on the
stage until an inordinate love of liquor caused him to lose
it. By reason, then, of what he had been, Currier was
looked up to by the members of Parrish's company as an
authority in theatrical matters. He was, certainly, pains-
taking ; and in the parts allotted to him always endeavoured
to be as literal in his make up as the characters would
admit of. In the *rôle* of Jonathan Wild he had to remove a
wig and disclose his bald head, so following out his
favourite theory he shaved his pate. The members of both
companies met as usual at the Bermondsey Hotel during
the time that Parrish was running, or attempting to run,
Jack Sheppard. Comparisons were made of the scenery,
dresses, and acting of the two establishments. ' Why,'
says one of Parrish's company, ' you never make up for
the parts as we do.' ' How not ? ' I inquired. ' Well,
look, for instance, at our Jonathan Wild here,' lifting off
Currier's wig, ' he has had his head shaved, you see, and
you haven't.' ' No, thank goodness,' I replied, ' my mind
hasn't been brought to that strait to require it.'

" Though we withdrew *Jack Sheppard* when Parrish's
company began to play it, yet, strange to say, they had a
mere dragging on with it. But it was, until the Lord
Chamberlain prohibited its performance, always a successful piece with us. We could generally count upon a good
house when that was down on the placards.

" Liver, our scenic artist, being allowed a benefit, asked
me what I thought would be a good thing to ensure him a

crowded house. I instantly replied, ' Play *Jack Sheppard*, and take Holloway's part for that night.' He spoke to his wife about it, but she wouldn't hear of it. She was ambitious for him to shine in nautical parts, and preferred that he should sustain Long Luke or Tom Cringle, two of my favourite characters. Now, Liver was a little man, of no presence at all, and for him to attempt characters usually sustained by a broad-shouldered fellow 5 feet 8½ inches in height, was almost certain to end in failure ; and another thing, he had never made these characters his study. But his wife had unlimited confidence in him, so he made his own selection of pieces. He chose as the first, *Breakers Ahead, or the Shipwreck of the Spanker*, and in lieu of a farce, *Tom Cringle's Log*. Two days before the benefit I said to him, ' Now, just to show you the certainty of success which you might have with *Jack Sheppard*, we will play it to-morrow night.' So I had small handbills printed—

Have you seen
JACK SHEPPARD ?
No.
Then go and see it at
W I L D ' S,
To-night,
For the Last Time this season.

Not a word more. Nothing about a benefit or aught else. The house was crowded to suffocation, and scores went away unable to gain admission.

" Well, Liver's benefit night came, and it was the worst night we had during the entire season. After all I couldn't but be sorry for him, because, as he was to have a third of the clear receipts, he might have put £5 into his pocket that night, instead of which he had very little, if anything, to receive. Such was the penalty the poor fellow had to pay for his wife's ambition."

CHAPTER X.

"Is John Audley there?"—"Tom Hexam"—Press Notices — Newspaper Controversy — Close of Season at Liver Theatre—The "White Abbey Lot"—Pritchard makes "Old Wild's" move on —Donnybrook Fair.

> Speak of me as I am : nothing extenuate,
> Nor set aught down in malice.—*Othello.*

"Notwithstanding his ill-luck with *Jack Sheppard*, and only an indifferent success with his pieces generally, Parrish did not leave Bradford until the close of the winter season I have referred to, nor for some days after we had played out our full term at the Liver Theatre. Nor did he afterwards, to the best of my recollection, remain at Bradford longer than the fair, during any of the seasons when 'Old Wild's' was located in that town.

"As may be supposed, the *Jack Sheppard* business— the forestalling incident I allude to—did not cause him to be very affectionately disposed towards us, but we made it a rule never to notice, or to appear that we noticed, spitefulness or animosity from whatever quarter it might proceed.

"Even during the fair season, when rival establishments sometimes sought their own welfare at the expense of ours, it was always our policy to be blind to their proceedings, and indeed to conduct ourselves generally as though in happy ignorance of their very existence. Though I will not say that at such times we did not occasionally make just a little more display outside than usual, and, as I have said before, show the varied resources of our establishment. But we never wrangled with our adversaries, and the noisy ones soon grew tired of having it all to themselves. Fair days were harvest days with us, and we couldn't afford to waste our time in useless controversy. Those were the days when we adopted the shopkeepers' motto, 'Small profits and quick returns,' and when we measured our successes not so much by the quality of the performance given as by the number of them that could be got through in a day.

"Those were the days, too, when 'Tom Hexam' and 'John Audley' used to be inquired for, very loudly and sharply, and always, bear in mind, when we were in the thickest of our business upon the stage inside the booth. 'Is John Audley there?' from the door at the top of the gallery came the question from one of our company. For we were not all down in the cast of characters for the fair days, and those who were not would repair outside when we were about half-way through a performance, while those who had got through their parts early would join them, and together they would endeavour to attract a fresh audience, to succeed that which we were entertaining within. This object attained, then came the question, as I have said, 'Is John Audley there?'* But on the stage we never appeared to notice this interruption, though, by hurrying through the performance, we always responded to the inquiry satisfactorily enough. For this, like the demand for 'Tom Hexam,' was simply a signal to us that there was another audience waiting outside, and that we must bring matters within to a *finale* as speedily as possible.

"Everybody didn't know these things, however, and it required some effort at times to preserve our gravity when asked by certain of the audience when the performance was over, who this 'Tom Hexam' was, and who this 'John Audley.' Were they recent additions to the company? Not by any means. But had they ever acted? Yes, frequently. Had 'Tom Hexam' been acting that day? He had acted that day (to which might have been added that he had acted very well, too, as he always did on fair days). Why, which was him? Now that was the point. Ah! they saw through it now—he performed under another name; that was it, for they had never seen 'Tom Hexam' on the bills.

"I think it was during our first season at the Liver Theatre—and how we came to occupy it for more than one

---

* This device was also employed by Richardson, who learned it from John Audley, the celebrated showman, with whom it originated. —"TRIM."

season I will explain by and bye—that *Oxberry's Weekly Budget of Plays* began to appear. Each number contained a copyright piece, the terms for the privilege to perform which were, in the country, half-a-crown an act per night, or two guineas for the right of playing a piece during one year. As these dramatic effusions were generally of an interesting, and oft-times thrilling character, we availed ourselves of the right to perform them by paying the editor of the *Budget* the stipulated fees. Amongst those which appeared in the journal in question we have produced and played, from time to time, the following :—*Ruth, or the Lass that Loved a Sailor, The Rose of Ettrick Vale, The Tables Turned, or Master Humphrey and his Clock, Grace Clairville, Ben Bruce, The Black Reefer, The Red Lance, Ada, the Betrayed.* This last piece, I may remark, was always a successful one with us, and, at one time and another, has brought us hundreds of pounds.

"In the *Budget*, which was also a 'Magazine of Romance, Whim, and Interest,' appeared notices of the London and provincial theatres, and the performances at the Liver Theatre were sometimes alluded to amongst the rest.

"In Number 30 of that journal, dated January 1st, 1844, appeared the following :—

BRADFORD, ROYAL LIVER THEATRE.—This prosperous little concern, under the management of Mrs. Wild, has been doing wonders lately— the sure effects of good management and good acting. Amongst other pieces, *Ruth* and several more of the copyrights which have appeared in the *Budget* have been got up in a highly creditable manner, and with great success.

"Again, under date January 15th, 1844 :—

BRADFORD, LIVER THEATRE.—We wish that Covent Garden and Drury Lane were doing as well as this theatre, under Mrs. Wild. It has performances twice a day, and the house is always crowded. On Saturday last we witnessed *Gilderoy* and *State Secrets*, admirably played. On Monday *Walter Tyrrell* was got up in a very superior style, and was followed by *The Queer Subject*, which elicited shouts of laughter. We cannot speak too highly in praise of Mr. Holloway, Mr. Lomas, Mr. Crowther, and Mrs. Finch.

"You will observe in the last notice that it is stated we had performances twice a day; that was on account of the fair.

"As *Oxberry's Budget* was open to all kinds of theatrical notices and correspondents, it is hardly to be expected that we, any more than anyone else, should find everybody speaking to our advantage. We have met with severe criticism as well as complimentary. Here is a little of both :—

BRADFORD, LIVER THEATRE.—*The Jewess* has been got up here and has had a run. Houses crammed every night.

BRADFORD.—In addition to the report already given, we have received the two following, which are so opposite in tendency that we must request to be enlightened on the subject :—

BRADFORD, January 21, 1844.

Sir,—You will oblige a party of friends to the drama by inserting the following in your valuable and popular work of the *Budget*. On Friday last we witnessed the Bard of Avon's masterpiece of *Othello* with a degree of pleasure. The part of the noble Moor by Mr. Holloway was played with great effect throughout. His jealous scene was truly beautiful and sublime ; he is a very clever man. Iago, by Mr. Harding, was excellent, and deserves much credit. Cassio, by Mr. Lomas, was good. Desdemona, by Mrs. Martin, was a chaste piece af acting. Emilia, by Mrs. Mansfield, was powerful and effective. The rest of the characters were all that could be. The performance concluded with the farce of *The Siamese Twins*, the parts well played, and elicited a deal of laughter. On Saturday *The Jewess*, for the third time, which has been got up with great taste, and better acting we have not seen for some time. The Eleazar of Mr. Holloway thrilled his auditors ; his conference with the Cardinal was truly great. De Brogni, Mr. S. Wild, was played with good taste and judgment ; but we would ask, Why was there not a better dress ? he was ridiculous in the extreme. Prince Leopold, Mr. Sharp, made all that could be made of it. On the whole it was very respectable. Karl, Mr. Crowther ; Mox, Mr. Finch ; Basil, Mr. Fraser, kept the house in roars of laughter. The first-mentioned gentleman is an excellent actor, possessing a deal of rich humour. Rachel (the Jewess), Mrs. Mansfield, was executed with a deal of judgment. This lady deserves much praise. Take it on the whole, we have not witnessed better acting. *The Jewess* was followed by the *Bath Road*. We did not stop to witness it. This theatre is crowded every night.

I remain, yours, &c.,

A CONSTANT SUBSCRIBER.

To the Editor of *Oxberry's Weekly Budget*.

Rochdale, January 21st, 1844.

SIR,—Having again received a letter with the enclosed from a Bradford friend, I forward the bill to you. From what I have heard, the less that is said about the performers and the performances the better. The company are so elated with their success, which can only be attributed to the briskness of trade at present in Bradford, that they care not in what manner they insult their audiences, by only indifferently, and, in some instances, shamefully playing the simplest and easiest dramas. I am given to learn that a report is prevalent among the play-going public of Bradford that your correspondent for Bradford was no other than one of the company, Mr. Macarthy who, in consequence of writing the article which appeared in No. 31 of the *Budget*, has got discharged. (We hope that this report is untrue.) If this be true it reflects very little credit on Mr. S. Wild, for, though the booth goes under his mother's name, he is virtually the acting manager.

Yours truly,   *   *   *

"The Mr. Macarthy alluded to in the letter of the Rochdale correspondent, who, we had reason to believe, was none other than Macarthy himself, was with us for a time as a utility man, but as my mother was very much dissatisfied with him she gave him notice to leave. Who the *Budget's* ' correspondent for Bradford ' was we never knew. It might have been Macarthy, but I do not think he was ever suspected. Though I cannot now remember even the substance of ' the article ' which appeared in No. 31 (for which number I have searched amongst my papers, I regret to say, in vain), I look at the matter in this way -— If Macarthy did write those articles, and penned the one (which appears to have been of an un-favourable character) for the thirty-first number of the *Budget*, after he had received his notice to leave, the latter circumstance would fully account for any severity in his remarks. On the other hand, if ' the article ' appeared, as the Rochdale correspondent suggests it did, before Macarthy received notice, I can only account for him doing such a thing out of pure malice, in which case the pro-priety of discharging so dangerous a character cannot, I think, be questioned.

"In the next number of the *Budget* a correspondent, quite unknown to any of us, though evidently having authority for what he wrote, thus referred to the Roch-dale letter :—

On perusing your valuable *Budget*, I find a letter from Somebody or Nobody—there being no initials attached thereto. I would ask this unknown to be more circumspect, "nor set down aught in malice" when next he wishes to make public the doings of a theatre. * * This wise-acre says the company "insult their audiences by only indifferently and shamefully playing the easiest dramas." * * The good people of Bradford are not so easily duped. The best criterion to follow is the theatre crowded nightly by a discerning audience, and the performances deservedly applauded. He likewise states that Mr. Macarthy, "in conse-quence of writing the article which appeared in No. 31 of the *Budget*, had got discharged." Here is another glaring falsehood, and if an expla-nation is required by him or his friend, whom I strongly suspect, I will give it. I would ask the Unknown of Rochdale, when next he receives the gleanings of his Bradford friend, to stick a little more to the truth. In respect to Mr. S. Wild, he had no hand in discharging Mr. M., nor was he (Mr. M.) discharged for inserting aught in your *Budget*.

"In No. 36 of the same journal, I replied to the Rochdale correspondent myself in the following terms :—

Bradford, 30th January, 1844.

SIR,—I cannot but express my surprise on reading an article in your *Budget* (No. 34), purporting to be from a Rochdale correspondent, containing at once the most impudent and malicious insinuations and assertions ever penned. He asserts the Liver Theatre is supported solely in consequence of the briskness of trade ; and insinuates that a late member of the company was discharged for having written a critique published in your thirty-first number. This insinuation is false, for neither myself nor, I believe, the members of the company, were aware of his leaving until he received his due notice. In answer to this assertion, I say plainly that the success hitherto attending the theatre is solely attributable to the pieces performed being put upon the stage in a manner never before witnessed by a Bradford audience. As for myself, I have nothing whatever to do with the management, Mrs. Wild, my mother, being sole proprietress and lessee ; it therefore appears to me that your correspondent must have been imposed upon, or that some person, having a private pique against the manageress, myself, or some member of the company, must have concocted that very abusive paragraph.

I am, sir, your obedient servant,

S. W.

"No further correspondence appearing, the subject then dropped.

"In regard to the objection of 'A Constant Subscriber' to my make-up as De Brogni, in *The Jewess*, I cannot now call to mind the dress he complained of. But I know we were always very particular, in characters of the Cardinal type, to be sparing of crosses, devices, and of everything that gave too close a resemblance to what, upon reference to stage authorities, we understood to be the reality. For the Catholic portion of our audience had, more than once before this time, hissed us for excess of zeal in that particular, and, once or twice at fair time, those enthusiastic people had cast stones at such of our banners and embellishments as bore upon them anything in the shape of a cross.

"Here is just another notice of the Liver Theatre. It is in No. 42 of *Oxberry's Budget*, under date March 25th, 1844, and helps to confirm what I have stated relative to our success at Bradford :—

BRADFORD, LIVER THEATRE.—This theatre still continues to be well supported. The benefits in particular have been crowded to excess. On

Monday last, for the benefit of Mr. and Mrs. Finch, first time, *The Bohemians*, and *The Bear Hunters*. Wednesday, for the benefit of Mr. and Mrs. Holloway, Shakspeare's play of *The Merchant of Venice*—Shylock, Mr. Holloway ; with a variety of other entertainments. Friday, for the benefit of Mr. Samuel Wild, a new drama, entitled, *Gallant Paul, or the Wreck of the 'Raven*,' and *The Red Indian and his Dog*. The house was immediately filled almost to suffocation, and many were turned back, being unable to obtain admittance. Saturday, March 16th, *The Bohemians*, and an afterpiece. The military amateurs of this town (70th Regiment) are going to play the leading characters in the drama of *The Ostler and Robber, or the Innkeeper of Abberville*, which is in active preparation. If I go, I shall send you a description of their performance.

" The animal which performed with me at my benefit, in *The Red Indian and his Dog*, was neither my famous dog 'Nelson' nor 'Tippoo' (of both of which I shall have more to say anon), but a little French poodle called 'Bob,' whom I had put through his facings just for that occasion.

" This was our last season at the Liver Theatre, and as I do not find, in any of the numbers (after 42) of *Oxberry's Budget*, reference made to the theatre being in our occupancy, I presume we should leave about the time when this last notice appeared. The allusion made to benefits supports this supposition.

" How we came to lose possession of the place was this. When the building was first erected it was intended, as I have said, to serve for the season only—some four months or so—at the end of which time Crabtree was to take it down and remove the timber to his own yard. But as the Corporation of Bradford did not require the land at the time, and, further, offered to let it to us, if the building were allowed to remain, at a reduced rent during the time the theatre was not in use, and as Crabtree said he didn't want the timber just then, it was agreed to leave the place standing until another season, paying of course the land rent to the Corporation and a nominal sum to the builder as a sort of acknowledgment. Unfortunately, as it happened, no written agreement was entered into with Crabtree to this effect. The second and third seasons having passed over without opposition from any quarter, we assumed, naturally enough, that we should be allowed to occupy the place in the future upon the same terms as in the past. In this, however, we were mistaken, for Crabtree first let the theatre—during the summer fair of 1844—to a circus proprietor, and afterwards leased it to Messrs. Mosley and

Rice (then managers of the Huddersfield Theatre), to whom the Bradford magistrates granted a licence.

" Though a short intimation to this effect appeared in *Oxberry's Budget* for July 22nd, 1844, strange to say, we never saw it. But about a fortnight or three weeks before our usual commencement of the season at Bradford, mother and I called upon Mr. Wagstaff, of that town, our lawyer, with instructions for him to apply for a licence for us in the usual way. He, having learned that the Liver Theatre had been engaged by Messrs. Mosley & Rice (though no company was playing there at that time, I believe), advised us to see Crabtree. We did so, and, much to our regret, found that he had let the building to them. Of course he was 'sorry,' and so forth, and excused himself as well as he could ; but after all the fault was ours in not having, after the first season, a proper written agreement with him about the theatre.

" So that winter we only went to Bradford for the fair season, and instead of taking up our old quarters at the Liver, we had to squeeze in with the other showmen, and make the best of our portable theatre.

" Messrs. Mosley & Rice opened the Liver Theatre that season as it stood, but altered it very considerably before the next. And in this altered form it remained until, many years ago, it was sold by auction by Mr. J. Buckley Sharp, who, standing behind the footlights during the time he was selling it, remarked, as I am told, that such being his first appearance upon the stage, he should want every encouragement from his patrons.

" But, before I leave the subject of the Liver Theatre, I may as well tell you a little about our patrons, or, rather, about one section of them, usually known as the White Abbey 'lot.' They came nearly every night, thirty or forty of them, lively fellows from the regions of White Abbey. They always sat together in the gallery in one place, and entirely to themselves, as nobody except strangers would venture to sit near them. They were full of practical joking when the act-drop was down, but still, after their fashion, stoutly contended for order. Almost all professions and callings were represented by this 'lot,' and a couple of chimney sweeps in good black, I remember, generally occupied a prominent position amongst them. Should any unfortunate individual, not of their company, but within reach of these last-named gentlemen, happen to hazard an observation to a friend upon the merits of a performance, and in doing so raise his voice anything above a whisper, switch came their sooty caps into the face of the critic, with a sort of qualified request that he would return them without delay, and give his thoughts no tongue. Nor did they think anything of propelling an offender from the back of the gallery down into the pit—which joined the gallery, by the way—nor of amusing themselves generally at the expense of others. A pretty 'lot,' these, but hardly a profitable 'lot,' I am afraid, for though they always gave their undivided attention to the performance, and applauded the loudest of any in the house—and always, too, at the right time—we couldn't get along with them at all without the aid of a policeman. We paid 18s. per week for one of those liveried gentlemen, just to keep these tykes in order. The policeman, somehow, was always able to manage them, but he went very carefully to work. 'Now, my lads,' and a shake of the head—that sort of thing goes down much better with the working men than 'Now, you blackguards'—and there was usually an interval of quiet, because they knew that if any of them were detected in any mischief they would be refused admittance into the theatre for at least a week afterwards, and a more severe punishment than that of keeping one of the 'lot' outside while his friends were enjoying themselves within could not have been devised. Sometimes they would get a little more obstreperous than usual, and then Tom and I, between the acts, would go up to them in the gallery, where the policeman would join us. We always hustled the offender out ourselves, so that there could be no direct charge against the policeman, and they never thought of retaliating upon us of the sock and buskin. Then, instead of declaiming against the ejecting party, their observations would generally concern the party ejected—'Sandy owt ta ha' been quiet.' Then 'Sandy,' every night until his term of exclusion was up, would present himself at the door of the theatre for admission along with the rest, and, being detected as a recent offender, would look very contrite, while a few of his friends would plead a little in his behalf; but we were obliged to be firm and refuse to have him in. At length, when we considered that he had fairly atoned for his sins of commission, he would be admitted under a promise of future better conduct, which was generally given with much seriousness. So Sandy would join his friends again in the gallery in great glee, and for a few nights all would go on pretty smoothly, until some-body else offended, when the same routine had to be gone through. Such was our experience of the White Abbey 'lot.'

"It was somewhere about the year 1844, I believe, that while we were stationed at Leeds, Pritchard, the lessee of the Theatre Royal, in Hunslet Lane, made us 'move on.' We stood in Vicar's Croft, and played simply by permission of the magistrates. As we always endeavoured to put our pieces upon the stage well, it was not often that we had to complain of a want of patronage. Indeed we drew, comparatively, better houses than Pritchard, and this annoyed him exceedingly, for he knew it. Thinking, probably, but indifferently of our capa-bilities and resources, he made a great point, as he fancied, in announcing that he would produce, at the end of a fort-night, the drama of *Margaret Catchpole*. Now, what we did in Parrish's case we did in his—we forestalled him. We procured the play, got up some good scenic effects, and on the third or fourth day after Pritchard's grand announcement, *Margaret Catchpole* was down on the pla-cards for 'Old Wild's.' As usual we had splendid houses every night, and continued to play the piece until the very day when Pritchard performed it for the first time in public, and then we withdrew it for a little time to let him have a fair chance. At the stated time the curtain at the Theatre Royal arose on *Margaret Catchpole*, but before the company had gone half way through the play, some of our 'gods,' who had gone to compare notes, cried out—very probably at what was considered by the lessee to be a 'taking' effect—'You should go to Old Wild's to see that.' This was the finishing stroke for poor Pritchard, who, knowing we hadn't a licence, opposed our playing without one (the fair season being over), and so compelled us, as I said, to 'move on.' The Act for regulating theatres gave showmen, in effect, permission at the times of fairs, feasts, and holidays to perform stage plays without a licence ; and if, in our case, nobody interfered, we frequently remained longer at the place we were located at

than the time allowed. But, as anybody had power to object
to our performing without a proper licence, the magistrates
had no alternative in Pritchard's case but to accede to his
request, the gist of which was, that we should no longer
be allowed to entertain the public of Leeds. For we had
not the slightest chance of obtaining a licence from the
authorities so long as he opposed our having one. We
were obliged, therefore, to leave Leeds and seek 'fresh
fields and pastures new.'

"About this time Edwin Hughes and his family were
staying at Dublin, his circus being at Donnybrook, about
two miles from that famous city. He had gone there for
the fair. Mother and I, in response to an invitation from
him, went over on a visit, Tom being left in charge of our
establishment. Donnybrook Fair commenced on Sunday,
immediately after morning service, and continued with
unabated vigour until the Saturday evening following.
We remained in the Emerald Isle the whole week, dividing
our time between Donnybrook and Dublin. During our
stay I donned the tights again, and went into the arena at
Hughes's along with my brother James, who was clown
there at that time. I did this out of respect to my brother-
in-law Hughes, though he afterwards insisted upon making
me a present for my services.

"However Pat may delight in fighting away from his
native soil, strange to say, I do not remember to have seen
a single blow struck during the whole of the time I was at
Donnybrook; and I leave you to judge whether the fair
was crowded or not when I tell you that the receipts at
Hughes's circus, of the first day alone—why it was really
only half a day—amounted to no less than £125.

There is just a little incident in connection with this
visit to Donnybrook which I may mention here. James
and I lodged in Dublin, and came to the circus every
morning on a jaunting car. We were rather late one day,
and the only vehicle that was to be had was four short of
its full complement of six (or eight, I forget which). My
brother jumped on to the car, and beckoned me to follow.
'Take us up to the 'Brook, quick,' said he to the driver,
'and I'll pay for the other two seats if nobody turns up as
we go along.' Forthwith Teddy started upon his journey.
We had not gone far before two persons hailed him and
took possession of the vacant seats. Arriving at Donny-

brook, Teddy, after duly receiving his fare from each of the last two comers, demanded of my brother four fares, including in the demand the two seats the fares for which he had just received. James very properly declined to pay for more than two places in the car, whereupon Teddy, who fancied he had a clear case, called two mounted police to his aid. Formidable-looking fellows those police were, in their helmets and dark blue coats, and armed each with a sword and a brace of pistols. Splendid horses they rode, too, and, taking them altogether, their appearance alone was calculated to frighten such people into doing right as had no natural leaning in that direction. Answering Teddy's summons they came towards us, and, after hearing that he had a charge against us, bade us walk beside them up to the constable's office. We did so, and Teddy followed to lay the information. Most of his friends in the jaunting car line, seeing us in custody, were ready to believe that we had done him some terrible injustice, and, full of sympathy for him, expressed a very lively hope that the ' poor bhoy' would make us, 'spalpanes' and 'blackguards' that we were, pay. At the constable's office, however, Teddy's charge not only fell through, but he was threatened with incarceration himself, for a barefaced attempt to swindle the public. As we came out from the presence of the chief constable—acquitted of all fraudulent intentions—Teddy was hurrying along before us to the party in whose charge he had left his car. The moment it was known that Teddy was at fault the tables quickly turned. There was now no longer sympathy expressed for the ' poor bhoy,' but the cries were ' bad luck' to and 'dirthy warther' upon him for wanting to rob the 'gintlemin.'"

CHAPTER XI.

A Royal train, believe me.—*Henry VIII.*

"In the early part of the year 1847, while Alfred
Bunn was the manager at Drury Lane, Edwin Hughes
was engaged by him to introduce his troupe of elephants,
camels, horses, and ponies upon the stage at that theatre,
during the nightly performance there of *The Desert*.
William Batty, then proprietor of Astley's, had been, and
still was, drawing crowded houses at the Amphitheatre
with *Mazeppa*; and Bunn perceiving the attractiveness of
performing quadrupeds, had determined to cater to
popular taste in that direction. This decision led to
Hughes' engagement and to the production of *The Desert*,
on a most magnificent scale, at Drury Lane. Hughes,
who, in addition to the quadrupeds, undertook also to
provide bipeds to control them, thought this would be an
excellent opportunity for me to see London, and to have
the honour of performing at Drury Lane. He accordingly
wrote to me while I was at Blackburn to this effect. I
did not hesitate to accept an engagement which seemed to
me of no little importance, and in due time had the
honour, along with my brother James, who was still with
Hughes, of appearing behind the footlights at that famous
theatre. Neither James nor I was overtaxed with speaking there, but as the leaders, each of a band of Arabs, we
cut prominent figures occasionally in the inciting of our
followers to make attacks upon caravans as they crossed
the desert, and by taking active part in the business ourselves. We also assisted in forming spectacles or stage

pictures, the main features of the drama; but I cannot suppose that we should claim a very great share of attention in the final tableau, for in that there were no less than 300 persons (including two bands of instrumentalists), sixty horses, fourteen camels, ten ponies, and two elephants, together with a gorgeous dragon chariot, and a Burmese Rath, all upon the stage at one time.

" But if, even in this subsidiary character of an Arab chief, I considered myself fortunate in my Drury Lane engagement, it will be easy to suppose that I regarded myself as more than fortunate in having, while there, the distinguished honour of performing in the presence of Her Most Gracious Majesty the Queen, His Royal Highness Prince Albert, the Queen Dowager, the Royal Children, and a host of the nobility and gentry.

" The Royal visit to Drury Lane was in the afternoon of the 22nd April, 1847—the first day performance of *The Desert* which had been given there. The Royal party occupied a private box at the side of the stage, and the moment Her Majesty appeared there, the orchestra announced the fact by playing the National Anthem. Then all eyes were upon the Royal box, and afterwards, during the performance, whenever Her Majesty chanced to draw aside the curtain, there was very little seen of the doings on the stage. The distinguished visitors had been previously announced, and the consequence was a house filled to overflowing. It had also been intimated that Mr. Hughes would do himself the honour to present to the Prince of Wales on that occasion a handsome white pony. And a pretty little animal it was too, and very gay it looked in its trappings of scarlet morocco—no unacceptable gift, in my humble judgment, even for a Prince of Royal blood. The presentation was to take place immediately at the conclusion of the grand tableau, in which the pony in question was introduced. During the performance, Mr. Hughes sent, by the hands of Mr. Alfred Bunn, a communication to the Royal box, asking permission for the young Prince to come upon the stage and receive the gift. But Her Majesty refused to allow his youthful Highness to appear on those classic boards, and the distinguished honour which Mr. Hughes had anticipated was unfortunately denied him.

" I did not, of course, hob-a-nob much with the players

at Drury Lane.   They were not as we strollers used to be,
' hail-fellow well-met' with all who appeared upon the
stage.   In this higher theatrical world there were distinctions, as in society, and in the eyes of the leading actors at
Drury Lane we horsemen were regarded as but one
remove from the lowest order of aspirants to theatrical
fame.   If we had required any consolation, which however
I hardly think we did, we might have found it in the
reflection that horsemen were necessary, aye imperatively
necessary, to the success of the piece ; and that, on the
occasion just alluded to, we shared, if only in a less degree,
the honour of the Royal gaze.   On my own part I was
satisfied with that honour, and the audiences at ' Old
Wild's' for a long time afterwards were as proud of it as
I was myself.

" Amidst these professional distinctions at Drury Lane,
it was particularly refreshing to find that Tom Barry, who
had risen to a very high rank as a clown, and was then in
the zenith of his fame at Astley's, was still the same jovial,
good-natured fellow he used to be when he performed at
our lesser amphitheatre years before.   He and I saw much
of each other while I was in London, and at Macintosh's
vaults, near Westminster Bridge—the rallying ground
of theatrical and other performers—we used to sit and
revive old recollections after our nightly labours were
over.

" After a very successful run, *The Desert* was with-
drawn from the Boards of Drury Lane and I rejoined our
company

" Before my famous dog ' Nelson' began to appear in
public, I had a performing retriever called ' Tippoo.'   He
played in such pieces as *The Forest of Bondy* and *The Red
Indian*, and also performed many wonderful feats ; but in
cleverness and intelligence, ' Nelson' afterwards far surpassed him   While our company was in Hull, in October,
1846 (I had not of course been to London then), William
Batty came over for a few days, and visited Pablo Fanque's
Circus (then located in that town), for the purpose, as he
said, of looking for novelty.   ' We can meet with none in
London,' said Batty, ' there is nothing for it but coming
into the provinces if we want novelty.'   It so happened
that while he was over, I appeared at Pablo's with
' Tippoo,' for the benefit of Little Beaumont the clown.

Batty was delighted with the animal and wanted to purchase him, but for a time I declined to sell him.   Next
day, after rehearsal, Pablo and he sent for me to have a
drive out with them.   I accepted the invitation, and had
the honour of being taken about Hull in the society of
these two great circus proprietors, in a smart looking trap
drawn by four cream-coloured horses.   After visiting Drypool and the garrison, we got out at the Wellington Hotel,
in Hull; my brother Tom and Old Finch were sent for,
and we spent a very pleasant afternoon together.   ' Now,
my laad,' said Batty to me while we were there, ' what are
you going to let me have that dawg for ?'   With a view,
as I thought, to prevent him importuning me again, I
named what I considered an excessive price.   But no
sooner had I done this than Batty threw down the money
upon the table, and said ' The dawg is mine.'   Of course
this was considered as a *bonâ-fide* sale and purchase, and
' Tippoo ' and I had to part company.   I told Batty, however, that I was afraid he wouldn't be able to make much
progress with the animal, whereupon he desired me to
accept an engagement for Astley's, and go up there and
perform with ' Tippoo.'   We couldn't agree as to terms
just then, and so he took the dog away with him.   In
reply to a letter from myself inquiring as to his arrival in
London, and how ' Tippoo ' was, he wrote as follows :—

Astley's Royal Amphitheatre, October 29th, 1846.

Sir,—I received yours and am glad to say I arrived here safe, and the
dog is going on well, but it is my intention to have a piece wrote for him
and which will be ready in about three weeks ; if you will write at that
time and say where you are, and whether you will be able to come up for
a week, I shall be glad of your services.

I am, yours respectfully,

WILLIAM BATTY.

Mr. Samuel Wild, at Mr. Smith's, 59, William Street, Pattery, Hull.

" In reply to that letter I wrote stating my terms,
which, however, he thought were too high, and for a month
or so the subject dropped.

" I had ' Nelson ' with me at the time when Batty came
over to Hull, but his education had then only just begun.
But I set myself to work with him, after ' Tippoo ' was
sold, and his training commenced now in right good

earnest.   He was a difficult dog to teach, but I succeeded
with him at last; nor did I regret any extra labour he had
cost me when I saw him turn out a finished performer.   I
taught him to vault through hoops; to perform on chairs;
to take an egg, without breaking it, out of a pail of water;
to fetch a living canary out of a box, and to bring it to me
in his mouth, without so much as a feather of the little
songster being ruffled; to open a letter box and take out a
letter; to pull off his collar, and, at the word of command,
to put it on again; to go up a forty feet ladder, fire off at
the top of it a 24lb. cannon, and come down on the other
side, and to simulate lameness and death so cleverly, that
he rarely failed to draw tears from the eyes of the
spectators.   Then I taught him also to perform in plays.
His first appearance as a stage hero was at Lancaster, in
the celebrated melodrama *Mungo Park*.   The original
version of this play made no provision for the introduction
of a dog, but I adapted it myself for 'Nelson' by writing
special parts here and there for him and by arranging a
few dramatic effects.   In the original text of the play, the
African traveller is released from his confinement by
Snowball, the cabin boy.   The alteration which I made at
this point was, that, while still preserving the character of
Snowball, I made 'Nelson' take part in the liberation.
This I did by teaching him (a prisoner and in chains like
myself) to slip off his collar and go unbar a door or wicket,
to let in Snowball.   The first time the cabin boy appeared,
however, sounds of some one approaching, caused him to
beat a hasty retreat, whilst 'Nelson,' to avoid discovery on
his part, put on his collar again and lay at my feet as
though nothing had occurred.   This piece, which always
went off with *éclat* (as did any piece in which 'Nelson'
appeared), remained a favourite one with the public for a
great many years.

"Batty having written to me again about going to
Astley's to perform with 'Tippoo,' I replied that if he
approved of the idea, I would go and take 'Nelson' with
me, and for a weekly salary of £10 would introduce
him there, nightly, in a piece, and display also his feat-
performing capabilities.   He offered me £5 only, which
I refused, because I knew as a fact that he had before
been paying £15 per week to a Frenchman, with a
performing dog called 'Camille,' which was not to be

compared with 'Nelson.' Batty again wrote me as follows :—

Astley's, February 11th, 1847.

Sir,—If you can now make it convenient to come to London for a few weeks to introduce your dog in any piece you may think proper—as I am given to understand you have two or three dog pieces you can bring with you, if not I have one—I shall be glad. Should this suit you, let me know what salary you require, bearing in mind you will have to pay your expenses up and down, and your living while here.

Let me know by return when you can come, as you will have to open on Monday night, and require a day or two's rehearsal previous.

Yours respectfully,

WILLIAM BATTY.

" In reply to this letter I simply repeated my previous terms ; and then the correspondence ceased.

" You will observe that Batty, in his last letter, makes mention of 'Dog pieces.' These were written expressly for myself (and 'Nelson') by Mr. C. R. Somerset, of London. Their titles were, *Home, Sweet Home, or the Labourer and his Dog ; The Lion of the Desert ;* and *The Slave, or the Blessings of Liberty.* They were all three-act pieces, and I had the sole right of performing them.

" At that time—and I have no doubt it is the same at this day—there were always to be found authors prepared at a short notice to write a new piece, or to adapt an old one to meet the capabilities of an establishment. It was simply necessary to state what talent you had, your scenic resources, and the extent of your wardrobe, and they would get you a new piece out in a couple of days. And right glad of the commission they seemed to be too, for, as they had never learnt the art of saving money, they were generally as poor as crows. Mr. Somerset, to whom I paid £2 2s. for each of the plays he wrote me, came down to Leeds to write *Home, Sweet Home,* so that he might see ' Nelson ' and study its characteristics and abilities. But as I paid the author's expenses of keep while he was over, he may perhaps be excused for having taken a fortnight to discover the dog's good qualities. I suggested the incidents of *Home, Sweet Home* to him ; perhaps they are not entirely original, I leave you to judge :—There is a rustic beauty affianced to a country swain, but secretly beloved by the village squire, who, after a course of systematic plotting with a view to obtain the hand of the maid, contrives to place the lover in durance vile. The agents employed by the squire, finding him somewhat chary in rewarding them for their part in the villainy perpetrated, fall foul of him at the trial (for felony) of the lover, and unmask him. The squire, wild with excitement at this disclosure of his dark doings, is just on the point of shooting down his accusers, when the lover's dog —which has been mixed up with matters all the way through the piece—seizes the squire and strangles him, to the general satisfaction of the audience.

"*The Lion of the Desert*, in which 'Nelson' appeared as that majestic animal, was founded upon the well-known anecdote of Androcles and the lion. The difficulty in this piece was to keep the dog from barking when, as the representative of the king of beasts, he had to spring upon, and despatch, the inevitable villain in the last act.

"The circumstances under which I came into possession of 'Nelson' were these. In 1845, or thereabouts, while staying with our company at Sheffield, my brother James, who had bought 'Nelson' at Monmouth during a visit there with Hughes, sent the animal to me (having himself few opportunities for training him), with instructions that I should bring him up well and spare no pains in his education. Whatever I charged for doing all this he would pay me when we next met, but in the event of his not requiring the dog I was to keep him myself. As I had a great affection for these intelligent animals, I readily undertook to carry out his wishes concerning 'Nelson,' and, as already hinted, spent considerable time in training him. But as James never came, or sent for the dog, I accordingly claimed him. He was a white Newfoundland dog with red ears, and had a little spot of the same colour upon his tail ; and though I cannot trace his descent, he was considered to be of a very valuable breed of Newfoundlands, and was only a very 'wee' thing when my brother gave £5 for him.

"Towards the close of 1847, 'Nelson' was in the enjoyment of a wide popularity. I find from an old programme of dances, that I introduced him at a grand dress ball given at Hull, on the 25th of October, in that year. The *Hull Packet* of the 28th of the same month and year, thus referred to myself and him :

HULL.—The great magnet here is Mr. S. Wild and his Newfoundland dog, "Nelson." He is a beautiful animal, and his feats are worthy the patronage of the most fastidious and aristocratic of our fellow-townsmen.

"Passing over to the year 1849, I come to the follow- opinions of the Press :—

BOLTON.—We have seen what have been considered crowded houses, but, really, the dense mass that inundated the theatre on the occasion of Mr. S. Wild's great Newfoundland dog, "Nelson's" appearance, was altogether beyond expectation, although a great house was expected. The performances of Mr. S. Wild and his really clever dog cannot be done justice to in our pages—they must indeed be witnessed.—*Bolton Free Press*, March, 1849.

THEATRE, BLACKBURN.—The principal attraction here is Mr. S. Wild's celebrated dog, "Nelson," who performed between the pieces. The astonishing display of comic sagacity exhibited by this highly-trained dog called forth the loudest acclamations ever heard within the walls of any theatre. His performances are almost incredible, and much spoken of in the provinces.—*London Era*, April 29th, 1849.

On Monday and Tuesday was performed *My Poor Dog Tray, or the Idiot of the Shannon.* Mr. S. Wild's celebrated dog, "Nelson," sur- passed anything of the kind hitherto witnessed on these boards. Of Mr. S. Wild's Idiot we can only say that, be the nerves of brass and the heart of adamant, they will relax and become subdued when contemplating this appalling wreck of all that is noble and immortal in man.—*London Era*, May 20th, 1849.

THEATRE ROYAL.—Mr. S. Wild's Living Pictures of Ancient Sculp- ture gave great satisfaction ; his herculean form and graceful and classical delineations of the marble statuary were universally admired.—*London Era*, May 27th, 1849.

Last night the house was uncomfortably crowded on the occasion of Mr. Samuel Wild's benefit. An additional attraction brought thousands to witness his inimitable dog's ascent up a forty-foot ladder, firing a cannon, and descending on the opposite side. A feat so astounding is really without a precedent, and the bursts of applause which hailed its completion were highly deserving and congratulatory to the beneficiare. —*London Era.*

"The foregoing reference of the *London Era* to the 'Living Pictures of Ancient Sculpture' reminds me that I have omitted, up to this point, to make mention of them. These pictures—suggested to me by the statues of Constantine and his friends, alluded to by Wallett— consisted of Hercules and the Neméan Lion ; Cincinnatus, the Roman, fastening his sandal; Samson slaying the Philistines ; Cain taking the life of Abel, &c. I performed in white tights to suggest marble, and was considered at that time a model for a sculptor. The pictures were represented on the stage at the end of the first piece, and Thomas Hanlon, our acting manager, used to stand at one of the side wings, and explain them to the audience.

Down to the very time when my health and business alike
failed, these pictures formed an incidental feature of the
performances at our establishment.   I'm afraid I couldn't
perform them now, nor would sculptors care much to see
me in tights, for my figure—like my occupation—is gone.

" But to return to ' Nelson.'

" In June, 1849, we were at Preston, in Lancashire,
and had erected our booth upon a piece of waste ground
called Chadwick's Orchard.   On the morning of the 6th
of that same month, two of the members of our establishment, Thomas Hanlon, just mentioned, and Richard
Craiston, our property man and scene-shifter—a young
fellow of about twenty-one—went for a little boating
exercise on the Ribble.   When they had been out some
time, and were making their return journey, they began—
quite overlooking the fact that a boat is not a thing to be
trifled with—to amuse themselves at fisticuffs, or in some
other boisterous manner, the consequence of which was
that Craiston, throwing himself suddenly backwards, fell
into the river.   It so happened that some of our company,
including myself, accompanied by ' Nelson,' were at this
very moment going down the river's bank to bathe—
it being a spring-tide.   Engaged in conversation, we had
not perceived the accident, but ' Nelson ' had, and in an
instant the powerful animal sprang into the river, and made
for the drowning man.   Hearing a plunge, I looked round
and saw ' Nelson ' in the water.   I knew at once, by his
excited manner, that somebody was struggling for life
there, and forthwith began to throw off my clothes to swim
to the rescue.   When Craiston (for I soon learned that
the unfortunate man was he), came to the surface of the
water for the first time, ' Nelson,' who had just reached
the place, seized his cap, which unfortunately coming off
in the dog's mouth, the poor fellow again disappeared.
Dropping the cap, the animal—almost frantic since his
first attempt at rescue had proved a failure—swam about
the place where the drowning man had disappeared,
barking wildly in his excitement.   The second time
Craiston rose, ' Nelson,' instantly at the spot, caught him
by the shoulder, but from a fear, apparently, of hurting
him, relinquished his hold.   A third time the poor fellow
came to the surface, when the animal—not to be disappointed in this, his last chance—laid firm hold with his

teeth of the man's coat collar. Then keeping Craiston's head above water as well as he could, the dog buffeted his way to the opposite shore, where, with those wonderful jaws of his, he drew the rescued one out of the river, and deposited him on the sand. As all this was done before I could reach Craiston, there can be no doubt that, but for 'Nelson,' he would never have been taken out of the water alive. He required, as it was, considerable care and attention before he could be brought round. The first thing 'Nelson' did after this noble effort of his, was to give himself a good shaking, and then to return to the place where the rescued man lay, and over whom he kept faithful watch and ward until further assistance arrived. And I may add that he continued to show a lively interest in Craiston until he was safely housed in the Ship Inn.

"The crowd which by this time had collected almost worshipped the dog for his bravery; and so great was the joy of Craiston's mother, on learning that 'Nelson' had saved her son from a watery grave, that when shortly afterwards we went to Kendal, where the good lady lived, she insisted upon the animal dining with her family every Sunday during our stay at that town.

"'Nelson' was now the theme of conversation everywhere, and his admirers were more numerous than ever. At the close of the week following the event just described, we were honoured with the patronage of the Mayor of Preston, as the following extract from the *Preston Chronicle* will show—

The performances on Saturday, the 16th, were under the patronage of the Worshipful the Mayor, R. Pedder, Esq., and the nobility of this town—present in order to witness the extraordinary feats of Mr. S. Wild's wonderful dog, 'Nelson,' who had previously saved a man's life in the river Ribble. The house was fashionably and respectably attended, and the performance of Mr. S. Wild and his truly astonishing dog was hailed with the most rapturous applause, and left an impression that will not easily be forgotten by the inhabitants of Preston.—*Preston Chronicle*, June 23rd, 1849.

"Opinions of the press began, so to speak, to shower upon 'Nelson,' and he occupied such a high position in the estimation of us all at the booth, that in our placards we ventured thus far in his praise—'The almost incredible feats of this noble animal stand unrivalled, and it is with confidence asserted that his parallel cannot be found either in ancient or modern history.'

" On the 10th of July, 1849, I performed with him at the Leeds Zoological Gardens, before 14,000 persons, and under the patronage of the Right Hon. the Earl of Carlisle, the Right Hon. Earl Fitzwilliam, the Right Hon. Lord Wharncliffe, Edmund B. Dennison, Esq., M.P., Wm. Beckett, Esq., M.P., James Garth Marshall, Esq., M.P., Jas. Brown, Esq., Col. Bush, and the officers of the Leeds Garrison. Upon this occasion ' Nelson,' in addition to his usual performances, drove four geese round a lake, during which a combination of brass bands played ' See the Conquering Hero Comes.' ' Nelson ' was now dubbed ' The Wonder of the Age,' and he was one of our most valued performers. Wherever we went we were well patronised, and frequently by those in the upper ranks of society. On September 28th, 1849, I find, from an old playbill, that at Penrith we were honoured with the patronage of Sir George Musgrave, Bart., Eden Hall, and shortly afterwards, at the same town, with that of Lord and Lady Brougham, Lady Mallett, the Countess Oskalin-skey, the Marquis of Douro (afterwards Duke of Wellington), the Hon. Mr. Vane, and others. Concerning the distinguished personages last named, and the honour conferred upon us by their presence at our theatre, the following particulars may not be uninteresting. Thos. Hanlon, our acting manager, a person of good address, waited upon Lord Brougham, at his residence, just out of Penrith, and solicited his patronage. His Lordship at once gave his sanction for a performance under his patronage and presence. The day before the one selected for his lordship's visit, the Marquis of Douro called at our theatre to see what description of place it was, and the sort of accommodation we could offer. I attended upon his Lordship, and conducted him round the place. My lord was hardly satisfied with the internal arrangements. He must have the pit and boxes (the seats of which were only carpeted) altered, and he must have hair-seated chairs for Lord Brougham and his friends, and a sofa for Lady Brougham, who was an invalid. ' But, my lord,' said I, ' while we feel ourselves highly honoured by your promised patronage, and that of Lord and Lady Brougham, I am afraid the proprietress, my mother, is hardly in a position at present to undertake the alterations your Lordship suggests.' ' Nor is it desired,' rejoined the

Marquis, 'that she should be put to any expense on our account. I will myself obtain the articles I require, and all I shall ask of you is that you will be good enough to send to the Royal Hotel for them.' I thanked his Lordship very much for his consideration, and assured him that his wishes should be attended to, and the suggestions he had made scrupulously carried out, upon which his Lordship retired.

"The next day—the great patronage day—there was no small bustle at ' Old Wild's ' betimes, preparing for the distinguished visitors. We did not fail to send to the Royal Hotel for the seats the Marquis had bespoke, and endeavoured to carry out to the letter all that he had intimated with regard to alterations. We charged our regular audiences double prices that night, and the gallery only was open to the public. Our patrons had previously selected the pieces for the evening, and these were *Every Inch a Sailor* and *Mungo Park*. They chose these because they wished to see as much as possible of ' Nelson,' whose fame had reached even their ears. At seven o'clock the carriages of our patrons drew up before the theatre, and the distinguished occupants were admitted by a private entrance. We had a capital house that night, and everything went off with *éclat*. The lords and ladies remained until the fall of the curtain at the end of the last piece, and went away with the same ceremony they came.

"In the afternoon of the next day the Marquis of Douro called again at the theatre, and asked to see Mrs. Wild. I was sent to him as her representative. His Lordship placed a sealed envelope, addressed to her, in my hand. I at once took it to her. The moment she opened it she found to her surprise and delight two bank notes, each for £5.

" Shortly after this the friends of the Humane Society presented me at Keighley with a silver medal, to commemorate ' Nelson's ' rescue of Craiston from drowning.

" I was proud of this medal, and wore it for the dog's sake.

" Some time after this presentation, Williams and I were travelling one day by train from Dewsbury to Halifax. We were both of us well dressed ; myself particularly so, as the following inventory will show :—

Frilled shirt, a massive watchguard, one or more rings upon my fingers, my hat upon three hairs, and last, but not least, 'Nelson's' medal glittering upon a vest of the newest cut. We were joined at Mirfield by some Irishmen, who were going to Liverpool, and thence to Queensland. They stared at Williams, my coloured companion, and at myself, scanning the jewellery with admiring eyes, and hinted to each other, in a low voice, that I was a foreigner of distinction, and that he (Williams) was my coloured servant. At length one of them mustered courage to inquire of Williams who I was. Overhearing the question, I whispered to my ebony friend, 'Say I am the Marquis of Douro, and Duke of Wellington.' They no sooner learned this than their astonishment gave place to admiration. Almost simultaneously, each of them produced a whisky bottle, and, first apologising for the familarity, asked if 'his Highness' would object to 'dhrink wid his counthrymin.' His Highness did not object, and the delight of the good-natured sons of Erin knew no bounds. Williams and I had to change at North Dean, but our enthusiastic friends kept their seats. Just as the train was about to start, they, seeing us still upon the platform, united in wishing us a hearty good-bye, adding, as the train moved off, 'Long life an' more power to yer Highness.' "

CHAPTER XII.

Some have greatness thrust upon them.—Twelfth Night.

" On the occasion of Sir Geo. Musgrave's patronage, the performances, upon the authority of the playbill before alluded to, consisted of *Mungo Park* and the farce of *Family Jars*, with a couple of songs (by Lishman and Williams respectively), and a dance by Tom's daughter (Selina) between the pieces. In addition to these names the following also occur in the programme of the performances :—Messrs. John (better known as ' Jack ') Holloway, Bateson, Noakes, Hargreaves, Hanlon, Hewitt, James, Sharp, and Sam Wild (the last named individual being then acting manager), together with Mesdames Sam Wild, Bateson, and Noakes. But this list by no means comprehends all the performers engaged at ' Wild's Theatre' (as we called the booth) at that time. There were also my brother Tom, Old Finch, their wives, Fraser, and several others whose names I cannot now call to mind. These were excluded from the programme simply on account of the insufficiency of parts, the *dramatis personæ* in both pieces being somewhat limited.

"As already shown, my sister Selina (Mrs. Bateson) and her husband were with us at this time. Bateson was by profession an acrobat, and had been attached to Hughes' Circus some time before he became acquainted with Selina. How the latter circumstance was brought about was this— Selina, while on a visit to her sister (Mrs. Hughes) in Ireland, appeared in the arena at the circus during Bateson's engagement there. There they met, were engaged, and, before Selina had, if I remember rightly, completed her nineteenth year, were married. They remained at Hughes' several years after this latter event, and then joined our company; he as a posturer for the outside parade (from which position he at length gained a place behind the footlights), she as an actress and terpsichorean artiste.

"Jack Holloway first came to us during the second winter season of our theatrical career. He was then quite a young man. My mother engaged him at Manchester, I believe, and down to the period under notice he had always been our leading tragedian.

"There were three brothers Holloway, tragedians all of them. Jack, the eldest, was always regarded as the most talented performer of the three, though James, next in age, possessed considerable ability. While Astley's was under Cook's management, he (James) played Richard III. there upwards of two hundred nights, and his fellow artistes presented him, at the close of his engagement, with a gold medal as a testimonial of their esteem. The youngest Holloway, Joseph, was a man of talent, too, and he, like each of his brothers, has performed more than once or twice before audiences at ' Old Wild's.'

"In the *Mungo Park* cast—to revert again to the pro-gramme—there was no character suitable for Mrs. Sam, and so, on the occasion first referred to, she appeared as Liddy O'Larrigan in *Family Jars*. Thoroughly successful as she always was in characters of this description, and in comedy generally, tragedy was undoubtedly her *forte*, Shakesperian characters were her favourite study, and in the impersonation of many of these she excelled. ' The Lady Macbeth of Mrs. S. Wild was finely conceived and well acted throughout,' remarked the correspondent of the *Era* in his notice, on 26th October, 1849 (only a month later), of the performances of our company before Appleby audiences. And this is but one of the many favourable opinions she gleaned during an eventful career upon the stage.

"Mention of Appleby (Westmoreland) gives me a cue to further incidents—unfortunately not of the pleasantest description—in our history.

"To the circumstances of this and a later time I would hesitate to allude at all, were they not in a measure inseparable from the history of my early proprietorship of the concern, because there can be nothing particularly interesting, I imagine, in a recital of family grievances.

"Upon leaving Appleby, at the close of the season just referred to, we went to Carlisle, at which place a large wooden building, with a tiled roof, had been erected for us. The season was a prosperous one, and we remained there four or five months. Our next port was Wigton, in Cumberland, but to this town my mother, having previously fallen ill at Carlisle, was unable to accompany us, and had to be left (the doctor's commands being that she must not travel just then) in the care of Mrs. Darling, the landlady of the Drove Hotel, in the last-named town. Before we started for Wigton, however, mother sent for Tom, and intimated that as she was prevented from going with us to look after the place herself, as usual, she wished him to take charge of the concern.

"Dissatisfaction with the new management having been expressed by Holloway and Noakes (both of whom threw up their engagements), and by other members of the company, the old lady wrote to me at Wigton, from Carlisle, on the 24th March, 1850—her letter is still in my possession—requesting me to take the whole of the responsibility in connection with the establishment entirely upon myself.

"I was much startled by this communication, and took the earliest opportunity to go over to Carlisle and see her upon it. She there renewed her instructions to me to take the management into my own hands, and hoped I should not fail to put in force the authority she had given me. This was, for me, an unfortunate business, for as Tom was the elder brother, I did not like, though anxious to carry out her wishes, to exercise the authority she had armed me with, for I foresaw a rupture with him would be the certain consequence of my so doing; and then any unpleasantness of this sort coming to my mother's ears (as it certainly would have done) might have seriously affected her in her then precarious condition.

"Edwin Hughes, who had retired from the circus business and was then residing at a snug retreat in Smithdown Lane, near Liverpool, and who had long wanted mother to give up business and withdraw from the concern, on hearing of her illness, at once wrote to her, requesting her as soon as she found herself sufficiently improved in health to undertake travelling, to go and stay with himself and wife (my mother's sister) until she had quite recovered. Her illness took a favourable turn, and in due time she went to Hughes' residence, intending, however, to make only a very short stay. Matters concerning our theatre were discussed during her sojourn there, and Hughes strongly advised her to give up the business to Tom and myself jointly, and remain there, at Willow Cottage, with her daughter. Though it required no ordinary amount of persuasion to induce my mother to abandon travelling life, she did ultimately agree to do so.

"The following Whitsuntide, while we were stationed at Preston, the old lady and Hughes came over to see how matters were progressing with us, and to broach the subject of a partnership to Tom and me. A partnership with Sam! Tom would never agree to that. Finding at length all argument and persuasion vain, Hughes suggested that the old lady should give us a fortnight to think over the proposal. She agreed to do so, and then returned with him to Liverpool. At the appointed time they came again. It was asked of me, was I agreeable to enter into a partnership with Tom, and take over the concern in our joint names ? I replied to the effect that I could not be otherwise than willing so to do. A similar question was put to Tom, but he stoutly opposed the idea of a partnership upon such terms, or indeed upon any. The old lady, however, was not a person to be trifled with : she had a will of her own. Seeing now no chance of the partnership she had so much desired being effected, she sent for our scenic artist, Fraser, and, as near as I can recollect, the following conversation ensued :—

" ' Now, Tom, I am going to ask Fraser to alter the names upon my vans. What is he to put in place of " Elizabeth Wild " ? '

" ' Thomas Wild,' replied the owner of that name.

"She gave him yet another chance, and said, ' Not " Thomas and Samuel Wild " ? '

" ' Certainly not,' replied Tom with considerable emphasis.

"Then, turning to Fraser, the old lady said, ' Rub out the name " Elizabeth " on each of the vans, and in place of it write only " Samuel."

"Her word was law. Fraser carried out his instructions, and I was made sole proprietor of the establishment.

"As Tom and his wife still remained at the place, it

will be quite easy to understand that neither Mrs. Sam nor
I had the cheeriest of times there, notwithstanding the
'greatness' which had been so unexpectedly 'thrust upon'
me.

"Shortly after the honour of proprietorship had been
conferred, the time drew nigh when we must remove from
Preston to Halifax; but the balance of money in hand on
the occasion of the old lady's visit having been given to
her then, I found my resources now desperately low, so
low in fact that I had to look around for a friend to assist
me.   My wife being a particular acquaintance of Mrs.
Norman, the landlady of the Golden Ball, Blackburn,
went over to that town and called upon her.   She no
sooner became aware of our circumstances than she
advanced to my wife, without scrap or scrip of any kind as
acknowledgment or security, a sum of £20.   But for this
timely assistance, Halifax Summer Fair, 1850, would in all
probability have passed over without anything being seen
or heard of 'Old Wild's.'   We did get there, however,
but it cost me £30 to bring the concern over.   Yet the
season proved such a successful one that I had no reason
to regret the expense.   Indeed, at the close of the final
performance, I found myself in a position to refund the
£20 to Mrs. Norman, and this I did not fail to do.

"I may say here that I made it a point to keep a
strict record of all my receipts and payments, because I
had previously seen the absolute necessity of so doing.
In addition to this, in acknowledgment of the trust she
had reposed in me. I determined to account periodically to
my mother for all transactions in connection with the
theatre.   There was necessarily considerable extra labour
involved by my new duties, and no slight responsibilities
to contend with.   Yet I could have struggled with it all
cheerfully had I not been continually subjected to annoyance from a source to which I have already referred.

"By and bye, we came to Halifax, and pitched, as
usual, in the New Market.   I was astonished one day in
seeing the White Swan 'bus draw up at our place, and
was still more surprised (never having received a line of
intimation that she was coming) to see my mother get out
of it.   Mrs. Mainley (Parrish's mother, by the way), our
wardrobe keeper, welcomed her very heartily to the van,
into which we helped the old lady, and her boxes and

packages.   At first we thought she had come on a visit,
but it soon transpired that she intended to take up her
abode with us.   Her reasons for leaving Willow Cottage
I could well understand.   Life there was too quiet for
her.   The thousand and one discordant noises of a fair
were, to the old lady, preferable to the seclusion of Smithdown Lane, and the few simple chattels of her own snug
caravan had more attractions for her than Hughes' grand
furniture all put together.   Then, again, she could do just
as she liked at the old caravan, and, in fact, could feel at
home nowhere but in it.   She had been accustomed to this
mode of life for many a long year, and it was in vain she
had tried, by availing herself of Hughes' kindness, to
wean herself from it.

"I was right glad she had returned to us again,
because I was very anxious for her to resume the proprietorship of the concern, as I had long been weary of
that dignity.   Other members of the company, too, were
glad for reasons it is scarcely necessary to explain.   But
the old lady insisted upon me retaining my position.
Upon this her decision becoming known, the annoyances
to which I have before alluded, and which I may say had
never entirely ceased, were now revived whenever a
favourable opportunity presented itself.

"In August, 1850, I engaged (in advance) the Riding
School, at Huddersfield, for three months, from November
1st, at a rent of £20 per month.   The improvement in the
appearance of things here served, upon our taking possession of the place, only to irritate what had already become
an old sore.   My proprietorship was questioned, and my
authority set at naught.   I thought it now high time to
have something like a definite understanding as to how I
really stood with regard to the concern—since my mother
would insist upon me having it—and if I had any rights
at all what those rights were.   I accordingly consulted a
solicitor in Huddersfield upon the subject.

"'Is the portable theatre at the present time known
by your name?' he asked.

"'It is known only as "Wild's," or, speaking more
familiarly, as "Old Wild's,"' I rejoined.   'The word
"Wild's," however, is all that is written upon the front.
But my name appears upon the caravans and upon the
bills.'

" 'Do you receive all moneys, and pay in your own name all expenses connected with the establishment?'

" 'I do, sir.'

" 'Is the Riding School here at present taken in your own name?'

" 'It is. Here is a letter from Mr. John Armitage, addressed to myself, stating that the committee of the Riding School agree to let the place to me on certain conditions, and I have already paid, in advance, the first month's rent of the place.'

" 'Then, I'll just tell you, Mr. Wild,' said the lawyer, after a few more questions relative to the booth, 'what is my opinion in the matter. The concern is yours undoubtedly, and you have, of course, the sole control and ordering of it. If it came to a point, the law would, I doubt not, warrant you even in taking your own mother by the shoulders and in putting her out of the place.'

" Being satisfied now as to my rights, I was determined, in consequence of what my wife and I had hitherto had to submit to, that something like system, regularity, and order should be henceforth observed at the place.

" I forthwith drew up a list of rules, the nature of which suggest a few of the difficulties I had to contend with up to this time.

RULES OF THIS THEATRE TO BE OBSERVED BY THE COMPANY.

1. Any Member being intoxicated in their business.........fined...2s. 6d.
2. Any person keeping the Stage waiting .... ,, 0s. 6d.
3. Any Person refusing to play the part given to them by the Manager, to forfeit their Salary.
4. Any Person being too late for rehearsal (a quarter of an hour allowed for difference of clocks)............... ,, 0s. 6d.
5. Any Person staying from rehearsal, unless having obtained permission from the Manager .... ,, 1s. 0d.
6. The Property Man not having all ready for the Night's Performance, if down in his Plot .... ,, 0s. 6d.
7. Any Person refusing to wear the dress ordered by the Manager .... ,, 0s. 6d.
8. Any Member found Smoking in the Theatre .... ,, 1s. 0d.
9. Any Musician not being in the Orchestra at the first tune (to be played at a quarter-past seven)............ ,, 0s. 6d.
10. Any Member taking any Stranger or Person not engaged in the Theatre behind the Scenes without permission from the Manager.......................... ... ,, 0s. 6d.
11. Any Member not wrapping up his dress after using ... ,, 0s. 6d.

12.	Any Bill Deliverer neglecting his duty ....fined...1s. 0d.
13.	Any Person going in front of the House in their Dress, or with Paint on their Face................................. ,, 1s. 0d.
14.	Any Person leaving the Theatre in their Dress, unless covered with a Cloak.................................... ,, 1s. 0d.
15.	Any Member or Members of the Company quarrelling during the Performance, or in the Theatre, so that the audience may hear them, each....................... ,, 1s. 0d.

N.B.—It is requested by the Manager that the Company will have Properties, and Dress their parts, as well and as clean as possible. The Treasury will open every Morning at half-past ten o'clock.

SAMUEL WILD.

Theatre, Huddersfield, November 16th, 1850.

"The publication of these Rules, together with a private intimation to the refractory ones that I was justified by legal opinion in the course I was pursuing, operated in producing a decided change for the better at the Theatre.

"We had a very prosperous season at Huddersfield, and, in addition to the never-failing attraction of 'Nelson,' we produced a Christmas Pantomime there. This is what the *Huddersfield Chronicle* said of both :—

THEATRE.—The performances have been varied during the week by the production of *Mungo Park* and the new pantomime of *Cherry and Fair Star*. In the former piece Mr. Wild's dog 'Nelson' took a prominent part. He is an exceedingly fine animal of the Newfoundland breed, and possesses in a high state of training all those qualities of sagacity and intelligence for which the species are so well known. The most difficult feats in posturing are performed by him with most astonishing alacrity and ease; nothing seems to come amiss—and, with a ready recognition of his master's wishes, he accomplishes his " characters" in a manner which obtains the rapturous applause of the house. In such pieces as *Mungo Park* he forms a very successful addition to the *dramatis personœ*. The new Christmas Pantomime is full of fun and laughter. The machinery and tricks are well managed, and the dresses are such as " fairies wear." Mr. T. Wild makes a good clown, and the Queen of the Fairies is well taken by Mrs. Jones, the nymphs being very creditably performed by the juvenile members of the company. On the whole the pantomime passed off successfully, and was well received.

"Towards the close of the period of our stay at Huddersfield, my mother was again taken ill, and upon our removal thence to Cleckheaton, we were obliged, as we had previously done at Carlisle, to leave her behind. The doctor, who from the commencement of her illness had attended her, finding that she was gradually becoming worse, ordered her removal from the caravan without delay. Against such a proceeding she protested as stoutly as she was able for some time, but as the company were just about to leave Huddersfield (our term at the Riding School having now expired), she at length submitted to the course proposed. For her new quarters she preferred, before all other places, the Guildhall Tavern, in Monument Street, on account, I suppose, of its homeliness and comfortableness, and because the landlady was one of her old acquaintances. I accordingly engaged two rooms for her there, and then went to fetch her in a hackney coach. When it came to a strait that she must leave her old quarters, probably thinking she might never return to them again, a feeling of reluctance began to show itself. At length this was overcome. Then there was, as might be expected, an affectionate leave-taking of her old friend Mrs. Mainley at the van, and, as one may suppose, of the old van itself. I lifted her into the coach, and taking a seat in it myself, we were soon on our way to her new lodging. Selina, who was to remain behind at Huddersfield to attend to the old lady, met us at the Guildhall and took charge of her; and the landlady having been duly instructed to see that nothing that money could purchase was wanting, I took leave of my invalid mother and rejoined the company.

"I came over every day from Cleckheaton to see how she progressed, and finding that she grew gradually weaker, I then came twice a day—starting off in the morning early, and returning in time to attend rehearsal; and again soon after dinner, so as to be able to spend a little time with the old lady and still go back to the theatre in time for the evening performances.

"My mother grew worse, and still worse, until her voice entirely left her, at which point the symptoms of her disorder became more alarming; so alarming, indeed, that upon my return to Cleckheaton, late in the afternoon of the 15th March, 1851, I expressed to the company my fears that she was fast sinking. As there was not a single person about the place who did not feel anxious to see the old lady, if possible, once more before she died, we agreed to have no performance at the theatre next day, but to go over to Huddersfield instead.

"We found her in a very precarious condition; unable to gladden our hearts, even for a moment, by a single word. We could only stand, a mournful group, about her bed, and look down into her poor old face and sigh to think how powerless we all were to relieve her.

"In the afternoon, when the other members of the company had retired, Tom and I (forgetting at a time like this our little differences in the past) went softly into the invalid's room together; our wives, Selina, and the land-lady, being already there. We resumed our watch over the dying woman, and none of us seemed to have courage to utter a single syllable. At length the silence was suddenly broken. It was the announcement that the old lady had gone.

"The funeral was a very large one—by some it was said to be the largest that had ever been seen at Huddersfield, but as to that of course I cannot say. In addition to our relatives and the company, who followed in mourning coaches and in cabs, there was a great number of our friends from other towns, while it appeared to me that all Huddersfield had turned out to see the last of the 'Queen of the Travellers.' Tournaire (I believe it was), a circus proprietor who had succeeded us at the Riding School, sent his entire company mounted on horseback to take part in the procession; and as a proof, I think, that my mother was held in some esteem by the Huddersfield people, all the shops, from the Guildhall to Trinity Church, were closed during the time the funeral *cortège* was passing.

"By all who knew her—and almost everybody did know her—my mother was much respected, and by many beloved. The thoughtfulness which she had ever shown for the less fortunate of that class of people to which she had for so many years belonged, caused her to be every-where known as the 'Mother of the Showfolk,' while her uniform courtesy at all times gained for her, as I have before said, the title of 'Queen of the Travellers.' As may be imagined, there was a fair sprinkling of show-people at her funeral, for her death had become almost the universal topic of conversation amongst them. But there were mourners there too, of a humbler class still—those whose necessities she had oft relieved in her lifetime. For her heart and hand were ever open, and, notwithstand-ing her business habits, she was never known to turn a deaf ear to distress of any kind.

"So bringing up the rear of the procession—but no

less sincere in the expression of their sorrow on that account, I imagine—these humbler mourners followed ; and, though last to arrive at the churchyard, they were amongst the last to linger about the grave of the old lady.

"In the town in which she had given me birth he died ; and in the same vault at whose side she had, thirteen years before, wept over her departed husband, she was buried—having, like him, attained the advanced age of sixty-seven."

CHAPTER XIII.

A Benefit for Hungarian Refugees—"Sam" Wild
fails to pass as a "Furriner"—Edwards's *versus*
Wild's—Old Finch (and Shakspeare) to the
Rescue — Finch a General Favourite — An
Adventure.

·His eye begets occasion for his wit.—*Love's Labour Lost.*

"After a very successful stay of four or five weeks at
Cleckheaton we removed to Keighley, some eight or ten
days before the spring fair. Shortly after our arrival a
number of Hungarian refugees came over to Keighley, and
several gentlemen, who had formed themselves into a committee to procure relief for them, waited upon me. I
offered to give a performance at the theatre for the benefit
of the refugees, and ultimately did so, upon which occasion the house was crowded to excess. The refugees were
introduced upon the stage between the play and the farce,
and one of the committee, who also appeared with them,
gave an interesting account of the circumstances which had
caused these, and a great many more Hungarians, to flee
their country. The audience evinced a ready sympathy
with the refugees, and listened to a glee, which they afterwards sang in their own language, with as much attention
as though they quite understood and fully appreciated
every word of it.

"Keighley Spring Fair was merely a cattle fair, and our
reason for going to that town was to put on the time until
Huddersfield fair came round. We had hitherto had it all
to ourselves at Keighley, but on the occasion to which I
have referred, John Edwards entered into competition with
us. He had a portable theatre, but it was upon a smaller
scale than ours ; and though no actor himself, he managed
to get together a good company and to secure the services
of John and James Holloway. Edwards's theatre arrived
at Keighley a day or two before the fair, but he had previously announced his coming by large posters, in which

the names of the brothers Holloway figured conspicuously. As the elder Holloway had always been our leading trage-dian during our previous visits to Keighley, I confess I was not without a fear that we should find in Edwards a power-ful rival, for in addition to this enterprising engagement of the Holloways, he opened with *Belphegor*, a piece we were then announcing on our placards as in 'active pre-paration.' We could not but smile at this stroke of busi-ness, because it served to remind us of our own previous dealings with Parrish and Pritchard, only we took good care not to produce *Belphegor* at Keighley that season, as we could not think of 'Old Wild's' playing second fiddle to Edwards's. Whatever fears we had of success, however, were dissipated on the opening night at Edwards's, for owing either to the popularity of 'Old Wild's,' or to the favourable impression produced upon the public mind by the benefit I have alluded to, we had a splendid house. Nor had we, to the very last day of our sojourn at Keighley, anything to complain of on the score of patronage.

" But these were stirring times with us, and we had to put on our best appearance, and spin out our programmes to their greatest length. In this latter particular we used to show a strength, in point of company, which not only our rivals but also our patrons could hardly give us credit for. At these times we invariably selected for performance pieces with an extensive cast of characters, allotting minor parts to Messieurs Jackson, Jones, Harrison, Green, Smith, Brown, and Walker. These were very useful men, always ready at a moment's notice to represent any character, and though we paid them no salary (for they never asked for any), still they remained with us year after year, and were never known once to object to the parts given to them, however simple those parts might be.

" And this reminds me that I have occasionally been responsible for another performer in addition to having duties to discharge in my own name. At the Theatre Royal, Whitehaven, in May, 1851, I represented the *Bronze Monitor* as ' Mons. Leon,' having previously appeared with ' Nelson ' on the same boards that evening as Sam Wild. At Whitehaven everything went off with *éclat*, and the *Whitehaven Herald* spoke highly of all the three per-formers. But when I returned to Yorkshire, the ' Mons.

Leon' business wouldn't go down with the public at all.
Just before my first appearance as that talented foreigner
there would be a breathless suspense as the curtain rose on
the performances of 'Mons. Leon.'   But it took very
little time to discover who that personage was, and a short
conversation like the following would sometimes be
heard:—'I say, Bob.' 'I'm hearknin' on tha, Jem.'—
'That's nooan a furriner, I tell tha.   That's Sam Wild!'
'Tha'rt reight, Jem; it's nobody else.'—And this, too, bear
in mind, when Sam Wild was endeavouring to look as
much like a 'furriner' as he possibly could.

"To return.   Two nights before Huddersfield Fair, we
pulled down our canvas establishment and went to that
town, leaving Edwards's company still at Keighley.   We
took up our position at Huddersfield this time in the fair
ground, and got together all the strength we could,
expecting Edwards to put in an appearance.   But though,
as we learned, he had taken ground, he never came.

"The season at Huddersfield being over, we went to
Holmfirth.   While here I had six gas lamps made for the
outside of the theatre.   They were octagonal in shape,
and very large, and each lamp was surmounted by carved
work tastefully painted.   These lamps, supported on
pillars five or six feet in height, were arranged at regular
intervals along the front.   They proved a valuable addition
to the exterior, and at night, when the gas was lighted, had
a grand appearance.   In addition to the lamps, I had a
new folding front made.   It purported to be a view of the
exterior of the great Palace of Glass, and on the strength
of its pretensions we called the theatre at that time
'Wild's Crystal Palace of 1851.'   These alterations, or
additions, were made chiefly because they were required;
but also because we fully expected meeting with Edwards
at Bradford, whither we were next bound for the summer
fair.   Our expectations were realised—Edwards set up his
theatre on the very next stand to ours.

"We were stirring early in the morning of the first fair
day, and fixed and tried our lamps, but the front we still
kept down, as we intended that for a surprise by and bye.
Between one and two o'clock in the afternoon, Edwards's
procession on the outer stage commenced; the members of
the company, to judge from their gay appearance, having
evidently ransacked their wardrobe for the best dresses.

The procession concluded, a long strip of calico, containing an invitation to the audience to 'Come and see the Brothers Holloway,' was flaunted about, and the prices, which were the same as ours, were then announced. The moment these proceedings were over, up went the new front at 'Old Wild's,' and our full company, from twenty-five to thirty (which, of course, included Messieurs Jackson, Brown, and others), appeared, bearing the flags of all nations, and attired in a gorgeous medley of Greek, Roman, and Old English costumes. The band, consisting of cornets, trombones, clarionet, and drum, heralded the approach of the company, the rear of which was brought up by Old Finch as clown. The crowd now made for 'Old Wild's' to see the doings there, and Edwards's place was quite deserted. In vain they shouted the praises of the Brothers Holloway, clanged their cymbals, and smote their drum. In vain they sounded their noisy bell, and groaned defiance from their trombones. The only move the audience made was up the steps and in at the side-door at 'Old Wild's' the moment we had finished our parade. Our rivals still kept up their noisy proceedings as the crowd continued to make its way into the theatre. Old Finch, who, without appearing to notice them, had his eye upon our antagonists, and saw to what little purpose they laboured, seized a large flag, and, addressing the members of our company, at the same time pointing to the advancing host of patrons, he exclaimed—

> Hang out our banners on the outward walls;
> The cry is still "They come!"

This, from Old Finch, was relished by the spectators, probably all the more because of his clown's attire; and a merry peal of laughter followed. But the opposition only groaned the louder, and its musicians united in producing unearthly yells, while the noise was made still more deafening by the incessant swinging of a huge bell. These latter sounds seemed to give Old Finch a fresh cue. Raising his voice to the highest pitch he exclaimed—

> Ring the alarum bell! Blow, wind! come, wrack!
> At least we'll die with harness on our back!

Being of opinion, in the first place, that Finch was now acknowledging too plainly the doings of the opposition, which was contrary to our custom ; and, in the next place, feeling that the members of 'Old Wild's' company would 'never say die,' I advanced towards him with uplifted whip.   Quick alike in action as in thought, he threw the flag over his arm for a shield, pointed the staff at me with swordsmanlike grace, and assumed an attitude of defence.

> Lay on, Macduff ;
> And damn'd be him that first cries " Hold, enough ! "

shouted the inexhaustible Finch, to the uproarious delight of the spectators.

"We had nearly finished our first house before our rivals had half filled theirs, and it did not astonish us to find on returning to the parade that they had reduced their prices.   We still maintained ours, however, and seeing we could command audiences without any difficulty, it would have been nothing short of downright folly had we lowered them.   Each of the three fair days we had a procession similar to the one I have endeavoured to describe ; but afterwards we had only one evening performance, and then we came out upon the parade at seven, dressed in character for the piece.   Though Edwards's company remained at Bradford until the close of the fair week, they did not renew the proceedings of the first day.   Old Finch's Shaksperian recitals had silenced them, without doubt.

Finch was a man who worked hard for the good of the concern, and he could never bear the idea of it being put down.   I remember once while we were in Leeds—it was the summer fair—Parrish's, Thornes's, and Holloway's theatres were arrayed in opposition to ' Old Wild's.'   As an outside attraction, Parrish had engaged four trapezists, whom he styled the Swiss Brothers.   Holloway, not to be behind Parrish, brought out the Italian Brothers ; while Thornes, who felt himself bound to follow the example of his contemporaries, engaged the Hibernian Brothers.   We found the doings outside our place completely eclipsed by the attractions of our neighbours, and poor Old Finch looked in a very despairing condition.   On the second day of the fair, while the front of ' Old Wild's ' was almost deserted for Thornes's, Parrish's, and Holloway's, Finch espied at the foot of the steps a collection of little sweep boys, apparently without funds.   An idea suggested itself.

He instantly descended amongst them, and, selecting four of them, from eight to twelve years of age, he brought them on to the parade. He had a short conference with them, and then put them through a few tumbling feats, at which he found the little fellows decidedly clever. Satisfied with his experiment, he gave the painter a hint, and the 'Sweep Brothers' were duly announced at 'Old Wild's.' Whether it was the novelty or the ridiculousness of the thing I cannot say, but crowds flocked to see these little darkies, whom, greatly to their delight, we engaged for the following days of the fair. Old Finch's ebony brothers proved a decided success, and it was generally admitted that they had put all the other brothers into the shade.

"A few words more about old Finch. He was a comical fellow, and as good hearted and honest as the day is long and light. He was a great favourite everywhere and his company much sought after. At seaport towns, both captains and sailors were fond of him, and were delighted if they could get him to go and sit with them and spin them a yarn over a glass of grog. At Knottingley he was an especial favourite with the captains of the small vessels which used to ply up and down the Knottingley and Goole Canal. I remember once, at the conclusion of a short but successful season at that town, we were going to Drypool Feast. The day being fine, Wilson, Finch, myself, and our wives, determined to walk to Selby, from which place we should take packet to Hull. I had been out fishing the day before, and had caught some eels, which Mrs. Sam had introduced into a pie. This I carried, countryman fashion, at the end of a walking stick over my shoulder. Old Finch must, of course, have a parting glass with his friends, and his anxiety to oblige them all resulted in his becoming decidedly ' altogethery ' before we started upon our journey. But we managed to get him along with us somehow. Passing through a village on our way to Selby some farm-servants began to make merry at Finch's expense, and ultimately threw something at him. This I could not endure, and being younger than I am now, while Wilson was a fine muscular fellow—we set upon the cowardly tykes and soon overpowered them. We then resumed our journey. It seemed, however, that the enemy had only retired to gather more strength. It returned in goodly numbers and attacked us now in earnest. I found it necessary at this point to use my walking stick. This I swung about me right and left, forgetful for the moment of the treasure attached to the extremity, and which more than once, came whack into the face of the foe. But the enemy was mastered at last, and we continued our journey in peace.

"As we went along, Finch suddenly espied in a stream by the way side a large bed of watercress, and being particularly fond of that dainty plant, he determined to gather some of it. He reached forward, but being as a consequence of his previous parting at Knottingley in that unfortunate condition known as 'boosy,' he lost his balance and fell into the stream. We hauled him out and set him on his legs again, having secured for him the much desired delicacy. As soon as we reached our usual posting house at Selby we put him to bed, and took care to have his clothes well dried. Next morning when we all assembled at breakfast we reviewed the adventures of the previous day, and though he was the subject of considerable merriment, nobody laughed more heartily than Old Finch."

CHAPTER XIV.

Now let's go hand in hand, not one before another.—*Comedy of Errors.*

"It was while our theatre was located at Armley in
September, 1851, that a change in the proprietorship
took place. Tom, being pressed for an explanation as to a
certain line of conduct, which, greatly to the annoyance of
myself and wife, he had pursued for some time past,
admitted at length his desire to become a partner in the
concern. Though I reminded him of the terms in which
he had, barely fifteen months before, protested against a
partnership with me, I did not attempt to deny him now,
but I intimated that it must be subject to Selina being
allowed a fair share of whatever the concern was considered to be worth. Then I put the question to him,
What did he think its value was? He should say from
£300 to £400. 'Well, then,' I rejoined, 'you give me
£70, and I'll forfeit all right to the place and take my
leave of it too. Because I knew very well that I could
soon start another concern, and that with my trusty dog
' Nelson ' to head the attractions, I should have little to
fear on the score of getting on. But Tom said he didn't
wish me to leave the establishment, he would rather I
remained and continued the management as before.
Selina, however, upon the subject been mentioned to her,
preferred to receive cash in lieu of whatever it was
intended should be her proportion of the portable property
of the theatre. She preferred money even before a
partnership, because she was anxious to join her husband
at Brierley's circus, to which place, I may here observe, he
had attached himself, in consequence of a tempting salary

offered him by the proprietor shortly after my mother's death.   The end of our various conferences was that Tom was admitted to a partnership, and Selina agreed to accept, and was paid, £60 in hard cash as her proportion. But before the partnership between Tom and I was finally settled, I reminded Tom that it would hardly be the right thing to overlook our brother James.   So I wrote to him upon the subject, offering him a share in the concern. James promptly replied that as he had been absent from the place for so many years, and had done really nothing towards getting it together, he could not think of having any share in it.   He strongly advised me, however, that whatever I decided to do, either in the shape of dividing the effects, or of taking Tom in as a partner, to avail myself of legal advice and assistance.   An agreement as to the purchase of Selina's share was prepared by Mr. Charles Grainger, of Leeds, solicitor, and on the 11th of September, 1851, Tom, Selina, and I met at his office to sign it, and to pay the first instalment of £20.   The remaining £40 it was agreed should be paid by monthly instalments of £10 each, to secure which, Tom and I gave our joint promissory note.   The new firm of Samuel and Thomas Wild commenced from that day, and on the next, I believe, Selina joined her husband at Whitworth, in Lancashire.

"On taking Tom into partnership, I not only gave him an equal share with myself in the concern, but also handed him in hard cash £129 12s. 8d., half of my previous savings.   I also had the place thoroughly renovated at my own cost, for I was proud of the establishment, and determined to keep up its respectability.   You would scarcely believe it, but 'Old Wild's' has been a wonderful place in its time, and I am not saying too much when I aver that it has been the nursery of almost all the strolling players that have appeared during the last half century.

"To go back in our history a month.

"While we were at Cleckheaton, in August, poor Old Finch fell ill.   For some time past he had showed unmistakable signs of growing worse for wear.   A thoroughly conscientious fellow, he had always been a hard worker, and the effects of a life of ceaseless activity, or more properly of rough usage of himself as clown, posturer, and performer— in any of which capacities Finch was always

ready to oblige—began now to be seen.   When his Shaksperian recitals were given at Bradford a couple of months
before, he was far from being well, and ever after that
event his funniosities as clown were delivered with a more
than usually serious face, and he had less of sprightliness
and activity.   But Finch still kept to his duties, and
wouldn't admit that he ailed anything at all, for he was
the last man in the world to give in.   At Cleckheaton,
however, our eyes told us Old Finch was failing, and we
decided now that he should have complete rest until he
was, as we ventured to hope, fairly restored to health.   So
we sent him before us to Holbeck, at which place we were
due, for the feast, in the course of a few weeks' time.   The
feast came, and with it ' Old Wild's,' but there was no
Finch on the outside parade, and his comic songs and
merry antics were missed within.   He still lingered at his
old lodgings—years before he had always put up at the
same house—but his salary was sent him every week, and I
do not believe we ever sat down to a meal without first
thinking of Old Finch.   But, as I have just said, he was a
downright conscientious fellow, and was incessantly
expressing regret, when we took him anything, that he was
unable to appear at the theatre as before.

"The feast at Holbeck passed away, but we still
remained there, never forgetting to call and see poor Finch
whenever an opportunity offered, for though fearing the
worst, we were all anxious for his recovery.

"But I was aroused early one morning at my lodging
in the caravan by a sharp knock at the door.   I opened it.
It was the good lady where Old Finch lodged.   Her
sorrowful face spoke for her.   Old Finch was dead!

"At his funeral we gave him all the honour we could.
The drum, at which he had so often laboured in his lifetime, was muffled, and the old instruments to the sounds
of which he had cut many an amusing caper, and by the
help of which he had sung many a droll comic song, did
their best to struggle through the 'Dead March' in *Saul*
as the company walked slowly to Holbeck churchyard to
see the last of him.

"Tomlinson, a deaf and dumb man, who had been in
the employ of the Wilds ever since my father's time, also
followed in the procession.   Old Finch and he used to be
greatly attached to each other; they frequently went out

fishing together, and Finch always stood his friend in a
time of danger.   Though poor ' Dummy ' (as we used to
call him amongst ourselves) couldn't hear anything of the
' March,' or of the funeral service which followed, he
looked very sad during the proceedings ; and when we
returned from the churchyard, he shook his head mournfully, and intimated to us in his mute language that poor
Old Finch had done with clowning now.

"Finch was missed everywhere.   The old fair frequenters missed him ; the captains and sailors missed him ;
the children, amongst whom he used to distribute ginger-
bread and sweets, they missed him ; our company missed
him—sadly ; but ' Dummy,' without question, missed him
more than all.

"A fund of amusement at all times, it was a sad heart
Old Finch couldn't rejoice, and that too without having
recourse to vulgarity, which he ever disliked.   We never
had such a man for the outside parade.   He could keep
the spectators amused for any length of time.   Whenever
Finch showed his face the mirth was sure to begin, and so
long as he remained, peal after peal of laughter might be
heard at something he had either said or done—for he was
a master of gesture and grimace.   I know he used to
make all the members of our company laugh who were
used to him ; and it was no rare thing, when he was
anywhere about, to find that the band had suddenly ceased
playing.

"Two more faithful servants than ' Dummy ' and Finch
' Old Wild's ' never had ; and there never was a man,
within my recollection, more highly prized at the theatre,
or more generally respected out of it, than Old Finch.

"He left a wife, two sons, and two daughters.   His
wife, who was a very handsome woman, was formerly a Miss
Butler, and a sister of Mrs. Mansfield—the actress I have
spoken of as having left our company, at the Liver
Theatre, Bradford, for Astley's, under the more attractive
name of Miss Rosa Henry.   Finch met with his wife at
Parrish's, with which company they both travelled for a
short season, before they joined our establishment, in ' Old
Jemmy ' Wild's time.   One of Finch's sons, named Alfred
after himself, is, I believe, at the present time the proprietor
of a circus somewhere in the neighbourhood of London.

"Soon after Finch's death, and while our company was

still entertaining Holbeck audiences, Mrs. Sam and I took
a week's holiday and went to London to see the great
exhibition. We visited Astley's and saw William Batty,
Tom Barry, and Miss Rosa Henry, just alluded to. They
were all very chatty and kind to us. We also went to
Vauxhall Gardens, where we quite unexpectedly found my
brother James performing at a circus there. Concerning
his history I may say that when Hughes was about to
dispose of his equestrian and zoological stock, in 1847, he
intimated to James, who had been one of his oldest and
most trustworthy servants, that if he wished to commence
the circus business on his own account, he was to make a
selection from the stock, and pay Hughes for it when he
found himself in a position to do so. But James, though
the best of servants, had no pluck to be a master. He did
buy four horses, however, at Hughes' sale ; and those were
generally engaged along with himself. After Hughes'
retirement James's first place was Charles Hengler's
circus, were he acted as clown, ring-master, and horse-
breaker. He afterwards joined Pablo Fanque in these
varied capacities, and ultimately went to Vauxhall Gardens
at the commencement of the summer season, in 1851. His
engagement there concluded the day following that on
which we visited the Gardens, and he had arranged to
dispose of his four horses immediately afterwards. When
he told me this I asked him if he had accepted any other
engagement. He replied no, he was going to give up
circus life. Thinking it just possible he might be
wishful for a change to the stage, I invited him to return
to Holbeck with us and join our company, but this he
declined to do. The fact was, though he didn't tell us so
then, he was going to be married, in anticipation of which
event he had sold off his live stock. But this reminds me
I have omitted to make mention of his first wife. She was
a Miss Sackie, a clever tight-rope dancer at Batty's circus,
and at which place he had first met with her. There were
three children by his first marriage, all boys. When the
eldest of them, James, was only five years of age the mother
died. Batty's was at Huddersfield at the time, and she had
been fulfilling an engagement there up to within a few
weeks of her decease. On the very evening when that
occurred, her husband, as clown, was delighting his
audience at the circus with his quips and jests, when some-

body entering the place in breathless haste incautiously called out to him, ' Mr. Wild, your wife's dead !' On hearing these words he swooned, and had to be carried out, nor could he perform at Batty's for above a week after that sad event. When Hughes had comfortably settled at Liverpool he sent for the younger James to be a sort of companion to his two boys, and the three went to school together. The little fellow had a good home at Hughes's, but unfortunately he did not enjoy it long. One day, as he and the two Hughes were returning from school, each determined to be the first home, and they commenced to run very quickly. James was the first there, but the exertion must have been too much for him, for as the poor little fellow was in the act of hanging up his cap behind the door he fell down in a fit and expired.

" My brother James's second choice was a widow, the landlady of the White Horse Hotel, Bristol. This hotel was an old-fashioned place, and, after his marriage, James determined, out of the means at his command, to thoroughly improve it. In addition to this drain upon his resources, he found to his surprise and regret that his wife was in pecuniary difficulties, and his accumulated earnings had to be employed in the liquidation of debts she had contracted during her previous widowhood. Then she had sons upgrown ; and they couldn't get on very well with James, as they had hitherto had it pretty much their own way in the place. So after four or five years of aught but a pleasant life, he gave up the hotel and returned to circus clowning and horsebreaking ; to which employment he remained attached to the close of his life in 1871. He was with Charles Hengler, at Birmingham, at the time of his death, but his wife, who survived him, administered to his effects, though I believe they had been parted up to that time.

" During our stay in London, Batty renewed his offer of an engagement for myself and ' Nelson,' but as neither he nor I would budge an inch from our old terms, nothing came of the negotiations. What was £5 a week ? I asked him, and to have to pay my own expenses out of it too. Why, I could make that at our place at a single benefit ! and I told him so ; but Batty, enterprising though he undoubtedly was, evidently couldn't see his way to a profit out of ' Nelson ' and his master on any higher terms.

and boxes. We were not disappointed in our expectations —we remained four months in that town. Of course we did our best to produce novelty. We had a pantomime at Christmas, and afterwards, in addition to other attractions, engaged my sister Elizabeth's daughter, Selina, for six nights, to perform between the pieces upon the slack rope. She was announced as ' the celebrated Pauline Violante, the first tight-rope dancer in the world.' Of this young lady I may have to say more anon. In addition to many of our stock pieces we performed—*Robert the Bruce; The Bottle; The Miller and his Men; Laid up in Port; The White Slave; The Vagrant;* and similar dramas.

"This may afford some idea of the class of pieces which were popular with our audiences, and of the sort of work our company was equal to in 1853. But every succeeding year marked improvement. We began also to pay some attention to our programmes, displaying everything to the best advantage. Sometimes we had a few words of introduction when a ' star ' was performing with us ; sometimes a short address to the public on our own account; sometimes we went in for a little of the descriptive, and not unfrequently for a little of the sensational.

"1854, May 1st and 2nd. 'Novelty ! Novelty ! ! Novelty ! ! ! First night of *The Will and The Way*, which has been in preparation the whole of the season, and is decidedly the best drama now upon the British stage.' Such is the heading of a placard of the performances at Wild's Theatre, New Market Place, Blackburn, followed by a programme, nearly a foot long, of the scenery and incidents of the piece. October 2nd. In the Market Place, Halifax. Duly licensed, Wild's Portable Theatre, *Green Hills of the Far West*, with terrific combats and imposing tableaux. Azeni, Mrs. S. Wild (in large characters). December 9th, New Theatre Royal, Bury. 'For the only time this season, the drama. with new scenery by Mr. Fitzgerald, dresses by Mrs. Meanley, properties by Mr. Bolland, the music arranged by Mr. Pickering, the whole under the direction of Mr. S. Wild—entitled *Raby Rattler*,' principal characters by Messrs. Fitzgerald and Adams. Heading the programme is the following announcement, which not only furnishes a specimen of the literary capabilities of the establishment at this time, but also serves to prove that it was the desire and object of the management to provide as far as possible for the comfort of the audience:—

The patrons of the drama, and the public in general, are most respectfully informed, that the above place of rational amusement will open for the season on Saturday next, December 9th, 1854. The whole of the theatre is newly painted and decorated; the gallery has been enlarged, and is seated to the back of the orchestra, this will add comfort to that portion of the audience, as there will be no standing places or promenade. The pit will be large and commodious. The front and side boxes are all well lined with green and red baize, the seats are newly cushioned and carpeted. The whole of the scenery, wings, &c., are entirely new. A new and elegant act drop will be introduced. The proscenium, stage doors, &c., are all newly designed and decorated, and of the most magnificent description. The superb embelishments have been designed and painted by Mr. Fitzgerald, artist to the establishment. The whole has been executed regardless of cost, and the public may rest assured that every exertion has been made to present a combination of chaste decorations that may defy competition. The managers feeling assured that the play-going world is still numerous enough to render it again, as in the olden times, the rendezvous of the intelligence and wealth of this populous and enlightened neighbourhood.

"The fact that we had a very successful season of at least five months at Bury is, I take it, evidence sufficient that our efforts to secure the comfort of our patrons, and to cater well for their amusement, were fairly appreciated.

"There is a little incident in connection with our first season at Bury.

"We left Rochdale to go there, and having no use for our portable theatre, it was packed upon waggons and allowed to remain in the fair ground at that town. While we were at Bury, 'Great Saturday'—usually observed at Rochdale as a holiday—came round. Tom, Adams, I, and several others of our company, went over there in the afternoon for an hour or two. Amongst the places of entertainment for the feast was Sangers's Circus. We agreed to accord it our patronage. As we made our way towards it, Adams suddenly recognised the property of Messrs. S. & T. Wild, in the two pairs of portable steps leading to Sangers' parade, and upon looking about us we also found several poles belonging to that same firm. Upon taking our seats in the circus we further discovered that most of our brackets had been employed in erecting the gallery seats, and here and there sundry other articles of ours put to profitable uses. Never having been asked for our permission, we considered this general appropriation of our property as a rather cool proceeding, but as the circus was such a poor affair—there were only three horses, and those not of the sprightliest sort, while I do not think the entire staff of performers numbered more than half a dozen—we rather sympathised with the proprietors than otherwise. But we couldn't resist the opportunity of having a little amusement at their expense. So returning to the money keeper (who was a Mrs. Sanger, I believe) I said, 'I find there has been some of our property removed.' What kind of property, and who was I? 'Portable property,' I rejoined, 'belonging to Wild's Theatre, of which I am one of the proprietors. And what is most strange, I find some of the missing property here; these are our steps, those our poles, and within, I find our gallery brackets have been utilised. A policeman might probably assist me in unravelling the mystery how these things found their way here.' Never was poor mortal in such a state of agitation. 'Stop,' she said, 'and I'll call Bill Chappell, our clown; it was him who brought them here.' Bill Chappell was called for, but he being then in the thick of his business within, intimated that he couldn't possibly leave the circle. 'Come at once,' said the money taker authoritatively, 'and never mind the performance.' Whereupon the clown appeared. 'Here is Mr. Wild inquiring about certain articles which have been removed from his waggons. Chappell looked very woe-begone, but excused himself by explaining the emergency of the Brothers Sanger, and the confidence they had in our readiness to lend the properties in question, and wound up by a few encomiums on the well-known character of the Wilds for kindness, and so forth. The clown stated his case so well that he was not only assured that there was no harm done – it was only our holiday fun—but permission was granted Messrs. Sanger to avail themselves, until we required them, of any other properties they might find of service to them.

"These were the Brothers Sanger, John and George, so poor that they had to borrow properties from 'Old Wild's' to build themselves a place to perform in, and look at their position now! the most wealthy and famous of circus proprietors. Does not this remind one of the adage, 'It is better to be born lucky than rich?'"

CHAPTER XV.

> The battle and the breeze.
> CAMPBELL—*Ye Mariners of England.*

"In addition to the fact that it always endeavoured to cater well for its patrons and give them money's worth, there is this to be said of 'Old Wild's'—it was never appealed to in vain to lend its services towards the promotion of any charitable or philanthropic object. Indeed, I may say it more frequently gave them without being appealed to at all, and this statement is, I think, to some extent corroborated by an announcement of performances at Bury on the 17th January, 1855 :—

☞ NOTICE! ☜

Messrs. S. & T. Wild beg to inform their patrons that Wednesday, the 17th, will be set apart for a Public Benefit in aid of the Patriotic Fund for the relief of the Relatives of the killed and wounded soldiers, sailors, and marines in the East!

The Entertainments will be under the patronage of Colonel Haliday and the Officers of the 36th Regiment of Foot!

☞ The whole of the company have tendered their services gratuitously!

All persons possessed of true English feeling towards our brave soldiers, who are fighting our battles against the tyrant of Russia, will have an opportunity of showing their sympathy by supporting this laudable undertaking.

And this is but one of many announcements which I find amongst our old programmes of benefits given for philanthropic purposes, local charities, and the like.

"The old folks set the example of giving in this way—it seemed, in fact, to be one of the conditions of proprietorship—and it was followed ever afterwards, so long as ' Old Wild's ' existed.

" But, to dismiss this subject for the present. The drama selected for performance on Colonel Haliday's patronage night was *Belphégor*, in which were introduced ' the court-dresses of Louis Philippe, late King of the French.' These dresses were first purchased by Mr. Edwin Hughes at Paris on 27th July, 1846, and at the sale of his stock in London on 4th November, 1847, were bought by my mother. They were of a most magnificent description, and, I need hardly say, were only mounted by our company on very special occasions.

" While upon the subject of dresses, I may here remark that our wardrobe at this time also contained a complete set of the Lord-Lieutenant of Ireland's livery. This was purchased for my mother, and at her request, by Mr. Hughes, during one of his visits to Ireland ; and a good round sum it cost her.

" From which facts it will readily be seen that Mrs. Wild never took expense into consideration when she set about making additions to her wardrobe.

" Early in 1855, to resume our history, we began to engage stars. As regards patronage, we had nothing what-ever to complain of then, but we desired to make ' Old Wild's ' as attractive as possible, and to provide good entertainment for our supporters.

" On the 22nd January, Mr. Butler Wentworth, a tragedian of whom both the *Times* and the *Athenæum* had spoken highly, commenced a six-nights engagement with us at Bury. His chief characters were Hamlet, Macbeth, Richard III., Othello, in all of which he appeared during his engagement, and the leading female parts in which plays Mrs. ' Sam ' was selected to perform.

" Mrs Loydall, under her maiden name—Miss Georgiana Stansbury, also made her *début* at our place on the first evening of Mr. Wentworth's engagement. Of this lady and of her husband I take the liberty of saying a few words, commencing with him. Mr. Henry Loydall was only a young man, perhaps not more than twenty-two, when, some years before the period under notice, he left John Edwards's travelling theatre to join ours. For a time he gave little promise of that ability which he afterwards displayed ; but he had come to a good training school, and he wisely sought to avail himself of the opportunities it afforded of advancement in the performer's art. He worked hard, studied deeply, and at length the results of his labours began to be seen, and it was upon 'Old Wild's' stage, and in the character of Claude Melnotte, that he achieved his first histrionic triumph. He afterwards aspired to Shaksperian characters, some of which he sustained remarkably well, *Hamlet* being one of his most decided successes. He left us during our first season at Bury, and went to perform at the Theatre Royal, Bolton, where he first met with Miss Stansbury, who, along with her parents, was then fulfilling an engagement there. She was only about seventeen years of age, but quite old enough, it appeared, to reciprocate Mr. Loydall's affection. At length, quite unknown to her parents, the nuptials were arranged between them, and Mr. Loydall left the Bolton Theatre and rejoined us on the commencement of our second season at Bury, two or three days after which Miss Stansbury also came over to Bury, where she remained until her marriage. As soon as she was missing from Bolton, her parents, knowing that Mr. Loydall had accepted an engagement with us, and probably suspecting her attachment to him also, wrote to me to know if she had joined our company. I replied in the negative, but ignorant of what was in the wind, I added my belief that their daughter was somewhere in Bury, for I think some of our company had seen her. But to end this little romance. Whatever further steps Miss Stansbury's parents took with a view of securing her return to them and to her duties at Bolton, they proved altogether unavailing, for not long after their letter to me Mr. Loydall and Miss Stansbury took each other 'for better for worse,' immediately after which event she appeared at our theatre as I have already stated. The happy pair remained with us several months, and then started upon a provincial tour, which proved to be a highly successful one. Ultimately, Mr. Loydall became the lessee of the Bury Theatre and, successively, of theatres at Rochdale, Bolton, and other towns, and his circumstances for a time were flourishing. But by and bye reverses came, and sent him behind the footlights again as a performer, and at the present time he is, I believe, starring in the provinces.

"At the conclusion of Mr. Butler Wentworth's engagement, and on January 31st, there appeared at Wild's theatre Mr. Watkins Burroughs, a man who in his time won golden opinions, and it is worth while, as furnishing a fair estimate of the man, to quote a few lines from a long notice of him, which appeared in the *Belfast Commercial Chronicle*, two years before this time:—' People speak of " Burroughs," and recollect the gentleman, the scholar, the artist, the man of genius: know dignity in its elegance, scholarship in its refinement, oratory without a flaw, and versatility of personation having no competitor.' His favourite parts were Rob Roy, Jock Muir, William Tell, and Alessandro Massaroni; and during his engagement with us he afforded our audiences the fullest satisfaction by the varied capabilities he displayed in sustaining these and similar characters.

" The terms upon which we usually engaged stars were, one third of the receipts of each evening, after providing for cost of printing and gas, and one half the receipts (subject to the same deductions) on a benefit night— always allowing the artiste one during his or her engagement.

" The constant topic of the newspapers at this time, and the theme of general conversation, was the Crimean War. The successes of the allies generally, and the bravery of the English soldiers in particular, filled every mouth with praise and fired every bosom with enthusiasm. The only news people cared for was war news; their only music martial airs and patriotic songs ; and the only sights they thought worth seeing were military spectacles and parades. It was impossible, amidst all these manifestations of loyalty and patriotism, for ' Old Wild's ' to remain indifferent. It must keep pace with the times; it must echo the national sentiment; therefore, well knowing that ' nothing succeeds like success,' it actually undertook to fight over again *The Battle of the Alma.*

" This piece, written specially for us by Mr. C. R. Somerset, was announced as in preparation at the foot of the programme of the performances on the evening of Colonel Haliday's patronage, and it was due to his kindness that when the piece was finally brought out at Bury we were enabled to introduce a genuine British sergeant and twenty-four genuine British soldiers upon the stage. That sergeant and those soldiers—the smartest and cleanest fellows I ever saw—used to march from the barracks to the theatre every evening, and crowds flocked to meet them and to cheer them on their way. The theatre was literally crammed every night to see those gallant fellows storm the heights of the Alma. Which heights, by the way, consisted of a series of stage rocks and passes commencing at the very footlights, and extending, rock above rock, and pass above pass, the entire length of the stage— a distance of at least thirty feet—and until rocks, passes, and soldiers alike became almost lost in the ' flies.' Right bravely those English fought against the supernumerary Russians, and loud and prolonged was the cheering when, having at length scaled those mimic heights and completely routed the enemy, they planted the standard of victory there. And then—after having availed themselves of the use of gunpowder and fireworks to such an extent that the spectators were lost to each other for at least five minutes after the curtain fell, not to mention the imminent hazard they nightly encountered of being suffocated into the bargain—when the victors took their seats in the pit, just before the commencement of the farce, it was worth all the money paid at the door to witness the hearty reception that was accorded them. The sergeant had every reason to be proud of his men, and he was. So much so, indeed, that he generously divided amongst them the money he had received from the management as a trifling acknowledgment of his own valuable services. This kindness on the sergeant's part operated unfortunately for the men, some of whom, on the third evening after the performance, failed to report themselves at the barracks as usual. This annoyed the Colonel exceedingly, but having given us his word that the men should come and assist us for the first six performances of *The Battle of Alma,* he let them come the week out. But when, shortly afterwards, we desired their services again, he refused to let them come. ' I have nothing whatever against the Messrs. Wild; personally, I am sorry I cannot oblige them,' said the Colonel to our representative, in reply to his request, ' but I cannot allow the men to come and perform again—and for this they have nobody but themselves to blame.'

" Anxious, as far as possible, to keep up our attractions, we engaged for a few nights, commencing February 5th,

Mr. and Mrs. J. Stephens, formerly of Astley's, and, shortly afterwards, while still at Bury, Mr. George Owen, the celebrated tragedian. His first appearance was on the 26th of February, as King Lear, and he was announced for ' six farewell nights previous to his departure for America.' In addition to King Lear, he played, I believe, Sir Edward Mortimer (in *The Iron Chest*), Falstaff (*Merry Wives of Windsor*), Othello, Louis XI., and Cardinal Richelieu."

" As our season at Bury began to draw towards a close, benefits came on. Mr. and Mrs. Loydall took theirs on 26th March, in *Taming of the Shrew*, followed by the (then) still popular play of *Jack Sheppard*. Messrs. Harding and Greenhalch had theirs, jointly, two days after that, and appeared in a sensational drama, in MS., ' founded upon the popular novel, recently published, entitled *La Vie d'un Ouvrier*, written by Emile Souvestre, a working-man of Paris, dramatised for the English stage by C. R. Somerset, Esq., called the *Life and Struggles of a Working-Man*.

" On March 30th, I appeared (but this was not the occasion of anybody's benefit) as Tom, the Dumb Man of Manchester — a character, it was announced, I had played upwards of 200 nights. Though, as the description of the character implies, there is nothing for Tom to say, there is, nevertheless, a great deal for him to do. Indeed, I may say, it is one of the hardest parts I ever performed ; but, then, as Macbeth says,

The labour we delight in physics pain.

" So where's the odds ?

" The afterpiece on the occasion last alluded to was *Black-eyed Susan*, with the principal characters reversed ; the ladies all taking male parts, and Messrs. Bateson and Hewitt sustaining respectively the characters of Black-eyed Susan and Dolly Mayflower. Of course, this rendering of the celebrated drama in question turned it into burlesque ; and this was especially the case when, as I frequently did, I happened to play Susan ; because, when I fainted in the last act, where my ' William dear ' (Mrs. ' Sam ') is condemned to be hung, it took no less than six persons to bear me from the stage.

" After leaving Bury we went to Blackburn for a short season, and there we produced, amongst other novelties, *The*

Sea of Ice, or *The Wild Flower of Mexico,* and *The Struggle for Gold!* Adapted from the French. The overture and music, entirely new, arranged for this theatre. Produced under the superintendence of Mr. S. Wild. This piece was at that time counted, from the success it had met with in the Metropolis, 'one of the sights of London.' The first night of its production at Blackburn was April 23rd, when Mr. John Holloway appeared in it; and—just to show the early age at which a performer's life may begin—my little niece, Kate Bateson (then not more than four or five years of age) appeared as Marie.

"At the foot of the programme of the performances for this date is an intimation to the following effect:—
' Messrs. S. & T. Wild can assure all parties who may favour them with their patronage that they may visit the Theatre with the greatest confidence, as all improper conduct (if any) will be immediately repressed—respectability combined with recreation being their object.'

" This, I submit, is evidence in itself that the desire of the management was, as far as possible, to secure the general comfort of the audience.

" In all the programmes I was dubbed lessee. This was done for the sake of convenience when obtaining a licence. The management and care of the concern, however, still devolved upon me. Tom never played except at his own benefits, and, I may say, I had every whit as much responsibility as when I was sole proprietor.

" About September, 1855, while we were stationed in the Market-place, Halifax, Mr. Hughes wrote to me to the effect that two camels (male and female), said to have been captured in the Crimea, were being brought to Liverpool for sale; and that if Tom and I thought they would be of any service to us in the way of increasing our attractions, we were to let him know, and he would endeavour to secure them for us. Tom said he would have nothing whatever to do with them, but I wrote to Hughes requesting him to keep his eye upon the camels, and I would run over in a day or two and see them, with a view, if they suited me, to their purchase on my own account. Having provided myself, out of my account with Messrs. Beckett and Co., bankers, Leeds, with a sum of £200, I accordingly went over to Liverpool. The camels were on board the steamship *Carnac* (then lying in the Mersey), in which they had been brought over to England by Captain Dubbins, as a consignment for Mr. Hulse, of Liverpool, the well-known dealer in wild animals, &c. I decided at once, on seeing the camels, to have them, and paid Mr. Hulse £150 for them, beside making several small purchases of guns, a dagger, and other reputed war trophies which had been sent over with them.

" For money at that time was more plentiful with me than it is now. I estimate that the balances standing at my credit at Messrs. Beckett & Co.'s, Leeds, at the Morley and Skyrack Savings Bank, and at a bank (the name of which I forget) at Blackburn, amounted then, together, to something like £2000. This was, of course, exclusive of my share in the portable theatre, which, at that time, from the improvements which had been made in it, was worth bringing into the reckoning. These were the days when I used to go down to Leeds and deposit £200 with my bankers at one time. I have done this more than once during our visits to Holbeck. On those occasions, I remember, I used to ride over to Leeds on horseback, booted and spurred, and dressed in the prevailing fashion. I generally left at the door of the bank my horse Jerry— a coloured horse, well-known at Leeds, because he was usually attached to the front of the band carriage—and when I came out, after transacting my business, I was sure to find a crowd about waiting to see if Jerry's master had come with him. Then, amidst the exclamations of those who recognised me, I used to throw myself into the saddle, give Jerry his head, and ride off at a brisk pace, making the pavement fairly resound again.

" I have no money in any of these banks now—though it is urged that we ought to thank Providence for all things— nor have I aught to remind me of my coloured horse Jerry, save a mane comb, a picker, and a pair of old spurs.

" ' Sam ' Wild never dreamed then that he would have to face poverty ; but as the navvy said when the old lady reprimanded him for not providing against a rainy day— the misfortune was there came two rainy days together. But of this in its proper place.

" To continue our narrative of the camels. I directed them to be sent to me at Halifax, and in this town they first appeared in public. The female, which I named Sultana, was quiet and tractable, but her lord and master,

Mohammed, was a rough, uncivilised customer; and it took me some time to fit him for good society. But I spent several afternoons in his company and succeeded at last. When I thought him sufficiently well-behaved to be introduced to the public, I erected a small booth by the side of our larger one in the Market Place, and I exhibited him and his mistress as the 'War Camels of the Crimea,' adding to the attractions the war trophies I had previously purchased. The exhibition was open from about two in the afternoon until ten in the evening, and was well patronised. I think the charge for admission was 2d.

"But I fancied I might do still better by the camels if I could engage them to circus proprietors and the like. I accordingly advertised them in the *Era*, and Mr. Hobson, of Leeds, responded with the offer of an engagement for the Leeds fair week. I asked £12 for the six days, but he would only give £10; as this was a first engagement, however, I closed with him on his own terms. The camels had been taught to fire off pistols, to lie down at the word of command, to walk upon their knees, to feign lameness, and to perform many other similar feats, but in order that everything might go off with *éclat*, I decided to send Bateson with them. As already stated, he was by profession an acrobat, and so he was sent, as 'Herr Wilmot,' along with the animals, to throw somersaults over them, to put them through their performances, and to offer the best explanation he could of the circumstances under which they were brought to England from the Crimea. I had a splendid dress made for him for the occasion, and, indeed, spared no expense to make the camels' entertainment, if possible, a success. The arrival of Sultana and Mohammed at Leeds was duly announced by posters and bills, and at the appointed time they appeared, adorned in cloths (striped with red, white, and blue), and laden with guns, bayonets, and other implements of warfare. Herr Wilmot, my son Tom, and myself, in private costume, conducted them through the principal streets, and I think almost everybody turned out to see them. This was on a Monday, early in November, and I remained at Leeds that evening to see how Herr Wilmot and the war camels were appreciated by the public. I was delighted to find that they were most

favourably received.   On Tuesday afternoon, first putting
my son in funds to pay all necessary expenses of lodging,
&c., I took my leave of the party, from which I vainly
anticipated great successes, and returned to my duties at
Halifax.   I had advertised in the *Era* the engagement at
Hobson's Amphitheatre of the camels, and on Wednesday
evening, the third of their appearance, several proprietors
of music halls from London, Birmingham, Manchester,
Sheffield, and other large towns, in search of novelty, came
over to Leeds to see Hobson's latest hit.   When the hour
for the performance of the camels arrived, Herr Wilmot
was not forthcoming.   A search was made for him, and he
was found in the pit amongst the audience, endeavouring
to sleep off the effects of Jamaica rum.   He was aroused
and sent on to the stage, but of course everybody saw his
condition, and, instead of receiving applause, as before, he
was hissed ; and the camels' entertainment was doomed.
This was the first and last engagement of the kind.

"Well, as I found all my hopes of success with the
animals in this direction extinguished, I decided to introduce them upon our own stage.

"On November 14, we produced at Halifax a new
patriotic drama, (written especially for us by Mr.
Somerset) entitled *The Fall of Sebastopol* ; in the second
and third acts of which the ' War Camels of the Crimea '
were introduced, and very warmly applauded.   They
appeared engaged in removing the wounded Russians, and
Mohammed was taught to seize and throw over his head a
counterfeit of one of the enemy, during an attack in which
he (Mohammed) and his gentler companion were captured.
They also appeared harnessed and drawing cannons, pon-
derous, formidable looking instruments of destruction,
which a child might have wheeled about with ease.   No
pains were spared to make this play attractive.   We
engaged twelve pensioners, besides other supernumeraries,
to assist in the last act in the siege of Sebastopol.   It was
in this act that I appeared as an English sergeant, and
defended myself, amid shot and shell, against six of the
enemy at one time.   This was the great fencing bout in
which two swords were brought into requisition.   During
the siege there would be some fifty persons upon the
stage blazing away at each other, and so filling the booth
with smoke with their red-hot shot and shells, that the

audience had to hopelessly abandon itself to coughing and sneezing for full ten minutes after the ramparts of Sebastopol had been destroyed.

"I come upon another instance of a performance given for a charitable object. It was at Halifax, on November 28th, and for the benefit of the Infirmary.

Messrs. S. & T. Wild, ever desirous to aid, as far as their opportunities will permit, institutions like the above, where human suffering is alleviated by the charitable and benevolent, purpose placing a portion of the receipts of their theatre for this evening at the disposal of the directors of the above institution; and trust that the facility thus given to the public to contribute to that excellent institution will be responded to by all classes.

"After leaving Halifax we went, probably in December, to the Theatre Royal, Wakefield, to put on the time for a week until a temporary wooden theatre, which was being erected for us in Bond Street, Dewsbury, was completed. We played our war piece at Wakefield, but the stage being exceedingly small, we were very much restricted in our operations; so much so, that during the attack in the third act, one of the camels, Mohammed, received a flesh wound with a bayonet, which caused him to be rather furious; and one of the pensioners we had engaged also received a wound in his shoulder, and had to lay up a few days in consequence. On the second evening of the performance of the war piece we dispensed with the use of bayonets; but our successes on the field were no less brilliant than before, and happily we had no casualties to report. Notwithstanding the attractiveness of the performances, we had a very bad week at Wakefield, and lost £15 by it. This was due to the fact that the lovers of the drama in that town had several times previously been imposed upon by amateurs, who had taken the theatre, and had announced themselves as some famous London company.

"Our theatre at Dewsbury being now completed we took possession of it without delay. There, amongst other pieces, we played on January 21st and 22nd, 1856, *The Fall of Sebastopol*, with camels and pensioners as before. At this time we had added to our company a Mr. Alexander Ramsden. In the above-mentioned piece he had, as an officer, to marshal his soldiers, previous to an engagement with the enemy, and he puzzled the old pensioners not a little by commanding them to 'advance three paces backwards.' It was an unfortunate slip of the tongue this, and our Dewsbury friends never forgot it. So long as Ramsden remained with us we never went to that town that he did not receive from one or more of the audience, the moment he appeared upon the stage, a command to 'advance three paces backwards.'

"While at Dewsbury Mr. George Owen commenced another engagement with us, on February 5th, at the conclusion of which I received from him the following letter :—

46, Albany Wharf, Regent's Park, London,
February 11th, 1856.

Dear Sir,—In leaving you, after a highly successful engagement, allow me to thank you and the members of your company, for the kind attention displayed by one and all in the production of some of Shakspeare's most difficult plays ; and, furthermore, permit me to bear testimony to your high business-like habits, and the very honourable character of all your transactions.

Yours truly,
GEO. OWEN.

Mr. S. Wild, Victoria Theatre, Dewsbury."

CHAPTER XVI.

Under the Patronage of "Billy Barlow"—Cats'
Entertainment — Benefit Night Novelties —
Grand Procession at Blackburn—How the
Prestonian makes Holiday—Lessee of Theatre
Royal (Falconer) objects to 'Old Wild's'—The
Camel summarily settles the Controversy—Loss
of one of the Camels—An Accident at Skipton—
"Where's my Wig?"—A Dissolution of Partner-
ship—Two Companies of "Wild's."

A pair of very strange beasts.—As You Like It.

"As it drew towards the close of our first season at the
Victoria Theatre, Dewsbury, benefit nights came on;
when, as is still the custom amongst performers, each
beneficiaire vied with his brother artistes to produce alike
the longest programme and the most attractive entertainment; being permitted, by time-honoured precedent, to
announce his benefit night as the best of the season. A
good programme is invariably half the battle on such
occasions, but to secure as patron a person of some standing in society is to give a sort of *éclat* to the general proceedings, and in most cases to ensure a crowded house.
Though at the period under notice we rarely knew what it
was to want public patronage, Messrs. Boardman and
Ramsden, amongst the first to take their benefit, were
perhaps excusable, for the first of the two reasons just
stated, in announcing the 'monstre performance' for that
occasion as under the distinguished patronage of 'Sir
William Barlow, K.G.' In addition to this attractive
feature of the programme, however, there was the promise
of two powerful dramas (of four and two acts length
respectively), a comic duet, a song of the same pretensions,
the presentation of a dress-piece, the distribution of
songs, and, finally, an intimation that Mr. Boardman
would be drawn across the stage by fifty-four cats in a
blaze of fire.

" The *beneficiaire*, like the poet, has a licence, and he uses it at times pretty freely ; but with the exception that Sir Knight failed to put in an appearance, and that fifty out of the fifty-four cats were not forthcoming at the time announced for their performance, the programme of Messrs. Boardman and Ramsden was carried out with tolerable fidelity.

"As to the cats' entertainment, though it always created considerable amusement, it was only an incidental feature of our attractions. The employment of domestic animals in this way originated, I believe, with Dicky Usher, a clown in London in Ducrow's time. He used to be drawn round the arena (as also through the streets on each occasion of his benefit) in a small chariot, to which were harnessed four favourite cats, whose training he had made his especial care. The animals had little more to do than walk before the vehicle, for inside it there was some mechanical power, and it was by this that it was propelled.

" Our feline corps, like Usher's, commonly numbered four ; but we might easily have had just as many scores. For when it was whispered to the stage-loving young gentlemen, who were always hanging about our establishment, that the exigencies of our performances, on a certain night, would call for a few cats, and that to each of the said young gentlemen who, on such night, appeared at the stage door with one in his possession a free pass would be granted, it was really surprising with what a number of feline candidates we were besieged at the appointed time. As soon as our requirements became known, the country was scoured in search of these domestic pets ; and sleek, well-conditioned animals were decoyed, heartlessly betrayed, enticed, or otherwise carried off, *nolens volens*, to ' Old Wild's,' there to await solemn adjudication as to their individual fitness, or want of it, for a stage career.

" It would be difficult to say how many of these household treasures were restored to their hearths and homes after the performances at the theatre were over ; their captors but rarely turned up to claim them. As for the rejected ones, they were released at the stage door the moment their services were declined, and were left entirely to their own nimbleness and knowledge of geography.

" The animals selected for the performance were harnessed with tapes to a stout rope attached to a miniature carriage, bedecked and bedizened to give it the appearance of a chariot, and in this the *beneficiaire* (usually attired as clown) sat, with as much affected pomp and state as the circumstances would admit of. In his left hand he held what purported to be reins, while with his right he flourished an apology for a whip. Little preparatory training on the part of the feline performers was considered necessary, but when the chariot had slowly started across the stage (being drawn by one of the company by means of the rope), it was then a tragedy began to be rehearsed. For the revolutionary proceedings of the domestic animals in question well nigh brought upon them all the horrors of strangulation ; and, therefore, I use the word ' tragedy ' advisedly. Nor did the explosion of fire-works attached to the chariot, and, simultaneously, the introduction of coloured fire at each of the side wings, contribute much towards reassuring the rebels, or towards inspiring them with confidence in the existing state of things. But the rebellion was usually quelled before serious consequences ensued, and a timely rescue of the revolters was made that instant the curtain closed upon a scene of an unaffected struggle for liberty.

" On occasions when distinguished patronage could not be secured, or otherwise was thought unnecessary, and when the public grew tired of knights of the Billy Barlow type, attention would be arrested by some novel announcement. Here is one which headed the programme of performances on the evening of the benefit of Mr. Naylor and Mrs. Bateson during the last week of our first season at the Victoria Theatre, Dewsbury :—

NOTICE TO THE PUBLIC.

All persons desirous of visiting the land of Golden Amusement will do well to take a berth in the old line-of-battle ship, the *Victoria*, granted by the Lords of the Admiralty, positively for this voyage only, and now fitting out at the Dewsbury docks, under the command of Captain S. Wild, manned by as jolly a crew of able seamen as ever stood the fire of public opinion. This noble vessel will be ready to sail at seven o'clock on Monday evening, March 10th, 1856. She can safely accommodate 2000 persons—helmsman, Mr. Naylor, being his 3369th voyage. First cabin, 1s. 6d., second cabin 1s., third cabin 6d., fourth cabin 3d. N.B. The captain has kindly consented to make for the Sea of Ice, where every person may gaze upon the frozen regions, and from thence direct to the British camp. Mr. Naylor and Mrs. Bateson have the honour to announce that their benefit will take place on Monday next, when the performances will commence with the powerful and romantic drama, now performing in London and Paris, entitled *The Sea of Ice*, &c.

" It may be interesting to know, in regard to the fore-going announcement, that the 3369th ' voyage ' of Mr. Naylor has reference to the number of times he had appeared upon the stage at our theatre.

" The giving away of songs was always an attraction, and on the occasion just referred to, the intimation that 200 copies of a song by Mr. John Holloway would be dis-tributed amongst the audience, went a long way towards ensuring a crowded house.

" Not that the writing of a song by Holloway was by any means a rarity, though his poetical effusions were always appreciated. He wrote frequently in this way, as did also Mr. Mellers, only the latter aspired more to a position as playwright. He dramatised several stories for us which had appeared in the *London Journal* and in other periodicals of that description.

" Indeed, I might almost say, and with truthfulness, that there was hardly such a thing as drawing limit to the capabilities of ' Old Wild's,' for its company has, from time to time, included men of varied accomplishments and gifts.

" Our first season at the Victoria Theatre, Dewsbury, was brought to a close on the 15th March, 1856. Mr. George Owen, who had accepted another engagement with us, played during the last four evenings of our stay to crowded houses, and we left Dewsbury with an intimation that when we returned there another season, we should, as an acknowledgment of the kind and liberal support of our friends, bring forward for their amusement ' every novelty that capital can produce or labour accomplish.'

" At Blackburn, where we next appeared, we produced dramatic versions of *The Lamplighter*, *Temptation*, and *Masks and Faces*. The original stories had previously appeared in popular periodicals, and the public having read them with avidity, flocked in hundreds to see them represented upon our stage.

" On the occasion of my complimentary benefit during our stay at Blackburn, we had a grand procession through the principal streets of the town. The order of the procession was as follows :—

Military Band—
(Leader, S. Wild) in richly decorated carriage, drawn by four horses.
Horseman in Armour.

War Camels from the Crimea, with Mr. Naylor and Mrs. Bateson in
      magnificent Turkish costume, as the Sultan and Sultana.
                        Horseman in Armour.
Platform, Victoria (18 feet by 8 feet), on four wheels, drawn by a pair of
horses, with Miss Wild and Mr. Greenhalgh as the Queen of England and
the Emperor of France ; Her Majesty seated on a throne ; other members
of the company in court dresses, as attendants on Her Majesty ; two
juveniles as Peace and Plenty.
                        Horseman in Armour.
Platform, Duke of Wellington, on four wheels, drawn by a pair of horses ;
splendid tableau of Britannia ; Britannia, Mrs. Holloway ; Messrs.
Holloway, Crotty, Thornton, and others as The Sons of the Sea.

" In nearly every town we went to about this time we
had processions similar to the one above described, and a
very great source of attraction they always proved. Such
a procession we had when, leaving Blackburn, we went to
Preston at Whitsuntide, 1856. There, curiosity to see it
was perhaps greater than in any other town we ever
visited. Our advent was duly announced by posters, and
on the day on which we made triumphal entry into the
town, many of the manufactories were closed for a short
time, and the employés allowed to come out and see the
pomp and pageantry about which all tongues were busy,
and to obtain a glimpse of which everybody betrayed the
greatest anxiety.

" From long experience I venture to opine that there
are few people fonder of sight-seeing than the people of
Preston, and as for holiday-making, why, commend me to
the Prestonian before all others. Just see how he spends
his Whitsun holidays. The swing-boats and merry-go-
rounds are at work as early as five o'clock in the morning,
and some of the smaller shows are entertaining audiences
inside soon after nine. We usually opened our place at
ten o'clock, nor had we long to wait for a house, even at
that early hour. We got through a good number of performances in a day at Preston, and on some days have
taken as much as £80 at the doors. But our company
always received extra salary at that town on account of
their extra services.

" It was during our visit to Preston in 1856, and on
Whit Monday morning, between nine and ten o'clock, just
as our company, headed by the camels, were about to leave
the theatre for a procession through the streets, that two
gentlemen applied at the gallery door for the manager. I
was at once sent to them.

" ' You are the manager, I presume ? ' interrogated one of the gentlemen.

" ' I usually act in that capacity,' I replied.

" ' You may not, perhaps, know me,' said he.

" ' I am afraid I have not that pleasure.'

" ' My name is Edmund Falconer,' rejoined the speaker ; ' and I am the lessee of the Theatre Royal here at Preston.'

" ' And may I ask what is your business with me ?'

" ' To object to your performing here,' responded the lessee.

" There was a momentary pause, during which we eyed each other attentively.

" ' It may be, sir, that you are not fully aware who I am,' I observed to the stranger.

" ' The manager, as I understand,' rejoined he.

" ' Yes,' I replied, ' and also the lessee of this theatre,' waving my hand towards it with as much pride as if it had been Drury Lane.

" ' And do you happen to know,' I further observed, ' that you are now standing upon my platform ?'

" ' I am aware of that.'

" ' Then kindly allow me to suggest that you and your friend will find a way down from it by the steps there.'

" The lessee of the Theatre Royal was evidently a man not to be spoken to in terms like these. He waxed indignant and attempted to remonstrate. As I have already stated, the procession, headed by the two camels, was waiting within, and time was of importance to us. Neither the lessee nor his friend having thought it worth while to act upon the hint I had given them, I threw back the sliding panels of the outer proscenium and gave the order ' Door !' Immediately the procession moved forward ; and Mohammed, the male camel, who was first, poked his nose with a touch of his old vulgar curiosity into the face of the lessee ; whereupon that gentleman, together with his friend, without waiting for further familiarities from Mohammed, or invitation from myself, took their hasty departure. We never saw either of them again during the fortnight we remained at Preston, though Mr. Falconer threatened to put a stop to our performances. But then we were quite used to that sort of thing. Lessees everywhere looked askance at ' Old Wild's,' and would have

put it down if they could without the slightest com-
punction of conscience. To guard against possible opposition at Preston I had taken the precaution, before we
removed our theatre there, to obtain permission from the
authorities to perform stage plays during our fortnight's
stay in that town; armed with which authority I feared
not to confront even Mr. Falconer, since better known as
the author of *Peep o' Day Boys*, and as one of the lessees
of the Lyceum Theatre.

" The above was not the only instance in which my
camels created consternation.   I remember once going
from Dewsbury to Burnley with our usual bag, baggage,
and paraphernalia, preceded by the camels.   Just as we
were passing Townley Park a troop of horse soldiers came
out for exercise.   At sight of Sultana and Mohammed the
horses began to snort, and rear, and plunge, and in a very
few moments general disorder prevailed.   Nor was the
re-organisation of the troops any light undertaking ; it
was nothing short of a task.   As we passed one of the
officers who had been rushing wildly about, brawling out
his instructions, and making himself very red in the face
in his endeavours to restore order, we perceived at once
by the indignant glances he cast upon us, and particularly
at the animals, that our little party was the especial object
of his ire.   The excited manner of the officer considerably
amused me, but I confess I was far from feeling exhilarated
when I heard him apply the epithets ' damned unsightly
brutes,' to my grand war camels from the Crimea, upon
whose majestic appearance I somewhat prided myself.

" During our stay at Skipton, in May, 1856, Sultana,
after only a fortnight's illness, died.   The farrier who
attended her pronounced the disorder to be disease of the
heart. This was a pecuniary loss I was called upon to
sustain alone, but I made the best of it, as I have ever
tried to do under reverses.

"Thinking the deceased camel might be acceptable to
the curator of the Halifax Museum, I wrote to Mr.
Alexander Campbell, offering to present it to that institution. The offer being accepted, Mr. Campbell came over
to Skipton (on the day of the Peace Rejoicing, I believe),
and, after dissecting the animal, packed the bones in
hampers, and took them away with him. The very day
after I had written, offering the animal to Mr. Campbell

a gentleman from the Leeds Museum, having heard of the death of the camel, came over to Skipton and tendered me £20 for it. I told him I couldn't entertain his offer, for I wouldn't have forfeited my word for £100; and at that time I never dreamed I should be in want of such a sum. So I let Sultana go to Halifax, the town in which we had always done so well, and which, if it may be said we ever had such a place, we always looked upon as our home.

"In the large upper room of the Museum of the Halifax Literary and Philosophical Society in Harrison Road, and on the left-hand side as you enter, you will find the skeleton of my poor Sultana, and attached to it a card bearing the following inscription:—

Class 1. Order 12.
Swift Camel, or Dromedary.
Mr. Samuel Wild.

"Notwithstanding the loss of Sultana, we still kept up our processions, and, as she couldn't very conveniently be replaced, we made the most of Mohammed. But at Skipton one day we thought we were going to lose him too, for he took fright at something during a procession and started off, throwing his rider (Mr. Naylor) violently upon the ground. A fall of eight or nine feet on a hard dry limestone road is no trifling matter, and so, while the capture of the camel was immediately set about, the wants of its unfortunate rider did not escape attention.

"Naylor, I may say, though only a young man, had lost his hair, but he endeavoured to conceal his misfortune under a black ringlet wig. This artificial adornment he, unfortunately, lost along with his equilibrium when the camel gave its first signs of apprehension, and in the fall he became so enveloped in his long, flowing velvet robe, with its 14-inch gold lace, that extrication for a time seemed hopeless. He lay upon the ground so quiet that fears as to his condition began to be seriously entertained. When, through the wealth of his purple and gold, he was at length arrived at, his speechlessness and the ashy paleness of his countenance caused the crowd to gaze upon him with the tenderest anxiety. At length, though somewhat tremblingly, he raised his hand to his head, and, finding, alas! that his borrowed glory had quite departed, his distracted feelings now found utterance, and in the agony of despair he exclaimed, ' Where's my wig!'

"Poor Naylor! he seemed to be more concerned for the appearance of his head than for the safety of it.

"On June 10th, 1856, my brother Tom and I formally parted company at Skipton. It had often been talked of before, and ever and anon the threat would be held out to me that he would have the establishment divided. So, while we were at Blackburn, just before this time, the old subject coming up again, I decided that a division should take place, and arranged for an early parting accordingly. I at once sent over to Halifax for Mr. James Bedford, and instructed him to make me two parade waggons, so that I might be prepared when matters fairly came to a crisis. This was, as I have already stated, brought about while we were at Skipton. George Pickering, the leader of the orchestra, was chosen arbitrator, and the properties were divided equally between us. According to a memorandum drawn up at the time, I find that Tom took as his share : – Skeleton waggon, inside stage and box waggon ; one half of the bills, plates, cuts, and lithographs ; one half of silver bands and tassels ; gas name ' Wild's,' and star ; one pair of large cymbals, six pairs of small cymbals for dancing, his own selection of playbooks and MSS., three pairs of banner tops and banners, one half of properties and swords, stage fixtures, large window piece, fireplace, cottage, two rock pieces and one ground piece, table, new frame for booth and new tilt, old stage front inside, old wings, old pipe for inside stage, four dress boxes, one half of dresses, gong, old jackscrew, new galleries, three Russian and three French guns and bayonets, belts and gun boxes, and one half of the scenery. My proportion of the properties consisted of a four-horse, broad-wheeled waggon, yellow-wheeled waggon, the old living waggon ; one half of the bills, plates, cuts, and lithographs ; the Court dresses of the King of the French (first equally shared, but Tom's moiety afterwards purchased by me) ; one half of silver bands and tassels ; gas bracket, ' V.R.' ; one pair of large cymbals, six pairs of small cymbals for dancing, remainder of books and MSS., three pairs of banner tops and banners, one half of properties and swords, large cottage and boat, two rock pieces and one ground piece, deck piece, new frame for theatre and old tilt, new stage front inside and new wings, new gas pipe, four dress boxes, one drum, half of dresses, new jack and handle, old galleries ; three Russian and three French guns, with bayonets, belts, and gun boxes ; platform, and one half of the scenery.

" While we were at Skipton I had, in my own name, as lessee, taken ground at Bradford for the fair season. On the day of our parting Tom complained of this, and said it gave me an undue advantage over him. Without hesitation I handed him the agreement for the ground. ' Take that,' I said, ' and try your luck at Bradford, and I will go to Keighley and put on until Halifax fair.' My new vans were sent to me at Keighley, and I lost no time in getting my place in order and in appearing before the Keighley public once more as sole proprietor. Nearly all the old company went with me ; there were Messrs. Armstrong, Harding, Greenhalch, Lister, Mellers, Smith, Pickering, Thornton, Crotty, J. H. Williams, Mesdames Armstrong, Banham, Mellers, Lister. To these I added Messrs. and Mesdames Blanchard, Johnson, Lyons, and James. These, with myself, wife, son Tom, daughter Louisa (who was our Terpsichorean artiste and whom we styled ' La Petite Louise '), brought up the number, with bandsmen and supers, to between thirty and forty. Then there were also the further attractions of the camel, and my trusty dogs ' Nelson ' and ' Lion.'

"Tom took with him Mr. and Mrs. John Holloway, Mr. and Mrs. Naylor, and Mrs. Bateson and her daughter ; but nearly all his company rejoined me afterwards on different occasions. He styled his establishment ' Wild's No. 1,' but mine continued to be simply called ' Wild's,' until I changed the title for ' Wild's Allied and Zoological Establishment.'

" I had a capital season at Keighley, though I had only what we termed private business, and only one performance per night ; but I took almost as much money as if I had been at a fair. The dogs, the processions (which I still kept up), the camel, together with a good selection of pieces, were sufficient attractions in a town like Keighley to keep the people always alive. Then, being fond of music, I believed in having a good band, and engaged as leader Mr. John Hope, formerly bandmaster of Her Majesty's 98th Regiment of Foot, India. Tom, though a musician, never seemed to care much for a band, and would content himself with a small orchestra. He would sometimes engage Germans for the evening—those delightful discoursers of music who, during the day, go out 'busking' in the villages.

"At Halifax Fair, both Tom and I put in an appearance—he in Red Tom's field, I in the Market-place as usual. His close proximity to Templeton's Theatre and to Johnson's compelled him to reduce his prices, but I still kept to my old terms of admission, and filled the place notwithstanding. For fairs in those days were far more thought of than now. All the public-houses about the Market here in Halifax—the Peacock, Saddle, Wheat Sheaf, White Horse, and Mitre—used to draw as much money during the Fair week as paid the year's rent. But fairs, considering how they have dwindled of late, must, in my opinion, soon become a thing of the past.

"So Tom and I, after many hints that we would do so, parted at last.

"And now, having arrived, as it were, at a new epoch in my history, my new experiences will more properly find a beginning in a new chapter."

CHAPTER XVII.

"Sam" Wild's new Enterprise—Visit to Armley—
A Real Tragedy — Wild's Villain not a
"Gentleman" — Samuel Eldershaw — A Fat
Ghost — Pantomime — Bill delivering extra-
ordinary—Umbrellas required for the Front
Boxes—Henry Nichols—Arthur Nelson—Miss
St. Clair — "Herr" Teasdale — "Monsieur
Wildermeich"—Diego objects to be Knocked
Down—The "Monkey" addresses the Audience.

The race by vigour, not by vaunts is won.—Pope,—*The Dunciad.*

"Though I was now sole owner of one of the largest
theatrical establishments travelling, with every prospect of
success before me, I will not deny that for some reasons I
regretted the dissolution of partnership between my
brother and myself, as I am quite sure he did when it was
at length fairly brought about. Still there was a spirit of
pride lingering in each of us, which taught us to avoid any
allusion, directly or indirectly, to the state of our
individual feeling in the matter, and which incited us to
make the best of ourselves under the altered circumstances.
I never lost sight of the fact that I had the welfare of my
wife and seven children to provide for ; and it may have
been this consideration, together with a passionate love for
my calling, that at this time inspired me with new
energies, and so led me on to success.

"The company I had engaged, and to which, as favourable opportunities occurred, I made constant additions,
was, for a travelling theatre, a most efficient one ; and our
repertoire of pieces as varied and attractive as money and
thought could make it. My wife and I, who, at that time,
occupied a proud position in popular estimation, did our
best to deserve it, and kept well before the public ; and
the dogs, which during the popularity of the camels had
enjoyed a sort of temporary retirement, emerged therefrom
into usefulness and public life again.

"But in addition to the stock pieces which were favourites with our patrons, I was ever on the look-out for novelty. I subscribed to the Dramatic Authors' Society, and obtained permission to perform the whole of the pieces licensed by the Lord Chamberlain, and kept up a correspondence with Mr. C. R. Somerset and other minor playwrights, who regularly advised me when they were engaged upon anything new, and whose pieces, if I thought they were likely to become popular, I usually availed myself of the first opportunity of purchasing.

"Then, again, I did not at all times confine myself to things dramatic. The performances of the acrobat on some occasions came in for a fair share of attention. So early in my career as the 3rd August, 1856, I engaged, while my company was at Bramley, Mons. Shenterina, a slack rope performer, to give variety to our entertainment by his eccentricities on the *corde elastique*.

"A few years since, ' Have you seen the Shah ? ' was, as you are aware, a very common inquiry, but certainly not more so than was ' Have you seen Betty Wood ?' twenty good years ago. To cater to the popular taste and to echo its whimsicalities in whatever was harmless was ever my ambition and delight, and in order that our friends and patrons might have an opportunity of answering in the affirmative all such inquiries as the latter, it was arranged that Mons. Shenterina should introduce the lady in question to our audience. An announcement to this effect put everybody upon the tip-toe of expectation to see her. At the stated time the Monsieur appeared in his place on the slack rope, and with him (though looking considerably out of hers) an elderly lady, not over gaily attired, but whom the audience was given to understand was none other than the veritable ' Betty.' Her position, though an exalted one, was hardly as dignified as it might have been, inasmuch as she appeared poised aloft on the shoulders of the Monsieur. Notwithstanding his burden, which seemed in sooth no light one, he set forth cheerily across the theatre upon his journey of introduction, giving every promise by his care and skill of making it in safety. But he had barely traversed one half the distance ere he wavered, the old lady lost her balance, and she fell headlong into the pit, and before the audience had an opportunity of manifesting sympathy for the unfortunate lady, it was discovered that she was, of course, a dummy.

"Edwin Waugh's beautiful song, 'Come whoam to thi childer an' me,' was at this time at the height of its popularity. It formed in the hands of Mr. Somerset a capital theme for a domestic drama, which, under the same title, we played on August 5th, to a Bramley audience, with immense success.

"Early in the month of September we paid a visit to Armley, where, pecuniarily considered, we had a remarkably good season; but I always remember that season with a degree of sadness, because with it is associated the death of one of my company under circumstances awfully tragical.

"Mrs. Banham, equestrienne, dancer, and vocalist, and a recent addition to our dramatic corps in the two latter capacities, was the daughter of Mr. John Hope, the leader of my band. In her youth, Miss Hope, a handsome, light-hearted girl, was apprenticed to Pablo Fanque to learn the equestrian's art. William Banham (better known as "Billy Pablo"), Fanque's nephew, and a man of colour, was at that time a tight-rope dancer, vaulter, and bareback rider there. Between these two persons a friendship arose, and in course of time Miss Hope became Mrs. Banham. With a tendency under all circumstances to be somewhat gay, she gave occasion to her husband to believe he perceived grounds for jealousy, and under the influence of the 'green-eyed monster,' he left her and went abroad. A young man, John Hannan, a tailor from Manchester, met with her shortly afterwards, an intimacy was formed, and, considering that her husband's desertion amounted to a complete termination of the old love, she unwisely lent her ear to the insinuations of the new. But the new love ere long lost its charms; and it was because of a persistent refusal on her part to entertain proposals of a return to him that Hannan, at Armley, on the 11th September, 1856, took the poor woman's life, for which dreadful crime he shortly afterwards suffered the extreme penalty of the law.

"Just before the close of our season at Armley I took a benefit, the performances on which occasion were under the patronage of William Ellis, Esquire. While appealing to the Armley public for further favours, I felt it my duty

to recognise their kind support in times past, so I started
my programme after this fashion :—

Mr. S. Wild avails himself of this opportunity most respectfully to
offer to the authorities his sincere thanks for their indulgence ; also, to
remind his kind patrons that he does not come among them as a stranger,
but as an old acquaintance. His father, as an equestrian and theatrical
manager, was in the habit of professionally visiting the good old town
of Armley for sixty years ; and, as regards himself, during the period
he has had the pleasure of catering for their gratification in the double
capacity of actor and manager, it has ever been his study to blend instruction with amusement, by producing pieces of a strictly moral tendency
and in all respects unexceptional. His efforts to please have hitherto
invariably been crowned with success, and he doubts not that on the
present occasion his old friends and well-wishers will rally round him and
afford him an additional proof of their kind feeling and appreciation of
his endeavours by giving him A Bumper at Parting !

" I had next a capital season of two months (October
and November) at Halifax ; and, in addition to some of
our favourite pieces, produced *Janet Pride* (now, with the
addition of one act, played under the title of *Madoline*, I
believe) and *Dick Tarleton*, which, by the way, was dramatised by our Mr. Mellers, and on this occasion of our visit
produced in Halifax for the first time. In fact I never
heard of any other company playing *Dick Tarleton*,
except my own. *The Will and the Way* we also performed once during this season, but only by particular
desire. Then we went in for a little of the sensational in
a drama entitled *How We Live in the World of London*—
founded upon Henry Mayhew's *London Labour and London
Poor*.

" In most cases we had one or more new scenes painted.
These were executed by Mr. Hope, the leader of the band,
who, I forgot to say, was, in addition to being a sound
musician, an artist of good ability.

" Then we also reproduced, with Mr. Tate as the
Mountebank, *Belphegor* (a piece that is still a favourite
with the theatre-going public), and introduced during the
performance of it a genuine horse and trap upon the stage.
This piece, if I mistake not, was written expressly for Mr.
Chas. Dillon, who is generally considered to be the finest
Belphegor on the stage. I have seen him play the
character once or twice, while both Loraine and Coleman
have, at different times, sustained that *rôle* upon the boards
of my own theatre ; but according to my conception of
the character, Tate was the best Belphegor of them all.

"Though we only played it on one occasion during this visit to Halifax, *The Will and the Way* was as successful a piece as we ever had, and George Adams as "Will Sideler" just as bad a character as you would care to see. While on the stage he was generally the villain of the piece; off it, Adams always dressed well and carried himself with somewhat of dignity. Still it seems he could never remove from the minds of our audiences the impression which his performances created. Once, at Holbeck, a person met Adams in the street, elegantly attired as usual, and, curious to know more about him asked of a native, who happened to be one of our 'gods,' who the gentleman was?

"'Gentleman!' exclaimed the party interrogated, with some indignation, 'that's t' villain at Wildses.'

"The arrangement as to the Victoria Theatre, Dewsbury, which was the joint property of Tom and myself, was that whether he or I occupied it, the weekly rent should be computed at £3, the occupier finding his own gas. The ground-rent, which was £25 per year, I paid, as it became due, to Dr. Fearnley—afterwards first Mayor of Dewsbury. In addition to which I had rates and taxes *ad infinitum* to pay. When the theatre was not engaged by either of us it was let for concerts, panoramas, and indeed for anything almost except theatrical performances. As neither Tom nor I had time to look after the place and attend to the lettings and so forth, we appointed our Dewsbury bill poster to the office of custodian. All receipts for the hire of the theatre I set off against the yearly expenses, and settled accounts periodically with Tom.

"As my brother did not require the theatre for the winter season (1856-7) I had it painted and redecorated throughout, and added to the proscenium a splendid new curtain of crimson and gold. I also had the upper and side boxes lined with red, white, and blue, and the seats covered with red and green baize. After all which labour and expense, I took possession of it on December 6th, 1856. I had a neat bill printed (I always believed in advertising), giving a list of the principal members of my company, and announcing that 'the standard plays of Shakspeare, Knowles, Bulwer, and other popular authors' would be produced in 'rapid succession' and in a manner that 'could not fail to elicit public approbation.' The terms of admission were—Front boxes, 1s. 6d., Second ditto, 1s. ; Pit, 6d. ; Gallery, 3d.

"I engaged as tragedian a Mr. Samuel Eldershaw, and until other stars outshone him he sustained the principal characters in most of the tragedies I produced. Originally a collier, a love of the drama prompted him to study for the stage, and he at length became one of the lesser lights in the dramatic world of the stroller. We produced *Hamlet, Macbeth, Richard III.*, and a Christmas pantomime, entitled *The Water Nymphs' Revolt*, a day performance of which was given on December 26th.

"In *Hamlet* I sustained the character of ' The Ghost,' and a pretty substantial one I suppose I made. I had a tight-fitting dress spangled all over, and which showed my form off to advantage, and I looked just about as comfortable a ghost as any one might desire to encounter. But the juniors in the audience seemed greatly dissatisfied with me ; they expected to see something more shadowy for their money, and in a tone of disappointment I heard one of them exclaim :—

" ' Well ! if that's a ghost, it's a fat'n.'

" So far as the limits of our establishment would allow, and to the extent of the company's talent, we always endeavoured to do justice to all the plays we produced, and especially to those of the Immortal Bard. When we brought out *Macbeth* during the season under notice, it was with all the scenery and incidents of the piece, and the original music of Locke. We had several capital voices in our company, but to give effect to the choruses several Dewsbury vocalists were engaged to assist.

" Mr. Hope painted the scenery for the pantomime ; the costumes were the joint labours of Mrs. Meanley and Mr. Greenhalch—the latter was as clever with his fingers as any woman— and the properties, masks, and tricks were the production of my son Tom and assistants.

"For the performance we had children engaged to appear as fairies in the transformation scene ; and, glistening with spangles and jewels, night after night they appeared, each reclining on the bosom of a cloud, with a host of stage stars twinkling above them. Mr. Greenhalch appeared as harlequin, Mr. Norris as pantaloon, Mrs. Norris as columbine, and myself as clown. I was what is termed a good tumbler in those days; I am a tumbler still, but the difficulty in resuming the 'as you were' is slightly greater now than it used to be.

"For six nights, commencing 26th January, 1857, Mr. George Owen accepted an engagement with me and appeared during that time in the respective characters of King Lear, Julian St. Pierre, Master Radcliffe, Wolsey, Hamlet, and Falstaff. The terms on which I engaged him were, that after £26 had been received at the doors, the remaining receipts for the six nights should be divided equally between myself and him.

"On the Monday evening, just as we were lighting up for the performance, one of our supers, who had been delivering bills all the afternoon, came in. I rated him soundly upon his long absence, which he excused by explaining that he had been to Hanging Heaton and Earlsheaton, and down two coal pits, where he had distributed bills amongst the colliers, several of whom, he said, had promised to honour Mr. Owen with their patronage sometime during the week. Under such circumstances I could only smile at his zeal and accept his explanation. Friday evening, January 30th, was a sort of fashionable night, but the weather was exceedingly inclement. The wind blew off during the performance a portion of the asphalting outside the theatre and immediately over the boxes, and the rain began to find its way through, causing several ladies who were seated there to put up their umbrellas. When the performances were over that night, Mr. Owen said to me, 'I have been at a great many theatres, Mr. Wild, both in England, and Ireland, and Scotland, in my time, but I never was at one where the lessee had his bills delivered down coalpits, or in which the ladies put up their umbrellas in the front boxes.'

"On the 10th of February I engaged, for one week, Henry Nicholls, tragedian, and also a Shakspearian reader; and, again, on the 23rd, for a similar period, Arthur Nelson, a great musical clown, together with Miss St. Clair, a vocalist who travelled with him. This Nelson was the same clown who, at Yarmouth, years before this time, drove four geese down the river, curiosity to see which performance resulted in the death of a great many persons. Nelson, who was clown at Thomas Cook's Circus, then stationed at Yarmouth, was to take his benefit

in the evening of the day on which this calamity
happened. To remind the public of the treat in store for
them, Nelson, in addition to the ordinary methods of
advertising, undertook to perform the feat I have mentioned. Crowds of people came out to see him. Seated
in the conventional washing-tub, drawn by four geese, he
made his way down the river, to the great delight of the
spectators and amidst much cheering. Just as he had
passed under an old bridge which crossed the river, but
had long been condemned, there was a general rush to it
to see him, when immediately the bridge gave way, and
over fifty persons lost their lives by the accident.

"Nelson, besides being a capital actor and clown, was
also a clever performer on the dulcimer; in fact, one of
the best then travelling. He also performed in a similar
manner on the 'Rock Harmonicon,' a rude sort of instrument made of polished stones laid across pieces of webbing.
He had the knack, too, of extracting the most delicious
music out of a few pine sticks laid upon ropes of straw;
upon which several instruments and contrivances he performed during his engagement with me at Dewsbury, to
the intense delight of his audiences. He also repeated his
geese-driving feat—happily without any casualty—and our
band, stationed on the bank of the river, greeted him at
the finish with the strains of 'See the conquering hero
comes.'

"The practice of engaging stars towards the close of a
long season in any town having once been begun, I usually
considered I had no alternative save that of continuing it
until such season had ended. Therefore, after Arthur
Nelson had successfully played out his short term with us
at the Victoria Theatre, I introduced to our Dewsbury
friends Mr. Harvey Teasdale. 'Herr' Teasdale this
gentleman dubbed himself while in the theatrical world;
'the Converted Clown and Man Monkey' he now styles
himself out of it. It is under his first title, however, that we
have most to do with him just now. Teasdale's engagement
commenced on the 9th of March, and his two daughters,
dancers both, appeared with him. The characters he
sustained were, if I remember rightly, Tom, *the Dumb
Man of Manchester*, Scaramouch in the burlesque of *Don
Juan*, and Mushapug in *Jack Robinson and his Monkey*;
the latter, owing to the scope it afforded him for the

display of his wondrous agility, was one of his favourite, as it was, perhaps, one of his greatest, characters.

"He drew good houses during his engagement, for he was, and had been for a long time, a favourite with the public. After leaving Dewsbury he went to the Theatre Royal, York, at which place I was, according to a previous arrangement, to appear on the occasion of his benefit. When he was about to publish the announcement of that event it is quite evident he considered that ' Sam Wild,' as a name, had hardly sufficient of the professional ring about it to be any acquisition to his programme, for he wrote to me inquiring if I would allow him to introduce me through that medium to the good people of York as ' Monsieur Wildermeich.' I had still a lively recollection of the difficulty I had previously experienced in endeavouring to pass myself off as ' Monsieur Leon,' and I did not anticipate any better success from a further experiment. So in reply to Mr. Teasdale I stated that personally I was quite satisfied with my name, as it had always done very well for me, and proved at all times sufficiently attractive to the public to draw crowded houses to witness its owner's performances; and further that, unless he cared to have me in my simplicity, he was quite at liberty to make up his programme without me. As he did not choose the latter alternative, I was duly forthcoming at his benefit. In order to make the performances as attractive as possible I took with me Messrs. Greenhalch and Williams; also the two dogs and the camel. The pieces selected for the evening were *Mungo Park*, in which both the dogs and the camel were introduced; *The Sailor and His Dogs*, in which ' Nelson ' and ' Lion ' again appeared, and *Jack Robinson and his Monkey*, with Teasdale in his favourite character, Mushapug. There was a splendid house that night, and the receipts at the doors amounted to over £70.

"While at rehearsal during the morning I suggested that it would be necessary for certain of the actors in *Mungo Park* to colour their faces for the evening performance. There was evidently too much of the Christy Minstrel element in such a procedure for these smaller stage heroes, and they rejected the proposal with scorn. When I explained, however, that the employment of colour was absolute necessary to the success of the piece, the refractory ones began to compromise matters a little by suggesting the substitution of black crape. Our transformation to men of colour was commonly effected by a plentiful application of burnt cork and beer. The prescription was no particular secret, so I imparted it for the especial benefit of the haughty ones, hinting at the same time that unless the piece could be played that evening, in perfect character throughout, inevitable failure must ensue. The manager overhearing this came forward and said he should expect his company to conform to all the requirements of the piece under rehearsal, and if any member declined so to do there was only one alternative— notice to leave. That decided the matter at once; the dignified ones gave their assent to the colouring process, and when evening came, took to my prescription kindly.

" But while the two first dramas went off successfully, and Greenhalch's song procured for him an encore, there was a hitch in the last piece of a far more serious nature than anything that had taken place at the rehearsal. The charm, if such it may be called, which attaches to the character of Mushapug, consists in his agility, his mischievous propensities, and the comparative ease with which he can reduce to a horizontal position the stalwart forms of his adversaries. Teasdale, who sustained that important character, acquitted himself well, and all went on satisfactorily until it came to Diego's turn to be humiliated, when, contrary to the demands of the piece, and in defiance of all stage laws and customs, he refused to be so dealt with. The secret of it all was that there was some shyness existing between the sailor (Diego) and the monkey, and the former sought to avenge himself for old indignities by taking the wind out of Teasdale's sails on his benefit night. The knocking down experiment was repeated, but Diego stood immovable. It was again repeated, with the like result. Mushapug then laid violent hands on the sailor with a view of forcing him down to the required level, but Diego was ' too many ' for his adversary, and releasing himself from the monkey's powerful grasp, jumped over the footlights into the pit, the exasperated Mushapug following at his heels. Diego crept under the seats and disappeared, and his pursuer, after a futile attempt at finding him, returned to the stage. Meanwhile the audience was very much divided in its opinions upon these proceedings; one section of it, familiar with the play, evidently thought this was a new version of it, and so applauded; another, who could perceive that beneath it all there was some private pique being gratified, simply gazed upon the strange and unaccountable doings with silent wonder; while another section of the audience, to which the piece was a novelty, thought everything was regular and in order, and expressed its perfect satisfaction therewith accordingly; especially at the culminating point where the sailor and monkey jump over the orchestra. Mushapug looked considerably put out when he reached the stage again, and he had good reason to be so, for his success was nipped in the bud. Advancing towards the footlights he addressed the audience to this effect:—' Ladies and gentlemen, I have to express my astonishment at the conduct of that man Diego. It was his duty to be knocked down by me, and, as you have seen, he resolutely refuses to be. He has left the stage, and I am unable to go on with this scene in consequence, but should he return again he shall have cause to remember his conduct.'

"That was the first monkey I ever heard speak in public."

CHAPTER XVIII.

An Old Actor and a New Calling—A Building
Speculation Abandoned—Templeton in Distress—
An Impersonator of Female Characters—A
Narrow Escape—A "Rousing" Process Success-
fully Concluded—A Costly Jump—Sale of the
Camel "Mohammed"—Mosley Opposes a Licence
at Halifax—The "Gallant Colonel" recalls the
Fortune-Telling Pony days and Signs the
Licence.

For the sake of Auld Lang Syne.—*Burns.*

"I believe I am right in stating that Harvey Teasdale's
first *bonâ fide* travelling engagement was with my father
and mother; though there is no allusion made to that
engagement in his 'Life and Adventures.' It was during
the visit of 'Old Wild's' to Sheffield, one fair season, that
Teasdale was brought under the notice of my parents;
they opened negotiations with him, he accepted their
proffered engagement, and afterwards travelled with them,
some twelve months or so, in the dual capacity of clown
and low comedian. After leaving the old folks, he entered
upon a successful career in the provinces, and his services
were in great demand by theatrical managers everywhere.
John Mosley, a former lessee of the Halifax Theatre, and,
as may be remembered, joint successor with Rice to the
Liver Theatre, Bradford, after we had been outbid for it,
was particularly partial to Teasdale, and preferred him to
almost all other stars, because of the overflowing houses
his performances never failed to ensure.

"It is some time since Teasdale left the stage. The
last occasion of my meeting with him was, I think, in 1875.
I was making my way down Boar Lane, Leeds, one day, as
well as my old rheumatic pains would allow me, when a
respectably-dressed person suddenly came to a stand
before me.

"'Isn't this Mr. Wild?' he inquired.

"'It is, sir, and you are?'

" ' Harvey Teasdale,' rejoined he.

" After mutual congratulations he inquired if I was still in the profession, or what I was doing, and after some further conversation left me with a pressing invitation to go hear him preach at Woodhouse on the following Sunday. I promised to go and should have done so, but unfortunately when Sunday came I was confined to the house with rheumatism.

" To return now to the account of our season at Dewsbury.

" It had often occurred to me that if I could find some good investment for my money, it would be much better than allowing it to lie idle at my bankers.' At Dewsbury I conceived the idea that a row of substantially built houses would be about as sound and safe a speculation as I could possibly engage in. So I arranged with a grocer, Mr. Denton, who was also a sort of land agent at Dewsbury, to purchase for me a plot of land on Mirfield Moor, Ravensthorpe, about a mile distant from that town ; my intention being to erect thereon, twelve houses, a shop, and an inn. At that time there was only about a dozen houses on the moor, but since, building operations have considerably increased in number there, and the value of the property has enhanced in consequence. A piece of land was selected, a price agreed upon, and the deeds conveying the property to me prepared ; but when I went to conclude the purchase, I discovered that I was being charged by the seller nearly £100 more for the land than was originally stated to me ; and I was so annoyed at the want of principle displayed in the transaction that I declined to carry out the purchase. But I have ever since regretted that I did not, as Mr. Denton advised me to do, secure another piece of ground on the moor and set about realising my desire with regard to building, for then I should have had my money employed, and could not have ventured upon those risky circus speculations which I afterwards engaged in to my serious loss.

" While the matter to which I have just adverted necessarily gave me some anxiety, I did not neglect the duties of the theatre ; I still kept up the attractions there.

" My next star was Mr. J. C. Cowper, formerly leading actor at the Amphitheatre, Liverpool, while it was under Copeland's management. His engagement com-

menced on the 16th March, 1857, and terminated at the
end of the week. His forte was tragedy, and his selection
of pieces comprised some of those which were especial
favourites with our audiences.

" But while I ever sought to cater to the best advantage
for the public, to pay my company well and provide for the
wants of my own family, it was always a pleasure to me,
as in times past it used to be to the old folks, to lend a
helping-hand wherever one was needed, and especially to
run to the rescue of a brother in distress.

" Robert Templeton, who was stationed at Birstall,
near Dewsbury, at this time, had met with only poor
success there, and was in a state of great need. Learning
this, I immediately offered to give my services on any night
he might appoint for a benefit at his theatre. He selected,
after many protestations of gratitude, the 18th March, on
which evening Mr. Greenhalch and I, and those canine
wonders, ' Nelson ' and ' Lion,' appeared on his stage. The
piece de résistance was *The Red Indian, or the Sailor and
his Dogs.* To help Templeton to make up a good programme I lent him my block (engraved, by the way, by Mr.
T. S. Fraser, formerly with us at the Liver Theatre) to
introduce at the foot of the synopsis of scenery and
incidents of the first piece ; and Greenhalch, who had
promised a song for the occasion, consented for the nonce
to be dubbed ' Herr.' There was, and nobody was more
glad to see it than I, a capital house ; every available seat
and standing place being occupied, while several of the
spectators were seated upon the stage. Under any circumstances such a thing as a person going behind the scenes
was not allowed at Wild's establishment, but Templeton's
theatre was only a small one, and after the scanty support
he had previously received he was glad to seat his audience
anywhere.

" ' General Hope ' and ' Colonel Expectation ' were what
might be termed stock patrons of Wild's Theatre, and
there was never any demur to their names being introduced on the placards on benefit nights or on other special
occasions. Messrs. Boardman and Greenhalch availed
themselves of the ' distinguished patronage of General
Hope,' when they announced for the 30th March their
joint benefit at the Victoria Theatre, but they also took
care to provide more substantial attractions. They

announced the popular drama of *The Corsican Brothers*, with 'new scenery and startling mechanical effects'; three songs by the same number of vocalists, a selection of popular airs by the Dewsbury Campanologians, a musical discourse by the members of the Batley Brass Band, and a new comic pantomime, with 'jests and gibes and rhymes and riles, quips and cranks and sportive wiles, producing panting roars and smiles,' and entitled *The House that Jack Built*, with new scenery, dresses, transformations, and all the glories of the harlequinade.

"In the last of these entertainments, Greenhalch appeared as harlequin, and, according to announcement, in a costume similar to that worn by Madame Celeste when on certain occasions she assumed that sprightly character. The chief features of this article of attire, if such it could really be called, were its shortcomings, it being framed so as to allow of the display of shapely extremities. Greenhalch's figure was tall and symmetrical, and he adopted the costume on the above occasion because it afforded him an opportunity of exhibiting his graceful limbs. It was his face and figure that made his impersonations of female character so highly successful always. Indeed it would be a difficult thing to compute the number of conquests he has made over the hearts of susceptible young gentlemen during the many times he appeared in our transformation scenes dancing the 'cachucha' in white muslin and silk fleshings.

"Then, again, Greenhalch's taste in all matters pertaining to ladies' attire was universally acknowledged, and his skilfulness in the manufacture of dresses, caps, and other articles of wear was so generally admitted that he might have had as many private orders in that line as any fashionable milliner or dressmaker. On one occasion, when Mrs. G. was in a state of delightful anticipation of a certain interesting event, he turned his skilful mind and hands to the construction of very juvenile attire, concerning which everybody seemed ready to admit that they were the perfection of needle art, and would do credit to any baby linen establishment out of London. The harlequin's costume, *à la* Madame Celeste, was also the work of his own hands. Nothing, in fact, seemed to come amiss to him. Mrs. Meanley and he were generally appealed to in all questions affecting the wardrobe, and most of the dresses and costumes constituting it were the joint production of themselves and their assistants.

"When John Greenhalch and I first met (to continue this digression) he was an assistant at the Black Lion Hotel, Leeds (landlord, Thomas Price), in the concert room attached to which he frequently sang. His style, appearance, and voice pleased me exceedingly, and while over at Leeds, during the month of July, in a now-forgotten year, I offered him, and he at once accepted, an engagement with our company. In September following, our establishment was at Holbeck for the feast, and while there the members of the company usually went over to Leeds during the daytime. John Price, an old acquaintance of ours, brother of the above-named Thomas, and, like him, an innkeeper in that town, was about to erect a public-house upon a piece of ground called the Bank. He had already decided that the contemplated inn should, when finished, be called 'The Old Arm Chair,' because of the delight he had experienced on hearing Greenhalch sing that, then, popular song. He further intended to make the laying of the foundation stone an event, and invited our band (in which Greenhalch was drummer) to assist at the ceremony. The invitation was accepted. On the day fixed we started in a coach and four from the Royal Hotel, Briggate, Leeds, to the Bank, playing as we went, and distributing, on our own account, programmes of the performances at Holbeck that evening. Arrived at the place of ceremony, we found Price and his friends there and everything in readiness. In addition to the crowd which had collected there, our band had attracted a large number of persons, so that there was no lack of spectators. We took up our position on the site of the proposed inn. There was a little of speechifying, chiefly of a humorous description, a bottle containing papers, facetious extracts, coins, and other trinkum trankums was deposited in the cavity prepared for it, and the stone was lowered into its place. Then Greenhalch, by request, sang the song which had furnished Price with a name for his house that was to be, and after that the ceremony ended. We then moved away from the spot, but had only gone a short distance when the outer wall of a cottage adjoining the site (which cottage, having been considered unsafe, was deserted) fell with a tremendous crash, covering with *débris* the very ground we had occupied barely five minutes before.

"Greenhalch remained in our company twelve or thirteen years, and left it to join Duval, of whom, ere long, he took leave, and engaged himself to a minstrel troupe — Butterworth's, I believe. Subsequently he accepted an engagement at the Prince of Wales's Theatre, Wolverhampton, and he is still there, I am told. About two years ago he came over to Halifax with James Taylor's *Simon* company, in the place of a performer who was ill. One afternoon during his short stay in the town he sent for me. I went and saw him, and we had a long and interesting chat together, chiefly about days lang syne.

"By permission of the Mayor of Pontefract, my company played a few nights in that town about the middle of July, 1857. Our booth stood in a field which belonged to a Catholic priest, but which was by him let to a publican and master butcher in Pontefract, with whom my representative had made arrangements to take it for a short time. As land for our purpose was difficult to meet with in that town, I instructed him to obtain a written agreement, which he did. It appeared, however, that the priest had not been consulted by the sub-tenant in the matter, for just as we were taking our waggons and fifteen horses into the field on the day announced for our opening, the priest came out and very naturally wanted to know what it all meant. He raised a protest against a temporary theatre being erected there; but my answer to that was the production of the agreement with the sub-tenant. Nothing, of course, could be said against it, and after I had talked the matter over with him, and had assured him that my establishment would be conducted in a proper and orderly manner, he seemed to take a more favourable opinion of the strolling company which had, it appeared, taken possession of his field unceremoniously, and, as he had imagined, unlawfully.

"During our stay at Pontefract he and I got along very well together. Of an afternoon, if he saw me anywhere about the field (which abutted, I may explain, upon his house and garden), he would sometimes come out and exchange a few words with me. Then, again, the interest he took in the dogs and camel brought about many little conversations between us. So that, while we sought to be on good terms with the priest, and, as far as possible, afford him no ground of complaint, his uniform courtesy towards myself and company showed us that at least he appreciated our efforts to deserve it.

"Mohammed, during our Pontefract sojourn, having no stage duties to attend to, spent the greater portion of his time each day grazing in the field. There was a peacefulness and simplicity about this which ill accorded with the severe tastes of our Mr. Adams, and, while seeking, primarily, his own diversion therein, he had an idea one day he should be doing the animal a signal service by 'rousing him up' a little. He therefore set about the business without delay. I warned Adams, however, to have as little to do with Mohammed as possible, for though the education of that animal had been my concern for some time past, I never approached him without being fully prepared to acknowledge, in a suitable manner, any compliment he might feel disposed to pass. But Adams was not to be intimidated in the discharge of his self-imposed duties, so the experiment of rousing the animal was repeated. At length a spirit of retaliation began to show itself in Mohammed. Suddenly he turned upon Adams who, finding his experiment of rousing him a greater success than, in his most sanguine moments, he had ever hoped for, as quickly turned upon his heel. The chase was an exciting one, Mohammed's rapid strides soon brought him up with Adams, whose prospects, considering that he had in a very few moments reached the boundary of the field, looked far from cheery. That boundary was a myrtle hedge enclosing the priest's garden. With the infuriated animal's nose close upon his shoulder, George had no time for reflection now. It was clearly a case of must be; so over the hedge he went. There was a loud crashing of glass, and when the worthy priest appeared upon the scene to ascertain what dreadful thing had happened, he found Adams planted to his knees in a cucumber frame, and the camel looking daggers at him over the hedge.

"Foiled in his attempt at revenge, Mohammed did not, however, allow his anger to subside without making a determined effort to work it off. He broke from his keeper as he was being led down the Market-place that same afternoon, and started away like mad, clearing the streets as he swept through them, and not deeming it worth his while to come to a stand until he had successfully overturned a donkey and cart, thrown its elderly female owner into a state of violent agitation, and had put to the test the firmness of sundry crockery and earthenware she was exhibiting for sale.

"While still at Pontefract, and on the 17th July, we were honoured with the patronage of the Worshipful the Mayor, on which evening we performed, at his request, the *Lady of Lyons* and the *Captain's not a-Miss*, a programme of which performances, printed on white satin, I had previously sent him.

"During the feast at Dewsbury, in August, I took my company to that town, but we did not occupy the Victoria Theatre, because at feast times it was better for us to be amongst the show people, and on those occasions, too, we always required our parade.

"Adams' leap, to which I have just alluded, reminds me of that of Mellers, which took place somewhere about this time. We were at Skipton, performing the pantomime of *Cherry and Fair Star*. Mellers was one of the demons in it, and while he was endeavouring to avoid a blow from the Demon King, he jumped over the footlights, and into my son Tom's double bass, which was leaning against the front of the orchestra. That unrehearsed effect put a stop to the bass-viol's performances for two months, and cost me fifty shillings.

"Though Mohammed had certainly acquired a popularity at Pontefract during our late visit to that town, elsewhere he had ceased to be a novelty ; so I thought I would dispose of him. I accordingly advertised him for sale in the *Era*, and amongst those who responded to the advertisement were Messrs. Sanger. In reply to their communication I named £55 as the price of the animal, but they evidently thought it too high. This is their letter :—

Mr. Wild,   Kilmarnock, Sept. 6th, '57.

    Sir,—In answer to yours, respecting the camel, we will give you £40 for him. The winter season is coming on, so he will be of no use to us till the spring. You must excuse us not answering yours sooner, but we did not receive your letter for a week after you sent it.

    An answer to Ayr (Tuesday and Wednesday), or Maybole (Thursday), will much oblige,

Yours, &c.,

JOHN & GEORGE SANGER.

Mr. Wild, Wild's Theatre, Armley, near Leeds.
    If gone to be forwarded.

" After a further communication from me, Messrs·
Sanger ultimately gave me £45 for Mohammed, and I sent
him to them at Carlisle, from the Wellington Station,
Leeds, while my establishment was located at Holbeck.

" When Sangers' circus visited Halifax some five or six
years ago Mohammed was still with them, and looking as
well as ever.   My family and I went to see him, and were
afterwards admitted to the circus to see the performance
free of charge.   I may here observe that the principal
clown there then was James Holloway's son, who had
married one of the Misses Sanger.

" In the early part of October I made application,
through my solicitor, Mr. Mitchell, to the Halifax magistrates for a licence to perform stage plays at my booth,
which I had, as usual, erected at the bottom of the
Market.   Mr. John Mosley, then lessee of the Theatre
Royal, Halifax (which, however, was closed, for his company was then playing at Bradford), engaged a solicitor to
oppose my application.   The case was gone into, and, if I
remember rightly, one ground of objection was that my
establishment, being only a canvas affair, could not be
licensed.   That argument, however, was set aside by the
production of licences which I had previously obtained in
other towns for a similar booth.   The Mayor that year
(1857) was Mr. Samuel Waterhouse, and he, Mr. John
Abbot, and another magistrate, whose name I forget, were
on the Bench.   Mr. Abbot, who, in years gone by, had
known my father well, favoured my application, and finally
signed the form of licence presented to him, whereupon the
other two magistrates did the same.   But as the signatures
of at least four magistrates were, by law, required,
while only three were present, the application was
adjourned for a fortnight.   Meanwhile, I took my company to Dewsbury, opened the Victoria Theatre, and
commenced playing there.   On the day fixed for the
adjourned hearing of my application, Mr. Mitchell and I
duly appeared in Court, as did also my opponent and
his legal representative, and as did, also, as spectators,
many who had been patrons of Wild's in times past, and
were likely to be such again, and to whom, I may say, the
application was almost as serious a matter as it was to
myself.   Upon entering the Court, I looked very
anxiously towards the Bench, and found there were only

three magistrates there again, and, unfortunately, the same three who had previously signed the licence.

"'I am afraid it will be a case of further adjournment,' I whispered to my solicitor, 'there are only three magistrates present, and they have all signed the licence.'

"Just as I had done speaking, Colonel Pollard came in at a little door which opened upon the Bench.

"'Perhaps the gallant colonel will sign it,' remarked my legal adviser, in a tone of voice sufficiently loud for that gallant gentleman to hear him.

"'What is that?' inquired the colonel.

"Mr. Mitchell presented the licence and explained.

"The colonel cast his eyes over the paper, and then looked at me inquiringly, at the same time observing to Mr. Mitchell,

"'But this cannot be the Mr. Wild at whose establishment we used, as boys, to pay our pennies to see a fortune-telling pony?'

"My relationship to the person referred to was no sooner explained than the colonel took a pen, and, without saying another word, or even sitting down, he subscribed his name to the licence. It was then read aloud by the clerk, an outburst of applause followed, and a stern demand for 'Silence in the Court!' succeeded that.

"Mr. Mosley, it is needless to say, left the Court looking considerably annoyed at his discomfiture.

"We had a capital season at Halifax—we invariably had good seasons here—and during the first month of it, on 26th October, I gave performances for the benefit of the Halifax Infirmary, which performances were previously brought before the public in these words:—

"'Mr. S. Wild, in announcing the above night, mindful of old times, assures his patrons that his heart and purse are ever open to render assistance to benevolent institutions; he therefore respectfully solicits their co-operation in the good cause, trusting that it will meet with general approval.'"

CHAPTER XIX.

CONCERNING SELINA BATESON (*née* WILD)—THE WIGAN
ROUGHS AND HOW THEY WERE DEALT WITH—A
NEW DRAMA—PLAYBILL LITERATURE—A TRUCE, TO
REPLACE BOMBSHELLS—AN ACCIDENT—BABY PER-
FORMERS.

War, war, is still the cry.—*Childe Harold*.

" Whether it was a desire for change, or a thirst for
military glory, or a feeling of indignation excited by the
harrowing accounts of the Indian rebellion, that incited
Bateson, my sister Selina's husband, to enter the army, I
cannot pretend to decide; but that he did declare his
ability, willingness, and so forth, to serve Her Majesty
Queen Victoria, Sergeant McCoy, if he be still in the land
of the living, can doubtless testify. For it was McCoy, a
recruiting officer stationed at the Saddle Inn, Halifax, in
the latter half of the year 1857, who conducted my
brother-in-law through the formalities of an enlistment
some time during that period, and drafted him along with
other recruits to Chatham.

" From Chatham, Bateson's regiment, the 84th Foot,
was sent out to Dumdum, whither he was accompanied by
Mrs. Bateson and her four children. But when that same
regiment, almost immediately afterwards, was ordered to
Allahabad, he had no alternative save that of leaving his
wife and family behind him ; and, as he died of cholera at
Allahabad shortly after his arrival there, they never saw
him again.

" The news of his demise no sooner reached her, than
his wife, leaving Dumdum, returned with her family to
England. She came to Halifax during the summer fair of
1858, and found me and my booth there of course. I say
' of course' because at that time the Halifaxonians used to
say it wouldn't be like Halifax Fair if Wild's show wasn't
there. Dependent now, as she was, entirely upon her own
resources for a livelihood, could I do less than offer my

sister an engagement? That I did then, and, as
opportunities occurred, gave her children little parts to
perform. In this way they were gradually trained for the
stage.

"Concerning my sister Selina's second daughter,
Harriet, now Mrs. Ellis, and a widow, I am told that an
accident happened to her some months ago at the Theatre
Royal, St. Helens. She was performing Hecate in
Macbeth, and was being drawn up above the 'flies' at that
part of the dialogue in Act iii., Scene 5, wherein occur the
lines—

> Hark ! I am called ; my little spirit, see,
> Sits in a foggy cloud, and stays for me ;

when the machinery suddenly broke, and she fell to the
stage, a distance of twenty-two or twenty-three feet.
Though her injuries were looked upon as somewhat serious
at the time, she is now, I believe, quite restored to health,
and is attending to her professional duties again.

"To continue Selina's history—

"She remained in my company until her second
marriage, which was with the leader of the band, Joseph
Pugh, and also for some time after that event. At length
her husband was offered an engagement at Croueste's
Circus as bandmaster there, and he accepted it. His wife
accompanied him to Croueste's, where she, for a time, acted
in the capacity of wardrobe keeper ; but ultimately she
appeared in the arena as an *equestrienne*. By her second
marriage she has had two children ; the first died in
infancy, the second, Samuel, is clown at the circus of
Messrs. Taylor and Hutchinson, with whose troupe his
parents also are now travelling.

"Taking with us our wardrobe and scenery, but leaving
behind us, at Cadney's Croft, Halifax, the remainder of
our theatrical property carefully packed upon waggons,
my company and I went in December, 1857, to the Theatre
Royal, Wigan, producing during the five months we
remained there some of our best pieces.

"Messrs. John and Joseph Holloway being in my company at that time, I only engaged another star, Henry
Nicholls, during the entire period of our stay at Wigan.

"It was fortunate for me, as well as for the members
of my company, that we were not without ready cash, as

the previous occupants of the theatre had, on quitting it, left many of the Wigan tradesmen their creditors to such an extent that the fraternity of players was there looked upon with the gravest suspicion, and everything we required had to be paid for cash down. From the timber merchant and the printer to the butcher and the baker, all were inexorable in their demands for prepayment. Elsewhere our credit was always good for a week at least; but, as we had the wherewithal, we offered no objection to those peremptory demands for cash.

" The audiences at the Theatre Royal, I soon discovered, contained more than a sprinkling of roughs. Their conduct was such that I found it necessary to administer a corrective. This I did, through programmes and posters, as follows :—

NOTICE.

Whereas, some disorderly persons have made a practice of throwing orange peel and other missiles from the gallery, to the annoyance of parties visiting the pit.

Mr. S. Wild hereby offers a reward of one guinea for the apprehension of any party so committing himself, or in any way damaging the property of the theatre.

N.B.—Anyone whistling, stamping, interrupting the audience or performances, will be immediately expelled.

Officers will be in attendance to enforce strict order.

" The nightly engagement of a policeman, the constant visits to the theatre at my request of other members of the Wigan ' force ' during the performances, and the inducements held out for the apprehension of offenders, worked wonders in a very short time.

" But I met the unruly ones in another way. I sought to make the Theatre Royal a place of rational amusement to the Wiganians, and to that end selected my pieces with care, and mounted them with the best skill I could, for I had frequently observed that the conduct of an audience is, to an extent, invariably regulated by the entertainment presented to it We produced the plays of Shakspeare, Lytton, &c., introducing other novelties occasionally.

" The New Year, 1858, we commenced with a pantomime, which brought out my daughter Louisa as Fair Star and columbine, and also my son Charles Henry (then only six years of age), and my daughter Elizabeth (not more than four) as fairies. That same pantomime also brought out Jenny Lind, not the famous warbler of that name, but a dark-bay Lilliputian steed, only 32 inches in height, which I had purchased from Mr. Edwin Hughes. Clown introduced her to the audience during the harlequinade, and the statement that he did so is, perhaps, sufficient to indicate that Miss Jenny's performances were chiefly of a humorous description.

"Mr. C. R. Somerset wrote me a drama during this season at Wigan, Greenhalch and assistants painted scenery for it, and my son Tom gave himself up to the study of pyrotechnics for some time in order to render failure on the first performance of the piece impossible. But it was bound to become popular for two reasons—first because of its intrinsic merits, and second because of the circumstances—then fresh in the public mind—with which it dealt. The massacre at Cawnpore, the storming of Delhi, and the relief of Lucknow—the respective subjects of the three acts into which the drama was divided—were powerful items in the large double-column programme I had printed to announce the production, on 15th February, of *The Storming of Delhi*. But the introductory portion of that same programme could not fail to arouse patriotic feeling, and so assist in bringing us crowded houses. It was after this style :—

The performances will commence with a grand military spectacle, with new scenery, dresses, decorations, and mechanical effects, produced in a style worthy the subject and its importance, and upon a scale unapproachable and, consequently, unexampled.

The manager has great pleasure in informing his numerous patrons and the inhabitants of Wigan and its vicinity that, at considerable expense, he has secured a dramatic version of this important action and its period, renowned in the history of the world and unparalleled in the annals of time.

All the unhappy circumstances and historical facts have been carefully selected from the papers of the present day.

When Thompson wrote the song called "Rule Britannia," little did he dream on the immortality for which it was destined—that it would be the rallying song of Britons in future times, and make millions of patriotic hearts leap in their bosoms at its inspiring melody. 'Tis a majestic image ; Britannia ruling the waves that dash her white cliffs. Surrounded by the eternal barrier she laughs to scorn foreign aggression ; and when in defence of other nations she has been called to assert her supremacy, her tributary waves have not been the only scene of her triumphs, as the well-fought fields of Agincourt, Blenheim, Waterloo (would we could at the present time boast another Wellington), and latterly Alma, Balaclava, and Inkerman testify. That Britons never shall be slaves in the most appropriate and degraded sense—the slaves of despotism or anarchy—that they will maintain their scrupulous honour—their high tone of morals—their reverence for things sacred—their ardent love of country—inherent spirit of freedom—intrepidity in fight—

humanity in conquest—and the thousand charities that make the perfect man—we may well be assured : and though the sufferings our brave troops had to endure by a campaign in the cold regions of the Crimea were severe, yet their bold hearts never gave way to despair. And now, 12,000 miles from home, surrounded on every side by treachery, fighting fearful odds, viz., five to one, they will read the murderous Sepoys such a lesson as will ring like a death-knell throughout the heart of the Indian Empire, and terribly avenge the massacre of our men, women, and innocent children, and show the supremacy of dear old England!

" In the last scene of the drama, in which the Princess Zobiede appeared upon a model Indian elephant bearing the standard of England, there were at least one hundred persons upon the stage, including in that number all the rebel Sepoys who, in the two previous acts, had been slaughtered at Delhi and Cawnpore. All through the piece considerable importance was attached to the use of gunpowder; and on the second evening of the performance of the *Siege of Delhi* we did such terrible havoc amongst the revolters that we had to proclaim a truce for the following evening, 'in order to replace fireworks, bomb-shells, and explosions.'

" During its last performance, on 28th February, at Wigan, I fell from one of the ' racks ' and fractured the cap of my right knee, in consequence of which I was unable to appear upon the stage for nearly a month.

" Mr. and Mrs. John Holloway took their benefit on the 15th March. The pieces selected for the occasion were *The Patriot of Rome* and *The Lion of Naples*. The programme, as usual, opened with an address to the public, whose ' praiseworthy judgment ' was expatiated upon ; then there came a sort of an apostrophe to the stage, and, by way of peroration, the following lines :—

In the Augustine age, when theatrical entertainments were the common amusements of the people throughout the Roman Empire, they would not have passed uncensured by our Saviour and His apostles, who went forth by Divine mission to reform all nations of the earth, had they been deemed immoral or irreligious ; but we find His doctrines absolutely recommended and preached from the stage. And St. Paul sometimes quotes the expressions of dramatic poets in support of his own sentiments.

" The season at Wigan terminated, if I remember rightly, about the end of March, 1858, on the 17th of which month I set apart the net receipts at the theatre for the I.O. Oddfellows, M.U., Widows and Orphans Fund; and on April 23rd (I had removed to Blackburn then) I made a similar provision for the Blackburn Infirmary Fund.

" It is gratifying now, in the day of one's adversity, in looking over our records of the past, to find that there was at least an effort made in the good old times to assist the poor, the needy, and the sick ; and that the successive proprietors of ' Old Wild's ' did not in their prosperity live wholly to themselves.

" ' Charity begins at home,' saith the adage; but during our Blackburn season it ended there, so far as Mrs. Sam and I were concerned, for I did not take my benefit until the very last night of the season, the 18th May, and my wife's special appearance before the Blackburn public dated only a few days previously.

" The pieces usually selected by Mrs. Sam for her benefit were those in which both she and I could appear, and amongst her favourites were *Black-eyed Susan*, and *The Sea, or the Ocean Child*.

" Concerning the latter, this nautical drama probably owes much of its attractiveness (especially with the gentler sex) to the character of Jack Helm Neptune, who, twice or thrice during the first act, appears in his baby robes. For more than a quarter of a century the *Ocean Child* was a stock drama at Wild's Theatre; but I never knew us during that time experience any difficulty in obtaining a suitable representative for Master Neptune. Sometimes we could supply the little hero from our company's own stock —my wife has furnished many a one—but when our olive branches had bidden adieu to leading strings we were compelled to borrow. Mammas, as a rule, however, manifested no reluctance, but rather delight at the idea of ' baby ' appearing behind the footlights; considerably more delight, I may say, than at times did the baby himself, for it was no uncommon thing for Master Neptune to begin piping his eye during the christening ceremony in the first act. But, then, we always took care to have mamma seated behind the scenes to afford him ready consolation in seasons of distress. Sometimes the baby was of the lovelier sex— the distinction didn't matter much then—and many, many years afterwards, as we have renewed our visits to the old familiar places, we have occasionally met Master Neptune in a more important character, and with a baby in his, or rather her, arms, she would ask us with a smile, ' What do you think of your " Ocean Child " now ? ' "

CHAPTER XX.

> And feel again as I was wont to do,
> When hope was young.—WELLS.—*The Old Elm Tree.*

" ' Wild's colossal establishment, the largest and most valuable in Europe—Wild's that has no rival.' Such were the terms in which I drew the attention of the playgoing public of Blackburn and Preston to my Thespian temple during the spring of 1858.

" The increased importance which I had attached to my establishment at this time was to some extent due to a new and stupendous front which had been painted for it. The five hundred square yards of canvas which mainly constituted it were covered by a pictoral representation of the storming of Delhi, executed at a cost of £100, and in the best style of art, by Messrs. John Whaite & Son, of Manchester, then looked upon by the proprietors of portable theatres and the show folk generally as the very tip-top artists of the day.

" Contemporaneously with the first unfolding of this front to the Blackburn public, at the commencement of the Easter holidays, was the appearance of my band in French costume, *a la* Julien.

" If, therefore, to these new attractions be added a company numbering over fifty performers, and as talented perhaps as any strolling company then before the public ; the smallest horse in the world, the cleverest dogs in the world, extensive and well-painted scenery, valuable properties, and a wardrobe second to none ; it will be seen I was not without reasons for thinking well of my establishment, and the pride was perhaps a pardonable one which prompted me to dub it what I verily believed it to be, 'the largest and most valuable in Europe.'

"But, notwithstanding its pretensions, I threw it open to the Blackburn public at the nominal charges of three-pence, sixpence, and a shilling, and had every reason to be satisfied with the patronage accorded me during my stay in that town.

"Nor did I alter the terms of admission to the theatre when, at the commencement of the Whitsun holidays, I introduced it and its attractions to the good people of Preston, and found a 'local habitation' in the Orchard there. The entertainment, however, I did vary, and that daily, presenting to our audiences the humour of comedy and roar of farce alternately with the sparkle of pantomime and the more serious business of military drama and tragedy.

"Ever changing our location like our plays, the months rolled past, and September found us at Armley.

"We had finished the season there on Saturday, the 10th of that month, and had been pulling down all night, in order to be able to start off early and reach Holbeck before church time on Sunday morning. Our task completed, we retired for breakfast and a short rest.

"Blanchard, who had been assisting, repaired to his lodgings, somewhat fatigued, as we all were. After requesting his wife to make him some tea and a little dry toast, he went to lie down. Mrs. Blanchard lost no time in preparing this simple fare and in carrying it upstairs for her husband. She spoke to him, but he did not answer; he had evidently fallen asleep. She called him by his name; still there was no response. Approaching more closely the place where he lay, and bending over him, what was her dismay to find that he was dead. She immediately despatched a messenger for me, and I as quickly obeyed the summons, for I could not credit the news of Blanchard's death, as I had seen him hale and hearty only half an hour before. When I reached his lodgings, however, I soon ceased to doubt. He was lying on the bed with his arms folded across his breast, his head inclined slightly towards the pillow, and the long black hair, upon which he so much prided himself, streaming over it. His face was calmness itself, and he appeared to have passed away without a struggle.   His distressed wife stood near looking at him and weeping and wringing her hands.

" 'Now that I have lost my husband,' she exclaimed, despairingly, ' I haven't a friend in the world, for I have neither relative nor child.'

" 'Softly, Mrs. Blanchard,' I interposed, ' so long as I have an establishment, and you do what is right, you shall never want a situation, and Mrs. Wild and I will see you never want a friend.'

" Barely six months after this she left us, and I am sorry to say the fault was not ours that she did so.

" Mr. and Mrs. Blanchard were first engaged by me, through the *Era*, while I was at Keighley, in June, 1856. During the trial of Hannon, at York, in that same year, Blanchard was the principal witness against him ; and it was perhaps the recollection of this that prompted Mr. Hope, Mrs. Banham's father, to offer his vault at Armley, where his unfortunate daughter lay, as a final resting place for poor Blanchard.   I regard it as a peculiar coincidence that on the same day of the same month, two years afterwards, and in the same village, in which Mrs. Banham so unexpectedly came to her end, poor Blanchard died.   A fairly educated man, and gentlemanly in all his transactions, he was well liked by the members of my company, and his sudden demise (from an apoplectic fit, so said the doctor who afterwards saw him) threw a gloom over us all.

" After an unusually lengthened stay at Holbeck we went to Burnley.   That being one of the towns in which we generally had a successful season of several months, I had a place specially prepared for us.   It consisted, however, of little more than a wooden shell, which we fitted, when we arrived there, with our own pit and gallery seats, stage, and scenery.   But I had a side box added for the *élite*, capable of holding forty or fifty persons.   This temporary building was ninety feet long and forty-five feet wide, and stood upon what is now the site of a covered market.   It was capable of holding from 1200 to 1300 persons, and a good house, at lowest prices, would bring me £21 or more.

" We were well supported at Burnley, as we anticipated from past experience there that we should be.   Under the patronage of Captain J. G. Irvine and the Officers of the

71st Fermanagh Light Infantry Militia, we performed, on November 30th, Buckstone's celebrated drama, *The Flowers of the Forest*, in which were worn the court dresses of the King of the French. Upon reference to a programme for the occasion, printed in letters of gold upon pink satin, I am reminded that I had trouble occasionally with certain of the audience, but nothing compared with that I had with some of our Wigan patrons. In serene defiance of the notice prohibiting smoking in the theatre, certain frequenters of the gallery persisted in exhaling the fumes of the forbidden plant, and I found it necessary, while laying stress upon my objections to their conduct, to state explicitly what my intentions generally were in the interests of the audience :—' Strict order will be maintained. It is the determination of the manager to eject disorderly persons, and to rigorously prosecute parties guilty of breaches of the peace. The comfort of the audience will be studied, and the interests of the theatre protected.'

" The resolute opposition of the few did not, however, deter me from catering to the best advantage of the many. All the resources of my establishment were drawn upon for their entertainment, and long before there was any danger of these being exhausted, I again set about engaging stars.

" Early in the new year, namely, on January 9th, 1859, appeared behind the footlights at Wild's Colossal Pavilion, Mr. McKean Buchanan. Macbeth, King Lear, The Stranger, Richelieu, Claude Melnotte, Richard III., Rob Roy,—these were the characters he sustained during the six nights of his engagement. At each performance the house was crowded to excess ; in fact, I never had a star who, during a similar period, brought me so much money as Buchanan.

" He was an American, I believe ; a finely proportioned man, and a gentleman I am sure. He stood six feet two inches without any help from his shoemaker, and never an inch of that height did he lose. Still the degree of dignity with which he carried himself seemed natural to him, and gave him at all times a commanding appearance. There was nothing of haughtiness in his nature. On an emergency he would pull up a scene or lend a helping hand wherever he saw one was needed. For the more effective

representation of the witching scenes in *Macbeth* he imparted to us most valuable information on the art of
manufacturing lightning, and on many occasions and in
many ways gave us seasonable hints. At rehearsals, too,
he took considerable pains with us, and especially with the
utility men. Under his direction, and by acting upon his
advice—as we all did save one—Smith, that remarkable
exception, might have improved no little; but, unfortunately for him, he was of that pedantic turn of mind
which ignores instruction, is incapable of receiving improvement, and to which a suggestion is tantamount to an
insult. As the Third Secretary in *Richelieu*, Smith had,
in the last scene of act five, to present documents to Louis
XIII., and at rehearsal Mr. Buchanan was so dissatisfied
with the manner in which this was done that he compelled
him to repeat the ceremony some half-dozen times. Third
Secretary Smith didn't like this; there was, he thought,
something very humiliating about it. He conformed, however, to the requirements of the Cardinal during the
rehearsal, but when evening came and with it the performance, Third Secretary Smith fell back upon his own
superior judgment, and approached Louis XIII. in his own
familiar manner. Buchanan noticed this, but never
remarked upon it afterwards; but Smith was jubilant over
the affair, and was heard to utter congratulatory remarks
to himself when the performances were over.

" Mr. T. H. Glenney, who, with his company, was at
the Halifax Theatre a few weeks ago, began a six nights'
engagement with me at the 'Theatre Royal, Burnley '—
such was my establishment dubbed for this occasion—on
January 17th, 1859. For this engagement, as for those of
most of my stars, I was indebted to the *Era*. The pieces
in which he performed were *The Black Doctor*, *Belphegor*,
Eustace Baudin, *The Life of a Soldier*, and *The Woman
of the World*. There were capital houses every night, but
as I always advertised more when I had stars, the extra
receipts at the doors were generally swallowed up in extra
salaries and printers' charges.

" ' The lessee, ever desirous of rendering the Theatre
worthy of the increasing patronage bestowed upon it, begs
to announce that he has entered into an engagement, at
considerable expense, with the eminent Shakspearian
tragedian, Mr. John Coleman, from all the principal

theatres in the kingdom. This distinguished artiste, admitted by the general voice of public opinion and the most competent critics as worthy to take the highest stand amongst the first exponents of the intellectual drama, will make his first appearance here in his great character of Hamlet.'

" In conformity with which announcement Mr. Coleman, on 31st January, did appear on Wild's stage as the Prince of Denmark, and on subsequent evenings in the characters of The Stranger, Don Cæsar de Bazan, and Belphegor. He also appeared in 'a new grand romantic play in five acts, by John Coleman, and never acted here, entitled *Catherine Howard.*' After the performance of the latter piece on its first production at Burnley, Mrs. Tate, of my company, received a very high compliment from Mr. Coleman. ' I have performed in this piece,' said he, ' at many theatres where the leading ladies have not played Catherine Howard half so well as you have done to-night.'

" Mr. Coleman was the first great actor I had seen who did not conduct his own rehearsals. A gentleman who travelled with him relieved him of that duty.

" Henry Loraine was another theatrical luminary I engaged during our stay at Burnley, and shortly after his appearance the season there was brought to a close, as we were anxious to be at Blackburn in time for the Easter fair.

" In the various towns and villages at which we stayed during our yearly peregrinations, I had for some time past experienced difficulty in obtaining lodgings for my family. It was a large one now, and required considerable attention ; besides which we carried a private wardrobe of more than ordinary dimensions, and bed and bedding specially for the younger children. Hence the difficulty in meeting with the necessary accommodation will readily be perceived. Under these circumstances I decided to have a van built, and, like other travellers I was constantly meeting with, be always at home wherever I went. There was still, it is true, the old van which my father had in his time, but Mrs. Meanley occupied that. She having, however, attained her seventieth year, I decided to pension her off, and let the old van go in part exchange for the contemplated new one. I broached the subject to Mr. James Bedford, at Halifax, during the fair, in June, 1858, and he engaged to carry out my requirements. I also agreed with him to make me another van for the scenery, &c. During the progress of the work I came over to Halifax several times, but it was not until the Easter of 1859, and while my company was at Blackburn, that the vans were completed, and that was the time, too, when I came over to fetch them. They were capitally made things, both of them. The living van was considered by competent judges to be the handsomest ever turned out. It was sixteen feet long by eight feet six inches wide, and full of cornices and carved work. The outside panels were painted bird's-eye maple, and stood out in bold relief against a groundwork of ultramarine blue. Inside, the van was oak grained throughout. It was divided into two compartments, bedroom and sitting, or more properly, living room. In the first were two large shelves, which, with the help of mattresses and blankets, were converted nightly into two beds. The shelves, being attached by hinges to the side of the van, were capable of being lowered or raised at pleasure. This arrangement enabled us to keep tidy, and, in a sense, enlarged our sleeping apartment during the daytime, when a large curtain effectually concealed our little berths from view. Then there was other shelving in the room, also a nest of drawers, a locker, and a couple or so of chairs. The windows were partly of coloured glass, were large and of oblong shape, with venetian blinds before them. The living room contained two small fireplaces, each boasting a chimney piece of its own, and over one of these was a large handsome gilt mirror. There were several lockers in this room, more shelving, two, I believe three, tiny cheffioniers, a side table, a rocking chair, an easy chair, and of smaller chairs a few. Full of business though I generally was, I always contrived to get into that rocking chair whenever I wished to have a good think about anything. Then we had gas fittings in both rooms, handsome brackets, and cheery-looking globes ; but these, of course, could only serve us, except for ornament, when we were located where gas was procurable. Then we had—in fine, we had well nigh every comfort we required ; certainly every convenience that a van of this description is capable of affording. The living van and the scenery, or as I afterwards called it, the 'colossal' van, cost me, inclusive of furniture for the former, over £150.

" But I forgot to state that when I came over from Blackburn to Halifax for them, my wife accompanied me. I decided to send the scenery van by rail, and to return to Blackburn by road in the living van, for which I had engaged horses.

" Hearing of my determination in the latter particular, the cavalry band, of which Bedford was a member, hired an omnibus and preceded me as far as the King Cross Inn, playing, amongst other things, as they went (and which was suggested by the fact that I was actually going), ' Over the hills and far away.' At the sound of music crowds of people collected to see us pass. My wife and I were seated in the van, but they caught sight of us, and young and old, gentle and simple, alike cheered, and that right heartily, for where was the little boy who didn't know us, or the adult to whom the name of ' Wild ' had not been familiar, perhaps a charm, in years gone by ?

" Mrs. Meanley did not like leaving the old van. She had lived in it in my father's time and had seen him taken out of it to be consigned to mother earth ; she had companioned with his widow, and had witnessed her departure from it, never to return ; then there was a host of pleasant associations clinging to the old place, so that to give up her favourite and for many years only residence was to her like relinquishing a part of her existence. But as I had provided her with a good home at Blackburn, and had agreed to allow her twelve shillings per week for the remainder of her life, she could not but see that reluctance on her part to leave her old quarters was a hindrance to me. Especially as I had reasoned with her that I wished to supersede the van, which now being considerably the worse for wear, and of no use to me, had only to be dragged about from place to place at great expense and risk ; and that, moreover, as I had provided for her at a time of life when she needed rest and quiet, it would be seen I had neither forgotten her former services nor had the slightest idea, now that she was old, of turning my back upon her. So she consented at length to be pensioned off, and in spite of the unquestionable difficulty she experienced in taking a last farewell of her old habitation, she survived the loss of it at least fourteen years, and lived to attain the advanced age of four score years and five.

" Mrs. Meanley, long before my mother's death, had

saved a good round sum of money, but the difficulties of her daughter's husband, Edward Parrish, who had a travelling concern like ours, while they served to prove the old lady's benevolent disposition, also brought about a reduction in her circumstances. Parrish and his wife died at Oldham within a few days of each other, and the establishment, towards the extension and support of which Mrs. Meanley had advanced so much money from time to time, was left to her by Parrish's will. With a view to the successful carrying on of the business, she engaged a stage manager and an acting manager, both of whom, however, so plundered the old lady that, her funds at length exhausted, the concern had to be publicly sold at Stockport to discharge an old account for horse hire ; and to provide for which account she had some time before put her acting manager in funds.

"She was a very stout person this Mrs. Meanley, and lamentably deaf, but, like many more deaf people, she was generally quick to hear anything we didn't want her to know. Then her deafness was always the most confirmed when aught was wanted in a hurry. One day six or eight of our company were engaged in combats before a Halifax audience, when one of the swords broke, and I sent to Mrs. Meanley, in the van, for a pair of new ones. The messenger stated his requirements clearly enough, but the old lady altogether misinterpreted them. She had been busy with her laundress that morning, and linen was uppermost in her thoughts, and when the express made known my desire, that she would be so good as to send me a couple of combat swords, her hasty reply was ' Oh, tell him they've gone to t'wesh.' For long afterwards it was a favourite inquiry of mine whenever I saw the old lady in a cheerful mood, ' Well, have those combat swords come from " t'wesh " yet ? '

"She had her peculiarities had our old wardrobe custodian, most old people have, but she was as honest as daylight and candid almost to a fault. She was once taken ill at Keighley, and a doctor attended her for a week or so. His medicines were so unpalatable that she only attempted to take them once or twice, and, afterwards, with the same regularity with which he sent them, she threw them out ; but gradually recovered health notwithstanding. When the doctor at length came to see her, he expressed his satisfaction at her speedy approach to convalescence, pluming himself, no doubt, upon the efficacy of his treatment. But her candour and honesty were displayed together when she told him that she couldn't take, and, consequently, hadn't taken, his medicines, but that she was quite prepared to pay him for them notwithstanding.

"After the old van had left my service its roving days were over, and it meekly resigned itself to a quiet, everyday sort of life. Its last days were spent at the bottom of New Bank, here in Halifax, where it was carefully deposited in the recess of a wall, and divested of its wheels; lest, I suppose, it should be tempted, in a moment of levity, to go off of its own accord, and gratify its old wandering propensities. It was then converted into a little shop, whose first tenant was, I believe, a tobacconist; it afterwards fell into the hands of a little greengrocer, and finally became the workshop of a cobbler.

"So, quoting Hamlet, you see

To what base uses we may return.

"We remained six or seven weeks at Blackburn in April and May, 1859, after which, following our usual route, we went to Preston for the Whitsun holidays. Thence to Halifax, forward to Wakefield, afterwards to Leeds, thence to Dewsbury, and finally to Hunslet. At which last-mentioned place we will stay a few moments, in imagination, while I endeavour to relate the details of the arrest of myself and six of my company, by the sergeant of the Leeds police and about twelve police-officers, while we were in the very midst of a performance.

"But the circumstances which led to that arrest (so far as I was able to make out) shall be stated fully at our next interview."

CHAPTER XXI.

Man, proud man !
Dressed in a little brief authority.—*Measure for Measure.*

"The piece of ground at Hunslet, known as Penny
Hill, whereon in times past many a histrionic triumph has
been achieved by 'Old Wild's' company, formed part of the
demesnes of the Lord of the Manor of Hunslet, by whose
agent for the time being it had been leased regularly every
year, for a considerable number of years, to the successive
proprietors of that well-known establishment. For
'Wild's' was always regarded as the presiding divinity of
feasts everywhere, and Hunslet feast in particular was
looked upon as a thing of naught without it.

"Armley feast following closely upon that at Hunslet,
the custom had been for our company to remain at the
latter village until the day before the commencement of
the Armley festivities, and as exception had never been
taken to our performing at Hunslet, after the feast, permission for so brief a period was but rarely, if ever,
obtained from the authorities.

"This had been the state of things from my father's
time down to 1859; in the August of which year I applied
for and obtained temporary possession of the ground at
Hunslet in anticipation of the feast as usual; concluding
the agreement of letting with the Lord of the Manor,
through the Chief Constable of that village, who, at the
time to which I am referring, acted in the capacity of
agent for him.

"It so happened—unfortunately for me, as events will
show—that the Chief Constable and the Highways Sur-

veyor of Hunslet were just then on rather [questionable terms of friendship ; a condition which possibly may have been induced by the conduct of the surveyor, a young man, by the bye, who, in the opinion of the constable, slightly exceeded his authority at times, and, in a sense, interfered with the prerogative of that gentleman.

" The feast at Hunslet, 1859, had ended, and my company was performing there by way of putting on time a few days until Armley feast. As we were always well supported at Hunslet, we arranged to play a few of our best pieces during our short sojourn there, and amongst them the popular drama, *It's Never Too Late to Mend.*

" Mons. Shenterina was one of our attractions at this time, and just before we opened the doors each night to admit the public to the performances within the booth, he gave a short entertainment on a slack rope outside ; at the conclusion of which the wondering crowds were duly apprised of what was provided for their delectation within.

" The parade proving insufficient for the extent of rope required by Shenterina, we fixed a pole near the curbstone of the adjoining causeway, temporarily removing one of the paving stones the better to secure the Monsieur's required support.

" The Highways Surveyor, as it soon appeared, was no friend of ours. He looked upon the strolling fraternity with aught but a favourable eye, yet was he powerless to interfere with the doings at the booth so long as we kept within our own boundaries. But it seemed that our emergency had placed us in his power—at all events we inferred that it had from his subsequent proceedings. Is it then possible to imagine the delight of such a man when he conceived that to be the case ? There was a good deal of gall mingled with his words when he insisted upon the immediate removal of my booth from Hunslet, and more than a modicum of haughtiness in his threat, by way of alternative, to summons me for obstructing the highway.

" The only course which seemed open to me under such ominous circumstances was to consult with the Chief Constable of whom, as already explained, I had taken the land at Penny Hill. I accordingly did so, and he and his deputy together advised me to ignore the threats of the Highways Surveyor. He was, they argued, simply seeking to flaunt his importance before their eyes ; but that he had no authority whatever to molest me, as all the land thereabout belonged to the Lord of the Manor. I could not, therefore, but look upon all this as very reassuring. Yet, I thought, in order to avoid any further unpleasantness from the surveyor, it would, perhaps, be best after all to take down the slack rope, remove the pole and restore the pavement; and these things I set about having done at once. As for leaving Hunslet immediately, that I made up my mind I would not do. I had previously settled to go to Armley with my company at the end of the second day after the memorable visit of the surveyor, and I decided now that no threats of his should disturb my arrangements.

"The danger of delay is proverbial. Within twenty-four hours after seeing that personage, and in spite of his disputed authority, I received a formal request; in other words, a summons, to appear on the following morning (the very day fixed for our removal to Armley) at the Town Hall, Leeds, the charge against me being the obstruction of the highway at Hunslet on a certain date.

"On receiving this I waited upon the Hunslet constables again, and showed them the summons. Their cry was still, 'Never mind what the surveyor has done or may do, we will stand by you whatever be the consequences.' With which promise I decided to trouble no more about the instigator of the summons, except that I would duly appear next morning in answer to it at the Town Hall, as required.

"Shenterina's performances outside were dispensed with now, it is true; but the mere announcement of the production, under the same title, of a 'dramatised version of Charles Reade's thrilling story, *It's Never Too Late to Mend*,' was sufficient in the evening of the eventful day on which I received the summons to crowd the booth without any adventitious means or expedient.

"We had got through the scheming and quarrelling, the arresting and parting in the first act, and were engaged in the second scene of Act 2. It was the corridor in a model prison. Tom Robinson, in felon's garb, had just released the boy Josephs from the slow process of strangulation to which Hawes, the governor of the prison, had mercilessly subjected him; and was endeavouring to console the youth, when Hawes himself entered, and, scarcely able to believe his own eyes, authoritatively demanded to know

Who released that boy ?

ROBINSON : I did.

HAWES : Oh ! Then it seems you are the Governor here, not I. What—ho ! without there !

(Enter two TURNKEYS.)

HAWES (to TURNKEYS) : Seize and strap up that boy again.

ROBINSON (assuming a threatening attitude towards the turnkeys) : Here, on his mother earth, will I stretch him who dares to lay but a finger of harm upon this youth.

HAWES (*indignantly*) : Pray what is that you say ?

ROBINSON : What I will do.

" And at this point in our version of the story, I, as Tom Robinson, lifted my hand to corroborate my verbally expressed intention, when simultaneously with the amusing exeunt of the stage turnkeys, was the more serious appearance upon the scene of officers of a genuine sort, to check me in my high career and to arrest alike the Governor and the turnkeys.

" I was puzzled for the moment at this new and unrehearsed feature of the piece, yet it seemed so like a part of the play that at first it was difficult to believe it was not so. But when I felt the firm grip of a practised hand, I perceived a startling degree of seriousness about this new business. It became now a case of which was strongest, and I wrestled with my adversaries for some time before I became aware that I was resisting Mr. English, the Chief Constable of Leeds, and one of his staff. Moreover the pitch of excitement and indignation which I, in my histrionic character of Tom Robinson, had attained just before the unexpected appearance of these persons, made resistance rather congenial to my tastes than otherwise. But when I saw other police officers arresting my company, men and women alike, I thought there must be some cause for these proceedings (though I was ignorant of any, save the obstructing of the highway), so offered no further opposition.

" Meanwhile the screams and protestations of the women, the struggles of the men and police, and the unusual commotion upon the stage, had caused the audience to exhibit wonder, sympathy, indignation, and recklessness by turns. The looks of blank astonishment were quickly succeeded by the rising of the ' house ' *en masse*, and this was followed by hooting, screaming, howling, dismal noises that beggar description, and a dare-devil readiness for anything, which only a disappointed audience knows how to indulge in and exhibit. The fall of the curtain during the struggle, concealing from the audience what was going forward, tended only to aggravate matters. A person in the pit whispered another 'to turn off the gas,' and who knows what might have ensued but for the presence of mind of one of my men, Connolly, who being in the pit overheard this suggestion, and went at once and removed the key from the meter?

" In the midst of this intense excitement I asked the Chief Constable to allow me to go before the curtain and speak to the audience, for if such a thing as silence could be obtained, I thought I should stand as good a chance as anybody of securing it. He would not consent to my doing this unless he went with me, so I appeared before the footlights in the custody of Mr. English and a police officer. There were mingled cheers and hooting, loud and prolonged. At length, when something like order reigned, I assured my patrons that the sudden interruption to the performance was every whit as inexplicable to me as doubtless it had been to them. That there was evidently some mistake (for the constable had not yet informed me what was the 'head and front of my offending'), and that though I was sorry they had been disappointed of their entertainment, I should be with them again to-morrow evening, and would give them a full performance without charge. I begged of them to quietly disperse and not on my account, or by any means, interfere with the police, who were simply acting upon instructions. Such an inter-ference, I told them, might lead to serious after conse-quences, and I wanted nobody to suffer on my account. These remarks were favourably received, but as I was being led off by the Chief Constable and his man, the hooting was resumed. Mr. English then advancing towards the footlights told the refractories (in which term may be comprehended almost the entire audience that night) that unless they left the place at once, and in a quiet and orderly manner, they might find themselves in trouble before long, for he must inform them that they were there in an unlicensed house.

" The two last words gave me a sort of cue to the cause

of the arrest, and when I asked Mr. English about it afterwards he told me that the Highways Surveyor of Hunslet had represented to the magistrates at Leeds that I was performing without a licence and against the wishes of the Hunslet public. I must confess that I found it somewhat difficult to reconcile this last objection with the recollection of the crowded houses we had nightly drawn at that village.

"The male and female performers being all arrested, except Peter Wood and Mark Kirby, who escaped by creeping underneath the stage, we were about to be conducted from the theatre, when Mr. English, looking towards the females as he spoke, said, 'I think we will not take the ladies.'

"'It would hardly be gentlemanly to do that,' I replied. 'I will hold myself responsible for them.'

"So the ladies were left behind, while Mellers, Lister, Smith, Charles, little Joey Thornton, my son Tom, and myself were conducted outside the theatre, where four cabs were waiting to convey us to a stronger prison than the one we had left behind us on the stage. The spectators, still uneasy and ready to break out afresh, had followed us from the theatre (I may observe that, the instant the place was cleared, my wife ordered all the doors to be closed), and they were about to create a disturbance as the police guarded us to the cabs, but I requested them, for their own sakes, to be peaceable and quiet.

"I had managed before I left the stage to slip off my prison clothes, for, beneath them, I remembered I had on a capital dress suit in which I had appeared before the mimic arrest of myself in the first act; but my six companions were all attired in the costumes in which they had been performing.

"Upon our arrival at the Town Hall, Leeds, somewhere near ten o'clock, we were conducted into a large room. It was sparingly furnished with a few forms, there was a long shelf at one end of the room (a sleeping place I suppose it was), and a cheery fire burnt in a low grate before which was an iron guard.

"We had barely time to study the characteristics of the place, limited though they were, before Mr. English appeared at a little wicket in the door, and, opening it, inquired for me.

" ' Perhaps you gentlemen, being of literary tastes,' said he, ' would like something to read, for I scarcely suppose you will sleep much to-night.'

" I answered him we should only be too glad of anything to while away the time.

" ' Then follow me to the library and you shall make your own selection.'

" The door was unlocked and I went with the constable to his room.   There I made choice of the works of Shakspeare, Douglas Jerrold, and Bulwer Lytton, laden with which treasure I returned to my fellow prisoners.   Some of us read —Mellers was an inveterate reader—while others simply turned over the leaves mechanically, their minds being too much occupied by other thoughts.

" My wife sent Williams after us to Leeds as soon as the cabs had moved off, as she was anxious to learn what had become of us.   She sent me money by him, too (she expected the business would end in a fine), for the only money I had about me was stage money, which, however valuable it may be upon the boards, is difficult to pass anywhere off them.

" On his way down, Williams called upon the landlord of the Templar's Hotel, Leeds, Mr. Thomas Long, who accompanied him to the Town Hall.   There Mr. Long offered to become bail for me, and the Chief Constable, who, while our introduction had been rather rough and unceremonious, proved exceedingly kind not only to myself but to all of us, as prisoners, at once despatched an officer for a magistrate ; but, unfortunately, that officer's mission was a futile one—all the magistrates within easy distance had either gone to bed or were spending the evening with friends.

" Next morning, early, our breakfasts were brought by the ladies, who also came provided with overcoats for us.

" I sent Williams, who had also come down, to see Mr. Ferns, a solicitor of good practice in Leeds, instructing him to lay before that gentleman the particulars of the affirmed obstruction, the summons, and the circumstances of our arrest, and to ask him if he would be good enough to appear for us in court that morning at the hearing of the summons.   Mr. Ferns, I may say, readily consented to defend us.

" When our case was called, my fellow prisoners and I

were placed in the dock. The ladies were in the gallery, and there, too, were scores of our old patrons, who, hearing of the wholesale arrest of our company, had come to see how matters ended with us. The only person who appeared against me was the Highways Surveyor, and the only charge preferred was that of having performed at Hunslet without a licence.

" Mr. Ferns contended in defence that my booth did not come within the meaning of that section of the Leeds Improvement Act under which the information against me had been laid. I had simply, he argued, performed at Hunslet upon the same terms as my parents had done in years past, and as I had hitherto also done myself.

" In spite, however, of his able defence, supported by a reference to a similar case, the Bench fined me forty shillings and costs, but my fellow prisoners were discharged, the opinion of the Bench being that as these were servants merely they were not, strictly speaking, fineable.

" It was further stated from the Bench that had I applied for permission to remain at Hunslet a few days after the feast it would have been granted.

" That was, I will not attempt to deny, the proper course for me to have pursued, and why I did not do so has been fully explained at the commencement of this chapter. The necessity of obtaining the magistrates' permission had never been mooted before this time, and probably never would have been but for the interference of the Highways Surveyor. My company and I had nobody but him to thank for our introduction to the Leeds police, to him seven of us owed our gratitude for a night's lodging at the county's expense, and it was due to his spontaneous action that at the cost of three guineas we were allowed an audience of the magistrates next morning.

" We left the Town Hall as soon as the hearing was over, and the first person we saw outside was a gentleman from Hunslet, who was waiting for us with his trap to drive us back to Penny Hill. I told him how sorry I was to be compelled to decline his offer just then, as I had one or two little things to attend to before I could return to Hunslet. But that if he didn't mind doing so, he should take me down to Sir Peter Fairbairn's works, as I wished to see that gentleman. The trap was at my service, so there we went. Arrived at the counting-house, I per-

ceived a whispering amongst the clerks when I asked if
Sir Peter was in.

"'He is, Mr. Wild,' replied the gentleman who attended
on me, 'but I am afraid he can't be seen just now.'

"'I should very much like a word with him,' I urged,
'if it is at all possible that I may see him.'

"'Several gentlemen have called this morning to see
him and have gone away without.'

"'Would you oblige me with a pen and a scrap of
paper?' I inquired.

"'Certainly,' was the ready response.

"Then, having written a few lines requesting a
moment's audience with his Worship (for he was the
Mayor of Leeds at that time), I gave it to the gentleman.

"'There, if you don't mind handing that to Sir Peter I
will wait.'

"The message was taken in, the door was closed, a few
moments elapsed, the door was opened, and I was ushered
into the presence of the Mayor, to whom I made my best
salutations.

"'Well, Mr. Wild,' he asked, 'and what may be your
pleasure with me?'

"I proceeded shortly to explain to him the circumstances of the previous evening, and the result of the hearing that morning at the Town Hall.

"'I know all about the affair,' he replied, 'I was in the
Court this morning twice during the hearing, but wouldn't
sit upon that case, for I must tell you I am rather inclined
to be fond of you strollers. But to business, what do you
wish me to do for you?'

"'All I seek is your Worship's kind permission for
myself and company to perform this evening at Hunslet,
so that I may give satisfaction to those of my patrons who
were disappointed last evening, and so that I can meet the
public again after this unfortunate affair.'

"'But if you think you will require a longer time say
so now, Mr. Wild, and don't have to come again.'

"'I simply ask for this evening, if it please your
Worship, as we have arranged to go to Armley to-morrow,
and had so arranged, I may say, before we ever dreamed of
this unpleasantness.'

"'Well, then, you have my full and free permission.'

"I thanked his worship very heartily and retired.

"My next place of call was John Cooke's printing office in Meadow Lane, whither my companion and I drove.

"It had occurred to me, when I found a moment's time to reflect on the matter, that I had no means of ascertaining who my patrons at Hunslet last evening were, and that the best plan to avoid any contention at the doors would be to charge as usual, but to give to each person paying for entrance into the theatre, a ticket admitting him to my establishment any evening during Holbeck feast in September following. So I had handbills printed to this effect :—

Mr. Samuel Wild having obtained the kind permission of the Worshipful the Mayor of Leeds, Sir Peter Fairbairn, Bart., will perform before the Hunslet public this evening in the great drama, *It's Never Too Late to Mend.*

Notice.—Each person paying for admission to-night, will receive at the door a blue ticket admitting him to Wild's establishment on any evening during the week of the feast at Holbeck.

"That evening, at Hunslet, the house was literally crammed, and we had a most enthusiastic reception at the hands of the audience ; while as a consequence of the arrangement I had made as to the giving of tickets at the door, we were crowded all during the Holbeck feast days ; for those who had received tickets at Hunslet generally took to Holbeck with them friends who had not, and thus we had overflowing houses nightly.

"To return. When we, at length, went forward to Hunslet from Leeds, Williams was left behind to bring over the bills from the printers. When these came to hand we got out the band carriage and distributed them through their principal streets at Hunslet, then went forward to Leeds ; and there, while our band was playing in close proximity to the Town Hall ' See the conquering hero comes,' we showered our announcements on the passers by.

"At the hearing at the Town Hall neither the Chief Constable of Hunslet nor his deputy stood by me as he had promised to do, nor even so much as tendered me a shilling towards the costs attending it. Not that I was short of money then, the expense was but a trifle compared with the inconvenience to which I and my company had been subjected. But there was the disgrace of the thing ; there was a blot as it were upon ' Sam ' Wild's character for which he was not directly responsible, and there was, too, the non-fulfilment of a promise made by those from whom he had been led to expect vindication and support even under the worst of circumstances.

"At the bottom of all this unpleasantness for him lay ambition. Two or three persons were contending for mastery, while he was made alike the instrument and sufferer. But these were persons holding public offices, and against whose unimpeachable characters no word could be uttered. As for 'Sam' Wild and his company, who were they? Why, merely poor strollers, nobodies in fact, or, if aught, then 'Corrupters of the public morals,' nothing better than that. It was clearly the duty of such persons to submit uncomplainingly to persecution, and to count it matter for congratulation that a local print— unlike the press generally, which would be kind to the strollers spite of all that a few prudish people might say— condescended with an admixture of banter and righteous indignation to misrepresent their grievances; though nobody was more willing to believe that the substance of those misrepresentations had been communicated by an interested party than was 'Sam' Wild, the principal person traduced.

"But bad as we were made to appear, not one of us would have exchanged places with the surveyor, for he had aught but a pleasant time of it afterwards. As he passed along the streets, his ears were assailed with cries of 'Poor Tom Robinson,' 'It's never too late to mend'; and a jingle was perpetrated by some Hunslet geniuses in which he was alluded to in terms which were far from adulatory."

CHAPTER XXII.

A consummation devoutly to be wished.—*Hamlet.*

" Far from having any adverse effect upon our popularity, the incidents narrated in the last chapter served only to increase it—if it may be said such a thing was at that time possible. We had excellent houses every night during our stay in the neighbourhood of Leeds, and continued, with but one exception (and that was due to inclement weather), to be so favoured wherever we went, until a change, to which I shall refer by and bye, was effected in the establishment.

" Nor did we, because of its recent associations, exclude from our *repertoire* of pieces *It's Never Too Late to Mend.* We played it everywhere, for, popular though it undoubtedly is at the present day, it was simply the ' rage ' then.

" I cannot say, however, that for some time after the occurrence of the events to which I have above alluded we ever played the piece without having—the performers all round—a quiet sort of laugh, or without being unaccountably half on the *qui vive* when Scene 2 of Act the Second was reached. And at that point in it where Robinson assumes an attitude of defiance of prison authority, I, who usually sustained that character, was generally advised in an ' aside ' to ' look out for the chief constable.'

" We could afford·to laugh now, for business with us was good, and it seemed to me that few persons thought any the worse of us because of the Hunslet affair, with the true version of which everybody seemed at length to have become acquainted.

" On faith of the support I had in times past received from the good folks at Keighley, and in view of a visit which I intended to pay them, I had a wooden building erected there (at a cost of at least £200), possession of which we took early in November, 1859. My expectations were fully realised. The season was a successful one, and extended over a period of eight or nine weeks. I am reminded, however, of a misfortune at Keighley, namely, the fall of the gallery.

" It happened one evening during a performance. I was on the stage at the time, when a tremendous crash was heard, and, directing my eyes to the place whence the noise had proceeded, I perceived the gallery, which was capable of holding 800 persons, had given way. The curtain was immediately drawn and a rescue set about. Though the gallery at its highest point (from which it gradually sloped to the pit) was only some eight or nine feet from the ground, I fully expected, judging from the screams which accompanied the crash, and by the struggling and general confusion which followed it, to learn at least of broken limbs, if not of fatal cases. Fortunately, however, nobody was seriously injured, and the only losses complained of were those of hats, umbrellas, bonnets, shawls, boas, &c. At the time of the accident the performances were approaching conclusion, but the order went forth ' Come to Hecuba.' I then appeared before the curtain and announced that a careful search would be made, and such articles as were found would, on the following morning, at eleven o'clock, and in the theatre, be handed to those persons who could satisfy us they were the rightful owners of them. It was astonishing what a number of things we found, and yet all were claimed save one—a policeman's staff—nobody applied for that, and it is hanging up now in a corner of my house here, still awaiting identification.

" Mr. McKean Buchanan and Miss Fanny Rayner appeared for three nights during this season. They were the only stars I engaged at Keighley, and but for the fact that Buchanan wrote to me stating that he was three nights short of making up his engagements, the probability is I should have had none, for things were so flourishing I had no need of them.

"Leaving behind us at Keighley the wooden building, which was shortly to be removed to Blackburn, we went to Skipton about the middle of the month, January, 1860, and put up our portable theatre in the Old George yard. We remained at Skipton some weeks, during the greater part of which time the weather was rough and wet, and the booth sustained serious damage in consequence. The tilt was several times blown off and torn, and the ridges, side rails, and rafters were shivered completely. An entire week was lost in making repairs and restorations, and the season proved an unprofitable one by reason of these mischances.

"But at Blackburn, in the wooden building which I then styled the 'Victoria Theatre,' we had four months of continued good fortune, for which, however, I was not entirely dependent on stars, so I only engaged three during the entire season. The first of these was Edmondson Sherra, a young tragedian of considerable promise, but who died at Manchester only a few months after his appearance at Blackburn. The others were Lilia Ross, the wonderful child actress, only five years of age (if under the term 'stars' I may include so very juvenile a performer), and her aunt, Miss Clara Lindon, who accompanied the little prodigy on her tours, and 'supported' her in her dramatic representations. I was, and to this I chiefly attributed my success, at considerable expense and trouble in getting up horse pieces, such as *Mazeppa*, *Timor the Tartar*, and the *Battle of Waterloo*, in each of which at least four horses were introduced upon the stage at one time. These new productions involved important additions to the properties, scenery, and wardrobe, and these I ungrudgingly made in order to do full justice to the pieces, as well as to sustain the character for thoroughness which 'Old Wild's' had so long enjoyed.

"At a printing office in Manchester, one day, I met with Professor T. P. Hutchinson, one of the brothers Hutchinson, so famous but a few years before for their athletic performances and their classical gymnastic entertainment. The 'Professor' was the elder brother, and

had now, as the Faculty had prognosticated he would if he
persisted in his severer physical tasks, completely lost his
sight; but he was still able to exhibit his 'Studies from
Ancient Portraiture'; and, indeed, poor fellow, he was
obliged to do so, whenever he could obtain an engagement,
for, except the charity of friends, he had now no other
means of a livelihood. Years before, and ere they were
half so famous as they ultimately became, the Brothers
Hutchinson performed at our place on several occasions;
and in the days of their popularity presented me with
a silver cup as a token of—and so forth. The Professor,
in his time, had done much, both at home and abroad, for
gymnastic art and science, had been alike professor,
teacher, and inventor of a new school for athletic and
scientific exercises, and had received first-class diplomas
from gymnasiums and schools of exercise at St. Petersburg,
Vienna, Paris, and Berlin; besides testimonials innumerable
from all the principal theatres, amphitheatres, hippodromes,
and circuses. To behold him now, almost destitute, and
groping, as it were, in the darkness of one eternal night,
was for those who, like myself, had known him when he was
in sound health and in the full tide of prosperity, a sight
not to be forgotten. I offered him, as common humanity
must have prompted any one to do, the relief that was in
my power, and arranged to give him a benefit at the
Victoria Theatre, Blackburn.

" The date fixed was the 16th of April, and for the performance on that occasion he caused to be issued a very
capital placard and address, In the latter, first having
acknowledged the generous support of the public in times
past, and when he was in ' the pride and plenitude of
health,' he appealed for assistance, in that his ' day of dire
misfortune,' and thus concluded :—

Always struggling for the honour and improvement of his art—ever
mindful of his duty to his less successful brethren—assiduously devoting
his time and means to mechanical and scientific pursuits in connection
with the profession he loves : after thirty years of toil, thirty years of
struggle, and thirty years of hope, he finds himself, by a dispensation of
Providence, suddenly shut out from his profession, the world, the excitement of life, and all its pleasures, except the pleasure of believing that
in the hearts of his countrymen he shall find a warm sympathy ; and in
the assistance of his friends a proof that misfortune cannot alienate true
friendship, nor loosen the bonds of fellowship.

" And now I must go back a little.

" Though for some time past I had had no serious reason for complaint on the score of ill luck, I thought it more than possible I could do better.   That is, I believe, not unfrequently a failing with persons who are doing well.

" For many a long year I had never seen such a thing as a travelling amphitheatre, and it occurred to me that to transform my booth into one would be to ensure a financial success, as also to place myself as an entertainer of the people on the topmost rung of the ladder.   The desire to see the performances of trained and educated horses was, like the love of the drama, nothing short of a national characteristic, and to be able to alternate scenes in the circle with the attractions of the stage was, I imagined, to be equal to the production of an entertainment which could be no less than 'a consummation,' perhaps not ' devoutly,' but certainly ' to be wished ' by the pleasure-seeking public ; and that was sure to open up a new and shorter path to fortune for the person who could so provide it.

" Whenever I fell into this way of thinking I generally had a vision of my brother-in-law, Edwin Hughes. In my mind's eye I saw him making his first humble start in life. I followed him, shortly as it seemed, until he became a wealthy circus proprietor, tracing him through brilliant successes down to his retirement.   Then I pictured to myself how nice it would be, as he had done, to retire before one was too old to enjoy life.

" I talked over the matter with my family and friends, and they all concurred in the belief that an amphitheatre, conducted as I proposed, could not fail of success.

" Well, then, this longing daily grew stronger, and I at length settled it in my mind to bring about a metamorphosis of my booth with as little delay as possible.

" The first step towards the realisation of these desires had been the purchase of ' Jenny Lind,' the Lilliputian steed ; but the next and most important one was that of ordering of Messrs. George Griffin & Co., of Birmingham, a three-pole tent, which was, when complete, to cost upwards of £200.

" Then I took a further step while the tent was in course of making, during our season at Keighley, 1859-60. The stud of horses, vans, and other effects belonging to

Harry Brown's circus, which had been tenting all the previous summer, were announced for disposal by auction, at Bradford, under a bill of sale.

" I attended the auction, which was conducted in the tent at the bottom of Vicar Lane, and there purchased three horses, together with a blue and gold dressing and saddle van ; giving somewhere near £100 for the lot.

" ' Jerry,' my favourite horse, 1 had had for years, ' Harry,' ' Jenny Lind,' and ' Railway ' (so-called on account of her speed) had also been in my possession some time. These, with the horses I bought at the sale, now brought up the number to seven. They were on my hands five months or so before I opened the amphitheatre, and their keep during that time was a considerable item of expense.

" I mention these particulars of outlay because, with what follows, they help to account for the ultimate reduction of my bank deposits to *nil*.

" At Bury Spring Fair I purchased more horses ; these I intended for the vans. A three-days' stay was what I intended to make at each town when the glorious amphitheatre times were commenced, and I foresaw the necessity of having van horses of my own.

" As a sort of preparatory training for my daughter Louisa, she and I, during our stay at Blackburn, went regularly every Monday, Wednesday, and Friday, each morning at nine o'clock, to the public park ; my daughter on her manege mare ' Jenny,' one of those bought at the sale, and I on my celebrated horse ' Jerry.' We used to ride about the carriage drives, and over a piece of level ground near the top of the park. The public soon got to know of this, and we had any number of spectators each day afterwards.

" I went over to Manchester about this time and bought a small but splendidly-built open carriage ; and this, afterwards, with ' Jenny Lind ' harnessed to it, my son Charles Henry, in Highland costume as whip, and my daughter Elizabeth and her brother William Edwin, decked out in their best, and the ' observed of all observers,' proved one of the great features of our processions.

" Just before I closed the Blackburn theatre with a view of entering upon a new career, one of the horses, a spotted one which I had but recently bought, died. Here was a loss to me of at least £40, for the animal was a splendid specimen of horseflesh, and had been thoroughly trained to the work of the ring. This it seems the proprietor of Astley's amphitheatre knew, for only a few days before the animal died he applied to me, through Edwin Hughes, to purchase it.

" I had given several members of my company notice that I should be obliged to dispense with their services, and was only waiting now the completion of the tent to enable me to start my amphitheatre business. At length, being apprised by telegram that the tent and fittings were ready for delivery to me, I requested Messrs. Griffin & Co. to forward them to Accrington ; and at the end of April, 1860, taking with me the old stage, a portion only of the scenery and wardrobe (the rest I left in the wooden building until it was finally decided what to do with them), I set out from Blackburn for Accrington to introduce to the public there my new venture.

" The tent was 100 feet long and 80 wide, the awnings and wallings were blue and white striped, and the former supported, as already suggested, by three poles. The middle pole formed the centre of the arena, immediately adjoining which, and at one end of the tent, was the stage; near this was the second pole, while the third was in the centre of the gallery at the other end. The pit and boxes respectively were arranged at the sides of the circle and at right angles with the gallery and stage. The prices of admission were 3d., 6d., and 1s., as usual. The first part of the entertainment consisted of scenes in the circle, including equestrian performances, and my little son, Charles Henry, as General Tom Thumb, in the manege act, on his tiny steed, ' Jenny Lind.' This was one of the most attractive features of the programme. ' Jenny Lind ' was considered equal in point of training to Pablo Fanque's famous mare ' Beda,' and that is saying a good deal, seeing that Pablo was generally considered one of the first horse trainers of his time. Then the dogs were introduced and put through their performances, and a short drama and farce concluded the entertainment. As our stay in town and village was to be so short, we did not trouble to get up more than half-a-dozen pieces ; and in order that all our arrangements should be conducted in a business-like manner, I engaged a person to act as agent in advance; and it was his duty to see that at every place we intended to visit our coming was duly announced by lithographs and posters some days before. Each day my brass band headed a grand procession, and Herr Shenterina appeared outside the tent on the *corde elastique* as a preliminary to the performances within.

"We did remarkably well at Accrington during our three days' stay there, but in all other towns we visited we met with nothing but disappointment and loss.

"At Preston, on Whit-Monday, the weather was very inclement, and my place was blown down immediately after the first performance, and before it could be put up again the night was far advanced. My receipts that day amounted to £4 odd; those that day twelve months past to £70 or more. Pablo Fanque's circus stood in the Orchard near my tent, and the temporary collapse of my establishment caused him to do an unusually good business. He took upwards of £100 that day, though his place was smaller than mine. I saw him the same evening, and while I was lamenting the morning's misfortune as concerning myself, he very drily offered me the consolation, 'It's an ill wind that blows nobody good.'

"Though we remained the entire week at Preston, we did really very little business, so moved in the direction of Wigan, but the repeated stoppages of one of my van horses lost us a whole day in the journey. At Wigan we did next to nothing, and at St. Helen's less than that, on account of the opposition we met with there from Hayes' circus. We then pushed on to Bolton, hoping in that town to meet with better fortune, but all in vain.

"One afternoon, while at Bolton, I was giving my son, Charles Henry, a riding lesson, when a reverend-looking gentleman, in good black cloth and white cravat, made his way into the amphitheatre and inquired for me. I approached him with feelings alike of wonder and respect, and begged to learn his requirements with me. Didn't I know him? was his first inquiry. Of course I readily answered in the negative, for my past dealings with grave-looking gentlemen of his supposed order were not difficult to compute. When, at length, he confessed himself, I had a vivid recollection of him; he had been a servant of ours years ago, and I remembered having had, as manager, occasion once or twice to discharge him for drunkenness. It may therefore easily be supposed that I was not a little puzzled to find him in such good feather, but I was more particularly at a loss to account for the white cravat. By and bye he admitted me into his confidence ; and, would you believe it, that drunken tyke of a servant of mine had actually turned temperance advocate ! After he and I had finally parted on the grounds above stated, he joined Her Majesty's 41st regiment, there attained the rank of corporal, and after receiving his discharge, which was sanctioned by no less a personage than His Royal Highness the Duke of Cambridge, he addressed himself to the work of a lecturer, and espoused the temperance cause. At that time he was carrying the country by storm. 'Corporal ———'s ' name was in everybody's mouth, and his eloquent advocacy of temperance principles was the theme of conversation generally. On the very day he called upon me he was announced by large posters to give an oration that evening in the Temperance Hall, Bolton.

"It is a pity, I think, he did not embrace some other cause where self-denial is not so much a question of principle, for the sequel to all this, and to which I may refer by and bye, is an unfortunate one.

"On the afternoon in question, and shortly after the meeting just alluded to, two persons were seated in a private room of a certain hotel at Bolton. They talked, they laughed, they drank, and their drink in no respect differed from that ordinarily served out at good hotels to their more respectable frequenters. Inasmuch, however, as what they drank was duly paid for, it perhaps, after all, concerns nobody to know who these two persons were. Yet were 'Sam' Wild accused of being one of those parties, he could not, I am afraid, conscientiously deny it, but who his companion was must for ever remain a profound secret.

"To return now to amphitheatre matters. Business at Bolton was bad, worse at Bury, and still worse at Heywood. I determined, at the latter place, that as no money could be made by my new venture I would give all the school children there a treat. But it seemed as if the elements forbad me success even on these terms, for just when the children were all comfortably seated and expressing their unfeigned delight with the performance, a severe thunderstorm came on, and in a terrible state of agitation and fright, my audience, one and all, scampered away.

"At Rochdale we were no better appreciated by the public than we had been elsewhere, and we left there for Oldham, only to meet with still worse misfortune. Through the folly of one of my men, I lost a valuable horse during our journey to that town. Anxious to pass another van on the road, simply for the sake of afterwards boasting he had done so, the driver brought his horse into such violent contact with one of the tent poles as to cause almost instantaneously the animal's death. At Oldham I received the sum of twelve shillings for him dead; at Bury, but a few months before, he had cost me £30. The weather was all against us, too, at Oldham, but I had rent and stabling and salaries to pay, notwithstanding the fact that nothing could be done in the way of giving performances. I was obliged to go over to Leeds and withdraw money from the bank to meet these various demands upon me. The balance at my credit was now, I may say, becoming 'small by degrees and beautifully less.'

"At Huddersfield, my native town, I did expect to receive patronage, but there, too, my hopes were crushed.

"In fact, go where we would with the amphitheatre, we encountered nothing but bad weather, disappointment, and ill-luck. What I had expected everybody would rush to see, nobody seemed to appreciate. The public didn't care for my grand amphitheatre, not they. It wasn't 'Old Wild's.' The combined entertainments by which I had hoped to become suddenly rich reduced me, and almost as speedily, well nigh to poverty. Though I had only had four months of amphitheatre life, I was quite satisfied. Remembering all my serious losses, and in face of more, it was, I thought, high time to clear out; and while at Brighouse Feast, in August, I came to the determination to do this. The tenting business accordingly ended there.

"I sold off my horses at that town; four of them Pablo bought for far less money than I had previously given for one; and two of them, 'Jenny' and 'Jerry,' he sent to Copenhagen to a circus proprietor there, who paid him £70 each for them, while I did not receive from Pablo more than £10.

"After duly crediting myself with the receipts of the sale, I estimated that my total losses by the amphitheatre speculation would not be far short of £1000.

"So abandoning all hopes of suddenly becoming affluent, I rigged out my portable theatre again, and recalled my company ; and at Hunslet, made memorable to all of us by the events of the previous year, we resumed our performances of the legitimate drama, and were glad to hear the booth called ' Old Wild's ' again.

"I may observe that I never saw anything of the Highways Surveyor this time, as for the Chief and Deputy Constables, their offices had been supplied by other persons.

"We issued our most attractive programmes and put forth now, and unmolested, our best efforts. The public soon acknowledged our exertions, and fortune seemed to smile upon us once again.

"The dog ' Tiger,' which, when he was only ten weeks old, I had purchased at Burnley in the winter of 1859, was now beginning to make himself useful on the stage. He was at the starting point of his career, while 'Nelson,' enfeebled by age, was rapidly drawing to the close of his. The carrying of a basket or bundle across the stage was about the extent of ' Tiger's ' capabilities at this time ; but he made as much fuss after this performance as though it had been a success unprecedented in the annals of the stage. As for my old stage favourite, ' Nelson,' he had almost lost his power to perform ; but, judging by the expressive movements of his tail, he took some interest in ' Lion's ' feats, and also in the efforts of his younger companion, ' Tiger.'

"But he began to fail rapidly as autumn advanced, and at length became so feeble as to be scarcely able to move about. A gentleman advised me to make away with the animal, but that, I felt, I could not do. For I had not yet forgotten ' Nelson's ' stage triumphs in years gone by, nor his gallant conduct in saving life. He had been at all times a faithful friend, and, as a performer, had been worth his weight in gold to me. Though now old and infirm he did not appear to have any pain ; and I determined, so long as he did not actually suffer, to let nature have her way with him. When at last, however, he quite lost all use of his limbs, and could take no food of any kind, I knew the chances then would be all against him. Upon a little bed which I made him near the fire, he lay for days as if in slumber, while 'Lion' spent his every spare moment watching him; just as a human being would watch by the bedside of a dying friend. He was thus attended to the day of his death, in his seventeenth year, which occurred on the 3rd of November, 1860.

"The *Era*, in a special notice of his demise, spoke of him as 'a well-known stage favourite who, in his time, played many parts, for which even our greatest histrionic artists would find themselves but incompetent representatives.'

"Though I had two paintings of 'Nelson'—I still possess them—I should have had him preserved, but as on many parts of his body he had lost his hair, had that been done it would have been almost a difficult matter to recognise him. So I decided to give him decent burial.

"Hearing of this, Mrs. Norman, of the Golden Ball, Blackburn, expressed a wish that he should be buried in the yard adjoining her house. This being acceded to, a flag was taken up, a grave made, and 'Nelson's' remains with all due ceremony placed in it. A member of a masons' club which held its meetings at the Golden Ball, volunteered to letter the stone; and, to this day, over the place where still repose the bones of my old stage companion, may be deciphered these characters:—

To the Memory of
NELSON,
The Hero of the Sea and Member of the Royal Humane Society."

CHAPTER XXIII.

THEATRICAL BUSINESS RESUMED—STRAITENED CIRCUM-
STANCES — BLACKBURN — WAKEFIELD — A REVERIE
PAINFULLY DISTURBED—HUDDERSFIELD—T. SWIN-
BOURNE—LORAINE—THE INFANT ROSCIUS—OTHELLO
AND THE CHANTICLEER—MATTERS BEGIN TO CHANGE
FOR THE WORSE— GEORGE OWEN—HOLLOWAY—
ENGAGEMENT OF MR. AND MRS. CHARLES MATTHEWS —
THEIR REFUSAL TO FULFIL IT THE DEATH BLOW TO-
' OLD WILD'S.'

> —Fortune was so low,
> That either it must quickly end,
> Or turn about again and mend.—*Hudibras.*

" A sum of money short of two hundred pounds ; the
booth and the effects belonging to it ; the tent and a few
trifling et ceteras pertaining thereto—these formed almost
the entirety of my possessions when I resumed the
theatrical business in August, 1860.

" For twelve months or so, and while I was enabled to
produce novelties, dramatic, scenic, and otherwise, affairs
with us wore a cheerful aspect. But after that a very
perceptible change began to take place.

" In addition to the fact that ' Old Wild's,' by reason of
its proprietor's narrowed circumstances, was slowly becoming less gorgeous than of yore ; counter attractions were
springing into existence on every hand. With the development of towns was not unfrequently the erection of
buildings as permanent theatres, while concert halls and
singing saloons, as if by common consent, started into
being, and flourished almost everywhere. In nearly every
provincial town a properly organised theatrical company
might be met with, or troupe of equestrians, or it might
be coloured minstrels ; or, perchance, a proprietor of a
panoramic or other exhibition, a concert party, a lecturer,
or a mimic. Then the increasing number of cheap trips, at
fair times and at feasts, militated seriously against us, for

they always managed to take from home a greater number of our old patrons than they ever brought us of new.

"So long, however, as I had means, I struggled in competition, if I may put it so, with all these innovations, but, my funds at length exhausted, what alternative had I save that of yielding to the inevitable? For when a man who has never known want finds himself stared in the face by something closely resembling poverty, it is then the life seems to go out of him.

"Hitherto I had rarely visited town or village twice without having, on the second occasion of my visit, something new wherewith to please my patrons. Imagine then how miserable must have been my condition when I found myself at length unable to indulge in the luxury of a new front, to make any additions to my wardrobe, now becoming dingier every day, or to treat my old supporters to fresh displays of scenic art.

"These shortcomings did not pass unnoticed by our patrons; they had been taught to expect novelty with every advent of 'Old Wild's'; they looked for it still; and were naturally enough disappointed as time after time nothing but the old faded pageantry was presented to them.

"Still the decadence of 'Old Wild's' was gradual.

"Patronage nights we had at first, though they were fewer in number, and perhaps a little less distinguished than of olden time; then we had stars now and again, and benefit nights set apart for charities, aye, even, as I may say, in the midst of want at home.

"But here let us take up our history again.

"After having, under the patronage of Mr. Alderman James Cunningham, ex-Mayor of Blackburn, given a benefit on 5th December, 1860, for the Infirmary, we brought the season to a close in that town, and set forth again upon our peregrinations. We visited several towns in Lancashire and Yorkshire, and finally dropped anchor in autumn, 1861, at Wakefield, where, according to previous arrangement, a place had been prepared for us in the Borough Market.

"I may here observe that meanwhile the dog 'Lion,' which had never done any good as a stage performer since 'Nelson's' death, had unfortunately to be made away with, because of the dangerous symptoms his fretfulness had brought on.

"The only circumstance which I can now call to mind as breaking in upon the routine of our life during the Wakefield season is one touching Williams and myself, in reference to a slight service we performed in a most distressing case.

"I was seated in my van one day musing over the past and laying down plans for the future, when I was suddenly aroused from my cogitations by shrieks, as of some one in pain. Hastening to the door I perceived, rushing along the street in a state of wild consternation, a young woman enveloped in flames. Hatless though I was, and coatless too, I was after the poor woman in a trice, and instantly coming up with her seized her garments with my hands and endeavoured to put out the terrible flames which darted furiously into the air several feet above her. While I was thus engaged, Williams came to the rescue with a rug, and by means of that and a coat or two lent by the spectators, the flames were at length extinguished. I then ran for a cab and brought it to the place where the unfortunate woman, in the utmost agony, still lay ; we lifted her into it and she was taken to the Clayton Hospital. There, however, she died next day. Apart from the painful circumstances preceding her death, her case was one of the most melancholy interest, I remember, from the fact that the following Sunday had been fixed for her marriage.

"The season at Wakefield ended, I opened the Theatre Royal, Ramsden Street, Huddersfield. The building had been formerly occupied as a riding school, but of late years it had been converted into a theatre. Mosley was my immediate predecessor, and under his management many eminent performers had appeared there. This was the last occasion of the place being occupied as a theatre.

"We had not enjoyed a very brilliant season at Wakefield, but I had some hope of success at Huddersfield, and determined I would do my best, in spite of decided financial disabilities to deserve it. I made my best bow to the public, and explained unreservedly what my intentions were with a special view to its entertainment.

In the formation of the company, great care has been exercised in the selection of such talent and experience as must be found efficient in rendering just representations of the works of our best dramatists. New pieces will be produced in rapid succession and from time to time, as opportunity and experience shall dictate. Additions will be made to the corps dramatique in the persons of various stars of celebrity, and in the production of the various novelties which will be presented during the season, every attention will be paid to completeness of detail. S. W., also being a native of Huddersfield, looks with perfect confidence for adequate remuneration and support from those kind patrons who have enabled him to hold the reins of management for so many years, triumphantly and successfully.

"Which things I endeavoured faithfully to carry out. As to stars, I engaged during that season T. Swinbourne, Henry Loraine, the Infant Roscius (Percy Roselle), and several lesser luminaries.

"There was a rather amusing incident on Swinbourne's benefit night. The *piece de resistance* was *Othello*, and Swinbourne, of course, the noble Moor. Suppose I endeavour to recall it?

"It is the last scene. The attention of a sympathising audience is rivetted upon the gentle Desdemona. Not unmoved they hear her declare her guiltlessness, and plead with her husband for her life. They watch, with feelings which it would be difficult to describe, the proceedings of the much abused Othello. They see him agitated, even to the verge of desperation, by the worst suspicions ; they hear ominous expressions escape him, and at length they see him carry out his terrible resolve. For a moment all is silent. Then out of that silence comes a sound, not of pain, not of contrition, neither of remorse as yet, but an ill-timed sound of triumph and of joy. 'Cock-a-doodle-doo.' Yes. 'Twas the voice of the chanticleer. Behind some unused properties in a remote corner of the stage he had found him a domain, and, taking advantage of a pause in the performance, sent forth thrice the shrill proclamation of his sovereignty there.

"An effect so unexpected turned the sadness of our patrons into merriment, and imposed upon Othello the obligation of smothering in turn his own laughter until the audience had sobered down again.

"For some time after that all pathetic scenes were invariably approached with fear ; for, sure as ever the telling point was reached, some mischievous wag would set up a crowing just sufficiently loud to affect the risibilities of actors and audience alike.

"After making our usual round with the booth, with lessening successes at each place we visited, we returned to Huddersfield in December, 1862, and stayed there five months.

" The Riding School having been converted into an Armoury for the Yeomanry Cavalry, I had a wooden place erected by a local timber merchant, and dubbed it ' Wild's New Theatre.' The cost of erection and of the timber amounted to £125 ; but my finances at that time being exceedingly low, it was agreed that I should pay the amount by instalments.

" I did my best, however, to make the place attractive ; produced several new dramas, domestic and sensational ; and, limited though my resources were, I even engaged stars.

" Moreover, I still kept up my annual subscription of £12 to the Dramatic Authors' Society, besides paying certain sums yearly to Mr. E. Stirling, of Drury Lane, and other authors for permission to perform their plays.

" By this time my company had considerably changed, and I am afraid, like ' Old Wild's ' generally, for the worse. Some of the older members had died, others, fitted thereunto by previous training, had accepted higher engagements elsewhere, while less experienced persons, but the best I could then obtain, had supplied their places.

" I have said I engaged stars. Amongst these were George Owen and James Holloway. Then I had a few others of less note. Holloway was styled ' The hero of a hundred nights,' and first appeared on February 9th, 1863, in a new drama, written expressly for him, and entitled *Break o' Morn,* and, afterwards, during his stay, in several Shakspearian characters.

" In his programme announcing the performance of *Richard III.,* on February 13th, allusion was made to the title *rôle* as having been sustained by him with ' unbounded success for upwards of one hundred nights at Astley's Royal Amphitheatre, being patronised by the Queen, Prince Consort, and Royal Family, Duke of Cambridge, Colonel Phipps, the Queen of Oude and Royal Suite ; and for his truthful delineation of which he received a gold medal.' Concerning which gold medal another of his programmes stated that it had been presented to him by William Cooke, Esq., ' as a memento of merit and appreciation of his histrionic powers, he having accomplished what no other actor in the world ever did, viz., performed the arduous character of Richard, the crooked-backed tyrant, for one hundred and four consecutive nights.'

" As all information concerning the Holloways must be interesting to those who have known and patronised ' Old Wild's ' in days gone by, I may add that the *News of the World*, speaking of a then recent performance of *Richard III.* at Astley's, remarked that ' the Richard of Mr. James Holloway, who is very much in the style of Charles Kean, would be by many preferred to that gentleman, as he seems to read his author with a due appreciation of the text, and is by no means deficient in energy.'

" George Owen's first appearance that season was on 16th March, in the Irish drama, *Thackeen Dhu*, but subsequently he appeared in some of his favourite characters, Richelieu, King Lear, &c.   Percy Roselle, also engaged by me during this season, made his *début* in *The Four Mowbrays*; but during his stay sustained, though but a boy, several Shakspearian characters, and appeared also in pieces written specially to display his versatility as a performer.

" When the last of the stars had played out his term, we were then left to our own resources.   I launched into the old broad-sword combats again, brought forward the dog ' Tiger,' now worthy, as a stage performer, to supply the place of ' Nelson,' and produced almost every variety of drama, from Shakspeare downwards; from the ' grand spectacle, displaying all the gorgeous luxury and splendour of the East,' entitled *Sadak and Kalesrade*, to the latest ventures in burlesque and things farcical.

" The *Era* from time to time took note of the doings at ' Wild's New Theatre,' through which source, I suppose it was, that the late Mr. Charles Matthews was induced to enter into negotiations with me for an engagement for himself and his accomplished wife.

" The engagement, though properly arranged as regards terms, fixing of dates, &c. (which letters, still in my possession, show), was for some reason or other never fulfilled, though both Mr. Matthews and his lady came over to Huddersfield on the evening previous to that announced for their appearance at my theatre.

" The complaint which Mr. Matthews made to me next morning, when he came to rehearsal, was that he thought the theatre was a permanent building, whereas it was only a wooden one.   That was true enough, and yet it was, as I submitted to him, the only theatre in Huddersfield then, and was duly licensed according to Act of Parliament.   I will grant this, however, that its proscenium was somewhat faded, because for lack of means I had long been unable to provide a new one.

"But it matters little now what were the reasons—of which you know every whit as much as I—of the non-fulfilment of that engagement. The fact is sufficient for purposes of this narrative.

"Setting down naught in malice, I simply state that the non-appearance at 'Wild's New Theatre,' on the evening of the 5th May, 1863, of Mr. and Mrs. Charles Matthews, after preliminary announcement that they would do so had filled the house to overflowing at doubled prices, was nothing more or less than the death-blow to 'Old Wild's.'

"The audience that night, though receiving back the money paid at the doors for admission, returned from the theatre disappointed. The manager's future efforts to please met with little or no encouragement, and from that time forth the glories of 'Old Wild's' began rapidly to pass away."

CHAPTER XXIV.

A Dreary Waste of Empty Benches — The "Corporal" proves a Draw—Loses his Ambition and Finds a New Field of Labour — Presents to Audience—Last Shifts at Existence—Pressure of Creditors—The Establishment Sold by Auction—A Prisoner for Debt.

Faith, this is more than I bargained for.—*Money.*

"To score any successes in the legitimate drama since the unfortunate fifth of May (1863) appeared to be quite beyond the bounds of possibility. Night after night the curtain rose upon a dreary waste of empty benches, and instead of thundering rounds of applause the only sounds we now heard were the echoes of our own voices, which the wooden walls threw back to us as if in scorn.

"While casting about in my mind for some new attraction, Corporal——— happened one day to present himself to me. 'Here,' I thought, 'is the very man to fill a house.' I immediately opened negotiations with him for his appearance at 'Wild's New Theatre,' and he at length agreed to give his famous and thrilling entertainments, entitled, *The Bottle, or Fifteen Years of a Drunkard's Life,* 'in ten living representations,' and *The Idle and Industrious Apprentices, a story of real life;* 'in eight beautiful groupings.' Each of these entertainments was to be accompanied by a descriptive lecture by the Corporal, and to conclude with a laughable sketch written by himself, and entitled *Intemperance, Moderation, and Sobriety,* while I agreed that my band should play appropriate music during the intervals. The programme issued for the two entertainments was a lengthy one, and besides being enlivened by opinions of the press on the Corporal's eloquence, was rendered still more attractive by the reproduction of testimonials from the presidents of various temperance societies, and by four lines of poetry written

by one of his admirers somewhere down south. To afford
every person an opportunity of hearing the Corporal, the
prices were reduced to 3d., 2d., and 1d. On both evenings
the house was crowded. The man of eloquence was
assisted in his entertainments by about forty young ladies
and gentlemen (members of local temperance societies),
who appeared upon the stage, the act drop and scenery
being brought into requisition for the *tableaux vivants*.
The Corporal himself appeared, as usual, in good black cloth
and unimpeachable tie, and, I may say, preserved his
appearance unsullied and his gravity unshaken to the close
of the lecture. But his corps passed through varied and
rapid phases, some of them advancing from juvenility to a
state of married bliss in a couple of *tableaux*, while others,
at a similar rate of progression, descended from a condition
of tip-top respectability to rags and tatters, and a simu-
lated wallowing in the mire. Eloquently severe was the
Corporal upon these latter—creatures of improvident
habits they and addicted to boozing; but he was exhaust-
less in his praises of the former—happy, rational, industrious beings, who made abstinence their watchword
through life.

"The entertainments being somewhat of a novelty to
me, and as neither my company nor I had to take part in
them, except the band, which gave a few appropriate
staves between the *tableaux*, I sat with the audience on
each occasion. There was no denying the Corporal's
attractiveness. Physically, nature had done much for the
man; but it was in his mental endowments that his
strength lay. His eloquence, sound reasoning, and descriptive capabilities were unquestionable. His ideas were
as original, and indeed sublime, as was his language chaste
and bold. Then his power of rivetting the attention of
his audience was simply marvellous, and his words seemed
to carry conviction to the minds of his hearers. In fine,
he was irresistible. It was a thing to be remembered to
hear him denounce in tones of thunder the drinking
customs of society; and to listen to him as in thrilling
language he enjoined his auditors, one and all, to attach
themselves, without loss of time, to that noble cause
whose claims it was his proud privilege to advocate.

"There can be no doubt that he made many con-
verts on those occasions; but I am afraid that his

co-*beneficiaire* (S. W.), though an attentive listener, did
not number with them. He, it is to be feared, belonged
to that class of beings who are indifferent to all reproof,
and with whom the chances of amendment are small; or
perchance one of those callous mortals he whom the cap
never fits, or hardened sinner who, in spite of all remon-
strance, still continues in the error of his way.

"But are there not extenuating circumstances in the
case of the stroller? Does not his wandering life throw
him (as travelling of a higher sort not unfrequently brings
its votaries) very much in the way of hotels and inns and
innkeepers? The inn is the rallying place of his wandering
brethren; he transacts his business, sees his friends, and
ofttimes concludes his professional engagements there.
Taking, therefore, all these things into consideration, there
is little surprising in the fact that as the years rolled by
the subject of this narrative became acquainted, almost in
spite of myself, with many mine hosts in his travels. It
may easily be supposed, too, that he knew, from long
experience, at what particular house in each town and
village the landlord was the jolliest, the company the
merriest, and the creature comforts the most toothsome.
And when, in his native town, a certain inn became famous
for a very superior quality of 'Old Tom,' it was almost in
the nature of things that the stroller should either find it
out or be introduced to it by one or other of his friends.

"It was only some two or three nights after the Corporal's last rousing lecture that the proprietor of 'Wild's
New Theatre,' forgetful of all that the man of eloquence
had said, was induced to enter that certain inn and to
ascertain, as a matter of curiosity, or for the private information of friends, if the before mentioned 'Old Tom' was
still as meritorious as of yore.

"Among the many who were eager to recognise the
stroller was a man with a flowing black beard. He was
rendered chiefly conspicuous by a dyer's blue smock which
he had on, and the won't-go-home-till morning condition
he was in. He wore a cap which was redolent of the mill
grease wherewith it shone, and trousers which careful
research might perhaps have proved to have been respectable once upon a time. His face, like his general appearance, was cloudy. Approaching the stroller with extended
hand he was anxious to know if 'Mish'r Wild' knew him.

To the best of his recollection 'Mish'r Wild' had never seen the party before.

"The blue smock whispered in the stroller's ear.

"' Nay, surely, can't be!' exclaimed the recipient of this confidential communication, at the same time starting back in amazement.

"' 'Sh no'b'dy elshe' rejoined the smock, with what was intended to be an air of dignity.

"And upon the stroller scrutinising the features of the man more closely, he found, sure enough, that he was—would you believe it?—none other than—the individual he had represented himself to be.

"But whence and why that transformation? That was perhaps only to be explained in the fact that genius is whimsical. This person, one of the favoured in that endowment, had it seemed at length, and for reasons best known to himself, scorned the respectable apparel to which of late years he had been accustomed, and had effected an exchange of his silk hat, surtout, unimpeachable—that is, other valuable articles of wear, for the homely garb of a practical dyer. This attire, together with a speedy consumption, through the medium of malt liquor, of the few shillings which the successor to his black cloth had given him 'to boot,' had brought about such a complete change in the appearance of the man, that though the stroller had seen him, been with him, in fact, but two or three nights previously (under widely different circumstances, however—let not that credit be denied them), he might have passed the man a hundred times had he not made himself known.

"After the Corporal's entertainments, the drama was then my only resource, and unpromising though things were, I fell back upon it. But by way of increasing the attractions I gave away a silver cup and made other presents; and, anon, introduced Sergeant Beaumont and the '*élite* of the Huddersfield fancy,' to display the manly arts. These were some of my shifts at existence in my native town.

"As a consequence of the exceedingly miserable business I had been doing for some time, I was unable to keep up the payment of the instalments due from me for the New Theatre. Pressure was put upon me for the money, and to pacify my creditors, the builders, I gave them a bill of sale upon the timber; under which bill of sale, I may observe, it was sold, and the theatre pulled down the moment I left Huddersfield for Elland with my portable booth.   The builders gave me credit, however, for the amount realised by the sale of the timber, but after so doing, I was still a debtor to them to the amount of £54.

" I remained at Elland until Halifax fair was over, for I hadn't somehow the pluck in the then faded condition of things at ' Old Wild's ' to show myself in a town where I had hitherto been able to put on a good appearance. I went to Wakefield summer fair, however, but just as I was about to leave that town for Knottingley I was served with a writ at the suit of the Huddersfield builders. To satisfy the demands of the writ within the limited time was quite out of my power, for I had just drawn all the money I had, £8 12s. 8d., out of the Skyrack and Morley Savings Bank. I consulted with my friends, and they advised me to sell the establishment as it stood, and the wardrobe and vans belonging to it. Therefore, in lieu of the customary programme on the side of the theatre, appeared one morning, while we were at Knottingley, the announcement that ' the whole of Wild's Theatrical Establishment, with vans, scenery, dresses, and other effects,' would be sold by auction in the theatre on a certain date.

" From thirty to forty persons attended the sale, and the whole of the portable property constituting ' Old Wild's ' was knocked down to Mr. James Hodskinson, of Blackburn, for £70 or £80. My company, self, wife, and family were still kept on to continue the theatrical business, but Hodskinson's name was put on the vans, and the outer proscenium was altered and read as follows :—' James Hodskinson, late Wild's.' His name also appeared at the foot of the programmes and posters as sole proprietor, but the booth was styled therein ' Wild's National Theatre '; for my friends, of whom Mr. Hodskinson was chief, would have me consider myself still owner of the place, as pecuniarily I had not been benefited by the sale.

" On the Monday following the sale old Joseph Thornton, of Huddersfield, sheriff's officer, and his son, accompanied by a bailiff, came over to Knottingley to levy an execution. Imagine their surprise at finding the aspect of things changed all of a sudden. But before showing themselves to me they inquired of the printer concerning the change, and who had ordered the bills; they also questioned the landlord of the hotel opposite the theatre; then various members of the company; then my daughter Louisa; and finally they came to me. I explained to them how matters stood, and they then saw at once that their journey was in vain.

"Leaving Knottingley we went to Hunslet. As Calver the marionette man had forestalled us at Penny Hill, we took up a position opposite the Exchange Hotel. There we blocked up an entire street with the booth; and the buses from Leeds had to run 150 yards round in consequence; but never a word of complaint did we hear from any source.

"Following our usual course we appeared next at Armley, thence we went to Holbeck, and subsequently to Keighley; producing novelties notwithstanding dwindling patronage, and giving presents frequently as an additional draw. At Keighley, keeping pace a little with the higher theatrical world, we produced *Colleen Bawn*, with the water cave scene and other effects; also *Lady Audley's Secret*, and many other plays popular at that time. Each of us, including Herr Shenterina, who was still with us, taxed his and her utmost energies to amuse, but things were so bad in November that we had to dispense with the boxes altogether. We had plenty to do to fill—in fact we never did fill—pit and gallery at the nominal charges of 6d. and 3d.

"On the 10th December the tilt blew off, and was torn into ribbons. This was very unfortunate, especially as we were going to do a little extra next day and introduce the splendid 'court dresses of Louis Philippe' in the play of *The Mountebank*.

"While at breakfast next morning a messenger came to the van to say that I was wanted at the Queen's Hotel. I immediately went and found Mr. Thornton, junior, from Huddersfield waiting for me. He shook hands and invited me to something at his expense; for we had always been on friendly terms when we met at Huddersfield. Taking me into a private room he produced an account for £54, the balance due from me for the Huddersfield theatre, and asked me if I was in a position to pay it. I assured him that in my then straitened circumstances such a thing was quite out of the question.

"'I am sorry to hear that, Mr. Wild.'

"'No doubt.'

"'And particularly so as I have been specially sent over to-day to demand payment.'

"'But how if I cannot meet your demands?'

"'There is but one alternative.'

"'And what is that?'

"'As my prisoner,' said he, 'you must go with me.

"'Where?' I inquired.

"'To York.'

"'When?'

"'To-day. At once.'"

CHAPTER XXV.

Life in a Debtors' Prison—Christmas Day in York Castle—Released—A Fresh Start in Business—The New Company—Shipley—Bradford—"Old Wild's" still held in Esteem — Shakspeare's Tercentenary—A Tempting Offer for the Dog "Tiger"—A Conflagration—The Ancient Order of Foresters—Penniless!

> O give me thy hand,
> One writ with me in sour misfortune's book.—*Romeo and Juliet.*

"Knowing that the young man was simply acting in accordance with instructions he had received, I did not long parley with him, but mentally prepared myself for the alternative. Asking him to excuse me until I went to furbish my appearance a little and leave a few necessary instructions with Mrs. 'Sam,' I retraced my steps vanwards. At the door of our little residence (town and country both) my wife was stood looking for me. As I approached, her first questions, asked in a tone no less of sadness than surprise, were, ' What is the matter now, pray, and what do those policemen want?' Quickly turning round, I was somewhat perplexed to find two gentlemen in a well-known livery standing but a short distance from the van and looking very anxiously after me. It instantly occurred to me that this was a precautionary measure on the part of Thornton, junior, and I didn't like it. It looked as though, having pledged my word that I should return, my promise couldn't be relied on. When I told my wife all that had recently taken place at the hotel, and whither I was now bound, she instantly burst into tears. Cheerless as our prospects had been for some time past, every ray of hope seemed instantly to vanish now that her husband was to be taken from her and sent to a debtors' jail. What was to become of her and her family (four members of it too young then to engage in any sort of employment), and how were they to exist? Even in the

hard times upon which 'Old Wild's' had fallen, her husband's name had sometimes helped to draw a house; but
now, as far as she could see, the programmes and posters
were to know it no more. Truly the outlook was dismal.
There had been times of trial before this, but the passage
through them had only left us worse prepared in every
respect for those which were to follow. Sacrifices of every
kind had been made to enable us to meet our engagements
and to procure the necessaries of life. Amongst the
earlier ones was that of jewellery. My wife's gold watch
and guard, which cost me twenty-one guineas, my own
watch, several guards, and five valuable rings (one of them
presented to me at Penrith, in 1849, by Lady Mallet), were
all disposed of to meet demands which could not be put
off. Then 'Jenny Lind,' the Lilliputian steed, had to be
given up by way of satisfaction of the amount which was
due from me for her keep, and in short, in one way or
another, our sacrifices and concessions became as frequent
(while the means lasted) as was rapid the march of poverty
upon us. Our condition at this time may well be imagined
when I state that the united funds of myself and wife
did not amount to half-a-crown, and negotiations were,
unknown to me, opened by my wife with Old Smith for
a loan of five shillings to help me to provide against any
little emergency during my journey to York.

"When, after a hasty leave-taking of my wife, I got
back to the Queen's Hotel, Mr. Thornton, senior, came in,
shook hands, and offered me the usual pledge of good fellowship. At length, all of us leaving the hotel, he accompanied his son and myself to Leeds. Arrived there, he would
insist upon me having some refreshment at his expense, as
the train to York was an hour and a-half short of being
due. He chatted about old times, and about my father,
whom he said he had known well, and by and bye, coming
to the circumstances of my arrest, he expressed regret that
so unpleasant a duty had fallen to the lot of himself and
his son to discharge. As the time for our departure to York
drew nigh, he took me aside. If I would promise him, he
observed, that I would accompany his son to York without
offering any resistance, he, Thornton, senior, would go
back to Huddersfield. I stared at the old gentleman
surprisedly as I delivered my reply. 'To offer resistance
under such circumstances would, I imagine, only be to

make bad worse. But, by the way, as I went to change my attire at the van, before leaving Huddersfield, I was very much annoyed to find two policemen at my heels.' 'Well,' rejoined the old gentleman, 'I must admit that that was my doing.' 'And with what object, pray?' 'You see,' put in the sheriff's officer, confidentially, 'I know you to be a smart fellow in all the manly arts, and it was our duty to be provided in case you should have felt disposed to make resistance.'

"When Thornton, the younger, and I arrived at York (for his father, satisfied by my assurance, had returned to Huddersfield), he determined that he would not deliver me at the Castle until the very latest moment; so we spent a few hours together, and parted on the best of terms. Being formally handed over, together with certain documents having relation to myself, to a Mr. Pashley, I was put into a room (No. 8) in the second-class prison, to which three other debtors, occupants thereof, gave me a hearty welcome. The room was not a very large one for four of us, but the folding bedsteads, square table, couple of chairs, and form which it contained gave it a furnished sort of appearance, while the barrenness of its walls had been relieved by a plentiful application of yellow-wash. I soon found that there was naught to complain of as to rations. We had each of us 10lb. of potatoes per week, 4lb. of oatmeal, 5lb. of beef, and ½lb. of cheese, and about every third or fourth day we received each a supply of new bread. Tea, coffee, sugar, and butter were forbidden articles in the second-class prison. We had to find our own candles, basins, plates, knives, forks, and spoons; but the prison allowance extended to that important item, coal, and we were never without a cheerful fire. There was an oven in the room, and we took it in turns to act as cook, as also to make the beds and sweep the floor. Once each day, and twice every Sunday, we attended service at chapel. I took the first opportunity to write to my wife, telling her of my prison life, and what was allowed and what was denied us, and also requesting her to send me my violin as soon as she could. A canvas bag, in appearance very much like a good-sized ham, was handed to me a few days afterwards by Mr. Pashley. It was his duty to inquire what was in it, and I readily informed him. I did not open the parcel just then, but laid it on my bed, as my

fellow debtors and I were engaged in conversation. After
the lapse of half-an-hour, Mr. Pashley came again. He
saw the parcel was still unopened, and said he was afraid
there was something more than a violin in it, and that,
sorry as he was to say so, it was his duty to be satisfied on
that score. Upon the package being opened in his
presence, I was more surprised than he was to find, along
with my old friend the violin, a jar of butter, sundry
parcels of tea, coffee, sugar, and, in fact, of all the forbidden articles. When Mr. Pashley took these things
away, I quite believe he experienced as much regret at
depriving me of them as I did in losing them, but his duty
fully exonerated him in my opinion. My fellow debtors
remarked that I had had time to put the articles out of
sight had I opened the parcel when I first received it, and
I wondered afterwards if the man's better nature had
for once gained the ascendant over his sense of duty,
and had so tempted him to give me an opportunity
to remove all grounds for suspicion before his second
visit. He told me as he was leaving me with the
little packages in his possession that if any of my
family or friends came to see me they could take
the articles away with them, and again excused himself on the plea of duty. The governor of the prison came
nearly every day to see us, and to ask if we had any com-
plaints to make, but I think we never had. Our food was
wholesome, and we had plenty of it, and everbody about us
seemed kind within the limits of duty. We, debtors in No.
8 room, were allowed to come out into the corridor
into which the doors of the other rooms opened, and I
frequently wandered up and down it with my fiddle, playing and singing snatches of ditties which carried me back
in imagination to the days of 'Auld Lang Syne.' And it
may be that my music had a touch of melancholy in it, and
so awakened the sympathies of the debtors of a higher
degree. For the moment the strains of my violin first
began to resound through the prison, those debtors—the
corridor to whose apartments communicated by a door
with that leading to our own—crowded about that same
door, and answered me by other strains ; and when, at
times, I broke into singing, they took up the refrain of
my song right cordially. Though I was unable to see
these debtors, or they me, our mutual sympathies were

thus drawn out, and when, by the kind permission of the governor, I was very shortly afterwards admitted to their society, we seemed to meet almost upon the footing of old friends. Amongst them were men of decidedly musical pretensions; the cornet, the flute, and other minor instruments were ably represented, while many of the non-instrumentalists had very capital voices.

" Christmas drawing nigh, this little constellation of musical talent, at the request of the governor, and with a view to the delectation of the good lady his wife, and her friends' anon, practised hymns and spiritual songs; awaking the slumbering echoes of the prison with its harmonies as a sort of experiment, preliminary to the awakening of Christians by and bye.

" The first-class debtors, whose restrictions were fewer and who were denied nothing their friends liked to send them, ' fared sumptuously every day '; and on each occasion of my visit treated me to the best of everything. In fact, we got along so capitally well together that they offered amongst themselves to defray all expenses if I would only go and take up my abode with them during my stay. But I had become very much attached to my second-class friends—many a long yarn did we spin together, seated about the fire—and I didn't care to leave them.

" Late on Christmas Eve the debtor harmonists were led out into the Castle yard and placed beneath the window of the room in which the Governor and his lady were entertaining friends and looking for the ' happy morn.' There, in the silence of that clear starlit night, the little band poured forth its melody to them, who, nothing loth to be thus disturbed, threw up the window and listened with manifest delight.

" As a consequence of my having taken part in this carolling and serenading, there were sent to room No. 8 on Christmas Day, and as a present from the Governor's good lady, a roast leg of mutton, plum pudding, with sauce (old style), and a liberal allowance of beer. To these things my fellow-debtors and I did ample justice; music and mirth followed, and, taking all things into consideration, Christmas Day in York Castle was not such a dreary affair after all.

" To return now to theatrical matters.

" For two days after my incarceration at York no per-

formances could be given at the booth because of repairs
being required ; and for a week after these had been made
little or no encouragement was given to the efforts of
' Wild's ' company.

" The members no longer received fixed salaries, but
were paid each a share of the profits, but as these on some
days came to *nil*, it was quite natural that the members
should be dissatisfied with their respective proportions.
Under such circumstances I was not at all surprised to
receive letters at my castellated residence from one and
another of my *corps dramatique*, stating their regretful
necessity of quitting my service. When they had all,
except my own family, forsaken the old place, the booth
was pulled down and put upon vans, while the scenery and
wardrobe were deposited, for better security, in an empty
room which my wife had engaged. My son Tom, then
recently married, took his wife with him to Huddersfield ;
his sister Louisa accompanied them, also the dog ' Tiger,'
and together they gave entertainments for a time in the
Gymnasium Rooms in that town. My wife, and the
younger branches of my family, Mrs. Hughes took under
her care ; but for her kindness I cannot see how they
possibly could have escaped the workhouse, as my elder
children had sufficient to do to keep themselves.

" I remained in York Castle about a month or five
weeks, and when Mrs. Hughes heard that I was coming
out, she sent me money to enable me to rejoin my family.

" As my company had dispersed and I had no present
means of resuming the old business, I accepted an engagement for myself, wife, and ' Tiger ' (for which I sent to
Huddersfield), and we all appeared for six nights, commencing 26th January, 1864, at Henry Pickles's Theatre,
Burnley. Joseph Holloway, lessee of the Royal Lyceum
Theatre, Blackburn, also gave us an engagement for six
nights, and we afterwards performed the same number of
evenings at the Theatre Royal, Rochdale, and at Hayes'
Circus, Preston.

" Mr. Hughes strongly urged me to try my fortunes
again, and asked me what amount I thought would start
me. I told him £20, and he readily lent me that sum.
My first care was to get a company together, which I may
say I had not much difficulty in doing. I next had my
vans, &c., removed from Keighley to Shipley, and in that

village opened my establishment at the old prices of 1s., 6d., and 3d. My new company consisted of Mr. and Mrs. Frank Brookfield, Mr. and Mrs. Morgan, Mr. and Mrs. Bell, Mr. and Mrs. Melville (these latter are identical with Mr. and Mrs. Fred. Wright, now travelling with the *Quarter of a Million of Money* company), Mr. and Mrs. Simpson, Messieurs Simmonds, Smith, W. A. Worrall (Mrs. 'Sam's' brother), Harcourt, Johnson, Ingham, Cartwright, Russell; the Misses L. Wild, James, Harcourt; adding thereto sundry supers, your servant, S. Wild, and his then consort Louisa, and, lastly, 'The Dog of Ten Thousand.'

"I may state, parenthetically, that I was still under the protection of the Court of Bankruptcy, and so remained until the 14th May, 1864, when I received, to the tune of £7 odd, my formal discharge.

"The weather was all against us during the Shipley season, and the field in which the booth stood was one pool of water most of the time. As soon as I saw a favourable opportunity I removed to Bradford, where, on April 22nd, I opened my 'Colossal Establishment.' The land, in Vicar Lane, upon which it stood, belonged to the late Rev. John Burnet. He consented to the ground being let to me, but had previously refused to let it to other travelling companies.

"Anent this instance of regard for the old place on the part of the Vicar of Bradford, I may mention the previous kindness of the Reverend Mr. Kendall, of Holbeck. He was asked by one of his parishioners to sign a petition to exclude 'Old Wild's' from the feast or to limit its stay (as also the duration of the feast itself) to three days. He declined to do this. Wild's booth, he argued, had been in the habit of regularly attending Holbeck Feast ever since he had succeeded to the curacy of St Matthew's Church, in that township, and, as he understood, for many, many years before, and he should not do aught to curtail the feast or the stay of 'Old Wild's,' or to prevent the strollers coming as heretofore.

"And a similar feeling of regard for the old establishment was continually being expressed down to the very last days of its existence.

"I recently came upon a letter received by me in May, 1864, from the Chief Constable of Armley. It is in answer to my application to him to reserve me our old ground as usual for the feast. Its cordial strain tends to corroborate to a certain extent what I have just stated. Here are a couple of extracts from it : —

I assure you that so long as I have the management, no new comer will have your ground, if you only apply in time, as you have done heretofore.

I hope you are doing well, and that your establishment may be prosperous, so that you will be able to furnish the public with good talent at a cheap rate, and develop more fully the legitimate aims of the drama, which, in my opinion, the increased intelligence of the working classes requires.

" Notwithstanding its decadence, the causes of which have already been assigned, 'Old Wild's' seemed to be held in general respect; doubtless because of what it had been, and maybe because of the associations which, in the minds of most adults, still clung to it.

" On April 23rd, the tercentenary of the birth of the Swan of Avon, and the second night of our opening in Bradford, we treated our patrons to things Shakspearian, and, if I mistake not, we were the only company of theatricals in the town at that time to do honour to the memory of the Immortal Bard.

" For some weeks we achieved very fair successes, and I did not fail to show my appreciation of these almost (as things had been of late) unexpected public favours. I produced novelties whenever I thought the stock pieces had lost their interest, and introduced the dog 'Tiger' frequently. Of his performances the public never seemed to tire, for no one could deny that he was in appearance a splendid animal, and as a stage performer then unrivalled. At this time he was almost at his best in every respect. His astounding feats never failed to bring down the house; and off as well as on the stage, he soon became an established favourite.

" One day, after rehearsal, I took him with me to the Junction Inn. There I met with a German merchant who, the moment he saw the dog, began to make a great fuss of him. The merchant and I fell into conversation about the animal. He had seen 'Tiger' perform, and should like very much to possess him. What would I take for him? Oh, I couldn't state a price. In fact I couldn't think of parting with him. The merchant took out a pocket-book, and counting down £100 in bank notes, offered me that sum for the animal, but tempting though the offer looked, I, nevertheless, refused it.

"In the afternoon of June 1st, while still at Bradford, Mr. Hope, our band master and scenic artist, was engaged in the booth upon a new scene. Though the day was intensely hot, his work obliged him to use a fire. While he was in the midst of his labour one of my company came in. After chatting a while, he lighted his pipe, and threw the scrap of paper he had used into the fire; the heat carried it up still blazing to the tilt, which, dry as tinder, immediately caught, and in a moment the place was in flames. Some masons who were working near the booth ran with buckets of water and rendered what service they could, while those of my company who were about, cut away the tilt so as to prevent the flames spreading to the stage and scenery. Several German merchants came out of their warehouses, and espying the residentiary van close to the front of the burning building, ran towards it, and laying hold of the shafts soon placed it far beyond reach of the flames. By and bye two fire engines appeared upon the scene and the conflagration was soon put out. The tilt and its supports, the curtain and a new act drop, painted by Mr. Hope, were entirely destroyed. Then there was a delay of four days, and no small expense in making necessary reparations, so that altogether my losses could not come far short of £50 or £60. Yet serious though these losses were in my then narrowest circumstances, I determined not to give way to despair, but started business again at the first opportunity. By and bye I gave presents, cups, timepieces, and the like, and even in the midst of hard struggle, I threw open my establishment, on June 16th, and gave my own and my company's services on behalf of the workpeople then suffering from a ' lock out ' at the Bowling Iron Works.

"In anticipation of the last night of the season, June 20th (and which, being the occasion of my benefit, I intended to signalise in some way or other), I solicited the patronage, for that evening, of the Brethren of the High Court of the Ancient Order of Foresters. But that court would not, either through its High Chief Ranger, High Sub - Chief Ranger, Senior Beadle, Junior Beadle, Treasurer, or Secretary, condescend to be represented at my booth, nor would it consent to lend its name as

patrons merely for programme purposes.   And this, notwithstanding the fact that I was a brother Forester, and
had been ever since the 20th day of February, 1844;
paying my subscriptions regularly, and declining in all
cases of sickness to throw myself upon the funds of the
Court.

   " When, at the close of the season at Bradford, I had
paid all dues and demands, I found myself penniless, and
it is extremely doubtful whether I should have appeared
at Halifax fair (soon after this) had not Mr. Joseph
Bentley, a bill-poster at Bradford, lent me £4 to help me
on the way."

CHAPTER XXVI.

A beggarly account of empty boxes.—Romeo and Juliet.

" The short season at Halifax, June-July, 1864, was a fairly successful one. I was enabled to repay the Bradford bill-poster the amount he had so kindly lent me, as also to purchase a horse for my band carriage. But my theatrical resources being still limited, I made the most of this last investment. I trained the animal, dubbed him ' Garibaldi,' and introduced him upon the stage to give a little variety to the performances.

" We made but short stays at Dewsbury, Hunslet, and Holbeck, after leaving Halifax, but going back to Dewsbury on October 3rd, we commenced a season there which lasted four months. Not that on this, our return visit to Dewsbury, the fates were more propitious than of late, but rather because the cost of removal thence was a terrifying item which I was not prepared to meet, and because, too, I had not much hope of doing any better elsewhere. It was this uncertainty of success with myself and company which made us, adapting the language of Hamlet for the occasion, rather bear the ills we had, than fly to others that we knew not of.

" We opened at Dewsbury at our old prices of 3d., 6d., and 1s., but before the season was half over we came down to 3d. and 6d. only ; and on some occasions two persons were admitted for one charge, which was, of course, equivalent to reducing the reduced price one-half.

But I determined to do my best under all circumstances, and being ever an advocate for novelty, studied to produce it still. As I had no means of providing new scenery, I had the old re-touched ; and when I thought it time for the production of a new piece, and found myself unable to go to the cost of one, I altered the title of some old drama, and so made the programme a little more attractive, though the audience not unfrequently remarked the strong resemblance of the new play to one they had seen before at ' Old Wild's.' Sometimes, through the medium of the programme, I was compelled to boast of an ' unprecedented success ' when, truth to tell, my company and myself were ' doing a starve.' As we are now approaching the time when ' Old Wild's ' ceased to be, I will give a few instances, in chronological order, of some of our efforts at this period in the direction of novelty, and in the way of programme making.

" October 10. ' Immense success of the New Company. First night of the Sensation Drama, *Peep o' Day*, written expressly for Mr. S. Wild. The whole of the scenery painted by Messrs. Heath & Woodford.' Yes, some time before. Four days later, ' First appearance of Mr. J. Wright as Claude Melnotte. Grand Fashionable Night.' A word about this young tragedian. Though unquestionably clever, his status was somewhat prejudiced by the fact that he couldn't read a line ; his parts had always to be read to him. Yet his memory was so excellent that he rarely required a part reading more than twice, no matter how long it might be, to enable him to sustain the character. Very extraordinary, but a fact nevertheless. On the 21st October a Grand Contest of Amateurs for a New Cornet. This contest had been announced many days before as going to be, for having spent three guineas in the purchase of the instrument, I felt myself bound to make the most of it. 28th, Selections of Music by the Band of the Dewsbury Rifle Volunteers in full uniform ; a kind and spontaneous effort on the part of that band to help me to draw a good house. Next evening, 29th (there is but one step, they say, from the sublime to the ridiculous), ' Dancing match for a pair of new clogs.' November 1st, ' Grand amateur performance by the gentlemen of Dewsbury of the nautical drama of *The Lost Ship*.' 14th, ' The greatest night of the season (half-prices notwithstanding) and engagement of Mr. Lionel Clare (vulgo Jack Johnson) for this night only'; also first appearance of Mr. R. F. Senior, native of Dewsbury, who had a passion for things theatrical, and who ultimately turned local preacher and declaimed against them. 18th, 'The great spectacle of the *Jewess*, with real horses'—the last in very large type, and represented in the evening by my horse 'Garibaldi' and a nag which I had hired in order to make the number plural. Also thirty supernumeraries – culled from enthusiastic young gentlemen who were perpetually hanging about the establishment, and whose ambition to appear on the stage was gratified for the nonce, their services being their own reward. Also 'gorgeous new dresses and new scenery'—slightly fallacious, I must confess, but, perhaps, excusable from long habit. November 25th, 'First night in England of the sensational drama *Ben Liel, the Son of Night*, with combats and explosions,' reduced terms of admission nevertheless. 28th, 'Great French drama, *Janet Pride*, with great sensation snow scene by gaslight'—paper lamps in flaring perspective down the stage, and fragmentary white paper distributed with liberal hand by two members of the company perched in the flies, whose lavishness having been duly provided for they were not reduced to the necessity of snowing another colour—I am thinking now of the story of the theatrical manager who, when informed in the very best part of a snow scene that all the white paper had been exhausted, hastily turned upon his informant and replied, 'Then, damn it, snow brown!' December 9th, Mr. R. F. Senior, the aforesaid native, as The Stranger. 12th, Messrs. Frank Newman, from the Royal Amphitheatre, Liverpool, and George Nelson, from the Theatre Royal, Leeds. 16th, Mr. Senior again, this time as Hawkshaw in the *Ticket-of-Leave Man*, and he was *par excellence* the best Hawkshaw that ever appeared on our stage. December 19th to 24th, Mr. James Holloway as Macbeth, Othello, Quasimodo, Rolla, Mazeppa, and also in his famous impersonation, Richard III. Still at reduced prices, though we went into five-inch type in the programmes on Holloway's account. 26th, *Christmas in the Olden Times*, by my own company, who, for reasons which hardly require explanation, were infinitely jollier in representing the Christmas revels of a hundred years ago than they had been in spending their own

Christmas the day before. To be in season as far as possible, the play was followed by that time-honoured institution, pantomime, with 'new scenery, new tricks, dances,' and all the rest of it. Sometimes between the various attractions above detailed 'Tiger' appeared, sometimes 'Garibaldi,' and, on some occasions, both. Mrs. 'Sam' supported all the stars. She still made up well as Pauline, and always bore off the honours in that character. Sometimes, when we had no stars she appeared in pieces of the *Valsha* class, and in which the interest of the drama was entirely sustained by her through three long acts.

"We began the New Year, 1865, with *Manrico*, a drama founded on the opera of *Il Trovatore*, with Mr. and Mrs. Frank Brookfield as the principal exponents of the piece. Then we had from time to time during the remainder of the Dewsbury season, miscellaneous concerts, coloured opera troupes, and amateurs of all kinds—we were glad to catch at anything. We were still down at half prices, and so remained to the end of the season, except when on certain occasions we halved them, in the absence of any special attractions. Sometimes we gave presents, legs of mutton, tea trays, and the like; indeed, we left nothing untried, so far as means permitted, to attract audiences.

"Soon after the close of the Dewsbury season (on February 7th) we tried our fortune at Cleckheaton for a week or so, but the weather being all against us, we took off the tilt, leaving the framework standing, and went to Brighouse. There we performed to threepenny and sixpenny audiences in an auction room in the Black Swan Hotel, to which place we had brought our scenery and a couple of galleries. The room, however, was so small that we didn't do more than just exist there, though we always put the best face on matters. Our cry was still 'a genuine success,' for that nothing succeeds like it nobody knows better than the theatrical performer. We varied the entertainments a good deal, fluctuating, according to popular demand, between the sublime, as represented by *Macbeth*, and the ridiculous, as embodied in the screaming farce of *Make Your Wills*.

"Next we had a three-weeks' stay at Heckmondwike, to the green in which village the booth was brought over from Cleckheaton. Mr. and Mrs. Brookfield in Shakspearian dramas, myself and 'Tiger' in plays nautical, were our particular attractions here.

"I saw that the old establishment was gradually dwindling down, in spite of all my efforts to uphold the honours of the drama, and I became low spirited in consequence. Some months before our opening at Heckmondwike I had appointed my son Tom acting and stage manager, and on the 1st of March he and I signed an agreement whereby I consented to lend him, and he to hire from me, the theatre and wardrobe (he keeping the same in decent order), for £1 per week. He also engaged to pay salaries to myself and to each of my family when we performed at the theatre. He had three months of sole management had Tom, but he found he couldn't do any better than his old father, so he threw up the reins of government. My family and I regularly received our salaries as they became due, but instead of the £14 standing to my credit for hire of the place, I received somewhere about ten shillings. Yet I couldn't blame my son; he had done his best, and couldn't pay when he didn't receive.

"About the middle of May we went again to Brighouse, but this time with the booth, which was erected on a piece of ground behind the Anchor Inn. The season there was marked alike by disappointment and loss. One evening during the first week the booth was blown completely down soon after the performance, and it took us a week to put things to rights again, as nearly all the timbers were broken. I recollect very well the first night of the re-opening; the lights were burning outside, and the band playing as usual, but not a solitary individual presented himself for admission. Pablo Fanque came to the town during our stay there, and, hearing of our ill-luck, sent us two shillings, which I looked upon as a very handsome present, seeing that Pablo's Circus, like 'Old Wild's' show, was gradually losing its popularity.

"In June we had a few days at Shelf, but things were only so-so with us there. I was determined, however, to draw if possible, to which end I resorted to various experiments—to wit: a day performance on the 17th of the month of *Uncle Tom's Cabin*, with 'Tiger,' or the 'Dog of the Prairie,' for the school-children, who were admitted at one penny each. For the same evening I had prepared great attractions for the adults. These consisted of a smoking match for a quarter of a-pound of tobacco, and an amusing exhibition of four boys eating (or rather attempting with laudable perseverance to eat) hot rolls and treacle for a wager. When an entertainer of the people has to struggle for existence, it compels him to study the popular taste, and he must cater to it also if he means to live.

"Towards the latter end of June, I opened my 'Colossal Establishment' in Cadney's Croft, Halifax. The lease of my former ground in the Market Place had expired in 1864, and I having overlooked the fact, and so neglected to make application for the stand, it was let to Stephens, a proprietor of a collection of wild beasts. Learning this as I was coming to Halifax, I applied to the Markets Inspector for a position in the fair ground, but found that the places were all occupied. Being short of funds wherewith to hire horses to transport 'Old Wild's' elsewhere, I set down my booth in Cadney's Croft; but notices having been issued by the Town Clerk requiring all shows, &c., to stand upon Corporation ground, and there only, my new quarters were objected to. Summoned to meet the Markets Committee, I attended at the Town Hall, and explained my reasons for the course I had pursued. The chairman of the committee expressed his regret that Wild's was not in its old place, and in the course of a short conversation concerning its visits in past years, he facetiously observed that in his younger days it was thought that without 'Old Wild's' a fair couldn't be. There was an undercurrent of sympathy in all that was said, and I somehow imagined I should be dealt leniently with. And so I was. All that was required of me was that I should pay a guinea to the Infirmary, as a sort of acknowledgment of the right of the committee to fine me for offending against the bye-laws, and that if I intended to stay in the town, as usual, after the fair, I must remove to my old ground when Stephens had left it. Which things I readily consented to do, and did. I opened at my old prices, 1s., 6d., and 3d., in the Market Place, but did only indifferently as regards business, though I was constantly announcing 'unprecedented attractions,' 'grand fashionable nights' and 'novelties'—the latter twice repeated, with an additional note of exclamation each time. *Damon and Pythias* and *'Twas I* were amongst my newer attractions; and the last performances at the booth of which I have any printed record were *The Lion of Naples*, in which Mrs. Sam and I appeared; *Ben the Boatswain*, with F. Brookfield in the principal character; and a song by my son Tom between the pieces. The date of the programme is July 22nd, 1865. I have gone a little into detail because, having now approached the end of 'Old Wild's,' the last expiring efforts of its proprietor may not be altogether uninteresting to those who have cared to follow me through my history. My company, exclusive of myself, wife, and son Tom, was now reduced to some fifteen or a score in number, the principal of which were Mr., Mrs., and Miss Brookfield, Mr. and Mrs. Cunningham, Mr. and Mrs. Pickles, Miss Percy, and Messrs. Smith, Flanaghan, Armstrong, and Woodford. We should have left Halifax long before the date just mentioned, and gone our usual round, but I was prevented from pursuing such a course by my usual drawback, lack of funds. So we remained at the bottom of the Market until the beginning of August, doing but little all the time. In anticipation of Hunslet feast, which I determined, if possible, we would attend (especially as a person at Leeds had promised to send me horses), we pulled down the booth, and packed up our paraphernalia as usual. But when I sent for the horses, the reply came that they were engaged elsewhere; so we missed Hunslet Feast altogether, and had to remain in the Market Place. Well, as there was nothing for them to do—for I hadn't spirit to open the place again, nor means to provide new attractions had I done so—my company left me. All remained packed up on the waggons, and the caravan was the residence of myself, wife, and our two youngest children, Wm. Edwin and Chas. Henry, until midwinter. But meanwhile I was not idle. I accepted engagements at other travelling establishments when my health permitted —for my misfortunes told upon me for some time—and occasionally went about with my violin entertaining the company in the parlour (by the kind permission of mine host, who always welcomed 'Sam' Wild), alternating instrumental music with song, and recitation with story. With all my efforts, however, I was unable to do more than just keep my family and myself from want—well, hardly that, as will be seen by and bye. Many a

seasonable help did we receive from Mrs. Grace Whitaker,
a good-hearted fish woman, who had a small stall near the
van, and many a loaf of bread has been broken for my
wife and hungry children by a generous little woman,
whose name I forget, but who kept a shop at the bottom
of the market. By December, I was £5 in arrear for
rent. The Markets Inspector applied several times for
the amount, but I could neither earn that sum nor borrow
it, so payment was out of the question. As it was contemplated to roof over the place where my waggons stood,
I was at length requested to remove them, and as soon as
I could find other ground and hire horses I did so. The
rent due from me the Markets Committee generously
forgave me—to their credit be it said. It was 'Old Wild's,'
as I take it, and they didn't like to be too hard on its
unfortunate proprietor. Affairs at the van just before our
removal from the Market Place, wore a cheerless aspect.
I remember, on one occasion, we had been without food
and fire for nearly two days; we hadn't even the consolation of a half-penny dip. I had gone out in the morning
of the second day to see what my old fiddle would do for
us; to try and make merry the hearts of others while
sadness possessed my own; to endeavour to put on a
cheerful face, though I had left my wife with a tearful one
in the van. About noon, and while I was away, a gentleman came to the door of the caravan. My wife's brother
and the two children were with her. She asked the
gentleman in and offered him a seat. He had heard, he
said, that she and her little ones were without food, and
he felt he couldn't sit down to his dinner without
ascertaining if such were the case. It needed but little to
satisfy him on that score, and he generously gave my wife
half-a-sovereign. She, staggered at so unexpected a gift,
burst into tears as he placed it in her hand, and couldn't
even thank him; while the joy of the little fellows at the
prospect of having something to eat was simply uncon-
trollable. He quickly diverted attention from the gift by
remarking, as he looked at her sons, 'You have two fine
boys there, Mrs. Wild. I think I could find them some
work if they would come to my place.' My wife, having
recovered herself a little, expressed her fears as to their
competency for the duties he might require of them. 'Oh,
never mind that,' returned the gentleman, 'we can soon

find somebody who will teach them.   And there's William there,' continued he, and motioning with his head to my wife's brother, 'I have no doubt we could also find him something to do.'   So next day the trio presented themselves at Savile Mills and began work, and my wife's brother and my son Charles Henry are there still.   This benevolent gentleman was Mr. Stanley Cooper, whose wife had been a companion of Mrs. 'Sam's' in her boarding school days.

"The earnings of the young people, though small at first, helped to feed and clothe them, and I made what I could by starring, in the lesser theatrical world, and by busking when engagements were not to be had.   In this way we managed to exist.

"I remember I had one day gone to the Saddle Inn, in Russell Street, to play for a party of quarrymen.   Though rough, from their employment, they are good-hearted fellows are these quarrymen, as I can well testify.   As soon as I received an invitation to the party I dressed as respectably for the occasion as I could.   Over a black waistcoat, which had seen better days, I wore a dark-blue overcoat of more recent date.   I invested threepence in paper cuffs, collar, and front, had a clean shave (I never took kindly to whiskers), and, altogether, had a bare and it may be a slightly youthful appearance.   My hat, specially brushed up for the event, was placed jauntily on one side ; and my locks, not so grey then as they are now, clustered about my neck beneath it.   I was standing outside the room door, during an interval between the music and the reciting, when I was thus accosted by a recruiting sergeant :—·

"'Young man, would you like to become a soldier and serve Her Majesty?'

"'Well,' I replied, 'if Her Majesty is in want of such men as me I have no objection.'

"At this point the sergeant called the landlord, and said, 'Here is a young man who wishes to enlist.'

"The landlord, Hanson Brearley, who knew me well, repressed a smile when he perceived who the intending recruit was, but kept mum.   The sergeant then took a shilling out of his pocket, and, looking at me, said: 'Are you free, able, and willing to serve Her Majesty?' with all the rest of the nominy in such cases.   Turning to Mr.

Brearley, I said, ' Landlord, please listen to what I say. I am free and willing to serve Her Majesty, if Her Majesty wants such men as me.'

" The recruiting sergeant, evidently not perceiving my object in appealing thus to the landlord, gave me the shilling, saying as he did so, ' You are now one of Her Majesty's men.' He then left me.

" As it was a general custom at that house for all recruits to spend the enlisting shilling there, I handed mine to the landlord, who, taking it with him into the room, apprised the quarrymen that their minstrel had enlisted.

" Sam Wild listed ? Everybody laughed. Nobody believed it. The bare idea of such a thing ! Nonsense.

" ' But I tell you he has,' said the landlord, ' and here is the enlisting shilling.'

" ' Well, then,' said the men, ' take it on account of a gallon of the best, and we will pay the difference.' The landlord did as requested, and the health of the recruit was drunk with the usual honours. By and bye the sergeant returned and came and seated himself beside me. At length one of the company said to me, loud enough for the sergeant to hear, ' Now as you're a soldier, Sam, you'll want a billet.'

" ' Oh, ay,' put in the sergeant, ' to be sure he will ; I'll go ask the landlord about it,' and thereupon left the room.

" He was not long before he returned, but it appeared that he must either have heard or suspected something, for he immediately demanded of me the shilling he had given me. I pointed to its representative, a jug of beer, and told him that as part of it was there and the remainder had been imbibed by the company, I couldn't very conveniently comply with his requirements. He waxed indignant at this. ' I'll find you a billet at the Town Hall,' said he, as he marched out of the room, leaving me in a state of doubt as to how the affair would end. By and bye he returned with Ben Tempest, a detective officer, to take me into custody. ' There,' said the sergeant, pointing to me, ' that's the man who has taken Her Majesty's money under false pretences.' Ben looked first at me, and then at the company, and then at the sergeant, and unable to control his risibilities, burst into laughter and left the room without uttering a word. The recruiting sergeant, not to be laughed out of it, again set forth in quest of somebody to arrest me. He was not long before he re-appeared, with Sergeant Holden. 'There he is,' said the recruiting officer, singling me out. 'Why, you fool,' said Holden, looking at the sergeant surprisedly, 'that your recruit? Why that's old Sam Wild!'

"Of course the officer was chaffed about the affair, but he couldn't endure it long, so left the room. As he was going out, one of the company called after him. 'If you want another recruit, here's one here,' pointing to old John Stocks, a man upwards of seventy years of age.

"The conversation after that incident turned for a while on military matters, and by general request I gave the company 'The Charge of the Gallant Six Hundred,' and as a testimony of the pleasure the recital had afforded them, they each handed me a copper.

"But that wasn't much to get on with, as the life-guardsman said when he cleaned his jack boots with a tooth brush."

CHAPTER XXVII.

THE DOG "TIGER" HELPS TO KEEP HIS MASTER—WARD-
ROBE LENT OUT ON HIRE—ANOTHER ATTEMPT TO
START THE BOOTH AGAIN—PROVES UNSUCCESSFUL—
"SAM" WILD AS A STAR—MEETS WITH JAMES NEW-
SOME—LOSS OF "TIGER"—DISTRAINT FOR RENT—
SALE OF EFFECTS—"SAM" MADE A STAGE MANAGER—
LAST ENGAGEMENTS — ANOTHER PARTNERSHIP — A
FINAL APPEARANCE—DEATH OF MRS. "SAM" WILD—
THE "FEMALE BLONDIN"—CONCERNING SOME OLD
MEMBERS.

> Nay then, farewell!
> I've touch'd the highest point of all my greatness.
> I haste now to my setting.—*Henry VIII.*

" The vans having been removed from the Market Place
to Lower Wade Street, to a piece of ground I had rented
there, I continued to divide my time between starring and
busking. Meanwhile my daughter Elizabeth, who had
returned from a visit to a relative, obtained work in
Halifax, as a short timer at a mill, and helped as far as
she could to improve the condition of things at the van.
Then 'Tiger' was taken off my hands for a while by my
son-in-law, T. Russell, who performed with him at concert
halls in London, and in the principal towns in the
provinces, and who made me a small allowance for the
animal's services. So that, these various items of income
united, we were just about able to keep the wolf from the
door.

" Early in 1866, a new theatre was opened at Dewsbury
by a Mr Joy. Sharp, one of his company and formerly a
member of mine, hearing the manager inquire about a
wardrobe, informed him that I had a good one and that I
should no doubt be open to lend it. The end of negotiations with me was the hiring of the wardrobe by the
manager at 30s. per week. He retained it for three
months at this figure, during which time my family and I

were enabled to live comfortably. Upon the return of the
wardrobe, however, it ceased to be a source of revenue for
some time, and I was thrown once more upon my former
means of existence.

"Tired, after a ten months' spell at it, of busking and
of starring, I determined to make another effort to open
my booth, and appealed through the *Era* of 10th March,
1867, to the 'profession in general' and also to the Royal
Antediluvians (of which ancient order I had been a
member upwards of thirty-one years) to assist me to
purchase a tilt. The result of that appeal was the receipt of
£3 11s. 6d., principally from Brother Buffs in the London
district and at Cardiff. To provide a suitable covering for
my booth, however, and such as I generally had, would
require at least £30; I was therefore unable to make the
desired start. So I continued to take engagements when
they were to be had, and between whiles took to the music
and reciting as a *dernier resort*. I have programmes of
my principal later engagements, but as in most cases there
is nothing much of a special nature to record, I shall content myself with little more than a bare allusion to them.

"In September, 1867, I performed six nights at Rowland's National Theatre, Cleckheaton, my terms being 30s.
for the week and half a clear benefit. Rowland, in
announcing the appearance of the 'old Cleckheaton
favourite,' stated that he had 'at considerable expense
made an engagement with the above celebrated artiste for
three nights.' By this method he ensured good houses for
the three first evenings, at the end of which time he
further announced, in large type, and with innumerable
notes of exclamation, a 're-engagement' of myself for
three nights more, and then attempted to give his 'excellent reason' for that re-engagement.

In consequence of the enthusiastic reception that has greeted each
performance, and at the earnest request of numerous parties, the
manager has been induced to retain the services of Mr. Wild for three
more nights, being positively the last nights he can appear in Cleckheaton this season.

"On October 12th (Saturday), assisted by my two
youngest sons and my daughter Lizzy, I gave an entertainment which was followed by a 'Grand Ball' (save the mark!)
in the large room of the Wellington Inn, Elland. Terms
of admission, well, 3d. and 2d. The vocal entertainment

lasted an hour and a-half, and then the dancing began, or,
as some would put it, the ball was formally opened. Except
an old musical clock,—whose strong predilection for hymn
tunes unfitted it for taking any part in the main feature of
the programme, namely, the dancing—I was the only
instrumentalist. But my friends were of that happy class
who can get along if there is only a noise at all, and they
required very little inducement from my old violin to make
them trip it on the light fantastic toe.

   "About this time a Mr. Richards, of London, took the
Theatre Royal, Halifax, and having previously advertised
in the *Era* for dresses, &c., I communicated with him, and
at length agreed to lend him my wardrobe, for which,
inclusive of my own services as custodian thereof, I was to
receive £2 10s. per week. Mr. Richards' company, which
included artistes from London, Liverpool, Edinburgh,
Glasgow, and York, first appeared before the Halifax
public on Saturday evening, 19th October. *Manfred* had
been previously announced as the opening piece, but by
reason of the great preparation required for its production
it had been postponed. On Monday, Tuesday, and Wednesday, October 21st, 22nd, and 23rd, Boucicault's drama
The Streets of London was performed, and on each of
those evenings there was a good house. On the Wednesday, after the performance, and when the salaries should
have been paid, there was neither money nor manager.
The latter, taking the former and his stage manager with
him, had sought a more congenial atmosphere elsewhere.
Next morning, at rehearsal, the members of the company
conferred together ; a Mr. Stafford was appointed stage
manager, and it was agreed to continue the performances a
week or so to enable the company to make good their
losses. I was asked to remain with my wardrobe, and
consented. *The Octoroon* had been in rehearsal during the
week, but the artiste who had been studying the *rôle* of
Wahnottee had left the previous night. I was requested
to undertake the part, and agreed to do so; for I was
active and knew nothing of rheumatism, then. Accordingly
it was announced, in large type, for October 26th :—' For
this night only, the celebrated actor, Mr. Samuel Wild,
will appear in his great character of Wahnottee, the
Indian.' There was a good house on the occasion, everything passed off with *éclat*, and I was thrice called before

the curtain.   The success of the piece induced the management to continue it two nights longer, on each of which occasions I received a similar honour.

"From November 4th to 9th, I was at the Theatre Royal, Castleford (lessee, W. H. Beresford), having previously been announced to the Castlefordians as 'the sensational and nautical actor, Mr. Sam Wild, who will appear in a round of his favourite characters.' Miss Finch, 'Old Finch's' daughter, was one of the company, and played with me in every piece.   She was a smart girl was Miss Finch, and I do not wonder that she afterwards became Mrs. Beresford.

"In the winter of 1867-8, while on a busking expedition to Bradford, I met with Mr. James Newsome, whose circus was then stationed near to where the present Town Hall stands.   On seeing me, he shook my hand heartily, inquired after my wife and family, and gave me half-a-sovereign.   He took me by the arm into the Commercial Hotel.   Some of the gentlemen in the parlour remarked to him that seemingly he had met with an old friend.   'Yes,' said he, 'I have; I have known this gentleman a long time, I knew his father too, and I knew his father's old trick pony "Billy."   "Billy" was the first animal I ever strode, and when I was a boy he and I used to be on very good terms.'

"The next public engagement I had (January and February, 1868) was with my brother Tom, who had had a wooden building erected for the season at Goole.   I took 'Tiger' with me, and we were to perform twelve nights.   Notwithstanding the fact that all strolling companies were at that time in a less flourishing condition than formerly, Tom drew tolerably good houses.   'Tiger' performed up to and including Saturday evening, February 1st, but on Sunday he was seized with an inflammation of the stomach, and died early on the Tuesday morning following.   His loss was a serious one to me; for since 'Nelson's' death he had been unequalled on the stage.   I sent the animal to Mr. Campbell, jun., at the Museum, Halifax, with a request that he would 'cure' it for me. This he did; but as I was never in a position to pay him for his labour, the animal never afterwards came into my possession.

"For six nights, commencing 2nd March, 1868, I appeared at Bacup, at Mr. Johnson Ambler's Royal Standard Theatre (the strollers are never at a loss for good titles for their booths), where, in addition to the nightly execution of 'terrific broad sword combats' and 'standard' dittos; the suffering of mimic shipwrecks, and the encountering of hair-breadth escapes, I also gave lengthy recitations before the curtain. So long as I was able, it was ever my aim to fairly earn my salary, and that I always did so cannot, I think, well be denied.

"My brother having bought my band carriage, I sent it to him one day towards the close of the month of March. About the second or third day afterwards I received from the owner of the ground whereon my van and other paraphernalia stood a demand for rent. They were evidently under the impression that as one of the vans had gone the rest would follow, as the children say, 'like Johnny Ringo's sheep.' Not being able to satisfy the claims of my landlord within the time stated, a distraint was on the 16th April made on the living van, three stage carriages, and the rest of my portable property, and it was subsequently offered for sale by auction; Messrs. Stanley Cooper and David Gaunt kindly bought in the whole of the property for me, which, on leaving Lower Wade Street, I took to a field at the bottom of Water Lane, where, by the kind permission of the Lord of the Manor, I was permitted to ruralise for a year and a-half rent-free. Seeing no prospect of 'Old Wild's' ever being resuscitated, and in order to pay Messrs. Cooper and Gaunt the money they had advanced me, I sold the entire effects by auction, and my family and I removed to our present dwelling in Caddy Field. My brother Tom's wife bought one of the parade waggons at the sale, and the living van which cost me so much only fetched £10. It was purchased by a proprietor of steam-horses, and was afterwards converted into a sort of travelling box for them. The scenery, wardrobe, galleries, rafters, poles, ladders, &c., were disposed of for merely nominal prices. And so ended 'Old Wild's.'

"In September and October I was at Tom's 'Mammoth Establishment' again in the threefold capacity of star, stage manager, and leader of the outside band, and all for a guinea a week.

" On January 16th, 1869, I appeared at Pickuls' Royal Alhambra Theatre, Todmorden, as Topac in the *Children of Cyprus*, and as Clown in the harlequinade which followed. That was the last occasion on which I donn'd the motley. A little later on I was made stage manager at Pickuls', but still continued to perform principal characters, and to give a recitation and song between whiles. For my multifarious duties here I had a share and a-half of the receipts, but did not get rich out of it. I was glad to be able to keep myself, and send a few shillings home now and then. The leading lady actress at Pickuls' Theatre at this time was, I may here observe, Wallett's brother's wife.

" In July I played for a few nights at my brother's establishment at Dewsbury, and on the 30th of that month I took my benefit. There was a good deal of local talent displayed on the occasion; several songs, a violin solo, and a cornet solo, while the Dewsbury Old Band volunteered their services for the *beneficiaire* for the sake of the good old times both he and they had known.

" Mr. Alfred Hillier had the management of the Britannia Hall, Keighley, in February, 1870, which was converted for the time being into a theatre. I appeared there for six nights, and, if the programmes go for anything, had an ' enthusiastic reception ' in that town.

" About or just before the month of July, my son-in-law, T. Russell, hired for a short season the portable property belonging to Mr. S. A. Pickuls, known as the ' Royal Alhambra Theatre.' From July 11th to September 20th my son Tom and I travelled with Russell's company, which from Skipton went to Bingley, Shipley, Hunslet, and Pudsey. I still played leading characters, and suggested and assisted in the production of standard pieces ; and at most of these travelling concerns I was more or less responsible for the *mise en scène*. Business was not very good, and so, while at Hunslet in August, Russell arranged that my name should be put on the programmes as lessee and manager, with a view to drawing better houses. On the 23rd of that month, it is just worth while mentioning here, I took my benefit under the patronage of the Lords of the Manor, the Bailiff, and the Constables of Hunslet. The following evening, 24th, was Mrs. ' Sam's ' last appearance on the stage. She sustained the *rôle* of Matilda Brightwell in *The Beggar's Petition*, the occasion being the benefit of her son Tom. Notwithstanding the subsequent engagement of James Holloway and Henry Loraine, the production of Shakspearian dramas and of sensational ones, and, withal, the presentation of gifts, things went off only indifferently well—the days of the strolling fraternity were evidently numbered. Russell gave up Pickuls' concern at Pudsey in September, and he and my son Tom joined Duval's at Chester.

" Pickuls at once resumed the management, secured the services of several members of the late company, and opened his establishment at Idle. While there he sent for me and my daughter Louisa, and we appeared before the Idle public (October 10th to 18th) in Shakspearian, Boucicaultian, and Tom - Taylorian dramas, and did ' a starve ' into the bargain.

"This last engagement rather damped my ardour for histrionic pursuits. I set out busking again, and did not appear on the stage for several months.

"The next programme I have is dated March 25th, 1871, and the place is the Theatre Royal, Dewsbury— Lessees, Messrs. Driver and Riching. In that same programme, the public's ' old friend, Samuel Wild,' is announced to perform ' two of his favourite characters, being his first appearance these seven years and his farewell '; and then it is asked ' Should auld acquaintance be forgot ? ' That the people of Dewsbury didn't intend that it altogether should was sufficiently proved to me on the evening of the 25th by a large and enthusiastic audience.

"Soon after this my brother Tom sent for me to undertake another engagement at his theatre ; and, after some conversation, and with a view to the improvement of his business, which had lately been only so-so, he wished me to join him in partnership. On April 8th an announcement to the following effect appeared :—

NOTICE !

Messrs. T. & S. Wild, having thrown into partnership once more, have great pleasure in announcing to the public generally of Stanningley, Pudsey, Farsley, Rodley, and the vicinity, that they will open their pleasant place of amusement for dramatic representations, at the back of the Huddersfield Arms ; and trust that their efforts to please will meet with the approbation of the lovers of the British drama ; as they are sparing neither trouble nor expense in securing the best of Histrionic Artistes, and all other accessories and paraphernalia necessary for the production of the first novelties of the day, and which will be put upon the stage in a manner that cannot be equalled by any other establishment out of London. They beg to state emphatically that their chief object constantly in view will be to hold the mirror up to nature, to inculcate in dramatic representations the moral " Vice to be hated needs but to be seen," and to forcibly pourtray the truth that " Virtue is its own reward "; while the performance will never be of that character which can call a blush to the cheek of the innocent.

" But the new partnership was of very short duration; points of difference between the partners brought about a dissolution in something short of a fortnight.

About a year after this Tom threw into partnership with an actor named Gledhill; and my last appearance on the stage, as Van Trump, in *Uncle Tom's Cabin*, was at their theatre soon afterwards.

" It was in 1871, I believe, that I first began to suffer at intervals from rheumatism. At length it assumed a chronic form, and down to the present time it has been a constant attendant upon my poverty; as it has, by depriving me of a means of livelihood, been also one of the main causes of it.

" The death of my wife on 18th January, 1874, was a heavy blow to myself and family; their loss was that of a kind and affectionate mother, mine of a loving and faithful wife.

" Since her decease I have managed to get along somehow. My old fiddle earns me a dinner now and then when I am able to go about, and when I am not my family are good enough to see that I don't want for one.

" And now a few words before concluding my narrative concerning some who have figured in it, and one or two of whom mention should be made.

" Mr. and Mrs. Hughes, whose past kindnesses to myself and family can never be forgotten, both died some five or six years ago; Mrs. Hughes surviving her husband only a few months.

" As to my sister Elizabeth—who in her parents' time married a member of the band named Young—she has been dead a very many years; but it is not long since her husband ' shuffled off this mortal coil.' Elizabeth left two daughters; the youngest was an invalid for a lengthened period, and I very much doubt if she be living. Selina, the eldest, was apprenticed to learn the art of tight-rope dancing; and twenty years ago was known on the Con-

tinent, as well as in England, as 'The Female Blondin.'
But her public career (an eventful one while it lasted),
was unfortunately cut short by a serious accident when
she was comparatively young.   Mrs. Hughes, her aunt, no
sooner heard of Selina's misfortune than she instigated an
appeal for her.   It resulted in over £300 being raised by
subscriptions.   I have here a copy of that appeal :—

THE FEMALE BLONDIN.

On Friday last, the heroine of the Crystal Palace in 1858, and of
the transit of the Thames on a tight rope, 2000 feet in length, in August,
1861, was removed on crutches from St. Bartholomew's Hospital, a
cripple for the rest of her life, from the accidental fracturing of the neck
of the thigh bone more than two months ago at Highbury Barn, while
obeying the morbid and romantic desire of the present age for perilous
adventures.   The fractured limb is three inches shorter than the other,
and perfectly useless.   The heroine, with a courage truly characteristic,
wished the surgeons to amputate the limb if it could not be rendered
serviceable, rather, as she observed, than have it dangling uselessly by the
side of the other one, and requiring support which she might find very
difficult to obtain for the maintenance of the sound one.   What renders
the case of this unfortunate artiste the more distressing, she was the only
support of an aged and infirm father and an invalid sister.   When English
sympathy can be so readily extended to the wounded in the hospital at
Spezzia, where the necessity for it is somewhat doubtful, we must not
altogether overlook the wise maxim, that charity begins at home, and
extend our benevolence to our less fortunate sister.

The very handsome sum which had been subscribed for
Selina enabled her to take a little shop in London, where
she afterwards married.   She is still in the metropolis,
though to fame unknown : the last I heard of her and her
husband they were keeping an inn there, somewhere on
the Surrey side.

"My brother Tom is still in the land of the living,
and, though the elder brother, is fortunately freer from
infirmity than myself.   His establishment finally collapsed
about five years ago.   At the present time he plays the
violin at Gledhill & Wallace's travelling theatre, and his
daughter Selina and her husband belong to the company.
Tom and I still correspond ; he also sends me a programme
now and then, and he visits us once a year or so.

"The only Wild of our family now upon the stage
is my son Tom, who is at present in Worcestershire.

"The famous ' Jack ' Holloway died some years ago,
but whether his brothers are still in existence I cannot say ;
I have not heard of them for some time.   Old Smith is
living still, somewhere in Leeds, I am told.   He cannot be

far short of eighty years of age, and yet I heard of his performing not more than two years ago at a travelling booth at Shelf. J. H. Williams is still alive, but he must be at least three score years and ten. He keeps to his old business yet, and when last I heard of him he was attached to Rhodes's establishment.

"The fabric of 'Old Wild's,' like those of its former contemporaries — Thorne's, Parrish's, Templeton's, and Holloway's, has dissolved, its glories have departed, and with the above exceptions, a few others previously alluded to, and your humble servant, 'Sam' Wild, the once better-known members of its company are all gathered to their fathers."

[END OF "SAM" WILD'S NARRATIVE.]

CONCLUDING CHAPTER.

"Last scene of all,
"That ends this strange eventful history."—*As You Like it.*

Owing to our removal from Halifax shortly after the completion of the foregoing narrative, we saw but little of "Sam," though several letters passed between us.

About two years after the first-named event he sent us a playbill which intimated that he was going to appear at the Gaiety Theatre, Halifax, along with his old friend Wallett, who had once again been induced to emerge from his well-earned retirement. We went. There was a crowded house, and loud and prolonged was the cheering when to the strains of "Auld Lang Syne" the curtain rose, discovering the old Stroller King seated.

When the applause had subsided Wallett appeared (to more vehement cheering), and he and Wild together recalled for a good half-hour their early experiences of the old show times.

Never were two persons more delighted, nor an audience more agreeably entertained.

"Sam" then said a few parting words, and leaning on a chair for support, concluded with a recitation which, of course, brought down the house.

This was positively his last appearance upon any stage.

The next news which reached us was an intimation, through the newspapers, of his demise on the 17th May, 1883, and that of his brother Tom two days afterwards.

The *Bradford Observer* of the 22nd of the same month thus referred to those events :—

DEATH OF A NOTED YORKSHIRE SHOWMAN.—Yesterday an inquest was held before Mr. Taylor, coroner, at the Junction Inn, Lowtown, Pudsey, touching the death of Thomas Wild, aged seventy years, who had been found dead in bed on Saturday last. It appears that the deceased, who has been a travelling actor, and well known in the profession throughout the north of England, had been residing in a caravan in the Market Place, Pudsey, since September last, in company with a grandson named James Donnelly, thirteen years of age, who states that his grandfather had been ailing for about three weeks, but had not been visited by a medical man. He saw him alive last about two o'clock in the afternoon of Saturday, when he gave him a drink of water, and then left him in bed while he went out to play. He returned at three o'clock, and found him dead in bed. The verdict returned was, "Died from natural causes."—The name of "Wild's show," or theatre, was a "household word" in almost every town and village in Yorkshire in connection with village feasts thirty to forty years ago, and it is somewhat singular that the two well known brothers and actors, Tom and Sam Wild, have both departed this life within two days of each other. On poor Tom's death-bed was found a letter, written by a niece, informing him of the death of his brother at Halifax on Thursday last.

And the *Halifax Courier* of the 26th of the same month had the following paragraph :—

DEATH OF SAM WILD.—The veteran showman, Sam Wild, died in a house in Wiscombe Bank, Halifax, on the 17th inst., at the age of sixty-seven. Wild's name is familiar to most of our readers, and in these columns there appeared some time ago an extended and interesting account of his career as a showman, written by an able correspondent. These facts we need not now, therefore, recapitulate. A few years ago, after an eventful life as an actor and the proprietor of a travelling show, Wild settled down in Halifax. Since then he has lived in very humble circumstances, and had it not been for the generosity of some of his old friends and admirers, he would have fared badly. With a little assistance in this way, how-ever, and by the aid of his fiddle, which earned him a good many shillings, he got along fairly well. He lived with his daughter, Mrs. Russell, in Caddy Field, and there many friends would visit the old showman, who would tell afresh the stories of many years ago, and recite favourite pieces to his visitors. He had a most retentive memory, and seemed to have fresh in his mind all the leading incidents of his life, and thousands of small matters, recollections of conversations with eminent actors, &c., which few could have remembered. For some time past his health has been failing, and he has gone about with very feeble step. Some two months ago, he removed with his daughter to Wiscombe Bank, and there he died as stated, retaining his consciousness to the very last moment. He was interred at All Saints' Church, on Monday. On the following day his brother, Tom Wild, also an actor, was buried, having died suddenly in a caravan at Pudsey. He was Sam's senior by two years. On his deathbed was found a letter, written by his niece, informing him of Sam's death.

With this quiet and almost simultaneous closing in of two lives of activity and bustle, the history of "Old Wild's" finally concludes.

There is, however, one little circumstance in connection with the death of the elder brother which is worthy of further notice. Found lying beside him was the letter announcing Sam's decease. That letter, to our mind, what-ever "natural causes" may be supposed to include, accounts for the suddenness of Tom's demise, and establishes the belief that, notwithstanding the occasional shynesses between the two brothers of which we have learned, they had still a deep affection for each other. This, we think, is more than hinted at in the opening of chapter xvii. They simply differed in their ideas of business management, and, in spite of little tiffs, and one or two partings in the old show days, were continually being drawn together again down to the very last.

"Tom and I," said Sam to us one evening, when touching on the subject of the second dissolution of partnership with his brother, "Tom and I could never agree, and yet I would divide my last loaf with him to-night."

Of the sincerity of which statement in the latter particular, the writer had several proofs during the progress of the foregoing narrative.

And now that the curtain has fallen finally upon the realistic drama of "Old Wild's," what have we learned from it? That while to that once famous Temple of the Drama our fathers owed much of their intellectual recreation and amusement, our indebtedness is still greater. For to its enterprising management in days of yore, and to the taste it everywhere created for the drama, has been unquestionably due the establishment of the Provincial Theatre.

Upon many of the scenes of its old triumphs, and in most of the towns where it was the only exponent of the dramatic art a well-appointed theatre now exists; in some instances two, and in others still more. For these "Old Wild's" assuredly prepared the way. And it is curious to reflect that by what may not inappropriately be termed its own progeny "Old Wild's" was ruthlessly elbowed out of the field.

W. BYLES AND SONS, PRINTERS, PICCADILLY, BRADFORD.

INDEX.